THE
PETROSSIAN
LEGACY

THE PETROSSIAN LEGACY

CLAUDIO B. CLAGLUENA

THE PETROSSIAN LEGACY

This is a work of fiction. All of the characters, names, incidents, organizations, and dialogue in this novel are either the products of the author's imagination or are used fictitiously.

iUniverse books may be ordered through booksellers or by contacting:

iUniverse
1663 Liberty Drive
Bloomington, IN 47403
www.iuniverse.com
1-800-Authors (1-800-288-4677)

ISBN: 978-1-5320-4439-7 (sc)
ISBN: 978-1-5320-4441-0 (hc)
ISBN: 978-1-5320-4440-3 (e)

Library of Congress Control Number: 2018904395

Print information available on the last page.

iUniverse rev. date: 04/05/2018

CONTENTS

PROLOGUE

Matt Burke sat at his desk at the technical division of his international IT company in Simferopol, Crimea.

He had celebrated his seventieth birthday two weeks earlier. His fingers stroked his short, steel-gray hair, a gesture usually indicating reluctance or doubt.

Despite his age, Matt was in great shape, an ardent swimmer and a passionate golfer when he wasn't in one of his offices.

Matt's company, Digital Security Solutions, was based in Canada, his homeland, but mostly operated in Southeast Asia, serving banks and large corporations. A few years before, he had made Igor Kuznechov a full partner, intending to transfer the company to the brilliant Russian sooner rather than later.

Now his protégé, several decades his junior, was enlightening him about a project he was developing for a Saudi-based bank that did business all over the world, particularly in Southeast Asia.

"How do you feel about this, Igor?"

"Well, it's child's play for me and enormous revenue for the company. I say we take it."

Khalij, the Saudi bank, wanted DSS to develop and integrate software to facilitate international transfers.

Igor understood that his boss and friend wanted him to maintain control over the software, meaning to hack into it and to monitor any moves that might endanger DSS.

Thus DSS received its biggest contract ever, although Matt had worries about the easy and maybe questionable money.

Igor was excited and wanted to start working on the system, which would provide the Saudi bank with a tool for trouble-free money transfers around the globe.

Igor had been Matt's partner since the older man's recruitment by Petrossian, a private and extremely clandestine intelligence firm formed during the Turkish-Armenian war, just after the Great War, with huge funding from its founder's family.

After spending several years in Libya and other places in Africa and enduring a failed marriage, Matt had grown bored with his life and had jumped at the opportunity to join Petrossian offered by an old acquaintance, a former KGB agent in Africa.

Matt hadn't cared much about the future of his company, which at the time provided surveillance systems to largely insignificant businesses, though that was at least a step up from his former job selling water filters to terrorists and other shady elements in Africa.

But when Matt accepted the firm's offer and began the intelligence schooling that would prepare him to become an agent at Petrossian's base in East Siberia, Igor, a young and extremely talented computer specialist, took over and transformed the modest Canadian company, Surveillance International, into an aggressive and sophisticated IT firm that was now on the technological level of its giant global competitors.

The training Matt had received at the Petrossian base still influenced his way of analyzing challenging situations. A healthy paranoia had saved his life more than once, and he was getting alarm signals now.

Matt and Igor had offices in Simferopol, Russia's Silicon Valley; Kuala Lumpur, Malaysia, and Jakarta, Indonesia, serving important corporations and organizations with their software.

Hand in hand with developing Internet software, Igor grew into a daring and expert hacker, a skill he used mainly to enhance elaborate security systems that were deployed by international corporations and leading intelligence firms.

The firm's links to government intelligence agencies like the CIA, the FSB in Russia, the DGSE in France, and GCHQ in Great Britain helped DDS secure contracts to develop or upgrade the organization's clandestine systems.

To verify security, Igor often hacked into the systems he had installed and then presented his findings to clients.

"Okay, we go for it, but I want you to keep a close eye on the activities of Khalij in Kuala Lumpur and Jakarta. Hack only when absolutely necessary."

"As usual, boss. I will monitor in the dark."

"I will sign the contract with Khalij next week in Jakarta," Matt said. "The Saudis will advance $1 million right after signing, and that's why I have some qualms. We've never received a down payment of such magnitude."

Matt stroked his gray hair again.

"I guarantee a close surveillance," Igor said.

He was excited and was ready to develop the code for a money transfer system that was just at the edge of legality.

Matt left Simferopol for Malaysia the next day, and Igor tasked his engineers to create the unique software that would allow customers to bypass the watchful eyes of the international finance authorities.

Under its mastermind, the Simferopol-based development center was able to roll out the product just three weeks later.

The Saudi bank, together with its partners in Indonesia and Malaysia, was more than happy to use the software to help its unsavory customers.

Igor flew to Kuala Lumpur where he hacked into his own system, uncovering transfers that he found slightly outside the norm.

That's when the trouble started, pulling Matt and Igor back into the dark, mysterious, and perilous world of intelligence.

CHAPTER 1

BALI, INDONESIA

I instantly realized something was wrong. My exceptionally well-developed sixth sense had never let me down in such circumstances.

The hotel lobby was deserted but for two girls behind the reception desk and three Arab-looking guys lounging in the rattan chairs.

I was carrying my golf bag over my shoulder and tried not to stare at the three Bedouins in dark suits. However, I felt their eyes on my back when I strolled to the elevators.

I regretted the three beers I had after a pleasant round of golf at Bali Nirwana. On the way to the hotel I almost fell asleep in the car, saved by the bumps in the Bali roads.

The elevator's metallic doors gave me a mirror view of the three, and I was quite happy when the doors slid open. The trio didn't move. That much I could see.

My heart had not raced so quickly in a long time. My room was on the third floor. Bali hotels have only three or four floors. Some building regulation dictates they can't be higher than the palm trees.

I walked to my room, unlocked the door, and for the first time put on the security chain after closing it.

It was three in the afternoon. My office was still open. I punched the speed dial on my mobile phone, but nobody picked up.

What the hell! I had a dozen staff members and an assistant, but nobody picked up the phone.

At that instant I realized something was wrong.

I called my assistant, Lisa, on her mobile phone and got the annoying instruction to leave a message.

I sat down and the ice-cold air conditioning soothed my nerves a bit.

About two minutes later my phone vibrated. I put it on vibrate while I'm golfing, because I hate to be disturbed by a ring tone while I'm concentrating on the next shot.

"Yes," I answered.

"Sir, it's Lisa." I hadn't recognized the number. Strange, but that's how I was feeling at the moment.

"Lisa, where are you?"

"Sir, I'm at the police station. They closed our office. My cousin, Nasurwin, let me use his phone to make a call. They took all our phones and ..."

"Hold on, Lisa!" I was calm now and realized something disturbing had happened.

"Who closed our office and why?"

"The police were here with some other gentlemen. They took all the computers and all the files."

For a minute, I was unable to think clearly and desperately tried to get a hold of myself.

"Were there any Arab-looking guys with the police?"

"Yes. They even ordered the police around. Nasurwin is really upset." Nasurwin was a major in the national police. That the Arabs had taken charge made me even jumpier.

"Please tell Nasurwin I thank him for letting you use his phone. I really appreciate it. He won't regret it."

I didn't need to say this. Nasurwin had been of great help before, and I had compensated him with a car, a golf club membership, and nice dinners.

"Lisa, listen. I might not be reachable for a few days. Just be calm and tell the others to answer any questions the police might have. We have done nothing wrong. Be honest and cooperative. Okay?"

"Understand, sir. They told us it might take some time. Hope all is okay."

"One more question, Lisa. Did you hear from Igor?"

"No, sir. I think he is still abroad. What shall I tell the police if they ask me about him?"

"Nothing. You don't know where he is. Understand?"

"Okay, sir. Take care."

Igor and I thought our latest project would have no bad consequences. How wrong we were.

"I'll call you as soon as I can. Just cooperate and tell them everything they want to know."

I disconnected and there was a knock on my door.

"Who is it?"

"Message for you, sir."

I opened the door a crack and the messenger boy slipped me an envelope.

The handwritten note simply said, "We would like to have a chat with you concerning Khalij. Come to the pool bar now."

Khalij Bank of Saudi Arabia. My nightmare.

The guys in the lobby didn't exactly look like bankers, although they were wearing dark suits.

My mind was racing. I'd been expecting something like this for a long time, but when nothing had happened I had started to relax and had tried to push the possibility to the back of my mind.

Luckily old habits never die, at least not with me. I never travel without at least one different passport and valid visas for the countries I visit. I opened the room safe and took out the emergency pack I always have with me. It contained Canadian and Swiss passports.

No time to pack. I would miss my next golf set.

My old briefcase contained my precious laptop, a dozen credit cards, and five thousand US dollars.

I made a mental note to call the hotel later to close my account and to store my belongings.

I opened the door. Nobody was there. This time I took the stairs rather than the elevator, descending slowly and carefully.

I remembered that one of the doors downstairs opened to the car park. There are no basements in Bali.

When I opened the door that led to the car park, there he was—the biggest and ugliest of the three Arabs.

"We are at the pool," he said, showing me his yellow teeth as he smirked.

Now one of the good old habits kicked in. Over the years it had saved my life on quite a few occasions.

I smiled back and put my briefcase on the floor.

"I want to show you something," I said, and while he was looking down at my worn briefcase, I kicked him in the balls with all my strength while my elbow connected firmly with his jaw.

I was out of breath but quite proud of myself as I watched him hit the ground hard without a sound. That was the trick in such a situation—no sound. The kick in the balls was usually good enough, but the elbow to the jaw finished the job.

I didn't take time to admire my handiwork but walked to the main road where I flagged down one of the many taxis that crowded the streets of Bali.

I smiled at the driver and told him to take me to the airport. However, I did not intend to catch a flight. My old schooling again kicked in almost automatically.

If my pursuers could get the Jakarta police to raid my office, it would be easy for them to find the taxi driver who dropped me off at the airport. Thus the airport was only my first destination.

I prayed the traffic would not cause too much delay, because the Arabs might have mobilized the police to find me. My second silent prayer concerned the injured Arab. I hoped he would sleep long and deep.

To my pleasant surprise the late-afternoon traffic was not bad, and I made the airport in less than half an hour.

I gave the driver a generous tip and hoped he would remember me when the police interrogated him. I waved at him as I entered the international departure hall.

When I saw he had gone, I left immediately to take another cab.

"Can you bring me to Mengwi?" I asked the driver, shading my face as much as I could. I sat behind him to the far left so he couldn't see me in his mirror.

"Yes, sir. No luggage?"

"It's already there in my house."

We spoke Bahasa, the Indonesian language.

I felt the urge to light a cigar. I love Havanas and always have some with me. That was the other important item in my briefcase.

He tried to make conversation, but I told him in a friendly tone that I was too tired to talk.

I sat low in the back seat, my golf cap covering my forehead but leaving enough room so I could scan my surroundings carefully.

Whenever I saw a police car I slid down a bit lower in my seat. While the two-hour trip was bumpy, it was uneventful.

Mengwi is a city to the north of Denpasar, the capital city of Bali, and halfway to Ubud, a famous and very beautiful mountain resort with great restaurants and numerous little villas for tourists who seek privacy. I was one of them.

I asked the driver to unload me at the busy street market. Street vendors were selling food, textiles of all sorts, and tons of souvenir rubbish for Indonesian rupiahs, or even better, for US dollars.

I strolled through this crazy tourist trap until I spotted a little shop that sold used mobile phones.

"You have a good phone for me?" I asked a bored-looking young man sitting on a wooden stool.

"I have Samsung only, sir."

I used English to sound like a tourist, although with my briefcase I might been mistaken for a lawyer on the run.

"I lost my phone. I need a SIM card too. You have?"

I showed him green cash, grabbing his attention.

"It's forbidden to sell SIM cards here."

"Oh, okay. Then I have to go back to my hotel and make arrangements there."

"But I think I have one for you. It's quite expensive, sir."

"How much? You would help me a lot."

"SIM card and phone two million rupiahs. Plus I can upload the card for you with XL. It's the best operator here."

"I'll give you two hundred dollars if you do that right now."

He opened a drawer in the old table on which his phones were displayed and brought out a Samsung Note, well used and probably stolen a long time ago.

"Here, sir. Very good phone. Almost new and pulsa [the upload] for more than 300.000."

The deal went quickly, and I pocketed my new means of communication.

Again, I operated according to old habits. Before fleeing the hotel, I had taken the battery out of my mobile phone. The Indonesian police, although terribly corrupt, are quite tech-savvy, and it wouldn't take them long to track a smartphone.

I thanked the young man and told him I was returning to the coast.

In fact, I was heading up the mountain. Taxis and other transportation were available in abundance. In my semi golf outfit, I looked too classy to take one of the minibuses, the angkots, that offered transportation for a few cents. I spotted a beat-up old cab. The driver was smoking and did not seem interested in customers.

"To Ubud?" I touched his shoulder, startling him.

"Okay, sir. Hundred thousand okay?"

"Sure. I'm not in a hurry."

I climbed into the dirty and worn back seat and again was tempted to light a cigar. I refrained, just in case.

The drive up the hills was spectacular as always. Deep bush left and right was interrupted only by emerald green rice paddies.

I enjoyed the ride despite my worries. Excited about his fare, the driver enlightened me about the area we passed. I played along and faked interest in every village and temple he pointed out.

I learned almost everything about his three sons, his two daughters, and all of his grandchildren. He was a typical Balinese and proudly so.

After an hour, we reached the outskirts of Ubud where about a thousand monkeys sat on the road or in the trees. I had been here years earlier, enjoying the fresh air and even the monkeys with my ex-wife. She was fascinated by the animals and couldn't stop feeding them bananas and nuts. It had driven me nuts.

"Where go, sir?"

I remembered a small warung, an open street restaurant found everywhere in Indonesia. It served great duck dishes and pork and was frequented by wandering tourists who wanted typical Balinese food and ice-cold beer. Duck is a Balinese specialty and is prepared like nowhere else in the world.

"The Bebek Manis. You know?"

"Very good food, sir. The owners are my cousins from my wife. You like good bebek (duck) there and very good cold beer."

He was happy with my choice because he would get commission from his cousins for bringing a tourist. In Indonesia, every business, whether small or large, is based on commission. The system works quite well.

The driver took a few turns that I didn't remember, and there we were. The warung was busy with tourists, a few Balinese, and Javanese girls in tight miniskirts. It was just about sunset, and the early night business was about to start.

I paid the cab driver $150 and asked him to wait for about half an hour. I intended to inquire about a private villa, pretending to be a writer who didn't want to be disturbed. The warung was the ideal place.

Suddenly, I was hungry. I felt quite safe here, and my earlier stressed mood was about to fade away.

I ordered half a duck glazed with delicious honey sauce and asked for an iced beer.

I asked the girl serving me whether she knew of a private villa for rent. I told her I was a writer and needed privacy. The girl and her boss gave me some options. Ubud is full of artists, painters, sculptors, and writers.

The boss mentioned three places, all family-owned and not too far away. He offered to show me the villas after my dinner, and I thanked him profusely.

I glanced over at my cab driver, who was again in a semi-catatonic state with a cigarette hanging out of his half-open mouth. He was waiting.

I had another beer, which tasted even better than the first, and then asked Wayang, the owner of the warung, if he could show me one of the villas.

We got into the ancient cab, and the two men greeted each other with great enthusiasm in Balinese, which I didn't understand. Indonesia has one national language, Bahasa, but in the provinces the people still speak their traditional languages, which only they can comprehend.

"Okay, sir. We have villa Kakatua [the bird] by a small river down in the valley. Very beautiful."

"You know," I said, "I would prefer something on high ground where I have a view of your beautiful city. This will give me inspiration and ..." I deliberately trailed off.

They quickly discussed the situation in their strange language. Then Wayang said, "We have a nice villa about a kilometer from here on a hill, a bit in the forest. Want to see?"

"That sounds great! Yes."

"But it's more expensive than Kakatua. One hundred dollars a night with the servant. She can cook too. Bebek is very good there." They both laughed.

About twenty minutes later we entered a narrow dirt road leading through dense forest. No monkeys, I noticed.

"No monkeys here?" I asked.

They laughed loudly.

"Monkey is very clever," Wayang said. "He knows where the tourists are. They all in one place. Get food and the people make money."

Of course, I thought. *Monkeys are smart, and the street vendors use them to attract tourists and to generate income from souvenirs, drinks, and T-shirts.*

After an abrupt right turn, we stopped in front of a typical Balinese house. The villa was located on a small hill overlooking a valley with a small river running through it.

"It has air conditioning and a small pool," Wayang told me. "Ketut likes to serve you." Ketut, as it turned out, was not the maid but the owner, or so I thought. The gorgeous middle-aged Balinese woman greeted us at the entrance to the villa, which had one of those ancient temple doors found everywhere in Bali.

"Ketut is my cousin," the cab driver told me. I still hadn't gotten his name.

They led me into the spacious villa. The living room offered a spectacular view. Right in front of it was a plunge pool with its outer wall at the edge of a deep canyon. Dazzling!

"I'll take it for one week," I said. "It will give me creativity to write and to think."

Ketut prepared iced fruit juice. I never found out exactly what it was, but it tasted just fine. She smiled at me, revealing shining white teeth between her full lips.

We sat outside enjoying the drink, and I was eager to get rid of the two cousins.

"We have beer and liquor here too, but you must pay extra," Ketut told me. "The food you wish is extra cost too but very reasonable."

She flashed her smile again.

Her English was flawless, which astounded me. I could hear a trace of Australian in there.

Finally, after almost an hour, I paid the cab driver, adding a handsome tip, and the two cousins left me alone with Ketut.

She showed me the spacious bedroom with a huge carved wood bed. A little balcony just off of the living room provided another stunning view of the canyon below.

"I'll leave so you can take a shower and refresh yourself."

Then she looked at me quizzically and asked, "Where is your luggage?"

I completely forgot I had nothing to change into. I didn't even have a toothbrush.

"It got lost on my trip," I replied. "I will buy something tomorrow."

"There is a robe in the bathroom, and you can use the pool naked. I shall not peek." Her smile enthralled me.

"Thanks a lot. I would appreciate it if you ate with me later. Whatever you have ready is good for me."

"I will open a nice red wine then. If you need anything, just call me."

Before any naked bathing I intended to make a few calls. Bali, like most of Indonesia, has probably the best cell phone coverage in the world for its mobile-phone-crazy citizens. You can get a signal almost everywhere.

I pulled my freshly acquired Samsung out of my battered briefcase and found immediate coverage.

Igor's number was in my head as were many other numbers. I punched it in and he answered after only one ring.

"Hello?" The hesitant tone was not like Igor. Of course, he didn't recognize the number I was calling from.

"It's me, Igor. Needed to change phones. Where are you?"

"Oh, good. I was worried after I couldn't get the office or your mobile. I tried Lisa but to no avail. What the fuck happened?"

"I'm not sure, but I am sure it has something to do with Khalij. Some fucking Arabs were in my hotel, and they didn't look too friendly. I had to take one out."

"Dead? Did you have to do it?"

"No, he's not dead, but he will have a headache and no sex for a few weeks."

Igor laughed, improving my mood.

"I'm in Simferopol in the lab," he said.

Simferopol in the disputed land of Crimea was the home base for our technical department. Listening devices, hacking tools, surveillance equipment—the Russians are good at this.

"Stay there and don't move until I tell you," I said. "We might have gone a bit too far with Khalij, but what the hell. Done is done. The fact that the Saudis—and I'm quite sure that's who they were—showed up means our findings were correct."

"Is your phone safe? I'm encrypted here, but are you?"

"Definitely not. I bought it in a market. Let's cut this short. I have to find out whether I have Internet access here. I'll mail you what I know. Don't try to get Lisa or anyone else. The Saudis managed to involve the national police. No wonder. Next week the king makes his state visit here and sends his harem to Bali. You know where I am, but let's not discuss this now."

I disconnected and started to get undressed. I felt sweaty and smelly and had no fresh clothes.

A soft knock on my door startled me.

"Sorry to disturb you, sir," Ketut said, almost whispering, "I have a toothbrush and some other things for you. I think I know your size. Tomorrow morning I will buy jeans and T-shirts for you and if you wish some underwear." She giggled, looking beautiful and shy.

"Thanks a lot, Ketut. We haven't been introduced properly. I'm so sorry for that. My name is Freddy Becker, and I really appreciate your help."

I used my Swiss identity. Switzerland's neutral status always helped in such situations.

"Please relax and enjoy the pool. The water up here is quite fresh, not like down at the coast. I'll prepare dinner and open the wine. Are you sure I should join you?"

For an instant, I had the salacious thought that she might join me in the plunge pool, but then I got a hold of myself.

"It would be a great pleasure! Please, let's have dinner together. You can bill me for two." Now I was grinning.

Ketut retreated and I continued to undress.

I brushed my teeth and then glided into the cool water of the pool. For the first time in hours I could lower my guard and relax.

I had been in the water for maybe twenty minutes, mulling over the day's events, when I heard Ketut calling me for dinner.

I greatly enjoyed my brief respite in the pool. I had cooled off and had returned to a state where I could think and make decisions again.

Other than my round of golf at Nirwana, the whole day had been a nightmare, but it had reawakened instincts I thought I had lost long before.

I replayed my encounter with the Arab at the hotel. How could I have reacted the way I did? I thought this reflex was long gone, and much more important, I hoped never to have to pull it out of the drawer again.

My life before establishing my business in Malaysia and Indonesia was often dictated by violent events that demanded reactions like hitting the Arab. Hitting and not missing.

I dried off and slipped into the soft bathrobe Ketut had provided.

"Are you ready? I made honeyed pork ribs."

Good, I thought. *No more 'sir.'*

"Yes, I am—if you don't mind me joining the dinner party in a bathrobe."

She laughed softly, a sound that ignited my appetite—for food.

I entered the living room/dining room and was entranced by the special atmosphere.

Far over the horizon behind the black bush was a spectacular sunset that I must have missed while I relaxed in the pool.

The flickering light from a chandelier over the dining table turned the room into a fairy-tale scene with me as the underdressed visitor and Ketut as the princess.

She obviously had bathed and had changed; her hair was still damp. The tight dress left no room for speculation. She was simply a beautiful sight.

"A Barolo 2004," Ketut said, offering me a glass of red wine. Immediately the tiny alarm antennae in my brain signaled me to be on the alert.

How could she have known? Maybe it was just a coincidence. Barolo was my favorite Italian wine, and the year 2004 had a special significance for me.

"This is lovely, my favorite wine and ..." I stammered, not quite in control of myself.

"I hope you enjoy it. I used to be quite a good cook, but I'm not too sure nowadays." She rolled her eyes toward what I assumed was the kitchen. The scent of the honeyed pork ribs signified she knew what she was doing.

"Now sit down and let me check on my work. I'm hungry too." We clinked our glasses, and I took a deep sip of the delicious wine. My little alarm system, however, told me to be careful with alcohol.

Her eyes drilled into mine while she took a sip. Then she said, "To Petrossian."

I almost expected that. I stayed calm and answered her stare without blinking. I swallowed the wine, and it helped me to recover from the initial shock.

"Okay," I said, struggling for the correct reply to her opening. "Who are you?" Genius that I was, I thought I had found the right words.

"I'm Ketut," she declared. "That is true. I'm originally Balinese but also Petrossian, like you. And yes, this is my house and Villa Kakatua as well. We have covered you since this morning because we knew about the Arabs. The only moment we lost you was when you left the hotel through the back door. But you handled the situation well, and from there we had you under close control."

She flashed her lovely smile again. "When you started to hack Khalij, the base was following." She hesitated for a second. "Maybe we acted a bit too late."

"The taxi?"

"Not the one you took at the hotel. No, that wasn't us. But we followed. When you went to the airport, for a moment we thought you would try to board a plane. Sorry. We should have known better."

"And from there?"

"We had two police officers on motorcycles following you. They reported on your whereabouts with their mobile phones. No radio." She trailed off a bit and smiled, again displaying her perfect white teeth. "You see, not all the police in this country are bad."

"And in Mengwi?"

"Wayang, the cab driver, is a trusted distant relative of mine. I had him park close to the market and gave him cash to bribe other drivers not to take you. He didn't have to because he was the only cab there. In Mengwi, even tourists take buses, not cabs."

I took another sip of the excellent wine. "So you are Petrossian. And the others? The cab driver, the bebek warung owner and ...?" I forgot the names of the cousins, a sign that I had become a trifle out of practice in this business.

"Only me. The cousins have no idea what's going on, but they were compelled to help me steer you in the right direction. Now let's eat and enjoy the wine. I will tell you all because you are a legend." She smiled again.

Ketut put her glass down and went back to the kitchen, emerging with a huge salad bowl. I went after her to help bring out the honeyed pork ribs. They came on a stone hot plate. When I saw them, I again realized how hungry I was.

We sat down, and I looked at Ketut with different eyes. She was a clever, beautiful woman making all the right moves. She was obviously still active in Petrossian.

"You were fifty," she said, opening our new dialogue.

She didn't refer to my age, which was far above that, but to my Petrossian identity. We all had numbers and never used names, not even false ones.

"Fifty is very high up, if not the top. I know that much." Again, she smiled at me and I realized I had better be careful around that smile.

"You are well informed, which means you are not at the bottom of the organization. Tell me about yourself. I'm retired and both touched and impressed that the firm still looks out for me."

Ketut told me about herself while we enjoyed her great food. Usually I'm a very quick eater, but that night I relished the food, her company, and her life story.

She had been married to an Australian banker for six years. He worked in Jakarta and had no idea his beautiful Balinese wife had a side job as an operative for the world's largest private intelligence firm, Petrossian.

Petrossian did not recruit people to spy on relatives or friends but hired individuals of great integrity, people who wanted to do something noble.

Southeast Asia is fertile ground for such efforts because millions of people suffer under massive corruption there. The conspiracy is deep-rooted and is comparable to organized crime. I knew Petrossian worked closely with the global anti-corruption agency, mostly to find those who had fled the countries where they committed their crimes.

Ketut was an activist before she met her husband. As a student in Jakarta, she raised her voice a tad too high against corruption in the courts, in the police department, in the parliament, and in business.

Two attempts were made on her life after she accused a supreme court judge of corruption. At that point, Petrossian contacted and hired her.

At that time, I was still engaged in operations in Libya and adjacent dirty places.

She had met her husband at her new job, which was arranged by Petrossian. He had been country manager for a leading Australian bank in the Indonesian capital, and Ketut, the sharp and beautiful Balinese activist, became his assistant.

Ketut kept her story short. In the sixth year of their marriage Peter was accused of financial misdeeds. This happened during the crisis of 1998 when many Asian banks went down. His Australian bank had no such troubles, but the Indonesians were looking left and right for scapegoats.

Ketut and her husband were trying to have a baby, and one morning while she was at the doctor's office she learned her husband had taken his own life by jumping from the roof of his forty-two-story office building.

"He never, never would have killed himself!" Ketut told me. Her smile was replaced by a grim look.

"We were planning a baby! I had trouble getting pregnant, but we believed one day we would be parents. We made plans for our daughter or son to attend the best schools in Australia, to live there after Peter's term here was over. We had already bought a house in Perth. I still own it. It's a Petrossian safe house now."

Ketut furiously wiped away the tear that ran down her cheek.

About three weeks after her husband's death, fifty-three approached her. That came as a big surprise to me.

Fifty-three was a longtime Petrossian, a good friend of mine, a comrade who had saved my life as many times I had saved his. Yevgeni Fedorov was a legend.

"He was a good friend of mine a long time ago. Do you still have contact with him?"

"That's why I'm involved now." Ketut flashed a lovely smile again.

"He is in Indonesia right now, but I don't know where. I suspect he is nearby. Don't forget, next week the king of Saudi Arabia is visiting, and the security is just crazy. Over a thousand Saudis—princes, princesses and other dark-veiled women, and crazy, carpet-riding Arabs—are invading Bali."

She took another sip of wine.

"They booked three major hotels on Nusa Dua."

Located on the southern peninsula, Nusa Dua was the newest Balinese holiday destination.

That would explain the well-dressed Arab goons in my hotel. They obviously were part of a special security detail, though they were quite clumsy.

"What is your involvement with the Saudis?" Ketut asked, her wine glass in her hand.

"It's a long story but it starts to make sense," I responded.

"Fifty-three wants to meet you, and he asked you to lay low. He said you know what that means."

I raised my glass to Ketut and started to tell her my story.

CHAPTER 2

KUALA LUMPUR, MALAYSIA, A FEW DAYS EARLIER

I have always loved Malaysia, Indonesia, and the adjacent countries in Southeast Asia. During my off-time with my former firm, Petrossian, I had often visited these beautiful countries with their warm and friendly people, who suffered constantly from corruption and violent crime.

Bali was my favorite destination for its natural beauty, the food, the golf, and last but not least its lack of Islamization. Balinese are Hindus, but now the Muslims from Java were playing an increasing role in Balinese culture and business.

Twenty years before one could not spot a mosque on the Island of the Gods, but now they were mushrooming, to the dismay of the Balinese. And the king of Saudi Arabia was visiting!

In 2013 I had finally decided to retire and to wipe the past from my memory when an old friend from Russia approached me. Igor had never been Petrossian, but we used his extraordinary skills on numerous occasions.

His family's roots in Russia went back hundreds of years. The Kuznechovs were Tatars, hated by the Russians and by the Ukrainians, who in fact were Russians for centuries.

Russia's interests in Crimea were too valuable to leave this land in Ukrainian hands. The Russians had a naval base in Sevastopol and the brain tank in Simferopol, regarded as Russia's Silicon Valley. Most of the sharpest minds in the growing IT industry were based there.

When Vladimir Putin decided to return Crimea to the lap of mother Russia in 2015, Igor was pleased and worried at the same time.

After his last relative in Crimea had died peacefully, Igor decided to come to Malaysia, a country he loved as much as I did.

He was twenty years my junior, and his relative youth convinced me to go back into business. We formed a company that provided all sorts of electronic security for businesses, mainly banks.

With my extensive contacts in Kuala Lumpur and Jakarta, we quickly became successful, and we expanded from a two-man office to a company with more than forty engineers.

Igor was happy, I was delighted to be active again, and our business was running almost effortlessly.

A building in downtown Kuala Lumpur, which we were forced to choose as our headquarters, was the main office of one of Malaysia's largest banks. It was a partner of one of Saudi Arabia's largest banks, the Khalij.

It was mainly Khalij that required our services. The bank carried out an enormous number of transactions involving Saudi Arabia, Dubai, Abu Dhabi, Kuwait, the United States, and Europe and now, of course, Indonesia and Malaysia.

That day in Kuala Lumpur when Igor entered my office his face told me something was wrong.

"What is it, Igor? What's bothering you?"

I grabbed a bottle of vodka from my fridge, but Igor refused, which got my full attention. We share the same affection for ice-cold vodka after a hard day's work.

"Not now. Let me explain first."

So it was serious. He usually sounded like that only when he had a problem with one of his elaborate codes.

He went into detail about the software he had installed at Khalij. Finally I interrupted him and asked, "What's the fucking problem?"

"I think I went in too deep. Okay, give me a vodka!"

For a few minutes, we sat in my office and drank.

"I think I know what they are doing," Igor said, breaking the silence. "Dhahabi Khalij is financing the Islamic State." His face turned crimson.

My worst fears, which had plagued me for more than a year, had been confirmed. This was a monster I had tried to push away whenever I closed my eyes.

I refilled our glasses.

"How? What have you uncovered?"

"Remember I told you about that French contractor for which Khalij wanted extra security?" Igor took another sip.

"The contractor that officially does consulting work here and in Indonesia for construction, railway, toll roads, harbors, airports, and the military?"

"Yes, you told me about that company, Alliance Ovest or something like that."

"That's the one."

"What's wrong with them?" I asked, though I already knew the answer.

"They have huge jobs here and there."

Igor paused and took another sip of the Stoly.

"And they have only three people here. Two Arabs and one Frenchman."

The Alliance Ovest office in Kuala Lumpur received euros and US dollars in the millions, mostly from Dhahabi Khalij in Saudi Arabia but also from other Gulf-located banks. Then the Kuala Lumpur operation paid foreign suppliers and contractors in Europe and the United States.

The only puzzle in this constellation remained the services those other companies provided.

We knew every transfer to Europe or the United States was backed by proper invoices and by progress and service status reports. The central banks and the financial regulatory authorities required this.

I needed another vodka.

Our company served Dhahabi Khalij with software and with documents stating that all these transfers were legal and based on work completed. Our software automatically provided the bank with the clearing documents. A clerk filled out the necessary transfer forms before Igor's brainchild kicked in and took over the rest.

The forms were legally copied to the central banks and there, again with Igor's creation, electronically checked and cleared.

"Did we build them the perfect laundromat?"

I eyeballed Igor, who took another large gulp.

"Yes, I'm afraid we did! At least that's how it looks."

"Oh shit!"

For another hour or so we exchanged ideas about how to proceed, how to hide, or how to disappear from the surface of the earth. We thought of bringing in Petrossian since going to the locals would mean prison.

We decided to continue as if nothing had been uncovered but to gather all the data we could through hacking.

Igor was a world champion at hacking into systems billed as penetration-proof, especially our own. He occasionally worked for the Russian FSB, which meant lucrative extra business for us.

I ordered him back to Crimea, where our main lab was located. He could access everything from there. We knew how to communicate. Our Internet-based operation was the safest in the world. Igor had set up a network of proxy servers that spanned the universe.

Special flagged e-mails could be seen only with elaborate passwords.

The flagging went via harmless text messages to our phones. We used girls' names programmed according to the importance of the e-mails, which never showed up on any server.

"You are aware, my half-drunk friend, that certain authorities are very much involved in this?"

"I wouldn't think otherwise," Igor said.

"That's why I want you out of the country. Hack what you can from Simferopol. We'll decide later when to involve Petrossian."

"What about you? You are in danger too."

"I'll manage. I think I can handle them. I don't necessarily trust my contacts, but I have some leverage."

"I could disarm the system with Dhahabi Khalij, just take it out."

"Let's find out first what they know. Then it might become a job for Petrossian."

That evening I was not in the mood for dinner and company. I decided to stay at my cozy house located right on a golf course.

I called my assistant and asked her to be at the office by six the next morning. She was used to my erratic and sometimes disturbing schedule.

Lisa gladly confirmed.

She was a single mother of two girls. A few years earlier, her ex-husband had swapped her for a much younger trophy wife. When she was on the market I grabbed her for her close connection to the national police and, yes, for her good looks.

Lisa was an efficient, hardworking woman, and my staff and I liked her very much.

Luckily, she lived in Malaysia, where family members were in abundance; her mother, sisters, aunties, and other relatives took care of her household, giving her time to work for a company that never had regular office hours.

Around 10 p.m. Igor called me from the airport.

"I got a seat on Qatar Airways to Doha. There's a connection tomorrow morning to Simferopol. I'll call you tomorrow afternoon. Please be careful. I'm quite nervous."

Well, so was I, but the difference between me and Igor was that I was used to critical situations that put my life in danger.

This, however, was a new situation.

I was used to a clear enemy that might be life-threatening. On numerous occasions I had been trapped in Libya, Chad, and other godforsaken places and had gotten out simply because I knew who the foe was, how he operated, acted and reacted, and killed.

But this was different.

It was too late to call one of my Indonesian banker friends, but I didn't have to. While thinking of him my mobile rang.

Mochtar.

Once in Malaysia and Indonesia, businessmen of Chinese extraction most often adopted Islamic-sounding names after they gave up their Fongs and Fus.

He called from Jakarta.

"Is it too late to talk?" Mochtar asked.

"Always good to hear from you, old buddy."

"Can we meet tomorrow for lunch at my office? In Jakarta, I mean. It's quite urgent."

I always loved to go there. He had his own kitchen at his workplace. Very Chinese, very spicy.

"Sure. What's up?"

"You are working with these French guys, Alliance something, right?"

Now that I knew he was aware of the French company, he had my full attention.

"Yes, we did their security system. Why you ask?"

"Tell you tomorrow. Not on the phone. Do you have security at your house?"

I put down my single malt scotch, which I preferred over vodka during late hours, and sat up in my chair.

"I have two national police officers moonlighting here every night. What's up?"

"Take an early flight and see me at noon tomorrow. I'll tell you all that I heard."

Mochtar hung up abruptly, which was out of character for him.

I checked on my security and made sure the maid was serving the officers food and coffee.

Yes, they were on duty and happy to see me.

"Selamat malam, Pak," they said, greeting me. They were chewing on something fishy, and the maid had placed steaming coffee on their little table in front of the garage.

I gave each of them an extra tip and asked them to be alert.

"Siap!" they shouted in military fashion.

I couldn't think of sleep and therefore went to my secure communications room. This chamber was specially designed so I could transmit and receive messages, phone calls, and texts without being overheard from outside the room or from the air.

Four screens displayed night sight views of my property from very expensive cameras that were equipped with motion sensors for immediate recordings. The technology was Russian and hard to get past.

All was quiet. I could move the cameras manually if necessary, but I never did. Now I shifted them around to cover all possible dead angles.

All remained quiet.

Just to be busy I started to check e-mails, which I had already done at the office. I read world newspapers and the latest entertaining news about the newly elected US president. I switched on the TV and tuned to Fox News. Always amusing.

None of this calmed me down.

Lately I had cut down on my cigar smoking. The coughing was getting annoying, and my doctor, another Chinese Malay, firmly advised me to stop altogether.

Well, I tried. But now with my nerves jumping like wild horses and my heart beating at a heavy metal pace, I decided a good Havana was my sleeping pill.

At almost midnight my mobile rang again.

Lisa. This couldn't be good.

"Sorry, sir! I know it's late, but I just got a call from my cousin, Nasurwin."

The major in the national police.

"He asked if you could meet with him tomorrow around lunchtime."

Now I would have two lunch appointments the next day—one in Kuala Lumpur and one in Jakarta. I wished I could split myself in two and become invisible.

Something certainly was going on. I had known Nasurwin for several years. He was a straight guy with a great career in front of him. I prayed I wouldn't become a tool for advancing his professional ambitions. Now I was thinking fast.

"Yes, no problem. I would love to meet him." I white-lied, feeling that an array of appointments would distract from my real plans.

Lisa sounded unconvinced.

"Uh, he said it's somewhat important."

"Thanks, Lisa. Tell him we can have lunch at my office."

We hung up and my brain started to race.

There was movement on one of the surveillance screens. I saw the green light go on, indicating recording.

A black SUV moved slowly toward the front of my home and stopped. Then I saw my two guards heading to the gated entrance. They had an exchange with the occupants of the SUV and pointed down the road. Then the SUV was gone.

I checked the camera angle and zoomed in on the plates. Diplomatic. Twenty-one Saudi Arabia. A coincidence? I didn't believe so. I never believed in happenstance.

I zoomed in closer and made out a three behind the twenty-one. Military attaché or Saudi intelligence. The Mukhabarat.

They certainly didn't ask for directions. They had a good look at my security. I was quite happy that my two moonlighters were wearing sidearms and in clear sight.

After a few minutes, the same screen blinked the green alert sign. The SUV was back, rolling very slowly past my entrance with the back window down. I didn't need to zoom in to see that some guy was filming or taking still pictures. My guess was he took a video.

Now I knew I had made the right decision to send Igor out of the country. We were in trouble.

I also believed my lunch diversion had been a brilliant idea. This allowed me to take another sip of my Macallan.

I realized sleeping was not an option. I sent Igor some e-mails, which were totally safe with the Russian encryption codes and with his set-up of multiple proxy servers. I traced the way my messages were sent. Starting in Helsinki, they went to Yokohama, Vladivostok, Zurich, Switzerland, and Cape Town. The routing was getting too crowded on my large screen. Anyway, the messages were delivered to Igor's mailbox within seconds. My sent box was erased immediately and was irrecoverable.

I decided to light another Ramon Alones, my favorite Havana, when more activity appeared on my surveillance system.

I was not surprised to see another dark SUV roll by slowly. I zoomed in. There! Twelve with the subnumber five.

The US embassy, cultural, military. All the numbers after two and three were CIA.

Now I definitely postponed my sleep to another night.

With nothing better to do, I switched to CNN. The new US president was talking about a great wall on the Mexican border and about a military buildup of historic magnitude. You could say about him whatever you wanted, but he had a relaxing effect on me, something like watching a B-movie with comic actors, like my favorites, Laurel and Hardy. However, I rated them A.

A Mexican wall! Had this guy never heard about Kublai Khan and the Great Wall in China? Or about tunnels?

I realized I had to take action. If I remained here I was a sitting duck. I rummaged through my personal belongings and packed for what I hoped would be a short trip and maybe even a nice one.

I called the twenty-four-hour service at IndoAirways, a private Indonesian charter company with offices in Kuala Lumpur, and asked the woman who answered whether a plane was available the next day. Where to? My mind raced. Bali. Yes, Bali, the place where I always went to recover from stress and to escape unhealthy situations.

Yes, a flight on a Gulf 500 was available for fifty-eight hundred US dollars.

"For whom might that be, sir?"

In such cases I used my Swiss identity. It was one of many, but Swiss always meant serious, no hanky-panky.

I gave her my Swiss name, Frederique Becker, my passport number, and my credit card information and said I would be staying with friends. I also provided my mobile number.

I told her my driver would deliver my luggage, consisting of one suitcase and a golf bag, in the morning. And just to nail the booking I casually mentioned that Frankie, the owner of IndoAirways, was a good friend of mine.

Frankie was indeed an old friend who had flown me on several occasions when I was active with Petrossian. He would notice the booking in the morning and would know that it required discretion.

I loaded my luggage into my Lexus SUV, proceeding quietly so as not to alert my two guards.

I would drive my Mercedes to the office and from there to the airport. At least that was the plan for the moment.

I didn't care about the time anymore. I called my driver and told him to come at eight, the normal start to a business day.

I instructed him to take the Lexus to a certain point and then to switch to a taxi to deliver my luggage to IndoAirways at Kuala Lumpur International Airport. Andi was loyal and did not need to be told that absolutely no other person should know about this.

He understood for several reasons. One of them was that I paid for the schooling of his four children.

Now it was time to move.

It was not quite five in the morning when I pushed the electronic gate opener and my two guards jumped from their chairs.

They would often see me come and go at all hours. I told them I was going to the office. They saluted and as I drove away I noticed in the mirror that the gate was closing again.

Kuala Lumpur's streets were never deserted. Even at this ungodly hour there was traffic, mostly buses and trucks. Nevertheless, it took me only twenty minutes to reach our office building. I didn't park in my reserved spot but in one of the visitors' spaces. My old and sometimes dangerous instincts were slowly kicking in again.

I opened the elevator with my card and sat at my desk on the thirty-third floor while the coffee machine heated up.

I was startled when Lisa entered before six with an anxious look on her face. She was out of breath, and I had seldom seen her so agitated.

"Good morning, sir. I see the machine is hot. I'll make you coffee. I also bought some pastries and croissants." There was a *tout les jours* bakery just opposite our office building. It was my favorite bakery.

I wanted to hug her because I realized I had had only vodka and scotch since the previous night. Lisa brought me coffee and delicious croissants, which I started to wolf down.

"Sir," she said, "Nasurwin came to my house this morning. He told me it would be good if you could lay low for a little. Is this the right expression?"

"Thanks, Lisa. I understand. Please tell Nasurwin I owe him one! This is also the right expression."

I smiled at her and that seemed to calm her down.

This meant my lunch appointment with Nasurwin was off. Good.

"I wanted you here so early because I know I better lay low for a while. You are in charge. I have sent e-mails to all our people explaining that I had to be away for a few days and that you are the person in charge of all administrative functions."

"Where are you going?"

"Better you don't know, but I'll stay in touch. Please make sure my house is guarded."

I arranged all the necessary paperwork for the next few days and instructed Lisa to hand it out to the engineers. None of our staff was involved with Dhahabi Khalij. Only Igor and I had worked on the project.

I wanted to make sure nothing incriminating would show up on my computer, but I saw Igor had already taken care of that.

Now, after three cups of delicious organic coffee and a few croissants, it was time to reschedule.

My old training taught me to change plans quickly in emergencies.

It was almost seven o'clock when I closed my office door and dialed Frankie in Jakarta. He picked up almost immediately.

"Hi, Fred," he said. (Frankie always used my Swiss name when I booked a plane.) "How are you doing?"

"I assume you have seen my booking for the Gulf. As before, can we keep this between us?"

"Hey, I know you. You can trust me. Don't even tell me about your troubles. I don't want to know. A woman?" He snickered.

"Now listen, Frankie! I booked the plane for the afternoon, but I really would like to leave around ten. Possible? I had to book for the afternoon because I wasn't sure my phone was clean. My driver will deliver my luggage before ten. He will arrive in a taxi. Please make sure he can enter. He will call your office when he is close. I will arrive in a cab too. Same procedure."

"Got it. No worries, mate! I will personally instruct the airport."

Frankie loved Australia and always tried to sound like an Aussie. He was the only outsider ever to enter the Petrossian base near Khabarovsk. He had flown me and my team there after a hot mission.

"You think Bali is the right location?" He sounded a little bit worried.

"You know, Frankie, when you don't want to be found, hide in the open. And with the woman trouble I'm having right now, a few rounds of golf will be good."

I had often found this an effective way of hiding.

I picked up my old briefcase, which contained three passports, several credit cards, my laptop, a few Havanas, and about five thousand US dollars.

"I didn't see your car when I came in, sir," the ever-observant Lisa said.

"It's in the visitors' parking area. I'll take a cab from here. I'll be in touch. Don't worry. And please call Nasurwin. Tell him I can't meet him today but I'll make it up to him. I appreciate his notice. And tell Andi to bring my car home."

I made up my mind to call Mochtar from the plane, telling him I was on my way to Hong Kong. He was a good friend, but in situations like this I couldn't trust anybody.

"Sir, be careful. Nasurwin will understand." Lisa looked worried.

I was quite sure he would.

I grabbed my things and left the office.

I strolled over to the bakery, sat down at one of the small outdoor tables, and ordered an espresso. My goal was to look unsuspecting and innocent as I started hiding in public.

I read the paper, which was full of news about the upcoming visit by King Salman of Saudi Arabia to Malaysia and Indonesia.

This might have been a coincidence, but I did not believe in such things. I should have seen the connection much earlier.

Saudi Arabia was a small investor in Indonesia, and most of its money went to building mosques. The Wahabi Muslims were on a mission to spread their fundamental Islam to other countries.

But what about the millions they transferred every month to Alliance Ovest and from there to Europe and the United States?

I had all the required information on a tiny flash disk, which was resting in my underwear. I had to talk to Igor as soon as I arrived in Bali.

I had made my hotel reservation early in the morning under my Swiss identity. People in Bali knew me as an enthusiastic golfer, a drinker, a cigar smoker, and a gourmet. I had even been there with one of my girlfriends. There weren't many after my messy divorce, but I was still a functioning male.

I finished my espresso, stood up, and flagged a cab. I hadn't seen anyone who looked suspicious, and I felt safe.

It was eight-thirty and the city traffic was in full swing.

"International airport," I instructed the driver, and he started his perilous race toward my destination. Cab drivers in Kuala Lumpur were all Formula One wannabes.

The airport wing that housed charter companies was quiet and appeared safe.

A security officer frisked me after I walked through the metal detector and asked me what flight I was taking.

"IndoAirways," I replied and a policewoman escorted me to the carrier's office just around the corner.

Frankie's local rep greeted me and told the policewoman I was an old friend from Switzerland.

"The Gulf is ready for takeoff when you are. Your luggage is already on board. Wish I could join you for a round of golf."

Xin Pi was not only the rep but a close friend of Frankie and, I assumed, a partner. We had played some enjoyable threesomes together all over Asia.

"Be happy that you can't. I would take your money again, and then my flight would be free of charge."

He slapped me on the shoulder. "Just take care, okay? If you need anything, call me or Frankie on our private numbers. We'll fly you out if your lifestyle becomes a hazard again, which seems to happen often."

We shook hands and hugged, and then an IndoAirways limousine brought me to the plane. The sleek Gulf, glittering in the morning sun, gave me new confidence, and I looked forward to the one-and-a-half-hour flight. That would give me time to enjoy a Ramon Alones.

We were airborne in less than fifteen minutes, and as the Gulf banked to the right, I sipped an orange juice and looked down at the golf course outside Kuala Lumpur where my house was situated.

In less than ten minutes we reached our cruising altitude of fifty-one thousand feet, much higher than the commercial jets. I lit a cigar and started to make phone calls, using the state-of-the-art communications system installed by my company.

I kept it short with Mochtar and simply told him a business emergency required my presence in Hong Kong.

"Pity," he said. "I needed to inform you about some goings-on that emerged with the central bank concerning Khalij. Is Igor available?"

"He is abroad, and I don't know when he will be back."

"Okay, take care. If you have time call me tonight. There is a lot of tension right now relating to Dhahabi Khalij. You know we have handled some transfers that were triggered by your software."

I heard more than just concern. Mochtar was alarmed.

Our software automatically directed the transfers made by Alliance Ovest to several banks with international correspondence permissions. One of them was Mochtar's Indonesia Union.

"There is nothing wrong with the software, my friend. Don't worry." I was testing him.

"Maybe not," he said, "but somebody started to inquire about the contracts of Alliance in Indonesia."

Like other institutions, Mochtar and his very straight bank made good money by facilitating the transfers. Alliance paid extraordinary fees to keep the remittances under the radar of any investigating party.

All such payments, except the ones to a bank in Delaware in the United States, were made in euros to avoid the regulation that came with sending US dollars via New York.

"I heard. Don't worry, Mochtar. Our software, as you know, is safe and accepted by the central banks."

"Have you ever investigated where the money really went?"

"None of my business, and I don't want to get involved with that."

We exchanged a few banalities and hung up.

This done, I opened my laptop while the pretty flight assistant brought me freshly brewed coffee and a clean, cigar-size ashtray.

I inserted the mini flash disk in a USB port and opened it with my password.

The bank in Delaware. I never had any doubt about the potential for trouble with transfers to the United States. Hey, paranoid American outfits like the CIA, the FBI, and the NSA, for which I had little regard based on past dealings, did almost nothing else but sniff around for hypothetical and real financial crimes.

I opened the information about the bank in Delaware, which was linked to a corporation registered there as a subcontractor of Alliance Ovest.

Here it was. Alliance Contractors, Dover, Delaware. Alliance again! I should have checked that much earlier. I delved deeper, and thanks to Igor's ingenuity I discovered Alliance Contractors was a subsidiary of an offshore company named Golden Trader registered in Belize.

Nothing wrong with that. I owned a Belize company for tax purposes. These companies were legal although they had a somewhat shady reputation for aiding tax evaders like me.

I needed to talk to Igor as soon as I arrived at the hotel. This situation was getting hotter, even sizzling.

The paranoid Americans allowed such transfers for almost two years without any serious inquiry!

We approached Bali's airport, which was built like an aircraft carrier and sat at the narrowest spot on the island with the seas north and south.

The Gulf made a smooth touchdown, and we taxied to the VIP parking area where a stretch limousine, courtesy of Frankie, was waiting for me.

I told the driver to drop me outside the airport where I would be picked up by friends.

I didn't want to leave too obvious a track. Frankie knew where I was staying, but why should a Balinese driver know?

He dropped me right outside the airport near the army of cab drivers eagerly awaiting tourists. I gave him a generous tip and waited until he was out of sight.

Then I slipped into one of those hot and uncomfortable taxis, telling the driver my destination, the Legian Top. I loved this hotel because it was small, discreet, and luxurious.

The traffic was exhausting, even worse than in Jakarta. I always wondered why tourists chose hotels like mine when reaching them meant being roasted for hours in a cab that hardly moved.

But once I arrived at the Legian, I forgot all the troubles with traffic.

The Legian Top was located at the spectacular Legian beach. Every suite had a balcony right over the water, and hotel guests were enchanted by the sound of huge waves constantly breaking on the shore.

I was greeted by the manager, who brought me to my room on the top floor. We did all the paperwork for registration there. That beat standing around in the lobby, which was deserted most of the time anyway.

"Have a good stay, Mr. Becker. If you need anything, call me directly."

The manager gave me his card, and I enjoyed the welcome drink, a mixture of champagne and fruit juice.

"Do you need a car tomorrow for golf?"

He knew about my passion for golf.

"Yes, please, and I'd appreciate it if you could make me a reservation for early morning. They can pair me with whomever."

"Consider it done."

We shook hands and I got into my swim trunks. I knew I would want to take a dip in the ocean after my conversation with Igor.

I turned on my super secure mobile phone, again courtesy of Igor, and pushed his quick dial.

"Hi, boss! I've been waiting for hours for your call."

Whenever he called me boss, I knew he was on edge.

I told him about the shady banking connections, the two SUVs cruising past my house late at night, the alarming information from Mochtar, and my escape from Kuala Lumpur.

Then Igor spoke for more than an hour. What he told me raised the hairs on my neck.

Igor probed the transfers made via our software. He hacked into our system because he had become more than suspicious. He apologized for not telling me earlier but said he had hoped his qualms might be unfounded.

However, what he found was more than disquieting.

Through elaborate hacking, he got deep into the intestines of Alliance Ovest.

A Marseille-based company, at least officially, Alliance Ovest was partly Saudi-owned. The French nationals listed as principals were mere puppets, although well paid. The company patriarch had lost his main interest years earlier and had been saved by Saudi investment.

The official owner of Alliance Ovest, Manuel Ortega, obviously was running a clandestine criminal empire for his investors.

"What are they really trading?" I asked Igor.

"That's the point, boss! Nothing. They are not into drugs, weapons, sex trafficking, or related things. No! They just send money around, and I know where to."

I was sure he did. Igor was the best hacker on the planet.

"So where does the money go, Igor?"

I suspected the truth, but I wanted to hear it from him.

"Mostly to Al Qaeda, Al Nusra, and the IS but to many other such assholes all over the world. Most of it lately has gone to Syria. Clever of the Saudis to use our software to launder the money. Once the money is clean, Alliance Ovest distributes huge cash amounts to Syria via Turkey. Yes, mostly cash. The company owns a shipping outfit that serves the whole Middle East. In Syria, the cash is transported by innocuous means—in Toyotas, on horses, in saddlebags. They could buy the whole fucking place.

"But there is just too much cash for all the Islamists. I suspect there are channels out of Saudi Arabia to other recipients. No clue yet who they might be, though."

Igor was breathing heavily now.

"But that wouldn't be too bad, right? Money for Al Qaeda, Al Nusra in Syria. Who the hell cares?"

He tried a meager laugh.

"What else have you found?"

"Another large bulk goes to AL Qaeda and IS cells in Europe and America."

That was bad. I had guessed right, but it was good to get confirmation from Igor.

And I knew what was coming.

"I don't want to tell you how I got it, but I have a list of recipients in Europe and America. Listen, boss, I have no proof, but I think the US authorities, or at least some of them, know what's going on."

That would explain the CIA car cruising past my house and would indicate that the Americans knew at least part of the story. Holy shit!

"Is the list safe?"

"Boss, you know me. Not even I could find it after three vodkas. It's in one of my clouds, one I call seventh heaven."

Now he was laughing.

"What are we gonna do?"

"I honestly don't know right now, Igor. Lay low. Stay in Simferopol. If things get hot, I'll call in Petrossian but not yet. We have to find out who will react and how."

I suspected my old firm might already have an idea of what was happening.

"But when we find out it might be too late."

Igor was not chuckling anymore.

"You are safe there, and I'll try to enjoy myself here. I'll play golf tomorrow. As you know, in these situations I'm Swiss. They are neutral, mostly clean and harmless."

At least on the outside, I thought.

"Maybe not, boss," Igor said. "Large amounts flow to a Saudi-owned company in Switzerland."

Maybe my Swiss identity was not as clean as I had thought.

"Okay, Igor, send me the list. I need to see it. It will be deleted after I read it."

"I'll make sure of it. Send, read, and auto delete after reading."

I told Igor to enjoy Simferopol, to have some caviar and vodka while I tried to contain the overflow of bad news.

I needed that swim. Right now any shark I might encounter seemed harmless compared with what we might face in the near future.

I walked on the almost unbearably hot sand toward the breaking waves and dived in head first. I felt a calm engulf me as I entered the ocean. I swam underwater until my lungs almost burst. I surfaced just before a huge wave threatened to break over me and push me under with all its force.

For the better part of half an hour I swam hard, dived, and let myself be carried by the surf until I saw I was about two hundred meters from the beach.

Too far out for these waters.

I attempted to ride the waves back to the shore, but in the low tide I had to struggle against the current flowing out into the dark green ocean.

It took me another half-hour to reach the shore where I lay on my back, now welcoming the hot sand. I took a cold shower and leaped into the swimming pool located immediately beyond the crashing waves.

After a delicious dinner that night, I slept like a stone. My internal clock awakened me at five in the morning.

Preoccupied with the rising troubles, I knew this wouldn't be my greatest day of golf, but I forced myself to go out and play, or at least to hack around. I was good at this form of hacking.

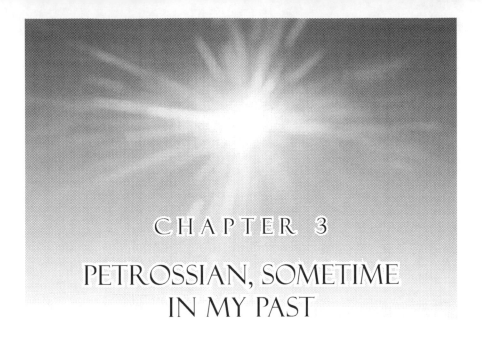

CHAPTER 3

PETROSSIAN, SOMETIME IN MY PAST

On December 25, 1991, the Soviet flag was lowered for the last time and replaced by the tricolor Russian banner.

Many intelligence personnel from the KGB, the Spetsnaz, the GRU, the Committee for State Security, and half a dozen other Soviet agencies became jobless overnight. Boris Yeltsin was not interested in reviving these agencies.

In March 1992, I was approached by Yevgeni Fedorov, a former high-ranking KGB operative with whom I had been socially acquainted during my time in Africa, mostly in Libya.

Fedorov was an adviser to the paranoid Libyan intelligence agency. We met in 1972 in southern Libya where I was selling portable water filters. As fate would have it, I became involved with shady characters from Black September, Germany's Baader-Meinhof Gang, and Italy's Brigate Rosse.

They were all in training camps east of Shabba in the hottest part of the Libyan desert—an ideal place to sell my water filters.

At that time, my closest ally and something like a friend was Colonel Jemal, head of the dubious outfit that called itself the country's intelligence agency. Leyla, the daughter of a former general in King Idris's army, had been my initial go-between. Her father had been executed by Gadhafi for having served a king. She had saved the rest of her family from the same fate by bribing everybody who could be corrupted. She came from old money that dated back to Italian colonial times, and she didn't want to give up her life in her home country.

We knew Jemal and his fearful bunch were tracking her, trying to find a reason to arrest, torture, and kill her. I tried on several occasions to take her with me to Malta or Rome, but she was always denied an exit visa.

I had wanted to smuggle her out of the country via Tunisia, but we were caught just short of the unprotected border by Jemal's henchmen.

I spent a night at an air force base in relative comfort while Leyla was transported to neverland.

Two days later Fedorov informed me she had been executed on the great leader's order.

He had told me he despised the Libyans despite being paid well and advancing his career with the KGB. That had convinced me to start working with him, naive as I had been.

We frequently met at the Uaddan, one of the oldest and most stylish hotels in town, for lunch or dinner. Fedorov had been on the Soviet embassy staff and therefore had unlimited access to vodka and other spirits that were strictly out of bounds in Libya. I enjoyed our get-togethers and fed him what I could, because I was still close to Jemal. I couldn't afford to do otherwise without giving up my vodka source.

Thus I became something of an asset for the KGB and my portable water filter business flourished.

This went on for years, and I enjoyed the special attention I received when I was abroad. The KGB put me up at the Excelsior in Rome and provided a generous allowance for my growing needs.

That's where I met my wife, a flamboyant Italian, sexy, loud, and insufferable in the end.

In 1977 I left Libya to live and work in Italy for her father's company, a job that soon started to bore me as much as my wife did.

Though she was Italian, she couldn't cook! Thus we became well-known guests in all the famous restaurants in Rome. Though these places were chic, I liked them only because of the food.

A few years later, with one daughter as the sweet fruit of our marriage, we decided to go our separate ways—she with a guy who fitted her better than I did, and I with myself.

Ariana, our daughter, and I were very close, and we stayed in touch throughout the years.

In 1992, I visited Prague for business. I had built a company, providing security for banks, cities, and corporations. It was successful but basically boring.

Prague was newly liberated from communism, and investors from the West were lining up to get a piece of the freshly baked cake.

One night I was enjoying a drink at my hotel on Wenceslas Square when a hand touched my shoulder from behind.

"Hello, old friend." The voice was very familiar, but I couldn't recognize the face. The man was bearded and wore sunglasses.

Fedorov.

I stood up and greeted him in Russian, which surprised him.

"You speak our language?"

"I studied Russian after my divorce, tovaritch. I had nothing better to do, and I could use words for her that she never understood."

We sat, had a few vodkas, and discussed the pretty girls in Prague. Then he came to the point.

"I'm still in the business," he said.

"FSB?"

He was a colonel in the Spetsnaz assigned to the KGB when we met in Libya.

The Spetsnaz was the absolute elite in military intelligence and was held in far higher regard than the KGB by its Western counterparts. It was considered cleaner, or so I thought.

"We are well financed and have a huge client list all over the world," Fedorov said.

I didn't know whether this was a recruiting approach or just small talk, so I let him continue.

"Matt, we could use a man of your talents." (He knew my real name; I had always regretted my French-Canadian mom's decision to give me an American name.)

Okay, a hiring speech.

"Our founder is Armenian, and not even I know his identity. He has recruited dozens of ex-KGB, Spetznaz, and CIA soldiers and formed the world's largest private intelligence firm."

He paused and looked for my reaction. I had none.

"Our clients are governments, the good ones, businesses, and individuals. And we are formidable. We have financial and technical resources that are on the level of any major firm in the world."

I still didn't react in any way to his oration, so he continued.

"It's no coincidence that we meet today. I have been following you and planned to see you tonight. I know you have your business, which is one more reason I approach you. If you are still not interested, we remain friends. I hope so."

Then Fedorov outlined his proposal.

My business would flourish after I became a member of his firm, as he called it. The organization would guarantee projects, finance them, and let my company grow while I worked as an agent.

There was one condition. I would have to undergo four months of training in Russia during which time my company would be run by a designated manager who was an expert in my field.

I was tempted. My business was like my former marriage—successful in the beginning and then boring. I was a restless guy. I was running from city to city to sign contracts, to assign my engineers, and to install stupid cameras and security systems. The IT world was in its infancy. Thus no complex high-tech solutions were required to fend off genius hackers and other weird personalities. It was all hardware. Intelligent software was a long way off.

I longed for action.

"Okay, you got me. Give me details."

Later that evening we met for dinner and Fedorov filled me in.

The founder, as he explained earlier, was an Armenian billionaire with business interests all over the world.

"The name of our firm is Petrossian, but I don't know if this is the name of our founder. Petrossian was a legendary figure during the Turkish-Armenian crisis, a hero in Erevan."

We discussed Fedorov's plan for hours, and he had me committed.

I was to return to Canada to meet the assigned manager. I would fill him in for about a week and then join Fedorov in Moscow. The training facilities were located near Khabarovsk, a few hundred kilometers north of Vladivostok, where Petrossian owned about two hundred square kilometers of untouched land. The firm had set up a state-of-the-art training center for prospects (or fools) like me.

I have to admit I got excited.

After my Libya adventure had led to the death of my girlfriend, Leyla, I had always wondered whether this kind of work might be my fate or my doom. Fedorov told me that I was very talented and that the KGB had wanted to recruit me in the seventies but didn't because I was somehow considered untouchable. That flattered me.

At the time, I would have flatly refused because I saw the KGB and its evil masters as the enemy based on my upbringing and on my strong belief in freedom.

The next day Fedorov gave me more information about clients, activities, and contacts but only after I signed an agreement stipulating total secrecy along with a very generous income.

Two days later I was on a plane to Zurich. From there I flew to Montreal where my company had its modest headquarters.

Louis Silverstein, an Israeli engineer who was my replacement as owner, CEO, manager, and slave master, was waiting for me at the airport. I liked the guy immediately. He told me he was a Mossad agent for more than twenty-five years before joining Petrossian. I told him I was a water filter salesman in Libya. We had a hearty laugh over that.

I introduced him to my staff, which consisted of two technicians, one bright Mexican boy who did whatever he was told, and my secretary, an elderly but efficient divorcee. After my failed marriage, I didn't want to have young, attractive women working with me.

It took me less than a week to make Louis familiar with my business. He was a smart guy and knew his assignment would last only until Petrossian took over my company.

The day before I was due to depart for Moscow, Louis brought a young Russian to the office whom he introduced as his assistant: Igor Kuznechov.

I couldn't possibly have known how close Igor and I would become many years later.

"Igor is what you call a genius," Louis said in introducing him. "He will bring your company to new levels involving computers and all kinds of new IT things that neither of us understands."

Louis, Igor, and I had a farewell dinner that night, and I gave Louis the keys to my apartment. He instantly transferred them to Igor.

"I prefer to stay in a hotel," he said. "No hassle with cleaning, house calls, and other domestic chores."

Igor, however, was happy to take over my apartment. I told him I had state-of-the-art TV, cable Internet, which was still very new, and a great view of the city.

That night would be the last one I slept in my apartment and in my own bed, and given my dreams I was sure I would never return.

The next morning I called my daughter in Paris where she was finishing her studies as a doctor and where she had fallen hopelessly in love, as she told me with some apprehension.

I told her I would check out her boyfriend before she took any more steps. Her sweet laughter rang in my ears all the way on the flight to Moscow.

Hell, I was close to fifty and was starting a new career that was more like an adventure. I thanked God I was free and without the burden of a wife, and I slept in my first-class seat until the captain announced we would be landing in half an hour at Sheremetyevo Airport in Moscow.

I was supposed to meet Fedorov at the Apartment Tsentralnaya, a small hotel a few kilometers away from the airport. We planned to stay the night there before boarding a Petrossian jet for the Far East.

My visa, which Louis had stamped into my Swiss passport in Montreal, proved to be valid, and I was through immigration in no time.

The last time I was in Moscow, the only time before now, was during Soviet rule. I had been interviewed by what were undoubtedly KGB border guards. "What's your business in the Soviet Union? Show me your hotel reservation. How much Western money do you have?"

This time the Russian officials were more humane than any US immigration officer. No questions, just a "Welcome to Russia," a stamp and I was out.

Wow, things had changed.

However, the ordeal of getting a cab remained unaffected by the new liberalism. I had to stand in line at an old-style taxi booking office where employees who looked like Soviet holdovers handed out paper slips with numbers on them. I paid twenty US dollars, which immediately gave me priority to the dismay of other waiting passengers.

My cab arrived after less than five minutes, and to my surprise it was an almost brand-new Toyota. The trip to my hotel took about half an hour and was totally uneventful.

My room was booked, the reception staff was friendly, and I took the elevator to the third floor at the top of the building.

The lift stopped at the second level, and two Russian gentlemen entered. They smiled at me and greeted me in English, saying, "Good afternoon."

Those were the last friendly words I would hear for some time.

My alarms were probably jet lagged and so was my reaction.

I was hit on the head with something hard and felt like I had suffered an electric shock. Then I felt nothing.

When I finally opened my eyes again, I had no recollection of the event in the elevator. I was naked on a cold, wet floor in a dark room.

"Why are you here?" a man with a heavy accent demanded to know.

I could only reply with a grunt. My head was killing me.

"You have two choices. One, answer truthfully and we let you rest, or two, keep quiet and we make you talk."

I grunted once again.

"As you wish." The voice created an unusual echo in my head.

Someone turned me on my back and put a wet towel over my face.

Waterboarding! The thought shot through my throbbing head. I had heard of this torture but had never experienced it.

One of my captors poured a cold stream of water over my covered face, making me choke and cough and creating the sensation of drowning. The pain was agonizing and the feeling of drowning something I wouldn't have envisioned in my darkest dreams.

Finally, after an eternity, the towel was pulled from my face and I started to vomit, almost completely clogging my respiratory tracts.

He or they—I still didn't know whether one or more torturers were working on me—pulled me into a sitting position.

"Now tell us why you are in Moscow." Okay, it was more than one. The interrogator paused and spoke in Russian to his partner in crime. I understood every word.

"Why don't we just kill him and forget about this worm?"

The Russians liked to use the term *worm* for their helpless prey. I didn't react to this. My brain had started to function again, and I didn't want them to know I spoke Russian fluently.

I now realized I felt pain when I tried to open my eyes, partly because a powerful flashlight was directed at my face. The light was so potent that I felt like a worm.

I tried to speak—in English. I remembered to use a Swiss accent, which was notably different from any other in the world.

"I want to visit Moscow and St. Petersburg. Museum and ballet ..." I couldn't speak clearly since my mouth was still partly clogged with vomit. My voice was fading, and I sensed I was not very convincing.

"You don't have a return ticket to Canada where you came from. Stop lying. Last chance."

I had established that there were two or more men in the room, but I quickly abandoned any idea of fighting my way out when the rough hands pushed me down on my back again.

The hands again put the wet towel over my face, and I came close to telling my captors a different story. But no one poured water on my face this time. Instead someone said, "Let's go have a drink. He can rot here for a few hours. Then we'll finish him."

Another guy was obviously amused, and with a hoarse cackle he agreed to his partner's idea. It seemed my captors had lost immediate interest in me.

I heard them opening a door, a heavy thump after the door was shut, and then the clanking of locks.

I didn't move for an eternity. Slowly and carefully I opened my eyes and found total darkness. Relief.

"Where are you?" I tried to establish contact, but there was no reply. Did they really leave for a drink?

I crawled around the wet floor and felt ceramic tile under my fingers. A bathroom?

Agonizingly I stood up and felt my way around my wet prison. Fixtures on one of the walls indicated a shower. I turned a handle, and cold water splashed over my body. Although I was freezing, even cold water was welcome.

A few centimeters to the right I found the other handle. Warm water! It gave me great relief. I turned the handle to hot, heating up my tormented body and my wits.

I was enjoying the hot water when suddenly the lights came on, and a metallic-sounding voice issuing from a speaker said, "The door is unlocked. Your clothes and belongings are on the other side. Enjoy your stay in Russia."

What the hell was that? Did they believe me? Was it over?

I looked around and I indeed was in a bathroom of some kind, albeit a primitive one—no toilet, no sink, just the overhead shower, and a single light bulb in the center of the ceiling.

Wet as I was, I went for the door. With great caution, I pushed it outward and stepped into a warm, luxurious room with soft leather chairs on which fresh towels had been placed. My suitcase, my old briefcase, and my clothes were on a soft settee on the far wall. Best of all, a large bar was situated to my right, stocked with all kinds of liquor and ice cubes in a silver bucket.

Again, what the hell?

I dried off and instantly began to feel better than I had in quite a while.

I dressed and sat down in one of the huge leather chairs. I was fighting the urge to pour myself a huge vodka when the door opposite me opened and Fedorov walked in.

"Hello, tovaritch. Welcome to Russia! Welcome to Petrossian!"

His Russian peasant face was beaming. That was my first impression when I saw him. This peasant was responsible for my suffering. I hated him. I wanted to hit him over the head and to waterboard him.

"You were great! You will be one of us." He poured vodka into two huge glass goblets and handed me one.

I stared at him, and he seemed to realize I was about to kill him.

"Listen first, my friend. This was a crucial test, and you passed with flying flags."

"Colors," I corrected him. "It's colors, not flags, you idiot. I almost checked out in there. If I get my hands on your two assholes, I'll kill them."

"We were careful with you! You were not hit on the head but were injected with an old KGB poison that has the same effect. Drink your vodka and then we'll go to our house where Irina is cooking the best food in the whole country."

The vodka did its job, and I started to feel healthy and calm again. And hungry! And somehow extremely proud and satisfied. I was a strange human being.

CHAPTER 4

ESCAPE IN BALI

K etut and I finished our marvelous dinner together with the Barolo.
An elderly maid cleared the table and served coffee.

"I think you should have coffee to stay awake," she told me. "Fifty-three might show up very soon. I know he was in Bali yesterday. He left a message and notified me about you. Just in case, he said."

"Let's call him Fedorov. I always hated our numbers and used them only in e-mails."

"Okay, Matt, I understand." She smiled. I was starting to like her.

Strangely enough, I felt a sense of relief to be part Petrossian again.

After almost twenty turbulent, adventurous years with the firm, I had returned to my old business with Igor. Today, however, we operated on a much higher technological level and on much more perilous grounds. Nobody could have imagined twenty-five years earlier how dangerous computers would be down the road. Igor always knew, though.

We sat in rattan easy chairs on Ketut's terrace, watching the dark sky and listening to the animal sounds coming from the nearby thick bush.

I enjoyed one of my Ramon Alones but stayed away from the cognac she offered.

"Maybe a wise decision." Ketut was cheerful.

After midnight we decided to try to catch some sleep. I kissed her good night on her cheeks and thanked her again for a lovely dinner and for being a great host.

However, I couldn't think of sleep. Earlier I had checked out the Wi-Fi strength on my newly acquired mobile phone. Though it had all the latest encryption Igor had developed, I didn't dare switch on this high-tech device, because even over Wi-Fi, a mobile phone, once logged, can be found.

I opened my laptop and it came to life right away. This machine was safe. I was sure of it.

I inserted the mini flash disk and continued reading its contents.

It was a time bomb, one that would detonate sooner rather than later.

The data more or less confirmed what I already knew, but then I arrived at a part of the document that made the hair on my neck stand on end.

It was not only Al Qaeda and Al Nusra but mostly the Islamic State the banks were financing and abetting.

I came to a page that contained videos of secretly recorded meetings. However, the videos were scrambled and could be opened only with the proper password. I would have to talk to Igor in the morning.

The names of the participants were scrambled too. With no way to read on, I hit the sack.

I fell asleep almost instantly. I entered a deep black hole undisturbed by good or bad dreams, only by a large hand that closed over my mouth in the middle of the night.

I kept still. Old habits kicked in again. I knew jumping up or trying to fight the intruder would be hopeless, for he had the advantage.

"Tovaritch, just be quiet."

Yevgeni Fedorov, now in his early seventies, released his hand, and I looked at his face for the first time in more than five years.

"I woke Ketut first. She is dressed and ready. She knows the area best."

"Nice to see you too," I said with a tired grin. "What's going on?"

"They found you. They are here. We have to move fast."

"Who are they? The fucking Arabs?"

"Yes, and more. I suspect the CIA, but I'm not sure. They want you and the flash disk."

How could they possibly have known about the flash disk?

I knew Fedorov would never joke about something like that in the middle of the night, and I got dressed in less than two minutes. I was again in my dirty garb.

The door opened and a fully clothed Ketut entered the room.

"There is movement on the road. I think it's a car without lights. No engine."

That made sense. The road to the house through the bush descended slightly, but the crushing of little pebbles under the tires apparently gave the intruders away.

"I hope you have good, solid shoes." Ketut looked at me in my sneakers.

"That's all I have. The rest of my stuff is at the Legian Top."

We didn't switch on lights, but the moonlight gave us enough illumination to move around and to prepare for a threat I still hadn't identified.

"Okay, listen," Fedorov whispered. "I don't know how many of them or whether they are close. We'll leave via your plunge pool right down into the canyon."

The plunge pool was located by a steep cliff.

"How the hell are we supposed to go down there?" I asked.

"I have a rope ladder hooked to the pool, and it can be released from the bottom. Come now."

Ketut looked more and more like a Petrossian to me. Her smile was replaced by a deep determination that reflected her professionalism. Had she trained like I had? Four months in Krylniy, the base, had left marks I hadn't seen on her yet.

I slipped my laptop into my old briefcase, which fortunately had a shoulder strap. The flash disk was in my pocket.

We crawled to the edge of the pool, and Ketut went first, lowering herself into the deep and dark gorge. Within seconds she was gone.

"Now you, tovaritch."

Fedorov gave me a little nudge, and I climbed at least twelve meters down the rope ladder. Ketut guided me into a shallow cavity made of palm leaves.

Fedorov came down with Ketut still at the ladder. She pulled hard on a little string attached to the ladder. With a soft click above us, the rope ladder fell into her arms. She had obviously practiced this way of escape.

We took shelter under the palm leaves, and Fedorov signaled us to be absolutely silent.

For more than fifteen minutes we heard nothing, but it was wise not to move. The thick shrub would have made too much noise for any movement to go unnoticed from above.

Then we heard a sharp crack. Someone was breaking down a door. Glass shattered and suddenly a bright light shone from above.

"Don't worry! They can't see us," Ketut said in a low voice.

"You see why I thought the CIA might be involved?" Fedorov looked at me.

Yes, I knew. This break-and-enter style was typical of the Americans, not of the Arabs, so it was safe to assume we were dealing with the CIA or people with CIA training.

"Just don't move." Ketut's warning came at exactly the right instant as someone pointed a powerful flashlight down toward our hiding spot. The light wandered right over us, then moved left and right, and vanished.

"No way to get down there." An unmistakable American voice from above confirmed our successful escape. *For now*, I thought.

We heard rummaging in the house, but nothing more got broken.

"Where is your maid"? I asked Ketut.

"I sent her home after dinner. I had this strange feeling. I didn't sleep at all. Then fifty-three arrived—sorry, Fedorov—and I knew something would happen."

She was trained.

Dawn slithered up slowly from behind the house. We knew we had to move from our cover while the darkness lasted. Fortunately, the light remained obscure down below for much longer than above us where we could already see the pool's lava stone wall.

It was risky but we had to make a decision. My old instincts resurfaced. I took over.

"We go one by one deeper down the gorge. Ketut, you go first, then Fedorov. Shit, we don't have a weapon. I want to cover you but with what?"

Fedorov took a black SIG handgun from his belt and gave it to me.

"Courtesy of the Indonesian national police. Your friend Nasurwin is in Bali and equipped me with one of their weapons. Don't shoot yourself! You are out of practice."

He gently slid down the steep bank toward the roaring river, which would dampen the sounds we made.

I listened intently for any sounds from above, but the thugs had left or were simply enjoying the view. I followed the two Petrossians down to the river.

CHAPTER 5

MARSEILLE, FRANCE

Alliance Ovest's headquarters was situated at Corniche du President John Fitzgerald Kennedy with a spectacular view of a storm-tossed Mediterranean Sea.

Manuel Ortega, the patriarch of the century-old family enterprise, stood at the floor-to-ceiling window scratching his head, which was covered with full white hair.

He turned and looked at his visitors, who were seated in high-backed leather chairs, ignoring the storm that raged outside.

The storm inside the luxurious conference room was becoming just as ferocious.

Ortega studied his visitors. He had hoped he would never see them in person, but now they were here, and his life's work, the expansion of his great-grandfather's business, was threatened. His freedom, his fortune, and his family were at stake.

He had deep regrets about his decision in 2001. At the time his business empire had been shaky, standing on thin pillars. He had lost two ships with illegal cargo of drugs, guns, and ammunition to pirates or the cartel. The Mexicans never admitted wrongdoing.

Naturally the ships had been uninsured, and therefore the loss was totally on his shoulders, which grew older and weaker under this heavy burden.

Then fortune showed up again in the form of a Saudi prince, or at least that's what he said he was.

Money was clearly not a problem for Al Anwar. He was staying at the Escale Oceania in the largest top-floor suite.

Ortega's daughter, Michelle, in the middle of a nasty divorce, bugged him to introduce her to the prince. He did, another regrettable move.

Al Anwar and Michelle hit it off, for a few months anyway. This special liaison handed the prince just the leverage he wanted.

The elaborate scheme he proposed had been more than tempting and proved to be extremely profitable. Ortega had been able to save his company, and somehow the dark forces around the prince even took care of the ever-intimidating and bullying Mexican cartel.

Soon after Alliance Ovest formed ties with several Saudi-owned banks and companies, Al Anwar dropped Michelle like a hot potato.

She was inconsolable for quite some time until she found her next prospect. Ortega silently thanked God that she remained childless. Her behavior was all his fault. After the early death of Michelle's mother, he had spoiled his only child rotten. She became an international socialite without the brains she desperately needed to maintain her lifestyle.

The Saudi plan was not simple and required a restructuring of his trading company. Thus he added a construction firm, a finance vehicle, and several international branch offices that took care of business that never really ensued.

Everything was financed by the Saudis, and Ortega was not required to dig deep into his pockets.

However, the price for all this was total dependence. He was rich again and practically untouchable. All he had done for the last sixteen years was sign papers, host dinners, and donate lots of cash to charities, mostly in France.

Now everything had changed. Al Anwar sat at the head of the conference table, drumming his fingers impatiently on the polished surface of the ancient mahogany.

"How could this happen?" Ortega struggled to maintain a stable voice.

"I'll tell you in detail later," Al Anwar said. "Now be calm and let us take over."

As if he hadn't done exactly that years ago.

"Sit down, Manuel, and listen carefully to what we have to say."

Al Anwar looked very much like the boss he was.

Two Americans sat to his left and three Arabs to his right. Ortega had never met them before. They looked grim and somehow dangerous.

These were not the type of people he was used to doing business with. Even the Mexicans had looked more professional when he had shipped drugs for them.

One of the Americans looked at him with a stern face.

"We have a serious problem in Jakarta," he said, as if Ortega didn't know already.

The other American explained about the hacking of information at one of the banks his office did business with in Jakarta.

"What do they know and who are the hackers?"

Ortega found enough mental acuity to ask the right question, surprising himself.

"Good question," Al Anwar responded. "It is a small company that specializes in software for banks and businesses in Jakarta. We are trying to get hold of the owner."

He glanced at the two Americans, and the apparent senior man said, "We have a lead on him, but he is still running. We consider him a fugitive. Our people on the ground should have him right now or before the day ends at the latest. However, the other problem is his Russian partner." He looked intently at Ortega. "The Russian is the real hacker. He has been on our list for some time."

"Again, what do they know?" Ortega asked.

"I'll discuss that in detail, but it looks like they know everything."

Ortega was too stressed to control his voice.

"Khalij?"

"Khalij, Dover, Belize, the Swiss banks, and of course, Alliance Ovest," the American said.

"How is this possible?"

"Well, we think the owner of the Jakarta-based software company has an entirely different background than just being a businessman with connections. We are researching him while hunting him in Indonesia."

"Why are you doing this only now? Why not before?"

"Easy!" The American's voice was commanding now. "His client was an Indonesian bank, not us. His company installed foolproof software that enabled us to shift money around without the bureaucratic hassle. Everything was safe until he or his partner, the Russian, started to dig around."

"By the way, who are you?"

Ortega felt he had a right to ask. He didn't like having some stranger take over his office.

"Anwar can explain that to you later. For now, let's concentrate on the issue."

Ortega was annoyed, and he showed it. He stood up again and walked to the window and then to the bar. He poured himself a tall scotch and added ice cubes.

"Anyone for a drink?"

They all had coffee. It was almost midday and therefore a good time to have a drink.

The Americans outlined the situation for everybody. It was serious, but there was no sign yet that authorities were aware of what was happening.

They concluded that, with any luck, this might be a simple blackmail case that could be dealt with. Blackmailers at a certain point must make themselves accessible, visible, and therefore catchable.

But Ortega feared this might be much more than simple extortion. It might be the end of his family empire, and he would do everything to prevent that.

It was lunchtime in Marseille and sunset in Bali.

The two Americans looked worried.

"Call!" the senior man told his junior partner.

Junior pulled a satellite phone from his briefcase and asked for a private space to make his call. Ortega offered him his adjacent private office.

After a few minutes, the American reappeared with a stern look on his face.

"Nothing yet," he said. "We have gone to the limits in a foreign country, and we have lost him—for now. That proves what we have suspected. He is more than just a business owner."

"What about the Russian? Are they together?"

"The Russian, Igor Kuznechov, is back in Russia. They operate an IT lab and their hacking base from Simferopol in Crimea. We'll work on him, but it might take a day or two."

A soft knock on the thick wood door startled everyone. Ortega's assistant stepped in and said lunch was served in the rooftop suite. This was Ortega's favorite spot. During the summer the suite could be opened, letting the breeze from the sea fill his lungs. Now, in March, the suite was closed, but it remained an attractive place. He would sit there for hours with his binoculars, watching his ships and others entering and leaving the harbor.

Finally, they could agree on something: lunch. Ortega had an in-house kitchen that produced food worthy of a Michelin-star restaurant.

Ernesto, his Italian chef, was in the suite when they entered, proudly presenting his seafood creations and touting the lamb entrée and the beef from the Bordeaux region, which he said was the best in Europe.

Even Al Anwar enjoyed the wines that were served. *So much for orthodox Wahabism*, Ortega thought, smiling inwardly.

Junior got up several times during lunch to make calls to Indonesia.

The third time he came back with a smile on his face.

"They have his location," the American cackled, "but he has help there.

And it looks like professional help. He and at least two others escaped from the house, but we know where they are heading."

Senior raised his glass. "So we might just get rid of the problem today. Our guys there are tops. I guess after coffee and a good cognac we will have solved a major problem. Salut!"

CHAPTER 6

SIMFEROPOL, CRIMEA, RUSSIA

It was midafternoon in Simferopol, and Igor was on the second floor of his lab on Kirova Prospekt in the center of the city. He was surrounded by a half-dozen huge screens, some with camera feeds from Jakarta and Kuala Lumpur, others with numbers, names, locations, and codes.

He was concentrating on the screen with a direct live feed from the Kuala Lumpur office and his partner's house. The cams were all hyper mini and were undetectable without sophisticated equipment.

Igor was alarmed. Just a few minutes before, people had entered the house. They'd locked Mirna, the maid, in a closet after beating her badly and threatening her in the style of Southeast Asian burglars. However, they weren't thieves but professional intruders. Unlike robbers, they went from one room to another and turned everything upside down systematically.

Where were the moonlighting police?

Feeling helpless, Igor found the video disturbing to watch, but he recorded everything. The intruders were Malays with specific training. The first thing they did was look for cams, but they couldn't find any, leading them to become quite careless. Their faces were clearly visible, and Igor recognized one of them. He didn't know his name, but he was sure he was a member of the national police. They must have gotten rid of Matt's security.

The sound track was flawless, and Igor heard them clearly. The leader gave clear commands, and his minions followed his orders.

Igor was not afraid they would find anything, but he was worried about Mirna. This north Malaysian girl was a good-natured person, working hard to get her two children an education, which his partner and boss financed.

It took the intruders less than twenty minutes to finish. To make the home invasion look like a burglary, they took paintings, silverware, two valuable carpets, TVs, and DVD players. Igor focused on the storeroom where Mirna was being held. On the way out the intruders unlocked the door but ordered her to stay there for an hour.

Igor returned to his other screens and was alarmed when he noticed he got pinged. *Impossible*, he thought. This must have been a major agency, most probably US-based. The NSA?

He didn't dare trace the source, not even with his sophisticated software.

His system was unimpregnable. It was used by the Russian military, the foreign department, and the FSB, descendant of the old KGB, and yet someone was in.

Igor frantically rerouted his proxies to an Estonian mother server, the birth server. The chiming sound of the pings was gone now.

He hoped and prayed they were too short for a location pinpoint, but he had engaged maybe just a bit too long with the cam screen from Kuala Lumpur.

Satisfied that the peeping had stopped, Igor tried to enter the IT system of Alliance Ovest in Marseille. This proved to be easy enough. There was no elaborate security, just a few firewalls that he broke down in less than ten minutes.

Igor accessed the cams, which covered the whole building. He focused on a bright apartment that looked like a rooftop setting and found five men lounging comfortably, sipping coffee and liquor.

Outstanding. There was one Arab-looking guy with a familiar face.

Igor hit the recording but had problems accessing the sound channel.

While recording and still desperately seeking the sound channel, Igor again tried to call his friend in Bali.

He was surprised at how easy it was to hack into this system. The cam quality was high grade, and he wondered who had installed the system with so few firewalls. *Probably just arrogance*, he thought.

Again, he tried to reach his friend in Bali but got only the operator recording telling him the phone was switched off.

As Igor watched the five people in Marseille, he began taking stills of their faces. *I might have to hack into the FBI's facial recognition software later*, he thought.

He was still unable to establish a sound connection, although he saw that the cams were linked to sound recording.

Suddenly one of the Western guys, the youngest, jumped up and grabbed a phone that looked like it was satellite handy.

The others were all looking at him, eyes wide, mouths open, and when he finished his conversation they displayed frustration and anger.

Igor's speakers started to crackle, a sign the sound system might just kick in. It did.

"… still at large. We now have half a dozen men in the area, but it's getting dark …" Crackle again.

It was clear to Igor that someone was looking for his friend and boss. Matt was seemingly on the run but from what or whom?

The sound quality was too bad to understand more.

They were now all standing, and talking in an agitated manner.

The oldest one, maybe the Alliance Ovest chief, was scratching his head with both hands when the door to the rooftop apartment opened. The young guy who entered gesticulated wildly, pointing his finger at Igor.

They had made him.

Now everything became hectic in Marseille. Pity he couldn't hear a word. The old man was shouting at the young guy who pointed his finger at the cam, and the others left the room in a hurry.

A few minutes later the screens with the Marseille feed went black.

Igor worked feverishly on his keyboard to redirect sources and servers.

When he was satisfied that nobody could locate his servers, he sank back into his chair and thought of having a vodka. But not here in the office. And first things first.

Igor had a creepy feeling they might be on to him.

He took the stairs down to the working lab and told his three engineers to go home.

"I will explain tomorrow. Just go home and be with your families now. We might have a situation."

They flatly refused.

"We have to finish the first phase of the FSB accounting code. Shukov is in town and wants a presentation tomorrow," his senior technician told him.

Igor played with the idea of conveying his worries to Shukov, but he dismissed the thought right away. It was not a good idea to disclose problems of another nature while doing business with a client.

He informed his guys that a foreign party was intruding after a leak in Kuala Lumpur.

"Be extra careful until we solve this problem. Lock the doors and leave the shop together. No one should go out alone. Understood? Take the baker's exit!"

This was not the first time they had worked under lockout and had been forced to leave via the bakery next door, which provided a hidden escape route. Matt had struck a deal with the Ukrainian woman who owned the bakery. When they had set up the lab, his professional paranoia had dictated that they always have a safe means of retreat. After all, they started out with commercial hacking.

Igor returned upstairs where his computers were combing through the FBI's facial recognition software, trying to identify the chaps in Marseille. He had gotten some high-quality stills, and they were being run through the program.

A few months earlier, somebody had planted Trojans in their system in Kuala Lumpur. It took Igor about a week to identify the source, the FBI. Since no sensitive data were ever stored on their computers, Igor recommended letting the Trojans do their work while he learned their code and then intercepted them with his own. He had developed a very successful program of this type for the FSB in Russia.

Once he had decoded the Trojans, they became his. He turned them around and got deep into the Quantico electronics. To maintain a totally innocent appearance, he never fought the original intruders. From there, tapping into the FBI system became routine.

The facial recognition software now came in handy.

Igor waited another fifteen minutes before he got his first hit.

The software identified one of the older Westerners.

Art Stiller. Former CIA operative. Fired two years previously for accepting bribes in Iraq. The source of the bribes was not disclosed, but Igor had an idea who wanted to buy a CIA officer.

Then the youngest one came up.

He was Brad Conners, a Yale graduate and a lawyer. He had been disbarred three years back for stealing and leaking court pre-rulings to a here-unidentified client, connected to or part of the US weapons industry.

Nice fellas.

Then the software displayed the client: Cohen Industries, United States.

The third Westerner was Manuel Ortega, the seventy-six-year-old patriarch of Alliance Ovest. No criminal records were listed for him.

The Arabs, zilch. No result.

Igor was in better mood now and jokingly thought of calling the FBI to report the holes in the bureau's software.

His piggyback Trojans were the FBI's own and were impossible to trace. Another field office appeared to be entering the system whenever he tapped into it.

Stiller was ex-CIA, not the CIA. That might change the picture.

A thought crossed Igor's mind: Cavity. The CIA had set up the super-secret black ops group to carry out actions it didn't want traced back to the

United States. He made a mental note to share his thoughts with Matt as soon as he could reach him.

He had to contact Matt to let him know that fake law enforcers, maybe belonging to Cavity or to an unidentified group, were after him.

But how could they dispatch the CIA in Jakarta to check on Matt's house? The situation grew more and more difficult.

Again, he tried Matt's mobile in Indonesia, and this time he heard a ring tone.

The squelch in the connection was heavy and noisy.

"Igor here. Can you hear me?"

"Igor, I can hear but we are in a ..."

He couldn't understand what his friend was saying. Matt doubtless was in a black hole for mobile connections.

"Where are you? Can you hear?"

"Check on Frankie. They got him ..."

The next sound Igor heard was beeping, indicating the connection was lost.

At least they hadn't caught Matt yet.

Frankie, one of their best and most influential friends in Jakarta, ran a successful private air charter company that transported mostly corrupt government officials around the country and abroad.

Check on Frankie!

Igor called Frankie's office at Halim Airport in Jakarta.

"Selamat malam. Blue Sky Charter. How can I help you?"

"Can I speak to Pak Frankie, please?"

In Indonesia, even in business, it's customary to use the first name of the party you want to talk to.

The line went quiet, and the operator was replaced by a gruff male.

"Who are you? I'm Colonel Aziz, national police."

"Uh, I'm calling from overseas. I want to book a plane."

"Call tomorrow morning. The office is closed."

The line went dead.

Igor frantically speed-dialed Lisa's number.

"Yes?"

"Lisa, it's Igor. What's going on?"

"I can't talk long, Igor. I'm with Nasurwin."

"What happened to Frankie?"

"Bad, very bad. He is dead. Someone killed him in his office, tortured him. I've tried to call the boss but cannot get through."

"Don't call him again until he calls you."

Somebody grabbed the phone from Lisa and in a harsh voice told her to shut up.

"Igor, if that's you, you better show up quickly. What have you guys done? The US embassy and the Saudis are all over me."

"I'm abroad and I have no idea what's going on, Nas."

"Where is Becker?" He knew Matt only by his Swiss identity.

"I guess in Bali. That's what he told me earlier."

"We know that. But where in Bali? He left the Legian Top in a hurry."

"Sorry, Nas, I wouldn't know. I haven't spoken to him in a while."

Nasurwin mumbled something Igor didn't understand and abruptly hung up.

"Boss, we are leaving."

Igor's guys downstairs apparently were finished with their task.

"Okay, take the bakery exit and have a coffee before you leave."

"We need a vodka." They were comfortable with the presentation prepared for Shukov and looked forward to going home.

Igor stepped to the stairs and shouted down, "Coffee or if you want, vodka first!"

"Okay, boss. Clear."

The boys had practiced crisis exits and were aware that their work required extra caution. Now was such a time.

Igor heard the clank of the heavy metal door that connected the bakery with one of Simferopol's most secret businesses. He lingered on the stairs until he heard the door close and get locked again.

Now, back to Marseille.

The screens were black. No cam connection. *Let's test them,* Igor thought.

He planted his Trojans in the Alliance system. The firewalls quickly crumbled. Igor was in.

But the cams stayed blind. *They must have disabled the cams manually, probably pulled the power cables,* Igor told himself.

However, he was in the core.

He went straight to the financial files and copied everything on an external hard disk without reading it. There would be time for that later with any luck.

Igor heard noise from the street. He walked over to the window but didn't move the blinds.

The commotion came from in front of the bakery café, but he didn't waste time finding out what was going on.

He knew it was time to leave. They were close, whoever they were.

Igor pocketed the tiny disk containing the financial intestines of Alliance Ovest and prepared to leave.

It was getting dark outside, but he didn't dare switch on the lights. Matt's expert paranoia had left a deep mark on Igor's behavior.

For a while he sat in his chair, not knowing what to do next. The bakery exit or the front?

He decided to use the bakery exit. Then he might sit at an inside table and take in the environment with an ice-cold vodka. Or maybe no vodka.

As Igor slowly descended the stairs to the hidden steel door leading to the café, his peripheral vision caught movement at the glass entrance door. To break the glass was impossible since it was FSB-grade bulletproof, but he knew trouble had arrived.

He felt relatively safe in his position because the lab was pitch dark and the bulletproof glass was mirrored so no inquiring eyes could see through it.

There were three men visible in the light from the café and from other sources. At least one of them looked Arabic. They tested the door carefully, but his guys had locked it.

It was time to go, and not via the front door.

Just when he was about to unlock the door to the bakery, his satellite phone beeped. He pressed "Answer" and said hello without identifying himself, because he didn't recognize the caller ID.

"Igor, it's me," Matt's said. "We are safe for now, but you have to disappear for a while. I can't talk too long. This is Fedorov's phone. It was useless before because we were in a deep canyon. Don't call me! We still have a serious tail …"

His voice broke off.

"Listen, Matt. Frankie got killed. I talked to Lisa and Nas …"

"Don't call Jakarta anymore. They're playing a double game. Shit! Frankie?"

"Yes, in his Halim office today or even just tonight."

"They are very serious, Igor. I know they are after you too. Go to your place in Alushta and wait for my call. Go now, Igor, tonight. I'll call tomorrow morning."

The connection broke off, and all Igor could hear was static and squelch.

Igor slowly opened the door, which led to a hidden spot behind the bakery café.

There Irina in her green apron pulled him farther back to the storeroom.

"Some strange people were here asking about you," she said. "I think they are Arabs or something like that. You better take the back exit. And be careful, Igor."

She whisked him out of her store via the well-hidden back door. Irina pressed a quick kiss on his mouth. "I mean it. Be very careful."

Irina and Igor had been something like an item before he spent most of his time abroad. Irina was Ukrainian and had been living in a politically hostile environment since Russia had taken Crimea. But Igor with his friends in the FSB had created a safe haven for Irina, a widow with two adolescent daughters. She could hold on to her bakery and her café license but not to Igor.

Igor kissed her back. "Spasibo, dorogoy."

The alley behind the bakery led to Simferopol's Kavulitsya, a busy road where taxis were available.

He didn't dare recover his car in the parking area.

He moved swiftly, carrying nothing but his satellite and mobile phones.

The time for a vodka had just expired.

Igor fell into a light run. Then he recalled Matt's warning: "When you must hide, don't hide. The best place to hide is in the open because there nobody looks for you."

The message was, don't attract attention! Igor was walking normally now, but he was perspiring heavily and not from his previous pace.

He played with the idea of heading to one of his engineers' homes and borrowing a car, but having regained his calm he realized that might leave a loyal coworker vulnerable.

The bus station. There was a night bus going to Alushta, Yalta, and Sevastopol. Igor again sped up his pace and reached the station just in time. He bought a ticket to Sevastopol. This was another Petrossian method. Hide in the open but cover your tracks.

In a few minutes Igor was on board. He took a rear seat, grabbed a newspaper from an overhead rack, and buried his face behind it.

The bus left on time and passed his office and Irina's café. Igor saw his three pursuers sitting at a roadside table with water bottles.

Once the bus hit the road for Alushta he settled back and tried to relax.

CHAPTER 7
BALI, AFTER MIDNIGHT

The three of us, with Ketut in command for directions, were holed up about fifty meters upstream from the famous Four Seasons Hotel. The creek rushed noisily beside us, allowing free conversation.

We had been hiding a full day in the bush flanking the river, unable to make a move.

Sensing Fedorov and I were getting tired, Ketut was forced to make a decision.

"Give me your phone." She took my slowly dying Samsung and dialed.

"Wayang, it's me, Ketut. I need your help."

She listened carefully. Her forehead wrinkled.

"Okay, understood. Try to get Wati at the Four Seasons. If she is working, tell her I need a room. Discreet, no registration. Call me back on this phone if all is set."

She looked at us. These two once-unbreakable agents had been on all kinds of missions. Provocateurs, combatants, and killers, at least in Fedorov's case, we were now defeated, tired, wet, and hungry. Yes, very hungry indeed.

"Ask Wati to send food to our room. Whatever," I said.

From my earlier visits, I knew the suite rooms were equipped with fully stocked bars, so drinks would not be a problem.

Though I was in the Balinese jungle on the paradise island, I felt cold and extremely uncomfortable.

The wait for a return call was agonizing, and my stomach agreed with my bad mood.

Then my phone vibrated.

"Yes?"

Ketut listened for a few seconds and said *terima kasih*. That meant

Wati was not Balinese, for the thank-you was in Bahasa, the Indonesian language.

"We proceed to the stream-side restaurant, which is deserted by now. There Wati will pick us up and bring us to our room."

The crawl through the brush, half of it in the water, brought us close to all our aging bones and muscles would allow.

It took us an eternity to reach the famous hotel, located right by the rushing stream with a spectacular swimming pool overhanging it.

I sent Ketut up to check whether her friend Wati was alone.

Fedorov for the first time took out his Makarov, which was equipped with a three-inch silencer, and got into position just in case.

Ketut walked up to the pool and disappeared behind the bar. We couldn't hear anything for a moment, and Fedorov whispered in my ear, "I don't like it."

I didn't either.

It took too long for Ketut to reappear.

A muffled scream from above made it more than clear we had been set up.

Fedorov desperately tried to find a target but, like me, couldn't see anything.

"Let's go!"

I pushed Fedorov into the water and followed close behind him.

Deep and very powerful, the stream carried us with incredible speed downward around a tight corner. My phone would be useless after this dip, and I hoped it could be revived once we hit dry ground.

Behind us a powerful searchlight came to life but too late to light us up.

We became part of the river, debris getting flushed down the canyon.

After a seemingly endless run in the wild river, Fedorov grabbed a branch and stopped me as I was rushing by.

"Let's get out of here."

We pulled ourselves to the narrow bank on the far side from the Four Seasons, but I knew instantly it was the wrong side. Our pursuers certainly would not make the side from where we entered the river their top priority.

I again noticed with some pride that my instincts were back.

"The other side," I screamed at Fedorov.

He nodded in agreement.

We both were back in our elements. It felt good and even banished our fatigue and hunger for now. Adrenalin was taking over.

We lowered ourselves into the river and were swooped away again twenty or so meters down the narrow valley.

A huge rock stopped our descent, and we climbed up the steep bank.

We lay side by side on our backs. I coughed up water while Fedorov inhaled air like a dying horse.

"We have to find shelter." Fedorov was at his limit, and I was not far from it.

"Do you realize that together we are over 140 years old?" He was laughing.

I helped him up. We were soaked, but I was more worried about my old briefcase, which luckily still hung over my shoulder. The laptop was secure since it was one of those military issues that were waterproof and could take the weight of a tank.

I checked the other contents of the briefcase—my passports, the cash, and the flash disks. They might need some drying.

Slowly we got on our legs and scrambled up the steep hill. Every minute or so we stopped and listened for threatening sounds. Nothing.

A small path led through the bush to a cluster of small houses and the inevitable temple.

We had no choice. The only way out of here was to get dry and to acquire some food and maybe a few hours of sleep.

A dim light was on in the first little house. We walked to the crudely carved door and looked at each other. Then I knocked once softly. No response. I pounded harder on the wooden door and heard movement inside.

The door swung open and an elderly Balinese wearing a sarong stared at us with drowsy eyes.

I took the initiative and greeted him in Bahasa, expressing our distress.

"We fell into the river at the Four Seasons. May we dry ourselves at your place? We won't stay long."

After a nudge from Fedorov, I said, "Maybe we could buy some food from you."

The man was very friendly and welcomed us into his small and extremely tidy household.

An equally old woman inquired from somewhere in the back and then showed herself. She wore a similar sarong wrapped around her bony body.

Her husband described the situation in Balinese, and she instantly got busy, firing up the wood stove and filling a pan with vegetables and white rice.

The old man said she was preparing nasi goreng for us. He led us back to an open bathing area where we found a typical Balinese water cistern with a wooden trowel for a manual shower. But we didn't need more water, and he brought us two towels labeled "Four Seasons Hotel." The Balinese network.

Fedorov and I took off our sodden clothes and wrapped our tired frames in sarongs. We hurried back to the main room where a fire was going in the stove. We stood close to the warmth, and gradually our focus returned to food.

Nyoman, the old woman, laughed when she saw us in our sarongs, saying something in Balinese that I didn't understand. Made, her husband, translated into Bahasa.

"She said you look like Vishnu, and she hopes you like her nasi goreng."

Vishnu was one of the Hindu gods whose images were housed in the thousands of temples on the island.

The fried rice, the veggies, and the chilly smelled wonderful. Made asked us to sit on the floor, and Nyoman handed us wooden bowls filled with delicious nasi goreng. We ate the hot rice with our bare hands and drank water from another wooden bowl.

We had no cutlery, but it was our best meal in a long time.

Our clothes were hung close to the warm stove, and so was my briefcase.

After the third serving, Made went outside and returned with an anxious look on his face. He exchanged some words with his wife, and they went to the door, talking rapidly in Balinese.

Fedorov fingered his Makarov, but I shook my head.

Made returned to the warm room, gesticulating wildly and speaking in Balinese. I had to ask him to switch to Bahasa.

"There are people on the other side of the river with lights. Are they looking for you?"

I was right to choose this side of the creek.

"Maybe," I said, "but it's better if they don't find us."

He seemed to understand and again talked in a fretful tone with his wife.

"They are bad people," I told him. "They want to hurt us and steal our things."

This was the time to show gratitude. I grabbed my briefcase and retrieved two hundred US dollars, which I divided between the two of them. Bali households are different from their Western equivalents. Men and women manage on their own, at least in most cases.

As did my ex-wife.

This was a lot of money for them. I was sure we would be safe at least for a few hours.

Made thanked me profoundly, and Nyoman did a magic trick, making her hundred-dollar bill disappear somewhere in her sarong.

Fedorov and I went to the door and watched the lights moving on the other side of the river. We heard some obscenities in English and perhaps in Arabic.

I hoped our pursuers didn't want to get wet by crossing the river, and the lights gradually moved up the bank opposite from us.

Hiding the Makarov under his sarong again, Fedorov dug in for more nasi goreng.

The couple offered us fresh sarongs and told us we could sleep. They would watch.

We decided to take the offer but to sleep in shifts, Fedorov the first two hours and after him, me.

I thanked the old couple and asked them to go back to sleep while we huddled near the fire in the stove.

Trying not to fall asleep, I went outside and watched the other side of the canyon, wondering what had happened to Ketut.

We had no choice but to leave her back at the hotel, but I would go after her tomorrow morning, actually today. It was two in the morning.

The silence of the night was disturbed only by the sound of the wild river about twenty meters down the slope. There were no more lights on the other side, no more voices to be heard. The sound of the roaring river kept me awake, although my stomach was no longer growling.

I walked around to the other houses. A single light was on in each of them. I didn't dare get too close for fear of waking the neighbors.

We warned Made and Nyoman to keep our visit to themselves. Another dollar bill would certainly seal their mouths for a while.

After three hours, I awakened my old friend. He was immediately alert and up and cursed me for letting him sleep longer than agreed.

I gratefully closed my eyes and fell asleep in an instant.

After a dreamless sleep, I felt Fedorov's hand on my arm. I was wide awake because his other hand was over my mouth.

"Police," he whispered.

Made and Nyoman were up. Daylight was working its way slowly over the back of the steep hill, but the houses remained in darkness.

"There are two uniforms outside," Fedorov murmured. "I promised the two oldies two more bills if they would keep their mouths shut. To underline the urgency I let them have a look at my SIG."

Made and Nyoman assured us of our safety and went outside. Fedorov covered them from behind the door with his semiautomatic while I put on my smoky but dry clothing. Fedorov was already fully dressed.

The policemen got closer, for I could hear their voices clearly now. They were inquiring about two dangerous foreign criminals. They were quite right. Fedorov and I were moving on old paths again, which made us dangerous when threatened. I had felt particularly threatened since yesterday, which revived my survival instinct, and therefore my killer instinct, rather quickly.

Made and Nyoman were hyper jumpy. My friend openly displayed his gun, and I told Made to go outside and talk to the policemen. Nyoman wanted to follow, but Fedorov, gun firmly in hand, pulled her back gently.

"Just go out and do whatever you do in the early morning," I instructed Made. "You haven't seen anybody. Just tell them you saw the lights on the other side last night. Do that and Nyoman will be safe. We are not the bad people. Don't offer them anything."

I looked into his eyes and thought he understood. We couldn't afford to have the police in the house.

Made slowly left his house and approached the two policemen, who were smoking cigarettes and lazily looking around. Their scooters were leaning on the house closest to our hiding place.

If worst came to wickedest we at least might have transport.

I watched Made through the half-open door. He conversed with the two officers, showing high respect. That was the way little Indonesians treated authority. Then they all laughed, and one of the policemen offered Made a cigarette, which he gratefully accepted.

He gestured toward the opposite bank, and I was convinced he had guaranteed our momentary safety.

They talked another few minutes. Then Made bowed his head and the two cops rode off on their scooters.

A trembling Made returned to his house where he collapsed on one of the woodblock stools standing in the big room where we had spent the night.

"They are looking for you. They said that you are bad people and that you almost killed a woman at the hotel last night."

He paused, his hands trembling in front of his old face.

"I know Ibu Ketut. What did you do to her?"

"Ibu Ketut is our friend, and she was attacked by the people looking for us."

I felt great relief at the words *almost killed*. So Ketut, the lovely, smart woman, was alive.

"Did they say where Ibu Ketut is now?"

"No, but they said she is with the foreigners up in Ubud. I don't know where but maybe in one of her villas. I sometimes work there for her. The Villa Kakatua."

It worried me a lot that our foes could involve the police in Bali. Security forces on the island were on high alert with the Saudi king arriving that day. The national police must have alerted the locals to look for us. However, the locals were not trained for thorough searches and interrogations. They were simple policemen doing their jobs to earn their salaries.

The undercover cops on the island were a different story. They hunted for drug dealers, addicts, pedophiles and other sex perverts. They were to be avoided at all costs.

Nyoman had prepared hot jasmin tea and another portion of rice for all of us. She seemed to be happy with the extra income and didn't look as worried as her husband.

"Come eat! I made breakfast."

I took another look outside and gestured to Fedorov to put away his gun.

"They wouldn't venture to arrest two dangerous guys like us."

I made the quote/unquote sign and smiled at Nyoman. She gave me a big grin that revealed an almost toothless mouth.

"I would like you to stay with us a few hours before we leave," I told Made, who nodded politely.

Nyoman fried some eggs, and the smell of the food was extremely comforting. We ate with great gusto and complimented her on her skills.

"We have to get in touch with Igor," I said. "He should be in Alushta by now. He is totally encrypted there, so with the satellite phone it should be no problem."

I fired up my laptop, which was unharmed by our watery adventure. The satellite phone was used as a tethering device, and we were online in a minute.

I sent a short message to Igor on our private message channel, which was so secure that it had never been hacked. A short beep signaled the text was received.

Igor: "I'm in the house now. [Even with our safe connection, we never mentioned locations or names.] They were at the shop yesterday. I don't know whether they entered or not. Took PT to here. Will send you video in a moment from our client's headquarters. The firm has a mole. Repeat, a mole! [The firm was the CIA]. Have about twenty GBs of downloaded fin info. Ex-firm employee involved and some oil [Arabs]."

Me: "We are okay for now. Get in touch with P head and mention the name Ketut. [No way around that.] She is P. Got abducted by the oil and probably police. We are gonna find her later. Contact P carefully, but don't send any info. We must find the mole first. Fifty-three with me. Saved my ass again. Send now compressed. I just store. No read. Bat life short. Send text when contact firm. Mention client name. Record and let me know reaction. Out."

I disconnected. This quick exchange took less than two minutes—too short to be identified by CIA and NSA satellite surveillance and impossible to unencrypt.

We had more tea while my Dell military issue received Igor's compressed files on a new connection. His super computer sent the whole batch in less than two minutes.

No time to read now. We had to find a safe house first.

"Any place on Bali?" I asked Fedorov.

"Never been here. No place. We must find something. Ketut?"

"Yes. That's next on our list."

"We can't move on the streets. They are hunting us."

He looked at me and gestured toward Made.

"Made, is there any transport we could hide in? Of course we shall be generous."

His eyes lit up for the first time since the confrontation with the police.

"I go find. My nephew has a truck. But I have to hurry. He works for the *koperasi* the whole day."

It was seven in the morning, and I asked him to leave right away.

"Tell him we pay extra."

I didn't want to mention a sum, but I thought Made got the hint.

Nyoman stayed as our guarantee if she was any.

After few more cups of tea and seemingly endless scrutiny of the immediate environment, a battered Toyota truck came rattling down the narrow dirt road that led to the small community.

Nyoman was edgy but not because of the truck or Made's nephew but because it was time to serve the gods food at the temple. Each day Balinese provide their gods with ceremonial nourishment in the form of a handful of rice and a few flowers served on nicely prepared banana tree leaves. When Made and his nephew entered the house, Nyoman left for the nearby small temple that doubled as a community center.

"This is Wayan," Made said. "He will bring you out now. But you have to hurry because he has to work."

We shook hands, and I told Wayan he wouldn't regret helping us.

"Now!" Made urged us. "People are at the temple and nobody will see you."

We checked the surroundings and indeed no one was in sight.

We hugged Made and told him we would be back after all this was over.

"Please make sure Ibu Ketut is secure," he said. "She is a very nice woman."

We promised and jumped on the covered back of the truck.

"Where?" Wayan's voice came from the cabin.

"Close to Villa Kakatua. But stop before so nobody can see us."

I shoved a hundred-dollar bill through the broken rear window of the cabin and told him there would be another one when we arrived.

The rusty old Toyota truck wound its way up the hill back toward Ubud, the picturesque resort village high above the crowded beaches of Bali.

I arranged the rubbery cover so I had a clear view of my surroundings. Fedorov was on his back and let me do the observing. We were a team again. Despite all the predicaments we had faced, that felt pretty good. I had always grasped that age doesn't change a person's calling.

This was our element. We knew how to swim, wade, and struggle in it.

Fedorov had a similar judgment of our situation.

"Not bad, huh? Being on a mission again," he said. "Petrossian was on to this for quite some time, and I convinced them to send me instead of one of the young dogs. We have quite a number of girls now too. They are deadly."

Fedorov smiled. His tone told me he thought these girls wouldn't be able to cope with what lay ahead of us.

I wasn't too sure of our capabilities. Together we were more than 140 years old. But I knew one thing. We were the best before and that would drive us again.

The driver turned his head toward us and shouted over the rattling engine, "I turn into the Kakatua road. Let you out after the next turn. Okay?"

"Make sure nobody is around before you stop," I screamed back.

After about three hundred meters the truck came to a halt with its earsplitting engine idle.

"Here is good. The villa is down in the valley. You can take the footpath left of the road. Nobody here."

I gave Wayan another hundred but warned I would take it all back if he told anybody about us.

His smile was wide.

"Ibu Ketut is our friend. Find her." (*Ibu* means "madam.")

We jumped off the back of the truck and headed toward the dense brush to the side of the road.

My briefcase was an impediment, but I hoped to deposit it somewhere after we had freed Ketut.

If she was there. But Made's hunch about Villa Kakatua was the only lead we had, and I had a creepy sense from my past that we were on the right track.

Fedorov and I became more light-footed as the day progressed and the tension rose.

Carefully but swiftly we proceeded down a narrow footpath toward the rushing stream that had bathed us the previous night.

After a few turns in the trees and the bush we could see the villa from above.

The beautiful Balinese dwelling was located right by the hated river. A sprawling terrace sat immediately above the water.

Everything was calm. No movement. No sign of inhabitants.

"We have to move to the other side." Fedorov pointed to the edge of the river where the road was hidden.

He was right. The entrance was on the far side. That meant we had to crawl even deeper into the brush and holding on to branches to avoid a rough slide down.

We were out of breath when we reached the viewpoint we needed. A Nissan Terrano was parked beside the villa. No other vehicle. It could hold at most four persons and, we hoped, fewer than that.

Fedorov checked his Makarov, and I longed for one. The Makarov was our standard weapon. It was the most reliable handgun on the planet with a history dating back to 1951. Dust, dirt, and water were her friends. She always worked. My SIG, equally reliable but more vulnerable to nature's power, would do.

The Makarov's predecessor was the Tokarev, which saw action during the Russian Revolution and was standard in the Soviet army until after Second World War. Equally dependable.

Fedorov showed me four spare magazines with twelve rounds each.

The Makarov was a heavy weapon and with the silencer attached weighed more than one kilogram. The gun's stopping power was impressive.

Fedorov handed me the gun. I had been always the better and quicker shot.

"You are the gunner. You always were."

It felt awesome to hold a Makarov again after so many years, but I hoped I wouldn't have to use it.

I checked the familiar weapon, reassured that the safety was on. I handed Fedorov the SIG, and we slowly slid on our butts toward the quiet villa.

About ten meters above the villa entrance we stopped our slightly painful decline and listened for any voices.

Still nothing.

There was a small window on the entrance side that might have given us access to a bath or storage room. But it was too risky to approach without intelligence.

We stayed where we were, Igor resting his head on my briefcase as I sat upright well protected by the brush and watched the property.

Then the door opened. *Finally*, I thought.

Two Arab-looking guys in suits (in Bali!) emerged, talking vigorously with each other as they approached the Nissan. They climbed in, and the car left the small landing for the access road.

"Did you understand?" Fedorov looked at me, knowing I spoke Arabic.

"I only understood 'French idiots and twenty-four hours.'"

Whatever that meant.

We had to make a decision. Two guys had left. That indicated maybe another two at most were in the house.

Fedorov again looked at me curiously.

"Shall we?"

"Yes. Now."

There was no reason to lie in these bushes while they had Ketut. She was Petrossian, and we had never abandoned one of ours.

We slid down to the deck where the Nissan had been parked, trying to avoid breaking branches or moving little stones and alerting whoever was still inside the villa.

We quickly reached the entrance door and took positions left and right of it.

Now we could distinguish voices. One was female, angry and agitated. The other male and clearly American.

Arabs and Americans. I stopped wondering and concentrated on the job ahead.

Fedorov slowly worked the brass door handle. It didn't make a noise.

I was on the opening side of the door with the Makarov pointed toward the slight gap between door and wall.

We now could hear the voices clearly.

"All you have to do is give me your handler," the American was saying. "You can go home and we'll forget we ever met."

We couldn't hear Ketut's reply, only a contemptuous laugh.

Tough lady, I thought. She had come from Krylniy where she was taught to withstand all sorts of torture.

The gap in the door opened a bit wider, and I could look inside. A small hallway led to a generous living room from where the voices were coming.

I nodded at Fedorov and he slowly and carefully pushed the heavy door so I could slide in.

I was inside in a split second, pressed to the wall. I held the Makarov in both hands and not downward as law enforcement agents would do but straight forward, ready to take my shot.

Now Ketut was sniveling. The asshole must have done something to her.

I stepped into the large living room and pointed my gun at the back of a bulky guy hovering over Ketut, who was bound with plastic cuffs.

She saw me and for a moment her eyes betrayed me.

The heavy guy turned around and faced my gun, pointed right at his chest.

He reacted quickly and professionally, dropping to the floor and trying to roll away from my range.

But my rejuvenated instincts kicked in rapidly, and without a second of hesitation I put a 9mm into his left hip. I could have killed him, but maybe we might have the time to ask him some polite questions.

A shot in the hip immediately immobilizes the victim, and he realized that after screaming loudly.

"Just lie still or you'll get one more," I told him. He obliged.

Fedorov took a large knife from a butcher block in the adjoining kitchen and cut Ketut's cuffs. She rubbed her purple wrists vigorously.

"Somehow I knew you would show up." She smiled and looked at me.

While my friend helped Ketut to stand up and recover, I had my gun pointed at the moaning thug. I encouraged him to show me his face, which looked somewhat grotesque given the pain he was in.

A bullet in the hip is no joke but is seldom deadly. It's hard to hit a vital blood vessel there, but a bullet anywhere in the body is agonizing and hard to ignore.

"Who are you assholes?"

My gun was still aimed straight at his ugly face.

"He is not alone. There are two more," Ketut said.

"We saw them leave. Arabs?"

"Yes. They are Al Mukhabarat Al A'amah, and this asshole"—she was barely able to control herself—"is somehow connected to the firm."

I cautioned her with a harsh movement of my free hand to keep any intelligence she had gathered to herself. We would have time later to discuss the information, which confirmed Igor's discoveries.

The Mukhabarat! Saudi intelligence, a rather inept service that consisted of a few princes and other royals who liked to play James Bond. The Mukhabarat was a CIA puppet without legs, arms, or a brain. But its agents could be dangerous, especially with a CIA operative leading them and letting them do the dirty work.

I handed Fedorov the gun with the silencer and set the American up against one of the heavy chairs.

No need to watch the entrance. We would hear any car approaching on the gravel road.

"Now listen to me very carefully. We don't have much time and I certainly don't want to waste it."

He seemed to understand I meant business and nodded his assent.

"Your buddies can bring you to a hospital after this if you make it through my questions. Capisce?"

Again, he nodded his head.

"I'll compress my inquiries so you can see a doctor sooner. But if I'm not satisfied, instead of a doctor you will meet the chief cook in Hades. Maybe you know who we are, and if so, you also know we never bluff."

He muttered something like "Got it."

"First, who are you? Second, what's your mission? Third, do you know who we are? And fourth, what was your plan for the lady?"

He hesitated to answer but only for a moment.

I looked at Fedorov and said, "He might be found in two or three days in the river about five kilometers from here."

That made him open his mouth.

"I'm a contractor for the Saudis. I don't know who they really are." He screamed when I probed his bleeding hip wound with Fedorov's knife.

"Do better or I might try to widen the entrance."

Fedorov's bullets were standard, and my shot went through cleanly. This would not have been the case if the Makarov had had devastating Russian softheads in her magazine. The entry would have been clean, but the exit wound would have been a gaping mess of blood and tissue.

He was turning white and panting hard, but he managed to put his life over such trivial matters as mission and sacrifice.

"Saudi intel hired us to go after you. I know you are Petrossian, and the Saudis wanted to use the girl."

"The girl!" I bellowed at him not because I was too agitated and emotionally involved but to demonstrate we wouldn't tolerate even a remote insult.

"This girl, as you call her, is a highly trained Petrossian agent, and I might just allow her to finish you off and throw you into the river."

I regained his attention.

"We were instructed to question her, and then the Mukhabarat would get rid of her. I wouldn't have been involved."

"Were you CIA in your former life?"

"No, never, but I contracted for them in Afghanistan and Syria."

"To whom do you report?"

"Art. Art Stiller. He is our boss."

Stiller was ex-CIA, a disgraced officer, a sadist with a pathological lust for power. We had crossed paths many years before when he was still with the firm and had set his mind on a great career. That ambition was abruptly crushed by his weapons and opium trading in the mountains of Afghanistan and by some shady deals in Iraq. The CIA could prove he dealt not only with the mujahedeen during the Soviet invasion but with the Soviets.

His fortune was parked all over the world, stretching from Switzerland to Panama to Thailand where he was a murder fugitive after killing some working girls in Pattaya and Bangkok.

Stiller was a perfect fit for the Mukhabarat if and when its agents had to avoid the real CIA.

Things were making more sense now, but I needed more convincing facts to get a clearer picture.

"Are you familiar with Dhahabi Khalij, the bank?"

"I don't know of such a bank. Never heard the name."

By now I was inclined to believe him, but a little nudge with the tip of the knife in his bullet wound helped me increase my trust in him.

He screamed again like the wounded animal he was.

"I'm telling you the truth, I swear."

I checked on Ketut to see how she took my refined interrogation technique. She wasn't even blinking. She had been to Khabarovsk and Krylniy. Now I was sure.

I hadn't asked the American for his name yet, but Fedorov was on my laptop communicating with Igor. He sent a few headshots of the American to Igor, who, I was sure, had the FBI's facial recognition software running that ugly face right now.

"Next question. When are your camel herders coming back and where did they go? Answer these questions as I posed them!"

Ketut nodded, showing she might be able to confirm what he would say.

"They were called to the St. Regis Hotel. The king is arriving today."

He still didn't understand my desire for answers to these questions.

"I told you to respond to the questions as I posed them. Back when and where to?"

I explored his wound a bit more with the knife, and after another scream he got it right.

"They said before two o'clock. They are high up in the Mukhab. Alief is a colonel and Ali I don't know, but I think one of the royals. In a way …" He started to blabber, which is usually good but often leads away from the real issues.

Fedorov waved me over to the laptop and pointed at the screen.

Mike Walters, ex-CIA. Got fired together with Stiller. Walters had been a desk handler at Langley. Here was the connection to a potential mole in the firm still leaking information to the slimy contractors.

I turned and faced my prisoner.

"Okay, Walters, let's continue."

He was visibly shocked that I used his name.

"How did you …" His voice trailed off.

"Never mind. You know who we are. Let's get back to business."

I showed him my knife.

"Not necessary. What you want to know? I need a doctor."

"First things first. How do you contact your two cronies?"

Ketut was getting nervous and a bit itchy.

"I think we have to leave," she said. "They might be back soon. I heard them saying they would hurry."

I played with my knife and turned back to Walters.

"Tell me how. Now."

"By mobile phone. I was supposed to call them if I found out more from the girl—the lady."

"Then I suggest you do that. Tell them she is talking, and ask them when they will be back. Where is your phone?"

In clear discomfort he pulled his phone out of his trousers pocket.

I told him what to say and to find out where they were. I again showed him my blade, which normally was used to cut meat, and he nodded.

"One wrong word, Walters, and you swim, which might be challenging with your hip."

We listened vigilantly for his tone, his words, and the way he described the situation with Ketut. I told him simply to say Ketut was talking. No details over the phone.

He finished his conversation and looked at me with hopeful eyes.

"You did okay. You just might live."

"Not once they find me here. I'm dead meat. Please bring me to a doctor. We have time. They need at least another hour."

I looked at Ketut, who nodded her head.

"We can drop him at a friend's place. She is a general practitioner.

That might be good enough for the bastard." She pointed at the suffering Walters.

Fedorov didn't like the idea of letting him live.

"Ketut, can you arrange for quick transportation?" I asked.

She was on it and confirmed that one of her cousins would be at the Villa Kakatua in a few minutes.

Lacking medical supplies, I grabbed a bottle of Arak, a Balinese liquor with an alcohol content that would kill a gang of sailors. I leaked some of it on Walters's hip wound, making him groan like a wounded bear. Best I could do. I wanted this guy to live, at least for now. We had hundreds of unasked questions for the slick ex-CIA officer.

Then a thought crossed my mind. "Are you Cavity?"

"You mean the black ops? No, I'm not part of Cavity."

Somehow I believed him. Cavity agents were hard-boiled bastards who would give up their lives rather than talk. I made a mental note to dig deeper into that possibility later.

A few minutes later we heard a car approaching on the narrow gravel road. The driver honked twice and Ketut ran outside. She brought back one of the young fellows I had met the day before at the little restaurant, the duck place.

We half carried Walters out to old Australian Holden and dumped him on the back seat. The car had at least forty years in its bones and sounded that way too.

Ketut was on the phone with her doctor friend and gave instructions to her cousin.

Fedorov and I sat in the back with our captive, and my friend found pleasure in making life more uncomfortable for him by giving him as little space as possible.

"We have good Internet at Mia's place, but sorry, I'm not fully back yet." Ketut realized we could communicate only via satellite phone tethering.

"The first thing the doc, Mia, will do is to give you a checkup," she told Walters

Earlier I had noticed a huge and ugly bump on Ketut's head that needed treatment.

"This dirt here comes second, and I might just stitch his sissy wound myself," Fedorov said.

With no hiccups, we arrived at Mia's house, which also served as her office. She was waiting for us and directed our driver to park in the backyard.

Walters made animal noises that were beyond my concern. I had the unwelcome task of helping him get into the house where I dropped him rudely on a chair.

Mia asked no questions, and I loved her for that.

"I have one more patient, but I will finish with him in a moment. He'll survive." She gave Ketut an intriguing smile and headed for the other room.

"We need to get in touch with Igor," I said. "He might have gone deeper by now. I have a feeling this is going to be bad."

I asked Ketut to stay with Walters while the doc treated him. I handed her the Makarov, which she took without hesitation.

We lugged the contract killer to the doctor's exam room, and I reminded him that whether we let him live depended entirely on him.

CHAPTER 8

ALUSHTA, CRIMEA

Igor sat in front of one of his screens and observed a team of goons searching his lab in Simferopol.

Four professional-looking, military-type guys were going through everything.

Good thing he'd warned his engineers to stay away from the office, although Shukov was pissed that their presentation of the new software had been postponed. Igor warned the engineers not to tell the FSB man anything about the company's problem but to delay the presentation for a day or so.

They were all holed up with their families or girlfriends and were probably safe.

Earlier Igor had been digging deep into classified files at a corporation in the United States.

Cohen Industries showed up on several occasions with the Saudis and with Alliance Ovest.

Cohen Industries, or CI for short, was a top military contractor involved in chemical warfare, operations in hazardous regions, and other dubious activities.

CI was a gigantic factor in the financial questions surrounding Alliance Ovest, the Swiss banks, the corporation in Delaware, and the Saudi bank Dhahabi Khalij.

Igor would have to spend the rest of the day exploring what CI was really into.

Then his com screen lit up. The boss.

"Hi, Igor. We got Ketut. Walters, the contract guy, ex-firm, is not talking fully yet. Check him out. We need to know whom he is working for."

"I'm on it, boss. It looks like CI is heavily involved in all of this. Some chaps are sniffing around at our lab right now, but they won't find anything." He paused for a moment. "I also think Cavity might be involved."

Cavity was a dark shadow from Matt and Fedorov's past. Was it alive again?

Igor paused and worked his keyboard.

"Walters, yes. He is working for CI. What the fuck are they doing in this?"

"We find out when I wash him."

Igor knew what that meant. Many years earlier his boss had been waterboarded, and since then he thought it was the most efficient way to open mouths.

"Any movement around your place in Alushta?"

"None so far but the boat is ready. Do I have to alert P?"

"Now is the time. Call Khabarovsk and fill them in about everything. Tell them where we are and that Fedorov is with me." Matt paused a moment. "And send them all the files."

"If Fedorov is there, they know, don't you think?"

Then he heard Fedorov's voice. The Russian came on the screen, his face more wrinkled than ever.

"Dobroye utro, Igor. They might not know I'm here. Just tell them everything. I was on the way to see Matt when all hell broke loose. I actually went to see Ketut and found him in her lap."

He snickered and that gave Igor confidence. Fedorov smiled or laughed only when he drank vodka or was totally laid-back.

"Are your cams and the surveillance system fully up there?"

The boss again.

"All functioning well. I don't think they have two teams up here, and I'm watching the one in our lab. They are not tech guys or at least not up to the task of breaking into my system. They are working on my base station where even I can't get in if I'm not totally sober."

"Anyway, they are big, Igor. If CI is involved and yes, maybe Cavity, you better be alert, very alert. They have a small army and connections all over the bloody universe. Make double sure the boat is running and ready to go."

"Copy that, boss. If I see movement I'm off to Sevastopol."

"Okay, copy me on all you find on CI and its relations. We're communicating safely for now, but my link will be down again shortly. I'll beep you when more com is required. First, inform P and call Fedorov's satellite phone with the reaction. And leave at the slightest alarm. These guys are dangerous and a real threat, and I have a feeling it's not just CI but something much bigger, like Cavity."

The connection was gone.

Slightly alarmed by his boss's stern warning, Igor double-checked his security system. All cams were working, and infrared traps for detecting the body heat of an intruder were running.

He stared for quite some time at the screen displaying the hidden boathouse with the powerful speedboat moored at the reinforced concrete ramparts. He loved to go out in the boat and to feel the cool spray of the Black Sea on his face. However, this time he might be riding to save his life.

A trip to Sevastopol, where Petrossian operated one of its many field offices in full agreement with the FSB, would take roughly two hours, going south first and then northwest up the coast. Igor even had special access to the well-protected Russian naval base but only at its fringe.

It was early morning in Alushta, and Igor was tempted to go out for a breakfast. He hadn't slept and hadn't had dinner the previous night.

He got up from his swivel chair and stretched. Yes, he was tired and hungry.

Right down the coast road was a small Ukrainian café bar that used to serve a great breakfast and brunch. The Crimea was his favorite hangout when he was in Alushta on a quiet weekend.

He checked the cams again, opened the steel door that led to the street side, and stepped outside.

It was early, and far behind the Black Sea the sun was sending its first signals.

The coast road was deserted but for a few parked cars and a delivery truck passing him on the way to the café. The Crimea was open, and he could smell the freshly baked bread and coffee. The aroma fueled his desire for food and maybe half an hour of relaxation.

Igor entered the café and grabbed a fresh newspaper from a table.

"Dobroye utro, Igor," the friendly Ukrainian woman said, greeting him. He always forgot her name, so he just shook her hand and muttered, "Good morning to you too."

He ordered coffee, eggs, bacon, and branosh with brinza, a typical Ukrainian dish. Igor was always amazed at how Ukrainian culture and cuisine survived the Russian takeover. He was a Russian, but he loved all things Ukrainian, especially the food and the women.

The woman, whose name he still couldn't recall, smiled at Igor as she watched him gobble down his food.

"You really are hungry. Did you arrive this morning?"

"Last night. Had to work the whole night."

Igor thought it couldn't hurt to be friendly and conversational with the woman who had fed him on multiple occasions.

"It's excellent food!"

That made her happy, and she disappeared into the kitchen with a big smile on her pretty face.

Half an hour into his breakfast Igor decided to head back to his house, which quite often served as a safe house for Petrossians.

With his stomach full and his mind at ease, he started to walk back when he saw a black SUV parked a few blocks up the street. The shiny new car didn't fit into these surroundings.

Igor quickly realized this was not good news. What to do?

If he walked into his house, they would identify him immediately if they had not already done so. He tried not to show anxiety and continued walking toward his house. Maybe they didn't know him from pictures and he could walk by the car, taking a different direction home.

A slight panic gripped him. He started to breathe heavily but continued his walk.

His boss would know what to do. But Igor was on his own right now.

He tried not to stare at the SUV, a BMW with Simferopol number plates.

As casually as possible under the circumstances, Igor walked past his house and the BMW. He faked interest in the car, forming an O with his mouth because it was a rare sight even in a resort town like Alushta.

Igor continued along the coast road until he found another café that was open at this unholy time. He entered the café and took a seat at the window so he could observe the car.

His mind was racing and the car was not moving. When he noticed cigarette smoke escaping from the driver's dark tinted window, he was sure the occupant or occupants of the car were watching his place.

Igor needed to reach the boathouse, a fortress under the main structure. There was no way to get in from the sea side.

He decided his only choice was to walk back and to make a dash for his place. He saw no other way to get down to the boathouse.

He hoped his pursuers were here only by car and not by boat too.

Igor finished his coffee and strode as casually as possible out of the place, walking toward his stronghold. He might be safe in there for quite a while. The few windows were bulletproof, and the heavy steel entrance door fortunately opened with a click on his coded remote. The situation was nerve- racking. They might have made him by now and could intercept him before he reached the house. This time when he passed the BMW he didn't dare look or show interest. He walked by on the opposite side of the street, and when he was close enough he activated the remote opener, which unlocked his door with a loud snap. The sound raced through his brain like a gunshot. He jumped up the short staircase, pushed the door open, and entered in a second, slamming the door behind him.

Igor was breathless, sounding like a horse after a mile race.

He was safe for now. The little fortress was practically invulnerable, but he realized the safest path would be the run to Sevastopol.

He checked all the cams, readjusting them to see the BMW up the street.

There was no action, no one storming out of the car toward the house. Cigarette smoke was still coming out of the driver's window.

Was he overreacting, paranoid? Matt, his friend and boss, had told him many times that paranoia was the way to keep alive in moments of doubt.

Igor calmed down but watched the street intently. The cams were well hidden and so small that they were invisible from the road.

Igor knew he had made a grave mistake by passing the suspicious car and dashing into his house. He had showed the watchers that he recognized them.

He had forgotten his boss's words: "Act innocent until you are forced to become guilty."

Igor was not a Petrosssian agent and had never received the outfit's training. He was an engineer. What else could he have done?

He fired up the ultra-secure connection and tried to get hold of Matt by beeping Fedorov's satellite phone.

He waited for more than fifteen minutes and then gave up. To his surprise, the expensive BMW was gone. While he was trying to reach his boss, he had ignored the screen for a moment and hadn't seen the car depart.

What the hell? Had he overreacted?

He was expecting a full-force attack on his house, but now everything was calm and almost normal.

Almost.

Igor was watching all his screens when he noticed movement on the water. Right and left of his house numerous boats were moored to decks that stretched out thirty meters and more into the Black Sea.

All the boats were resting peacefully at their piers or anchors, rolling slightly in the mild surf that ran up onto the beach.

One boat, however, was not moored to a pier or anchored but was idling about fifty meters out, starting to reflect the sunlight as it broke through the dark, low-hanging clouds.

Cloud!

That thought woke Igor out of his daytime nightmare. He had to make sure all his hacked findings were in seventh heaven, a secure cloud he had created to protect them from a dangerous cyber world.

He frantically checked all his uploads and was satisfied that everything was protected. His incredible software, an engineering masterpiece, could run all preprogrammed surveillance even with all the base equipment shut down and dead. The surveillance would continue and be uploaded to seventh heaven for later retrieval.

The unmoored boat worried Igor, and his fears were confirmed when, using his powerful night scope binoculars, he saw that he was being observed from the vessel. He almost dropped his binoculars when he glimpsed the opposite spotter with his field glasses directed at him. But then Igor realized he couldn't be seen. The bulletproof windows had additional mirror film that made it impossible to see through them.

What to do? The programs were running smoothly. The upload capacity to seventh heaven was nearly unlimited and would easily store recordings for days.

Igor had to make a decision. He had no doubt anymore that he was being watched from the boat. The vessel was a rather plump thing riding high in the water and probably not very fast. He could outrun this fatty and be on his way to Sevastopol within minutes.

But he wasn't too sure he could beat bullets.

Then an idea struck him like lightning. They obviously had everything. Expensive cars, boats, manpower. What if they had a helicopter too? Then he was fucked at sea.

Igor's coffee machine was bubbling, providing him with a welcome distraction. He had to stay awake and alert.

While he was sipping hot coffee another lightning bolt hit his tired brain.

He forgot! Matt had told him to call Khabarovsk.

Igor opened the secure tab on his main computer and punched in the code for Petrossian. He had contacted the organization only once before, and he remembered the soft, friendly female voice answering the call. It was a video call, but Igor could see only the digitalized form of the woman talking to him.

The same now. She answered after not more than a second.

"Hello, Igor. I was expecting your call. What held you up?"

Calm now, Igor explained that Matt had asked him to call Khabarovsk. A thought shot through his mind again. Matt and others in the know constantly referred to Khabarovsk. But was Petrossian really in Khabarovsk? Igor suspected that this spot in eastern Siberia was a mere code and that the powerful Petrossian center was located somewhere else. But never mind. He continued to relay all he knew, saw, and heard.

The digital girl asked him to immediately send files relevant to the case. Igor confirmed. Then he said, "Fifty told me to leave for Sevastopol. Can you confirm?"

"Yes, that's correct, Igor, but not in daylight. You are quite safe in the house for now. You should even try to get some sleep. We checked the house perimeters and the security system. It's safe during daytime. Thank you for your information. We'll start to communicate with fifty. Please tell him that. Fifty-three is already on the ground in Bali together with our local asset, seventy-one. Take care and rest."

She was gone, and Igor felt great relief. Suddenly he was extremely tired. He checked the security system and assured himself nobody could break into the house without using RPGs. He was quite sure such option was out during daytime at least.

One further check was necessary. The mother server, well hidden in the hills of the Crimea, was the core of their communications and hack structure.

To the south of Alushta was Roman Kosh, the highest peak in Crimea.

Petrossian had built a secret server station just below the peak that it used for communications and hacking; the lab had access to it. The servers there split global communications between satellites and ground-based proxy servers so no perp could pinpoint a location of the sender or receiver of any kind of messages.

Igor made sure the Kosh server was working properly and then fell half dead on his bed in the upstairs bedroom.

He fell asleep almost instantly but was shaken by violent dreams in which demons were trying to get into his fortress.

A loud bang awoke him after more than six hours of not very calm sleep. He shot up into a sitting position, sweating and still traumatized by the nightmares. Was the thud that shook him back to reality part of a dream?

No, it was not. Igor heard alarming sounds from below. The boathouse! How did they know? The boathouse was well concealed and hardly visible from the seaside. The heavy hydraulic door was camouflaged as part of the wall, appearing like stone.

Igor rushed to the screens downstairs on the ground floor. The cams were working fine. He switched to the seaside cams and was surprised that he couldn't see anything unusual. However, taking a second look, he noticed the boathouse door was slightly damaged. A small dent in the surface indicated an attempt to destroy it. This couldn't have been done with an RPG or a similar large explosive device, or the damage would have been considerably more extensive.

The sun, or what was left of it, was now behind the house, shining a mischievous light on the dark clouds over the Black Sea.

Igor knew the house had not been infiltrated. The fortifications were too strong for a simple break-in.

He swiveled the cams out over the ocean but couldn't find the boat he had seen in the morning. He decided to go down to the boathouse to check for damage.

The cams gave him an all clear, and with his remote control Igor opened the door to the watery basement. The sound of softly moving seawater outside the heavily armored door broke the quiet of the boathouse. *Blue Thunder* was undisturbed and ready to go. He climbed up to the nose of the elegant vessel to see if there was any damage to the hydraulic door. Igor could spot nothing from the inside. After all, the door was made of a special titanium alloy, which, combined with the stone camouflage on the outside, gave it a thickness of almost thirty centimeters. Once the boathouse door was down, *Blue Thunder* had a maximum of five seconds to clear the opening. As soon as the cigarette racer was out, the boathouse would be shut.

Igor figured they had used a grenade of some kind, hoping for a quick entry. Somehow, they must have acquired blueprints of the house, which would imply that Igor's fortress had been hacked.

As Matt said, "Never take your skills for granted! There are other geniuses out there competing with you."

Cohen Industries certainly would have virtuosos in its employ.

Igor was somewhat shaken that he had been hacked without noticing it. This was a matter of pride. He had to find the people responsible.

Satisfied that the house was still safe and his escape route open, he went back upstairs and raked through his firewalls, booby traps that were a vital part of his programming. Igor never used the term *hacking*. For him, it was all about writing code, programming, and entering and leaving unseen.

He checked all the surveillance screens and tried again to reenter the Marseille offices of Alliance Ovest. Dead. They were good there. He made sure all the recorded material was in seventh heaven, and then he concentrated on the cyberattack on his system.

He found the attacker after half an hour of hard work. As he suspected, the origin of the hack was CI, Cohen Industries, in Alabama.

He sent this information right away to Matt and Fedorov.

Igor didn't shut out CI but limited the hacker's access to less harmful matters, making it appear the hack had not been detected. He let the foreign search engine, which was quite impressive, circle around a lot of data in his system, but he blocked cam access, which was not yet penetrated anyway.

The sound of the doorbell broke Igor's deep concentration. The doorbell was a harmless-looking device installed in houses all over the world, but when this one rang, the main screen focused on the entrance and its immediate and wider surroundings.

The pretty middle-aged woman from the Ukrainian café was standing outside with a small package in her hands.

Igor activated the door communications system and asked how he could be of help.

"You were so tired this morning, so I thought I'd bring you some food. I have chiboureki [a delicious Tatar dish he liked very much] and some fresh sarburma [a Crimean meat pie]."

Igor frantically checked the cams but couldn't see any movement nearby.

"That's so nice of you, spasibo. I will be down in a moment."

He slowly walked to the entrance door, another titanium alloy hard to penetrate but disguised as a traditional Tatar-style wooden door. He clicked the remote and the door opened soundlessly. He should have taken the Tokarev pistol that was always handy in the control room adjacent to the spacious living room. But it was just a woman at the door.

"Dobryy den," he said, greeting the woman whose name he never could remember.

She somehow sensed that and said, "Dobryy den, Igor. I'm Oksana. I thought you might be hungry."

She glanced curiously into the living room. Out of instinct Igor invited her in.

"I was just thinking of making tea. Would you like to join me for a cup?"

"Spasibo, yes, that would be nice. It's quiet at the café right now, but earlier a few strangers asked questions about you."

Now she had his full attention.

"They said you were old friends, but they would not disturb you now because you must be tired from last night. They said they will be back tonight."

"What were they, Oksana? Russian, Ukrainian?"

"One of them was definitely Ukrainian. Two others I think were foreigners, European or even Amerikansky. Another didn't speak."

"Did they ask you to come and visit me?"

"No, but I thought this was strange. Their behavior made me feel uneasy. I have a good eye for weird people. You know I'm Tatar. The Russians hate me and so do the Ukrainians. I keep a low profile, but I have studied people for a long time."

The kettle gave its familiar whistling sound, and Igor got up and filled two cups with dark Russian tea.

"I'm very grateful, Oksana. I might be in trouble with these people, and you have helped me a lot. I don't want you to be in the line of fire—don't worry; this is just a saying. After we finish our tea, go back to your café. If they ask why you came over here, tell them I ordered some food."

Instead of looking worried, Oksana's face lit up with excitement.

"I understand. I'm experienced in such situations. I brought my entire family out of Russia a few years back only to be in Russia again. They live up in the mountains with other Tatars. I bring them food and money and have already arranged fake identities for three of them."

Seeming to realize she had said too much, her face turned a deep purple.

"Please keep this to yourself, Igor. I do my best. I will call you when they show up again."

"No, don't do that. I will be safe here. Just act normal, and as you said, I ordered food."

Igor led Oksana to the door, though not before checking on the screens in the operational room.

All clear.

He again thanked her profusely for the delicious food and almost shoved her out.

Just before Oksana stepped away, she turned back, looked into his eyes, and said, "Count on me, Igor. I'm Petrossian."

Before he could recover from the shock she was gone.

It was time to holster the Tokarev.

When Igor reentered the operation room his main set was beeping.

Matt and Fedorov. Igor still wondered why Petrossian had sent Fedorov for this task. He was even older than Matt and supposedly retired for ages. The organization might have its reasons.

"Yes, I'm here. Ready. Go. I met Oksana. She is Petrossian."

"Igor, I'll go into details from here later. Right now you must get out. Our guest spilled the beans. They know where you are, and they have gathered artillery to get into the house. Don't disable anything. We are protected, but leave the house by water quickly. Is the *Thunder* ready? And yes, we know Oksana. She is the best—and deadly."

"Copy that. Yes, everything is ready. I think I can outrun them. They have a boat, but it's no match for the *Thunder*."

Before Matt could reply, Igor said, "CI hacked me. Not deep but they are in. There was a half-assed attack on the boathouse door this afternoon. That means they have blueprints or other info."

"Okay, that confirms what we were able to extract from our boarder."

Igor snickered. "Boarder, good expression."

"We have access to the mother on Kosh. P is in now. They contacted Fedorov and handle him. Not me, though. I'm just some kind of asset. Whatever you have loaded up to Kosh, we will get it."

"Already done. Dinner is served."

Igor was in good spirits again after talking to his friend and confirming that Matt, Fedorov, and Ketut were safe.

"Sevastopol is alarmed. They will send an interceptor out on your route at about sunset. So be ready to leave before dark."

"Yes, boss. Don't worry. I'm on my way."

The connection was cut, and Igor prepared for his sea trip.

He placed water bottles, dry food, and a bottle of vodka in a cooler he carried down to the boat. The vodka would be for the moment when the interceptor escorted him into the harbor at Sevastopol.

Igor's satellite phone beeped.

"Da." He couldn't recognize the caller, but he recognized his boss's voice.

"Igor, it's me again, fifty. This is Walters's phone, which we'll use for the next few hours. P has noticed some tracking movement on our own phone."

Igor heard heavy breathing on the Bali side.

"Where are you?"

"We are on the road, so to speak. Heavy guns showed up. Ketut and Walters are hidden for now. P confirmed a jet. We are on the way, but that's not the reason I call."

Again, Igor heard loud inhaling as if they were running.

"Get out of there now! Not by boat. We have intel that the boat way is covered, and you would be a sitting duck. Let the boat go full throttle on auto, heading a hundred degrees southeast, close the door, and leave the house on foot."

"What?" Igor was in disbelief. "On foot? Where the hell could I run?"

But he already had an idea.

"Yes. The only way you can get out of there is by foot. P is about four hours out. They don't have assets in Ukraine. Come from the east."

Russia.

"Can't talk longer. Get out and send a text when you're safe. Godspeed!"

The connection was gone, and Igor was panting like he was already on the run.

He trusted Matt with his life and therefore prepared accordingly.

It was getting dark outside, and maybe this was the right time to fake a boat escape.

Igor again went down to the boathouse, which would provide him with the only safe way out of the house after the boat was gone.

He tucked some clothes into a plastic bag, made sure he had his passport, satellite phone, and what else? His mind was racing.

Igor knew that they were up to something very big and that he was facing a small army of CI killers.

He was tempted to take a sip of vodka to calm himself but dismissed the attraction and worked hard on the final planning.

The boat was ready. Its autopilot was set on one hundred, which would let it pass Yalta by a huge margin.

He took action.

The heavy door fell softly and almost silently to the ground, leaving the path open for a racing *Blue Thunder* on auto pilot.

The two engines picked up immediately, and after releasing the monster from its mooring, Igor pushed the controls full speed forward. He almost fell into the water but held on to the railing. A huge spray of seawater gushed over him when *Blue Thunder* left the cave. He had made sure no positioning lights were switched on so the cigarette would blend perfectly with the falling night.

Igor didn't waver in taking his next step. He closed the boathouse door with his remote, which he slipped into a plastic bag, and jumped into the wild sea. With the plastic bag fastened around his neck, he dived out of the boat shelter and swam to his right as far as he could underwater. His lungs were almost bursting when he broke the surface and found himself about ten meters from the shore in front of a neighbor's building. A holiday house like his own, it was dark and deserted but maybe too close to be a hiding place.

His head was bobbing just over the water when he saw movement in the supposedly uninhabited holiday house. Flashlights, no doubt. They were very close.

The clatter of rotor blades overhead led him to dive again.

Matt was right. They were fully equipped and meant business. A chopper was following *Blue Thunder* out over the Black Sea. That strategy had worked just fine. Another fast boat was pursuing the *Thunder*, but Igor knew no other boat could catch his *Thunder*, which was probably racing at more than 120 kilometers an hour toward Yalta.

He swam slowly down the coast toward the Ukrainian café run by—what the hell was her name?—Oksana. After about ten minutes he was floating outside the café's summer terrace, which was supported by fragile-looking pillars stretching into the water below.

Igor couldn't see any movement on the terrace or in the empty café.

He made a decision.

He carefully approached the deck that overhung the coast. It was designed so summer guests could enjoy Ukrainian lunches while looking out over the Black Sea. He held on to one of the pillars and listened for any suspicious noises from above. Nothing.

Igor didn't dare use his flashlight, so he felt his way around toward the dry ground under the terrace, climbed up, and took some deep breaths before exploring further.

He watched the sea but couldn't make out any immediate cause for alarm. Evidently, they were following the *Thunder* with the chopper, and at this speed it might take a while even for a helicopter to catch up. Then what? Would they sink the boat? His baby! He somehow took comfort in the fact that such thoughts of loss were creeping into his mind. P was generous and might compensate him.

Igor felt around the outside wall of the café and found a small window facing the sea behind which might be a cellar or a storage area. He didn't switch on his flashlight but listened intently for any sounds.

When he heard a car engine start on the road and doors close, he took the opportunity and broke one of the tiny glass panels.

The shattered glass made a hell of a noise. Igor didn't move for several minutes. No reaction. He might have gotten away with it.

Igor cautiously inserted his right hand into the opening and felt for a lever, which he found. The window was old and undoubtedly hadn't been opened for years, if ever.

He turned the handle and pushed the small window forward, creating a gap wide enough to climb through.

Once in the cellar, which indeed was a storage room, Igor sat on the concrete floor, shivering from the cold. He had to get out of his heavy, wet clothes. But before he could get undressed, the door leading to the café upstairs opened, and in the bright light from the staircase he could see Oksana.

"Igor, I know you are here. You are safe."

He was dumbfounded.

"Oksana, I …"

She interrupted him.

"I have cameras installed, and I saw you break my window. The cameras react to noise and movement."

She was smiling.

"It's the high-tech century, and the café has been burglarized more than once. Just beside that window you broke is a door. You could have tried there."

Igor was stunned. This seemingly simple woman was into many things. She had a top-flight surveillance system and had forged identities, undoubtedly with the help of Petrossian. Who knew what else she could do?

"I was sure they were after you, so I kept a lookout. I wanted to warn you about the helicopter that landed earlier behind the Villa Bon Maison."

Igor knew the place. The hotel was up on the hill and had a helipad behind it. The breeze from the sea made it impossible to hear the chopper earlier.

"Come up and change into something dry. I have closed the café. We are alone."

Oksana resolutely took Igor's hand and pulled him toward the lit staircase.

"And don't worry. I've lowered all the blinds. Nobody can see in."

Igor followed her, climbing the narrow stairs up to the empty café.

"Where is the screen?"

"In my bedroom. I don't want anyone to know I have surveillance."

That was a good idea given her side activities.

She led him to a heated room furnished with a bed and a TV.

"I'll prepare some food. Then we can talk."

She provided him with a fluffy bathrobe and some towels, shut the door behind her, and was gone.

"I'll fetch you in a few minutes," she called from the stairs.

Igor went to the window but was unable to look out since the heavy shutters were closed. *Maybe that's better for now,* he thought.

It took him a few minutes to get dry and to put on the clothes he had placed in the sealed plastic bag. The satellite phone was also dry and operable. He heard it beep.

"Da."

"Igor, are you safe and away?"

"Yes, I'm out and safe and ..."

The connection was gone.

CHAPTER 9

BALI, DAYLIGHT

The questioning of Walters was easier than we expected. He was no hero and had no such aspirations.

An ex-desk handler at the CIA, Walters had been entangled in a murderous conspiracy involving Cohen Industries, Al Qaeda, and several other radical Islamist groups in Iraq and Afghanistan.

At that time Al Baghdadi, who would become the leader of the Islamic State, had been released from Abu Ghraib prison in Iraq, mostly based on falsified analyses concerning the future terrorist chief.

CIA operatives in Iraq had warned Langley against releasing Al Baghdadi, but their warnings had been suppressed by the handling agent, Walters. He had been paid handsomely by Cohen Industries to keep the alerts from Baghdad on his desk until Al Baghdadi had disappeared into Iraq's northern desert.

Two days after the alerts, Walters was officially sick at home, and the detailed notes from Baghdad had landed on the desk of a furious but naïve CIA director, a political appointee.

The CIA usually didn't operate like that. Secure channels to all levels were open all the time. However, Walters had made a small but deadly error, which he later blamed on his deteriorating health. He had shut down all message-forwards before seeking the safety of his modest home.

Two new stars had been added in the CIA lobby shortly after Al Baghdadi's departure from Abu Ghraib. Wondering why there had been no reaction from Langley, agents Al Summers and Herb Brooks had been killed in their attempt to hold Al Baghdadi.

Entering the Abu Ghraib prison, the two agents had been shot from long distance, too long a way for any Islamic terrorist. The bullets recovered from their bodies had been US military grade and had most probably come from an M40 A3, a sniper rifle issued to the US special forces.

The shooter had never been found, but many years later the rifle had been recovered by the Iraqi armed forces during a raid on an IS stronghold.

Walters had been interrogated, but his doctor had attested that the desk handler had a severe flu with a tendency to acute pneumonia.

After days of hard grilling, the CIA discharged him on grounds of severe negligence. No legal action had been taken against him.

The same month he had joined Cohen Industries and had moved down to Alabama where he had run into several other ex-firm guys hardened by failures to protect the United States of America.

These men had mostly been stationed in Turkey and Lebanon where they had handled delicate transfers of oil from the IS-held areas of northern Iraq. More often than not, they had engaged in skirmishes with the US army, the Iraqi forces, or even their former colleagues.

After his stay at Abu Ghraib, Al Baghdadi had been transferred to Camp Bucca where he was supposed to be held indeterminately. However, nudged by Cohen Industries, the Pentagon decided to cut the supposedly harmless preacher loose.

Walters had been a small but vital cog in the CI machinery, and therefore Michael Cohen, the owner, chairman, and near king of CI, had assigned him to a luxurious post in Istanbul. As a former CIA desk handler, he had the experience to run the CI agents on their often-deadly missions.

Bali was his first task in the field after years of desk handling from a safe house in Istanbul.

He knew all along about the reputation of Petrossian, which used to hire clean CIA or GCHQ dropouts, and he was not shocked to run into two who had already been labeled as legends during his time at Langley.

Porter Goss, the CIA director at the time, used to engage Petrossian for joint missions on which the firm had been underrepresented.

Walters knew Petrossian's services were hugely expensive and therefore effective.

He had been assigned to the Al Mukhabarat Al A'amah, the Saudi intelligence firm, which was a mere subsidiary of the CIA and was mostly unable to move on its own.

According to Walters, the Mukhabarat or its renegades maintained close contacts with the Islamic State and, with the help of CI and other foreign contractors, ran a sophisticated global network to finance the terrorists.

There we were! Everything fit nicely into the complex plot Igor's software had uncovered but had not yet exposed.

That's why they were hunting us like animals here and in Crimea.

I wondered if we should unload at least part of our hacked findings to the CIA, but I dismissed the thought right away, not knowing who else at Langley might be a CI mole or even a Cavity operative.

It was time to work a bit harder on Walters. I offered him a relatively luxurious stay until the US Justice Department could get its hands on him or a more painful one if he wouldn't talk.

He immediately spilled the beans.

I was never a sadistic guy, but I felt a slight disappointment that I didn't need to waterboard this scum. Maybe later.

The Langley mole was Art Shipper, an assistant director for special ops. *Fits*, I thought.

Walters told us Shipper had recruited him for CI just before the Al Baghdadi mess in Iraq. The money was too good to refuse, and lonely, divorced Walters desperately needed a break.

Well he got one. With us.

Fedorov recorded everything on Mia's video cam, and after another hour of interrogation we uploaded the video to Igor's seventh heaven cloud via the tethered satellite phone.

While we were working on Walters, a jumpy boy whom Ketut had sent to watch Villa Kakatua returned on his scooter.

"They are there. I saw them. Two Arabs with a big car."

"Calm down and sit here," I said. "Tell me. What have you seen? Only two of them?"

"Yes, two. One big Arab and one not so big but with a big gun."

He was excited, and I told him he had done a good job. I gave him fifty US dollars and warned him to keep quiet if he valued his life.

"How much time do we have left?" Ketut asked.

She seemed calm but I could feel her anxiety.

"We'll wait for Petrossian's confirmation on the jet, and then we'll be off to the airport. Maybe half an hour?"

"We should leave right now. I don't want to underestimate the Mukhabarat. I'm sure the CIA or the bad guys there are working on this too."

I knew she was right, but we had unfinished business here. I wasn't quite sure what to do with Walters. Pointing at him, I said, "We can't bring him with us and he's heard enough."

"I'll drop him somewhere in the bush," Fedorov said.

"Just let me live," Walters said desperately. "I won't tell them anything."

That produced a healthy but coarse laugh from all of us.

With Walters alive, Mia's life was in great danger. I made my decision.

"Mia is coming with us. It's not safe for her to stay here."

Mia looked confused and more than worried.

I checked again with the boy, who confirmed that the Arabs had left in a hurry in their big car.

"We bring Walters back to the Kakatua and let him rot there until he is found," I said.

We all agreed and I started the satellite phone.

It was about six in the morning in Washington, DC, but I didn't care about the time difference.

"I'll call Mark Shearer. He is the only one there I trust."

Shearer was a retired CIA assistant director and maybe not as inactive as he liked to appear. The firm, at least the good part of it, still relied on his sharp mind and on his even sharper tongue when agency leaders were arguing over a sensitive project. He was one of the few straight, down-to-earth operatives I had ever encountered.

Fedorov agreed, although we might be jumping ahead of Petrossian's plans. But we were retired too and fully capable of making our own choices.

As I suspected, I awakened Mark. It was six in the morning. He was grumpy but alert when he heard who was calling.

"This better be worthwhile. I thought you had been out of the business for a long time."

"Good morning again to you, old friend and foe. I think somehow they always get us back in."

I filled him in, and Mark never interrupted. His willingness to listen was one of the traits that had made him a great CIA officer.

After my short but thorough briefing, he simply replied that he would work on the problem right away.

"Walters! That asshole! Why don't you just get rid of him as we should have done years ago?"

Sadly, the satellite phone didn't have a speaker function, so I was unable to add to our captive's terror.

It was getting late, and I tried again to reach Igor, but to no avail. I was sure that by now he was out on the Black Sea enjoying a speedy ride in *Blue Thunder*.

We were running out of time. Ketut convinced Mia to pack a few essential things for a short trip. Mia called her nurse and told her she wouldn't be in the next day and to move all patient appointments to the following week.

We grabbed Walters and dragged him to Mia's car where I dumped him into the trunk.

Ketut drove as nightfall quickly descended on Bali. We arrived at her villa in no time. A few phone calls to some of her cousins completed the plan.

They would show up the next day and would untie Walters. She made sure they would be armed at least with knives, telling them he was the guy who had abducted her.

She locked the villa, and we were back in Mia's car and on the road down the coast to the airport.

Halfway down my satellite phone beeped.

The woman who always seemed to handle sensitive communications told me a Dassault Falcon 7X with an ETA of 10:12 p.m. at Denpasar Airport needed about thirty minutes to refuel and to prepare for takeoff. It was our task to get to the plane. She apologized for not being able to help us there.

Resourceful Ketut had another cousin—or was it an uncle?—who worked security at the airport. Luckily, he was on duty and quite high up in the security pecking order.

He agreed to meet us at the long-term parking area with one of his airport security vans. "Don't be late," he said. "My shift ends at ten."

We hadn't talked about the trip we were about to take, but Fedorov and I had already decided on our destination. Petrossian might have had different plans, but once on board and airborne we would command the plane.

Our destination was Simferopol, Crimea.

To my surprise, the airport was almost free of tourists. I forgot that this was the day King Salman of Saudi Arabia had arrived in Bali. Ketut said that only VIP travel was allowed and that numerous planes carrying hundreds of Saudis had been arriving the whole day. These people required and received top security.

I was a bit worried we might run into some imbecile Mukhabarat agents cruising the perimeters of the airport, and that's exactly what happened when we entered the almost unoccupied parking area.

Two Indonesian national police officers armed with HK submachine guns and wearing heavy vests stopped us rather aggressively. They pointed guns at our car, and one of them strolled over to the driver's side. At that instant, another heavily armed figure emerged from the parking cashier's office.

Mukhabarat. I identified him instantly.

He waved the two Indonesians aside and approached us with the arrogance for which Arabs are well known. I had experienced such treatment several times before.

"Where you go? Airport is closed."

Ketut took over, increasing my admiration for her.

"We are scheduled on a VIP flight out tonight. No commercial airline.

My two guests and the secretary"—she pointed at Mia—"have their plane landing right about now. You can check."

This rattled the Mukharabat slightly, and just then Ketut's contact arrived with his security van.

I could see now that he was her uncle. He was at least sixty and had two stars on the epaulettes of his green airport security uniform.

"Asalam aleikum," he said, greeting the Arab.

"Aleikum salam," the Mukhabarat agent replied.

They exchanged a few words that we couldn't make out. All the while I was aware that Fedorov had a tight grip on the Makarov.

The Arab asked us to show our passports and closely inspected them. Mine was Swiss and Fedorov's Khazak, something I hadn't known. The two Indonesian women had honest papers.

"Where you fly?"

"Just to Jakarta tonight."

I jumped in to appear decisive so we might avoid more questions.

He was talking on a sophisticated communications device with a big M printed on it for Motorola.

After some rapid Arabic of which I understood only parts, he ordered us to park the car and to use the van to enter the airport.

I nudged Fedorov to put away the Makarov and hoped we didn't have to pass metal detectors.

Ketut again grasped the situation before I could open my mouth.

"Arie will bring us straight to the plane. He is a brother of my aunt and I trust him."

Okay, that made him an uncle. Bali is one enormous family united in protecting its own and sometimes friends.

A gate with razor wire on top swung open and we were on the tarmac. The small Bali airport could not accommodate the Saudi planes looking to park there. Thus, after unloading their royals and hundreds of domestics, the planes left for Kuala Lumpur to be on standby there.

With the airport closed for commercial traffic, we found the tarmac almost empty except for the sleek Dassault, which was being refueled.

"I'll drop you right at the stair," Arie said. "It's lowered. Hurry up. I don't want anybody else snooping around."

He turned his head and said with a grin, "If you were terrorists here to assassinate the king, I would be even more motivated to help you. We really don't need the Saudis in Bali."

Arie drove us to the stairs and wished us good luck, and we were out of the van, climbing into the comfortable belly of the Dassault. I noticed the plane was registered in Switzerland. The HB printed on the fuselage made us slightly more neutral.

I checked my watch and figured Igor must be in Sevastopol by now, although I was a bit concerned that there was no message.

The captain, a genuine Swiss citizen, came out of the cockpit, shook hands with us, and smiled at the two ladies, who looked somehow displaced in the luxurious and very expensive cabin. I led them to two soft, wide leather chairs and told them we were safe. However, as was often the case in such situations, my hypersensitive alarms were sending shrill tones to my brain.

The captain told us to relax. Refueling would take another few minutes, and then he could ask the tower for taxi and takeoff instructions.

A pretty girl in a uniform stepped out of the galley and offered us refreshments—champagne, juices, tea, and coffee.

Fedorov asked for an iced vodka, but I shook my head.

"After takeoff," I told the flight attendant, who was Thai.

"Bad feelings?" Fedorov asked.

"Very bad," I replied.

He placed his Makarov on the chair beside him, testing the Thai girl.

She obviously was company and had no reaction whatsoever. She brought us juices, and I told the girls we would have champagne after takeoff.

Ketut, seasoned professional that she was, sensed my hyper-alert state and took a seat at one of the big oval windows, giving her a view of the tarmac and of the main building.

The captain announced that refueling was completed and that we would be on our way shortly. Suddenly a black Toyota SUV pulled up beside our plane. *Mukhabarat*, I thought, slightly relieved. Any other law enforcement agency would have put its vehicle in front of the plan.

The captain, doubtless a professional too, announced he was lowering the stairs for three "visitors." We heard the electric hum of the stairway descending to the tarmac.

The captain received the three Mukhabarat agents, now clearly identified, and asked if there was a problem.

"Your passengers. Out of the plane. Now!"

The leader seemed slightly out of his league, screaming at the captain and waving his gun wildly in the air. He aimed a Glock automatic at us, shifting it from right to left, showing us he was not an elite professional.

The two behind him held their weapons casually, pointing them toward the floor.

There were two quick plops, inaudible over the engine noise. Fedorov had taken out two of the Arabs with shots to the heart. The third was about to lift his gun, but when he saw Fedorov aiming at him, he dropped his Glock and raised his hands. It looked as if he had some experience doing that.

Ketut was out of her seat in a split second and pulled the two dead Arabs away from the open door.

We needed clearance. We couldn't possibly take off without consent and instructions from the tower.

I grabbed the surviving Arab, took the Makarov, and pointed its warm barrel at his head.

"Cooperate and you live. We have nothing to lose. What do you have to report? Make it quick or I'll pull the trigger."

"We have to check on you. Your papers, your passports ..."

I knew he was lying. I underestimated him. The little camel herder was courageous.

We had no choice. We had to count on the poor coordination skills of the Mukhabarat.

I ordered the captain to pull in the stairs and to get immediate takeoff clearance.

My guess about the lack of coordination was right. The tower didn't know a thing about the recheck of the plane and instructed the Dassault to proceed to runway twenty-eight.

The plane moved rapidly toward the runway. The captain reported his position and said he was ready for takeoff. The tower gave permission with a friendly "Have a safe flight."

We couldn't relax as we raced to our takeoff speed of 160 knots. Fedorov, Ketut, and I were watching the activities on the tarmac, which was now alive with flashing blue-and-red lights as police attempted to get close to the speeding plane. After a seeming eternity, we felt the sensation of a rapid and steep takeoff that in seconds took us out of rifle range.

No time for champagne yet. What to do with the two bodies and the visibly scared survivor?

I instructed the captain to level off at three thousand feet and to open the fuselage door but not before I told all those on board to fasten their seat belts tightly.

Fedorov took care of the shivering Mukhabarat agent by showing him the Makarov.

The captain announced we were at three thousand feet with a minimum airspeed of 120 knots. The door was open, letting in a stream of cold air that filled the cabin with a devilish rushing sound.

Ketut got up from her seat and helped me move the two bodies to the door. I kicked them out while holding on to the door handle. The corpses disappeared into the dark night over the Indian Ocean. They would descend for about forty seconds before hitting the black waters below.

I shut the door and bent over the remaining Arab.

"You are next. You will enjoy the flight more than your buddies did, because you will make it alive."

"Rajá, rajá, please." He was in deep shock and spoke Arabic.

I replied in his tongue, "You might live if you tell us all you know."

His face lit up and he nodded. I soon found out he knew nothing and had no part in our case. I knew Petrossian planes had parachutes on board, the newest glides that let you maneuver and land on the spot you choose.

His name was Akeem. He was twenty-six years old and not a royal. Coming out of CIA training, he had joined the Mukhabarat only year earlier. His parents were proud of him, he told us, and he was supposed to marry just after the Hajj season that year.

I let him blabber while Ketut fetched one of the three glider parachutes.

Akeem had jumped before but never at night and not once from a jet. Still, he was very grateful we were giving him a chance to live.

I told him we would let him go over Surabaya where he could find the airport easily and make a safe landing. Because their lack of communication skills was well known, I was not afraid of swift action by the Indonesians or the Arabs.

Just west of Surabaya, the captain lowered the Dassault to six thousand feet, with the airspeed back to 120 knots, and opened the door.

Akeem looked at me and muttered, "Shoukran. Bark Allah fit." Thanks. God be with you.

I gave him a gentle shove and even hoped the chute would open. Akeem was gone and probably safe.

The Dassault reacted like a racehorse when the captain pushed the throttles full speed forward, leading the sleek and powerful plane into an almost vertical ascent that lifted us to our cruising altitude of forty-eight thousand feet in a few minutes.

Fedorov poured clear and delicious-looking vodka into two crystal tumblers, which were agreeably iced.

"What now? Where to?" Ketut joined us with a vodka while Mia, starving, gobbled down appetizers served by the Thai attendant.

"I'll tell the captain to change all flight plans and to direct this bird to Simferopol."

After a heavy gulp of iced vodka, I went to the cockpit.

"Captain ..." He interrupted me with his hand in the air.

"I know what you want but I have instructions. I'll drop you in Phuket, Thailand. P forty-nine is waiting for you there."

Petrossian forty-nine was the highest-ranking member of our firm. Long ago, the numbers had started with one, two, and so on. That was before World War II when Petrossian was fighting everybody—Stalin in Russia, Hitler in Germany, and Franco in Spain, and before that the Turks in Armenia. The operatives who held those first numbers were all dead now, and the numbers were never reassigned. There never was a new number one. The newest operative simply got the next digit.

I had been told that my number, fifty, would eventually lead me to the top, but after the horrors I had encountered, I had different plans, and so I retired peacefully. Now I was fifty again.

"We have a situation in Russia," I told him.

"We know, and it's being taken care of while we speak."

I headed back to the cabin and activated my satellite phone. Nothing from Igor. Not a sound. Not a sign.

At this altitude, forty-six thousand feet, the phone connected easily and I got dial clearance within seconds.

"Hello, boss."

Igor's voice filled me with relief.

"Igor!" I almost shouted. "Are you okay in Sevastopol?"

"Boss, I'm still in Alushta but not in the house. They are here and in force. I'm at the café beside my house with Oksana. She is Petrossian, but you know that already. I'll use my reliable Internet connection to send you all I have. Lots of video. *Blue Thunder* is gone. Autopilot. A helicopter is chasing …"

The link broke and all I heard was static and sounds.

As I tried feverishly to reconnect with Igor, the captain announced we had another two hours to our destination.

After a while I gave up and noticed how bloody tired I was—too tired even to eat the excellent food Chimlin, the pretty flight attendant, was serving.

I fell into a deep, exhausted sleep, and the last thing I felt was Ketut's hand on my arm.

CHAPTER 10

ALUSHTA, IN THE MIDDLE OF THE NIGHT

Igor was beat after the day's events. Oksana brought some delicious Ukrainian food to his room. The woman he'd never really noticed had changed into a lovely angel, albeit a middle-aged one. She gave him shelter, food, and safety while knowing he was Russian. It must have been his sex appeal or something close to that, he surmised, smiling for the first time in hours.

She sat down with him and they dined together. She didn't appear too old for him right now, just pleasant and attractive.

"Oksana, sorry to trouble you even more. I need to access your Internet. I could link to my house, but they might be in. Hope you don't mind."

"II give you the access password. No problem, Igor. I have good communications equipment here too."

"I'm so grateful for what you're doing for me, Oksana. I hope I won't disturb you much longer."

She gave him the access pass, but he had gotten it after he unpacked his ultra-thin, waterproof Fujitsu laptop from a plastic bag. He had immediately accessed her home network, which took him only seconds via the command prompt and his preinstalled software. But he wanted her to know he was going to use her Internet.

Then his satellite phone beeped.

Matt.

He was relieved to hear his boss was on a plane out of Bali. No, he told Matt, he was not in Sevastopol. And then an explosion next door had led him to drop the phone.

Igor was amazed at the connection Oksana had in her little café. This was not a mere home network but at least a semi-professional hot spot with a speed of fifty-six megabytes on download and more than forty on upload.

Then he remembered how she had produced fake identities, helping her relatives and maybe others. She was an active Petrossian.

Never mind. The Internet speed was fantastic, and he would be able to upload the video from his house to Matt.

"The explosion—my house. This was at my house," he stammered.

"Stay here. I'll check what's going on."

In her mysterious way, Oksana immediately took over and told Igor to calm down. As if she had known.

She left his room, and he went to the window that faced the sea, not his house. Nothing. No fire, no smoke. He went to the door behind which Oksana had disappeared a few seconds earlier.

She came up the stairs with a decanter of wine in her hands.

"I'm afraid they entered your house by blasting through the boathouse door."

At that moment, they heard a chopper approaching from the sea, flying right over their heads, low and aggressively.

"You think they got your *Thunder*?"

How the hell did she know the name of his beloved boat?

Igor now was on high alert, aware of the explosion and suspicious about Oksana's knowledge of certain things to which only he was privy.

"Who are you really?"

He faced her and took her by her sturdy arms.

"Igor, I told you I've been Petrossian for a long time. I have been asked, or ordered, the better term, to look out for you. Petrossian financed my café. They support me in bringing my relatives to safety. They did a lot for me and my family. I only repay now and then a little bit, and although I consider myself retired, I do jobs for them, very delicate ones. All my life."

She looked up into his eyes and gave him a strange but reassuring smile.

"I don't know what you are doing there at your house, and I don't want to know. I simply have to make sure you are safe."

Igor was about to shoot a thousand questions at her but refrained when Oksana led him back to his chair and told him to finish his food.

"You are safe here. I have been told that P will extract you tomorrow morning. They are now in Simferopol and wait for daylight to travel to Alushta without arousing suspicion. Your enemies have involved the police and seem to be quite resourceful."

She was right, and Igor was grateful for the Petrossian connections around him.

As if she knew his thoughts, Oksana looked at him with a stern expression and said, "Petrossian made my life worthwhile. The organization helps my family and has given me a life, a future I could never have dreamed of. I do whatever is needed here."

Looking up at him, she added, "And I got the proper training too. For many years."

With that, she handed him a black Makarov PM, the standard weapon of Petrossian agents all over the world. It wasn't as sleek and as high-tech as a Glock or a SIG, but it was very reliable in the worst circumstances.

Igor had to upload his info to Matt now.

"Is that why you have such fast Internet here?"

"Use it. Do what you have to do, and don't forget to catch some sleep."

She left his room and he heard her light steps going down the stairs.

Igor opened his Fujitsu and started to upload the surveillance video from his house, which right now was in the hands of the enemy.

Just when he was ready to send, there was a commotion downstairs. He heard glass breaking, a door cracking, and Oksana's voice penetrating the otherwise calm night.

They were here.

Igor opened the window, threw his laptop into the shallow surf of the Black Sea, and quickly followed his computer into the water. The leap from the second story was not life-threatening, and the sea's soft swell gently swallowed him. He surfaced briefly to catch some air and then swam to the next house, where a big boat was moored.

The shooting at Oksana's café was more than alarming. He wondered why the explosion at his house and the gunshots had not alarmed the ever-present police or at least some neighbors.

But his pursuers obviously had connections and enough money to bribe a few provincial uniforms. Besides, it was the off-season at the coast, and so most of the houses lining the shore were empty.

He swam toward the big old boat, which was tied up at two solid wooden pillars anchored deep in the seabed.

Igor had a feeling he might be caught if he tried to enter the house beside the café, so he swam around the timber hull of the boat, looking for a way to get on board. He found no ladder or rope that might facilitate a climb, so he tried one of the poles, which he climbed like a drenched monkey going for bananas.

Once up the pole, Igor realized he would be easily seen from the shore if he couldn't get on board quickly. He swung on the cable that fastened the ship to the pole and landed on the polished deck. He kept low behind the solid railing and crawled toward the deckhouse. The noise from the café had stopped, but powerful searchlights were aimed over the water in his direction. He could now see the name of the boat, *Nadezhda*, carved into the wood panel over the door of the deckhouse. It was written in Cyrillic letters, indicating a Russian owner.

Activity in the immediate neighborhood increased. Lights pointed in all directions, and Igor heard commands shouted in English. He didn't dare move closer to the deckhouse, so he stayed on his belly on the mahogany deck.

"Check the fucking boats. He must be here somewhere!" The hoarse voice sounded from close by on the shore.

The flashlights bounced off of his boat and the others berthed beside it.

"Shit. We can't get on this one. It's too high."

The flashlights moved to the other boats, and the house that belonged to the *Nadezhda* had been cleared. They were moving farther down the coast.

Igor crawled forward toward the deckhouse. He knew he had to get out of sight quickly. If the chopper showed up with its searchlight, he would be exposed and helpless.

As expected the sturdy door to safety was locked, and it was probably impossible to break in. Still on his belly, Igor crept around the structure, which would give him at least temporary shelter, and found a window on the lee side. Now he needed explosions or gunshots to mask the noise of shattering glass.

Then he got what he prayed for. The noisy helicopter swept low over the coastline, aiming its formidable searchlight all over the neighborhood.

Igor didn't waver and hit the window hard with his elbow. The glass shattered, and he cleared the shards from the frame. He threw his laptop inside and leaped through the window. Shit! If they lit up the *Nadezhda* again they might be able to see the open window. He had to hurry. Inside the spacious cabin he felt around for something he could use as a provisional cover. Luckily the numerous searchlights outside provided some illumination in the dark and spooky interior of the *Nadezhda*.

A chest-high cupboard just beside the window was the only item that might do the job. Igor pushed it in front of the broken window. This done, he tried to access Oksana's Internet with his wet but intact laptop.

He had a connection, weak but workable.

Frantically he typed a message to Matt, explaining his situation and Oksana's and noting his location and the name of the boat.

"Lay low, Igor. Fedorov already alerted P. Just don't move."

Then the connection was gone, and Igor instantly knew why.

They must have monitored any movements on Oksana's hot spot and now had found him.

It took them only a few minutes to surround the *Nadezhda* with their small boats, and when Igor heard a rope ladder being thrown over the railing he realized he was done.

They entered the cabin with force, placing a few rounds in the lock on the door.

A flashlight filled his vision for a moment, and darkness followed.

CHAPTER 11

OKSANA VOLOSHYNAIN

Oksana was born in 1959 in the Soviet Ukraine to parents of Tatar heritage. Her birthplace was totally insignificant to the Soviets and to the Soviet Ukrainians. Oksana opened her eyes for the first time in a small hamlet near Shcholkine on the Kerch peninsula that didn't have a name and consisted of just half a dozen miserable huts.

In 1974 when she was still a teenager, the Soviets caught Oksana smuggling caviar, beef, and other hard-to-come-by goods from the northern coast to the Ukrainian mainland. She had been quite resourceful, riding her bicycle with two baskets attached to the front and the rear. At the top of the baskets were bread and veggies destined for markets along the coast. Hidden underneath the produce lay the costly contraband imported from Azerbaijan, the Soviet republic famous for its centralized refrigerator manufacturing and its caviar. She had no idea where the iced steaks came from, but she always got one after a successful delivery in Nyzhnyohirsky, the largest city in the area.

Her mother, her father, and her two little sisters relished the weekly steak dinner, although her mother was frightened about Oksana's repeated runs for the smugglers.

On that September day, she was stopped by what she thought was a routine patrol. The officers thoroughly searched her body as well as the baskets. Oksana was a pretty girl and normally enjoyed the enthusiastic stares of boys her age and older.

Her natural charm had convinced the illegal importers in Kersh to employ her for small deliveries. She soon found out they were running dozens of girls and boys like her.

Oksana never had to accept cash from the recipients. Everything was prearranged. She would always deliver to the same address, a small house in a low-cost zone of Nyzhnyohirsky occupied by clerks and blue-collar workers employed by the Soviets in the city.

When they found the contraband, the police kicked her bicycle into the gutter and loaded her into their car, a second-generation Moskvitch, black as they all were and stinking of cigarette smoke.

They didn't speak a word to her during the long trip to Simferopol, Crimea's capital city. She had never been there but had heard the evil Soviets held their hunters on a loose leash to chase and to exterminate the loathed Tatars. She was one of them.

Strangely enough Oksana didn't panic. She was calm and worried only about her mom, her dad, and her sisters at home. Luckily, the Tatars in Crimea didn't have identity cards or any other official means of identification. She would keep her mouth shut, and the Soviets would never find her family.

After almost three hours in the stinking car, they arrived in Simferopol where they entered a large compound behind an electric gate garnished with barbed wire.

The three Soviet officers shoved her rudely into a small room with a table and two chairs.

"Sidet!"

The oldest of the three, the one with the cleanest uniform, gave her a devilish smile, revealing his yellow teeth.

"I have to go to the bathroom," Oksana said, a bit less confident than before.

"Later. Sit and be quiet, little Tatar whore."

After almost an hour she was defeated. She wet herself, feeling horrible and relieved at the same time.

Then the door opened, and a tall, thin civilian, wire-rimmed glasses on his beak nose, entered the now slightly smelly room.

"So you had to pee. You can clean up later. Now just answer my questions. Then we'll send you home."

He tried unsuccessfully to grin, which gave him the look of the hungry rats they sometimes hunted for food at home.

Oksana regained her confidence and lied in response to every question.

"Name?"

"Anastasia."

"Where do you live?"

"At the Fabrika in Kesh." This was a shelter for homeless teenagers and Tatar kids.

"Family?"

"All dead."

"Who gave you the goods?"

"People at the Fabrika. I don't know them."

"Where do you deliver?"

"I must wait at the market in Nyzhnyohirsky. Some man picks up the goods when he sees me."

"What do they give you? Now the truth!"

"One of the steaks." Her mouth watered just talking about it.

"Relatives?"

"None that I know."

This went on for two hours. Then two guards grabbed her under her arms and escorted her out of the room and down the stairs where a cold, dark cell awaited her.

"What about the ...?" She glanced at the wet floor.

"You have plenty of time to clean up your mess. If you remember anything useful we might let you go."

The interrogator, quite frustrated by now, stood on the other side of the corroded bars that confined her.

"Humor me. You are too young to rot in here forever."

With that, he left, and she was alone in this frightening place.

For hours, nothing happened. Oksana got no water, let alone food. She played mind games. She imagined eating steak with her family and taking a sip of her father's self-distilled vodka—just a sip when they were all happy with the little they had.

Night was falling, and a guard shoved a bowl of half-cold borscht and water of the same temperature under the iron bars.

Oksana didn't dare use the toilet, the dirtiest place she had ever seen. She peed like a boy, standing up.

A mattress in a corner looked like a breeding place for all sorts of little animals. But after a few hours Oksana didn't care anymore, and exhausted, she lay down and fell asleep.

She dreamed of a ship that brought her to far shores where palm trees lined the coast and people ate delicious food, listened to exotic music, and ...

A hand shook her awake—a gentle hand, not one of the guards' rough mitts.

"Oksana, wake up. Be quiet."

The hand was now over her mouth and stayed there until she nodded her assent.

Who knew her name here?

"Listen, Oksana, I'm Yevgeni Fedorov, a major with the KGB. I'll get you out of here, but you must be quiet. Understand?"

Oksana nodded again. *KGB!* she thought. *I'm not a spy!*

"We tailed you for quite some time, and we know what you do. It's not a big crime, but the police are following every track that leads to the smugglers."

"Why the KGB?" she stammered.

"If you agree we'll bring you to a safe place where you can study, go to school, have friends ..."

"My parents and my sisters need me here."

"We shall take care of them. I promise. We know where you live. Your father is Ayur and your mother is called Culpan. You are Tatars."

"Are you going to kill them?" Now Oksana was petrified.

"No. We will protect them and will give your father a job if you come with me. You won't be able to see them for a long time, but I assure you they will be fine. Better than ever before. Just nod your head if you agree."

Somehow this man was different. Oksana had a feeling she could trust him. She nodded her head with her blond hair flying. *Was that too much?* she wondered.

"Now we are leaving. The watch commander is asleep. I helped him have a deep nap. The guards are all in the barn outside, gambling."

He took Oksana by the elbow and led her out of the filthy cell.

"We have to cross the yard. My car is parked outside. Just be quiet and hurry."

They went up the stairs with Fedorov checking all directions.

"It's clear. Come."

They hurried across the yard, which was filled with police cars and motorbikes, and when they reached the huge gate a guy in a gray uniform pushed it open for them to sneak through.

She recognized the hated uniform. KGB. The enemies of her family, of all Tatars. Oksana hesitated a moment but Fedorov nudged her on.

"Come quick. That's our car."

It was a black Chaika. She recognized the car, luxurious and available only to assholes in the party. Oksana got suspicious. She would ride in a Chaika? That usually meant death or deportation to Siberia.

Fedorov pushed her in the back seat and followed her. The uniform, a lieutenant in the KGB, quickly took his position beside the driver. Another uniform.

Oksana was sure now that she and her family were dead.

"Where are we going?" She was so tense she could hardly form the words.

"To the airport. Again, Oksana, you have nothing to fear, and your family will do well."

The Chaika sped through the deserted roads of Simferopol. No police officer would ever stop a Chaika no matter how fast it was going.

They entered the airport, a gate swinging open as if it were operated by a ghost. The Chaika sped over the tarmac to a huge airplane, something Oksana had never seen before.

"This is my plane," Fedorov said. "You will get good food on board and plenty of time to sleep."

She was flabbergasted. To fly on an airplane, to get food, to sleep. She was too thrilled even to think of sleep.

"This is a Tupolev 154, one of the most modern airplanes in the world. It's not just a plane. It's a command center of the KGB division I head."

KGB again. All her excitement was gone, replaced again by naked fear.

"Come, get out of the car now."

Fedorov led her to a steep staircase connected to the plane and gently pushed her upward.

"Once we are airborne I shall tell you all, Oksana. Tomorrow morning a gentleman, not KGB, will visit your parents and will offer your father a good job. Your family will relocate to a nice house in Kesh, and your sisters will go to school."

Too good to be true, Oksana thought. But so far nothing bad had happened.

When she entered the plane a nice woman in a blue uniform took her by the hand and led her to the rear.

"Here are clothes, towels, and soap. If you need something else, press this button."

She showed her a tight but very clean bathroom that even had a shower. Oksana had never taken a shower before. She looked around, and the friendly woman seemed to understand.

"This is for hot water," she said, pointing to the left faucet, "and this is for cold. Take your time. Wash and change into the clothes here. When you are ready, come out and I'll provide you with dinner."

Oksana closed the door quietly and stood in front of a huge mirror that let her see herself in full. She was filthy, her clothes were torn, and her blond hair was streaked with dirt.

She had heard of a shower but wasn't sure what it was. She turned the left faucet, which brought a stream of hot water on her body. She shrieked and jumped back. But she quickly got the hang of it, and turned the two faucets to produce a mix of hot and cold water.

Oksana tore off her dirty garments and again looked at herself in the mirror. Her breasts had started to form. Other girls her age already had big breasts while she still looked more like a little girl than a woman. She cupped them in her hands, pushed them upward, and there they were. Bigger but dirty too.

She carefully turned the faucets—right for cold and then left for hot—until the water was pleasantly warm. She couldn't remember later how long she had stood under the warm water, rinsing her body, washing her hair with something called shampun, and checking her breasts again.

A knock on the door startled her.

"Are you okay, Oksana?" the friendly woman asked.

"Yes, I'll be ready in a minute."

Oksana realized she probably was taking too much time, but it was so wonderful. Now the doubts returned. What if all this was an illusion, a trick, and she woke up in a gulag?

She dressed hastily. All the sizes were perfect. She had even been given a bra. Oksana didn't know how to wear one, so she left it off. Her breasts were okay without it, she thought.

She rubbed her shoulder-length hair with one of the towels. They were soft and smelled good.

Okay, hurry, she told herself.

Her hair still damp, she emerged into the cabin in her new clothes. Fedorov was waiting, drinking vodka, she thought, from a big frosted glass.

"We are taking off in a few minutes. Moscow just gave us clearance. Sit here until we are in the air, and then we'll have dinner."

He led her to a huge leather chair and strapped her in.

Oksana was not sure whether to be happy or worried. She had never worn brand-new clothes. They felt good! She was cleaner than ever before. Her parents' hut had only an outhouse and water from a faucet right beside it where they all washed, using wooden bowls to wet their bodies. In the winter, her mother heated the water once a week.

Oksana was alarmed when the plane lurched forward with its incredible power, pressing her back into the comfortable seat. She gripped the armrests with all her might. The noise was earsplitting, and the plane rocked. Then suddenly the shaking and bumping stopped. The plane was in the air. She looked out the small window and saw the few lights of Simferopol slowly disappear beneath her.

After a few minutes, there was a clinking sound, and the nice woman opened her seat belt and asked Oksana to follow her.

Oksana was very excited and suddenly extremely hungry.

The flight attendant led her to the forward part of the cabin where a few men and women sat at small desks with TVs attached. However, no news or movies appeared on the screens, just things she could not understand—numbers, lines, schemes. All of the people wore headsets and spoke into microphones fastened to their necks.

"Here you are. Come with me. We are all hungry, and our cook has prepared food."

Fedorov took her by the hand and brought her to a lavishly furnished room. An oval table stood in the middle with six chairs around it. Plates and glasses were ready to be filled.

Valeriya—that was the name on the little brooch she wore—put Oksana in one of the soft chairs, which were anchored to the floor like everything else.

"We'll eat now, Oksana. Then we'll talk and then you'll sleep." Fedorov held a glass filled with a purple liquid. He sensed Oksana's question.

"This is wine from the Crimea. Your homeland is very rich, but I understand most of the people there are very poor. You don't get wine but water and juice."

"My father sometimes lets me have a sip of his vodka. He sells it..." She stopped abruptly. Distilling and selling vodka were highly illegal in the Soviet Union.

"We know. We studied your family before I took you out of the police prison. As I promised you, they have nothing to fear. Now eat."

Valeriya served things Oksana had never dreamed of eating. She knew these foods existed but believed they were only for the rich. Smoked salmon was one of the goods she had been trafficking until this morning, and then there was a dish called beef Stroganoff.

Oksana felt like she was in culinary heaven. She didn't want to disturb paradise by asking questions, so she dug in and filled her stomach to the limit. The pirozkhy with applesauce and the bliny with honey almost didn't find a place inside her, but she ate everything.

Fedorov poured a brownish liquid into a glass that looked like a small lantern.

"This is cognac, but it's only for adults. It comes from France and helps with digestion. It is excellent."

Whatever, Oksana thought. This was the best meal she had ever eaten.

"Now let's go to the salon. It's a special room where we talk, plan, and execute."

The salon was adjacent to the dining room and featured plush leather chairs where they took seats.

"Oksana, we have scrutinized you now for a couple of months. We have known for some time about the smuggling, which is not a big deal, although smugglers will go to prison. You could have skimmed some of the goods on your way, but you never did. We know that because the person to whom you deliver is one of us. You delivered the smoked salmon you just ate."

She looked frightened but Fedorov put her at ease.

"You are honest and did all this to support your family. That's why I freed you and am bringing you to a place that will ultimately make you a successful and happy woman."

"I'm just fifteen, I'm a girl, and I can't read or write well."

"You will go to school and be trained to be one of us."

"The KGB?"

"No, Oksana, not the KGB. You should know that not all of us are bad. Russia will change in the coming years, and maybe, just maybe, the hostilities with America and other countries will subside and the world then might be a better place."

He looked deeply into her eyes and found big question marks.

"I want to tell you about a secret society that needs young and intelligent people to fulfill its long-term dreams. In 1920 the Turkish army invaded Armenia, a territory the Turks had lost to the Russian empire in two wars in 1855 and in 1878.

"The war in 1920 was one of the cruelest and most painful the world has ever seen. Tens of thousands of Armenians were slaughtered by the Turks during their campaign. Then a new state, the Soviet Union, again took away Armenia from the Turks and made it a Soviet republic in 1921."

Fedorov paused and took a large gulp of his cognac.

"The Armenians stood no chance against the powerful Turkish invaders, but a few people in Armenia fought back. They sabotaged the Turks wherever they could and killed their commanders, even their generals, but in doing so helped open the way for the Soviet invasion. I won't go into too many details now because you will learn about all this in our school."

He poured himself another cognac and filled Oksana's glass with delicious orange juice.

"During the war, one man in Armenia—a hero, a freedom fighter, a scholar—never stopped protecting children, bringing families to secret hideouts, feeding them, and inspiring them with hope. His name was Petrossian."

Fedorov carefully observed Oksana's reaction. He knew she must be exhausted and could fall asleep in seconds, but she appeared alert and interested.

"Far away in the east of our country, Petrossian, who was a rich man, acquired land, an area almost as big as a country, which he secured only because he was a master at pretending to be what he wasn't. He was never a convinced Soviet or even a communist, but he used his associations with the Soviet elite brilliantly. Under the pretense of building and running an elite school for Soviet leadership, he created an institution that has placed many well-educated men and women in high positions in Moscow and continues to do so today."

He waited a minute and studied Oksana's face closely. She remained highly alert and was clearly eager to hear more.

"Petrossian educates and coaches two sorts of people," Fedorov continued. "The official sort goes to the Soviet Union, taking important positions as diplomats, KGB officers, pilots, or officers in the Red Army. The other 20 percent become Petrossians. They are not antagonists or enemies of the state, but they have chosen a different path. They are similar to KGB officers but follow different ideals, taking necessary actions here and abroad. Many Petrossians are successful agents in other countries and sometimes even cooperate with the KGB and other such institutions.

"Some of us are KGB officers, engineers, generals, and other important members of Soviet society. We are not dissidents, and we are not working against the regime in Moscow. That would be the end of our establishment. We are a supplement, but we make our own decisions about how to operate and how to deliver results for our clients."

He raised his voice slightly at the term *clients*.

"We use our own judgment if and when we have to operate abroad. Petrossian was extremely rich and invested all his money in his institution, but he has been gone for many years now. He died peacefully in Khabarovsk. You might not know where this place is, but you will love it. Khabarovsk is the capital of Khabarovsk Krai in east Siberia. It's close to the Chinese border, which is very convenient for our agents. You will learn why once you are in school."

Fedorov noticed they were now more than three hours into the flight, and he decided to stop the introduction to let Oksana rest.

"We have another five hours to fly, and I want you to sleep now so you are fresh when we arrive tomorrow morning. And, as I promised, Petrossian agents, not the KGB, will talk to your parents tomorrow. They will be safe, your father with a job, your sisters with a new house and school. Now I'll show you to your quarters. Come."

Oksana felt half dead but had enough enthusiasm after Fedorov's talk that she thought she might lie awake until the morning instead of sleeping.

Fedorov and Valeriya put her to bed in a small, clean cabin where she could stretch out. Despite her excitement, she was asleep within minutes.

A gentle hand touched her after a bottomless sleep filled with the wildest dreams. Her mother was serving her smoked salmon and blinyis, while her father was dressed in a suit and ...

"Wake up, Oksana. We have one more hour to go, and I have prepared breakfast. Do you like eggs? There is fresh bread too."

Oksana opened her eyes, and for a moment she didn't know where she was. Yes, on an airplane with people she had met only last night. Panic seized her. She sat up and scanned Valeriya's smiling face. She remembered her name now. It was still displayed on the pin she wore on her uniform.

"Oh, good morning. Where are we?"

"We are close to Khabarovsk, and you should eat something before we land. Another long trip awaits you."

Oksana climbed out of the narrow, bedlike folded chair.

"I'll give you time to dress. Then come forward to the dining room."

With that, Valeriya left and Oksana put on her new clothes, slowly realizing where she was and what had happened the previous night. The plane hit some turbulence that made her stumble, but her confidence was gradually building again.

Fedorov was at the dining table and told her to sit and to strap on her seat belt.

"We have some rough weather out here, but it will be over soon. There is coffee and juice. Just choose what you want to eat."

A variety of food—including omelets, eggs, bread, and something that looked like vomit—sat on fastened trays. Fedorov was amused when Oksana stared at the last item. "That's muesli," he explained, "a Swiss specialty made of fruits, oatmeal, and milk. Try it. It's very good."

He helped her with the food and loaded a big spoonful of the muesli onto her plate. *Yes, he is right*, Oksana thought. *It is good.*

Coffee! She had never had coffee before. Oh, it tasted delicious.

Now awake and alert, Oksana asked with her mouth half full, "What do I have to do for all this?"

"After we arrive we'll take a long trip by car to your new home, the school where you will make new friends and learn."

New friends? She didn't even have old ones. But Oksana enjoyed her breakfast and thought, *I'll worry about that later.*

Then the pilot announced they would arrive in fifteen minutes and said they should strap on their seatbelts for the landing.

Oksana sat looking out a small window, amazed by the emptiness below. There were no buildings, no trees, and no people, just brown and gray dirt. *This must be Siberia*, she thought. Then the plane banked sharply to the right, and her window filled up with structures scattered over the landscape. She could see a long stretch of gray concrete that must be the landing strip. The plane turned again and was now upright and straight. The ground below grew closer and then, with a gentle touch, the plane was on the concrete, moving more slowly until it stopped.

She saw two black Chaikas pull up beside the plane, and Fedorov fetched her.

"Come now," he said. "We have arrived in Khabarovsk. It's almost noon here, and we better hurry if we want to be home tonight.

"I got confirmation that my people talked with your parents," he added with a smile. "They are moving to Kesh today. They know now that you are safe."

Oksana was too dumbfounded to reply, just very happy inside. She would work hard, be good, and do whatever was necessary to please this man.

She rode with Fedorov in one of the Chaikas to a big, ugly building where they changed cars. A strange- looking vehicle was waiting for them.

"This is a Zlin all-terrain vehicle that will bring us to our destination. It's old but very reliable, which is good because the roads are not the best where we are going. Hop in. We need about five hours to reach Kriylny, a place in the north built by Petrossian."

Kryilny was not found on any map and was so secret that only a handful of KGB officers knew of its existence. It was not a city or a village where farmers lived and worked. It was a dwelling built mostly underground. Only a handful of innocent-looking huts were visible from above, so the place seemed to be a collection of meager farms with a few livestock grazing in the immediate surroundings.

Oksana settled in her seat, which didn't match the luxury she found on the airplane. She was seated in the back of the vehicle, while Fedorov and a driver in civilian clothes took the front seats.

The trip was hard, long, and exhausting. They made only one stop in the vast, uninhabited land they were crossing. Oksana wanted to relieve herself, but there were no trees to go behind, no bushes, just brown earth.

"We won't peek," Fedorov said, laughing. "Just go ahead."

After that pee stop they were bumped around for another two hours before arriving at a huge electric gate. Beyond the gate a long and much better road led through a lush forest, the first trees Oksana had seen in hours. Tall fir trees lined the blacktop road, which led to a large but shabby-looking building.

Where am I? Oksana wondered. *Is this the school he was talking about?*

The Zlin stopped beside the building, which looked like a dilapidated farmhouse. She saw no people. The place appeared to be deserted.

"Come, Oksana. Let's go inside and get you acquainted with your new home."

Again, Fedorov smiled. He could see and feel her anxiety by the way she looked at the structure, which didn't appear inviting.

He gently nudged her toward the big wooden door, which they reached over half a dozen worn timber steps. Fedorov pushed the door and let Oksana enter in front of him.

Her eyes widened instantly under her blond hair. She was stunned to say the least. A huge hall opened before her with fireplaces, lounge furniture, and one wall covered with books, thousands of them from floor to ceiling.

She stood near the entrance, amazed at what she saw. She couldn't read, but here were all these books.

Then a woman in a blue dress approached them. She looked pleasant enough, a bit round with heavy breasts.

"Dobro poshalovat domoy, stary drug!" (Welcome home, old friend.) She gave Fedorov a bear hug, which he countered by kissing her cheeks.

Oksana observed that she said "stary drug," not "tovaritch," meaning "comrade," which was common in the Soviet Union.

"This is Oksana."

He nudged Oksana forward, and the woman extended her hand to greet her.

"I'm Larisa Sokolova. I'm the headmistress of the school and the commander of Kryilny. You will never use my name here because nobody here has a name. I'm to be addressed as forty-two. We use only numbers here and around the world. Understood?"

Oksana nodded and forty-two reprimanded her.

"'Yes, forty-two.' That's how you answer. You will get your number tomorrow. Understood?"

"Yes, forty-two. Understood."

"You are one of the youngest here, and your work will be hard, but if you succeed you will live a life you couldn't even dream of. Clear?"

"Yes, forty-two. Clear."

Oksana's voice was firm now, all the tension gone. She would prove to be a worthy student.

Fedorov faced Oksana.

"You are home now, Oksana. Make me proud of my decision to bring you here. We won't see each other for a long time, and when we do, I will know you made it."

He shook her hand firmly and strode out of the huge hall, leaving a young girl who now felt homesick and frightened.

Oksana had begun an ordeal of schooling and training that would last for five years.

CHAPTER 12

PHUKET, THAILAND

The Dassault carrying us from Bali neared the airport in Phuket. It was 2 a.m. and raining hard when the sleek plane made its final approach. The turbulence shook us, but the pilot brought the plane down smoothly, taxiing to the airport's main building where a customs and immigration van was waiting. Private jet passengers were picked up and given VIP treatment.

The procedures were done in a few minutes, and our passports were stamped without being inspected. Then the van brought us to the curbside at the arrival hall where two Toyotas were waiting.

"Good morning," the driver said, greeting me, Fedorov, Ketut, and Mia. "I have instructions to bring you to the Blue Canyon Hotel. It takes only ten minutes from here."

He started the car, and I checked whether the other Toyota with the pilots and the Thai attendant was following. It was.

The Blue Canyon brought back nice memories. I loved this place and had visited it quite often. A luxury hotel far away from the customary Thai beach resorts, it featured one of the greatest golf courses in Asia.

The rain was pounding, and I looked forward to a comfortable bed in a luxury room. However, I knew this might not happen, at least not right away.

Forty-nine was here. That could only mean huge troubles and most probably another sleepless night.

Fedorov and I were only two of a handful people who knew forty-nine's real identity.

Galina Mikhailova, the daughter of the late Larisa Sokolova, the headmistress at Krylnyi, was sharp as a freshly ground meat knife. I recalled that she was also quite attractive. I hadn't seen her for many years and wondered what to expect. Her mother was killed in the late eighties when renegade KGB troops tried to storm Kyilny to save communism in the far east of Siberia. The KGB gang was no match for Larisa and her band of highly trained agents, who were skilled assassins. However, Larisa was killed by a suicidal KGB major who couldn't imagine a future without the Soviet Union.

We arrived at the Blue Canyon. The two women had brought small bags, but other than that we had no luggage. The manager greeted us like we were royalty.

"Welcome to the Blue Canyon, Mr. Becker. So nice to have you back."

He recognized me, and I forgot I had used my Swiss identity the last time I was there.

The manager escorted us to the elevators.

"We'll do all administrative things in the morning. Your rooms are on the top floor. Here are the key cards. If you need anything, call me personally. Madame Foster is expecting you in the top suite."

Madame Foster. She was using her US identity, which I recalled from exercises in Libya and Italy.

The top suite at the Blue Canyon was huge. The living room could host at least forty guests or a big family, and there were three bedrooms and a grand piano. After winning a prestigious amateur golf tournament at the Blue Canyon about twenty years earlier, I had decided to spoil myself with the top suite. Encouraged by a few single malts, I had played the piano, annoying other guests until the manager, a different guy at the time, politely asked me to refrain from pretending to be a virtuoso.

Galina was waiting for us outside the elevators with her usual grim expression.

"Welcome and thanks for stopping here."

As if we would had a choice.

"Go to your rooms and have a rest." She pointed at the two women, Mia and Ketut.

"You did very well, seventy-two," she said, looking at Ketut.

So Ketut was seventy-two. I had never asked her about her Petrossian ID.

"You two, please join me for a nightcap." She aimed her index finger at Fedorov and me.

I nodded at Ketut and Mia, wished them a good rest, and followed Galina, forty-nine, into the top suite.

Galina, now in her late fifties, was as gorgeous as ever. Her simple but elegant dress—which I thought was a Pucci, my ex-wife's favorite— emphasized her nearly perfect body. Italian designers knew how to dress women.

Fedorov and I sat on a sofa in the piano room and sank into the soft fabric, yawning and stretching to make it clear we were tired.

"I get your message. You are exhausted, and I'll make it short."

She filled two large tumblers with vodka, which she took out of a freezer ingeniously hidden in a mahogany cabinet.

"So Igor has opened a wasp's nest. As you can imagine, we have monitored his moves closely and followed him into the Khalij bank as well as Alliance Ovest in Marseille. At first, I wanted to stop him, but when we could tie the ends together, I decided to let him get it all. He is a genius hacker."

With that, Galina raised her glass.

"I'm proud and happy that you still have it, Matt."

She addressed me by my name, and I wasn't sure whether this was good or bad. After all, I had been out of Petrossian for quite a few years.

As if reading my reflections, she continued, "Your intervention in Bali was as professional as ever, and the information you extracted from the ex-CIA scum is pure gold. We have all the reports from Igor's servers in Simferopol and Alushta."

Galina paused before breaking the news. "Igor was captured by the other side. I don't know whether he is alive or not. However, in a few hours one of our teams will be on the ground in Alushta."

Then she addressed Fedorov. "Oksana got shot in the raid."

Fedorov, who was always unemotional, even cold, sat up straight, almost spilling his vodka.

"Shot! Is she …?"

"No. It's Oksana, Yev. She got away but is injured with a bullet in her hip or maybe a clear in-and-out. She contacted the base but couldn't give a clear location. All she said was that she was alive but that Igor had been taken away from her café. The perps are obviously Arabs and Americans. The Americans are part of the CI army that operates in Afghanistan and Iraq. Hard and merciless fellows. I'm afraid Igor has a bad time if he is still alive. It might be Cavity."

We had already concluded that.

Staring at us, she continued, "We know Cohen Industries is involved …"

"Involved?" I said. "They are pulling the strings."

"Matt, let me finish. Then you will see the whole picture."

Now I needed a vodka.

"CI is only a contractor, and guess to whom?"

Her expression showed expectation and excitement.

"Your old foe is back—Cavity. We don't have the proof yet, but all signs point in one direction. Cavity, the disbanded Pentagon and CIA contractor, is back in action."

That changed the picture dramatically. We thought the notorious contractor had folded years earlier when its leader, Maximilian Cahill, had died an unusual natural death.

"We think Maximilian's widow, Eileen, has reformed the firm to advance her political ambitions. But I'll let you find out in due time."

A revival of Cavity could radically complicate matters because this used to be a band of hardened and murderous professionals.

I glanced at Fedorov, knowing his protégée Oksana was probably the only person he ever had feelings for. Years back over some drinks, he had told me her story and had said how happy he was that she had become one of Petrossian's greatest assets—one with a big heart too.

"That's why we should be in Russia right now and not in Phuket," I said, thinking it was time to take my stand.

"You will be but later," Galina said. "May I remind you that you two are not young anymore? My people are well equipped to help Oksana and Igor, once they find him. Now you might want to know why we're meeting in Phuket."

She stared at us like a schoolteacher at her pupils. We nodded in assent to her question.

"As you know, the Saudi king is visiting Bali. His delegation includes more than 1,500 people of whom about 250 are intelligence and security. The Mukhabarat."

She smiled mischievously at me, knowing my opinion of the Mukhabarat after several encounters.

"The king's entourage has arrived in no fewer than fifteen planes for which the Bali airport is much too small, as you certainly know. Therefore, some of the Saudi planes have been redirected to Kuala Lumpur where they are parked with their full crews on standby. The airplanes are guarded by another small army of Mukhabarat agents.

"After we received Igor's evidence about Khalij, Alliance Ovest, and CI, we had to react quickly. Thus Kryilny for quite some time now has futilely tried to trace huge amounts transferred between the Americans, the Saudis, the French, the Islamic State, and some other party we haven't yet identified."

Each of us took a mouthful of the Stoli, and I wondered what she had up her sleeve.

"The Mukhabarat's number two was in Kuala Lumpur with the last plane."

Was?

"I know your next question, so just listen."

Galina gave me her stern look, and I decided not to ask.

"Hyder Fatah, a semi-royal in maybe the sixtieth degree but much more a commoner, is now the coleader of the Mukhabarat, and you know him quite well as I recall." She pointed toward me.

Hyder Fatah, a pain in the ass in my former life, was responsible for at least three assassinations that happened in France and in Tunis while I was assigned to track Wahabi zealots. Our client at the time was the CIA, which couldn't be involved in any action against the Saudis. We had proven the Saudis were financing Al Qaeda, Osama bin Laden, Al Nusra, and other Islamic fanatics. For several reasons, the Americans were not in a position to humiliate the Saudis, but they wanted leverage, which we had provided.

"Hyder Fatah is now here in Phuket in our safe house, compliments of Petrossian's travel service. I want you two to bring him to the base and to start negotiating with our new client."

I wasn't shocked that we were taking on the Saudis as clients. This meant leverage, control over one of the richest nations on earth. The golden era when we could afford to work for the CIA, the DGSE, MI6, and the Mossad were over. Petrossian needed fresh capital, and the Saudis would provide a strong financial foundation for our firm.

Our firm? Hell, I had been out for more than twelve years. But I would always be a part of the firm that had offered me the opportunity for my life's greatest achievements. I was part of the family, and blood kept me in line.

Galina refreshed our drinks and resumed her instructions.

"You two are seasoned negotiators, the best at destabilization we have ever had. I want you to strike a deal with Hyder that we can present to the Saudis. I don't want the Saudi renegades to continue financing the Islamic State, and I want them to comprehend that we will expose them to the world if they don't cooperate. Like you and probably the rest of the world, I want the Wahabis to sever ties with Al Baghdadi and to let this Islamic scum starve to death."

I stood up and poured myself some mineral water from a cooled bottle. The vodka was soothing but wasn't providing me with the proper nutrition to deal with this.

"So we bring him to the base? Then what? They will know their number two is missing. How can we negotiate with him while he is officially missing?"

"This is not the first time Hyder will have vanished for days or even weeks. His weakness for young boys is tolerated in Riyadh, and eyes and ears are shut when he disappears for a while. After all, he is the kingdom's best assassin. You have at least four or five days to work on him and to find out how to approach the Saudis with our proposal."

"That's more than enough time," I responded, "but what about Igor and Oksana in the meantime?"

I had already formed a plan to get the Saudis on our side and to use Hyder as a tool.

"We'll take care of that. As we speak, one of our most efficient teams is on the way to Alushta. If Igor and Oksana are still alive, we'll get them out. And our team is better than the Saudis or the CI filth—or Cavity."

We looked at each other, and no one had anything more to say.

"The full briefing is on this." Galina handed me a memory stick. "Read it tonight and be ready to fly off tomorrow morning. I want you at the base by tomorrow afternoon. A chopper is waiting for you at Khabarovsk. Once there, confirm your arrival and we'll discuss strategy further. Hyder will be delivered to your plane no later than 8 a.m."

Galina dismissed us, and Fedorov and I looked forward to a few hours of sleep.

We left and walked down the hall to our rooms adjacent to the top suite.

I didn't bother to read the briefing but fell on the bed in my clothes, embracing a deep and dreamless sleep. I guessed I might have time to read on the plane the next day.

CHAPTER 13

IGOR, CRIMEA

All Igor saw were dark, masked troopers wearing bulletproof vests and night goggles. They stomped onto the boat, aiming their automatics and small machine guns at him. He had the nerve to throw his laptop overboard before they got him. His satellite phone was still on him, down the back of his trousers.

"Search him," the leader, an American, commanded.

The troopers patted him down, found the satellite phone, and kicked him in the stomach. Igor vomited on the polished mahogany deck and lay in a fetal position, expecting them to apply their boots again.

An Arab-looking guy without the luxury of a vest grabbed him by the collar.

"Where is the bitch? Where is she hiding?"

Igor was unable to respond, his mouth still full of vomit and his brain playing color games.

"Take him down. Then we are off. Look for the bitch from the café and terminate her." He pointed to two or three of the men.

In military fashion they confirmed the order, grabbed Igor by the arms, and lowered him into the water. There two other mercenaries grabbed him and carried him to the stony beach. They half carried, half kicked Igor over to his house where he saw his entrance door blasted open. Without another word they pushed him into the control room. Although he had shut down the system, the screens were lit, displaying all sorts of harmless programs and the cams around his house.

Someone must have tried hard to enter the system but had gotten only common stuff.

Igor glanced at the wall in front of his mainframe. It looked untouched.

"Now you will guide us through, and I promise you might live a while longer," the leader said.

"Why should I if you're going to kill me anyway?"

Igor's quick reply cost him another fist in his stomach.

"It's easy. You cooperate, and all will be painless. Should you be a hero, we might hurt you a bit. Now open everything you have transmitted. No tricks."

He feigned gently stroking Igor's head for a second and then delivered a powerful blow to his face that brought back the colors Igor saw earlier.

They sat him down in front of his main console where the largest of his visible workstations was located. Igor hit some keys and brought up a transmission report to an address that officially didn't exist. The receiver side was a dummy in Estonia, one of the proxies that he used for delicate hackings. The proxy server was encoded and therefore instructed to respond to certain commands, exactly for a situation like this.

Igor showed them the surveillance video, which was uploaded automatically to Estonia, with banal text attached to it explaining that he thought he was being watched. There were no files to show, no data besides the video and his report.

"Where is the server located?" the leader demanded.

"It's in Paris, France." This earned him a blow to the nose.

"We know where Paris is, asshole. Who is there? Who is reading this?"

"There is a Paris in Illinois and one in Idaho."

Igor got bolder by the minute. This time there was no whack.

"Okay, France. Who is there receiving your messages, and where in Paris is the server?"

"I don't know the answer to either question. I was instructed to send there, and that's what I did."

"Who gave you the orders?"

Another blow, this time even harder.

"It's a company I sometimes work for out of my Simferopol lab. Some of my work is labeled confidential, although any child could do it."

"What's the company's name and who is your client?"

"It's called Petrossian something. I think it's Russian. We always get paid in cash. No records."

Igor decided it was time to give them something true, though they probably had this information.

"With whom from Petrossian do you deal? I need names."

"It's always a woman, a Russian. She introduced herself as"—he dithered for a second—"Larissa Tcharkova."

One of the CI mercenaries went through a little booklet and nodded at his leader.

Larissa Tcharkova was real. Igor had met her once when Petrossian had brought him for his one visit to Khabarovsk some years back. He didn't go to the base but had spent two dull days in the city lecturing Petrossians about computer and smartphone security. Larissa was a bright young lady and at the time was an IT teacher at the base. She also was a political destabilization expert. She must have been about twenty-five back then, and Igor hoped these thugs would never find her.

They were obviously in a hurry. The leader ordered his men to destroy all the equipment. No fire. They had already tested the patience of the coast town to the breaking point.

Igor faked protest and lamented that this equipment was vital to his work. He realized they were going to kill him, but if they didn't find his mainframe, Petrossian would always have the necessary proxy connection. And the young ones at the base were becoming cyber experts.

He managed to ask one more question before they dragged him out to one of their cars.

"What happened to the lady from the café? She had nothing to do with me. She made me food."

"How well do you know her?" The leader didn't smack him this time.

"Not at all. I seldom go to her café. I like the one up the street better. She brought me food tonight, maybe because Alushta is so quiet this time of the year."

This all sounded sincere because Igor earlier had no idea who or what Oksana was.

They seemed to believe him but pushed him roughly into a Toyota where another mercenary pressed a submachine gun into his ribs.

The car climbed the hill to the Porto Mare Hotel, the first address in Alushta.

The hotel was deserted with only the lobby lit. A night manager was waiting for them.

"The chopper is ready, sir. I checked with the pilot."

He obviously was expecting a tip, but all he got was a cold stare.

"Get out," the leader snarled at Igor. "You come with us. That might give you one more night to live."

In pain, Igor climbed out of the car and started walking with two escorts holding onto his arms.

Then something strange happened. The guy on his left suddenly let his grip go and fell to the ground. A second later the one on his right followed him. It took the leader two or three seconds to react, but it was too late. He fell like the others in front of Igor's feet.

"Igor, here!"

Oksana appeared from behind the shoulder-height stone wall that flanked the hotel entrance, holding a very long gun in her hand, the Petrossian home brand, a Makarov with a stubby silencer attached.

She limped over to Igor and pulled him hastily behind the wall.

"The others are not far away. We must hide. I know the place well. Follow me."

She was limping badly, and Igor noticed blood on her right leg. He had heard the shooting when he was hiding on the *Nadezhda*.

"You are hurt. Let me help you."

He grabbed Oksana under the arms, and they disappeared up a steep stairway.

"Why are we going up?" Igor was not used to Petrossian tactics.

"Think, Igor. Where would you look first? Not up, right?"

"Tel me about your role in Petrossian."

"Later, Igor. It's my duty to keep you safe, so just move as fast as you can."

A tough lady, he thought. *Blood running down her leg, yet she is leading the way.*

"It's just a scratch. They got me in the leg. Just muscle, but I need a doctor fast. That's why you have to move your ass and do exactly what I tell you to do. They will come for us with brute force, but I'm a match. Trust me."

She grinned with her blond hair flying over her face.

Igor had the crazy notion at this irrational moment that she might have been quite beautiful when she was young. She was now a bit on the heavy side with big breasts and slightly wide hips, but otherwise …

When they heard shouting below them he was quickly brought back to reality. The mercenaries were running down the stone stairs like a herd of buffaloes. Oksana had correctly predicted the direction they would take.

Oksana and Igor reached the top of the stairs under a dark and unfriendly sky.

"Now we have to create another distraction. Follow me. We might just make it. I have a car on top of the hill. We need to get there while they are busy."

"But they might hear the car, and they have a chopper."

"Just do what I say. They won't hear the car. Trust me."

They staggered out to a clearing where Igor saw a Zlin Jeep parked under some fir trees.

"It's my old Zlin. Over forty-five years old. I drove it through Russia from east to west, and it's very dear to me. I want you to drive it while I provide the entertainment for our enemies. Don't crash it or I'll kill you."

She sneered at him, and he again thought she must have been an attractive though rough woman in another life.

"Now sit behind the wheel. The key is in the ignition, and she will start like a sports car. When you hear the shooting, start the car and wait for me."

Oksana went over to the steep ridge, which provided a clear view of the coast road, Igor's house, and her café. She had her smartphone in her hand and pressed some keys. Igor was more than itchy—he wanted to get out of there.

Oksana turned and smiled at him, no smirk this time but a sweet smile.

Then shooting started down in the village, staccato explosions that sounded like submachine guns letting loose wildly.

She limped to the Zlin. Igor had started the engine. Nobody would be able to hear the roaring sound the old but apparently fit engine made.

Oksana took the seat beside Igor and directed him to an opening in the clearing. From there, a narrow road led farther up the hill to the vineyards.

"June 12 fireworks. My customers usually enjoy my fireworks on Russia Day."

She laughed but stopped when the pain from her leg crept upward toward her chest.

"It was a rush job, but it worked. I store my fireworks in the house opposite the café. I just needed to make a connection to my other phone. Listen! They are shooting back."

Oksana laughed again, and indeed Igor could hear submachine fire from below.

"By the time they find out what they are fighting, we will be halfway to Khrel where a good doctor is ready for me. I need to get this bullet out."

Igor heard agony in Oksana's voice, but he didn't dare look at her. He had to concentrate on his driving. The gravel road was narrow and ran roughly parallel to the main road to Simferopol. He had heard about Khrel. The huge vineyards there produced great red, white, and sparkling wines for export, mainly to Russia.

When Crimea was still part of Ukraine, the produce was exported to Europe in exchange for euros. Now the main market, as in the time of the Soviet Union, was Russia.

Oksana held on to the handle mounted above the door frame and tried desperately to stretch her leg, which was impossible. The Zlin was so tight that even Igor, who was less than 1.8 meters, or about five feet nine, had problems sitting comfortably.

"Take the next left. It's only about two hundred meters from here."

The night got very dark in this territory. There were no lights to be seen, and Igor feared someone might spot their headlights.

Oksana seemed to read his mind. "Make a left here. I should drive but I can't with my leg. So just follow my instructions and switch off the lights."

Igor entered the even narrower road and pushed the ancient light switch back into the dashboard. Total darkness engulfed them but not a minute too early. He heard the chop-chop of a helicopter somewhere far behind them.

"About fifty meters, and then you see the forest on your right. Drive in there and switch off the engine. They reacted quicker than I anticipated."

Unable to see a thing, Igor was feeling his way along the road.

"Here, turn right. Don't be scared. It's almost flat."

All he could make out was Oksana's hand in front of his face. She pointed to the right toward a black hole, an apparent vacuum in the dark night.

He trusted her and took a right turn that shook the Zlin violently. The road was not as flat as she said but straight down a steep hill.

"Don't use the breaks. Stay in the lowest gear. Break lights are as visible as headlights in the darkness."

She moaned at every bump and held on to the door with all her strength.

"There. Drive in there." Igor saw a dense forest ahead and was tempted to hit the brakes, but Oksana warned him again.

"Just let her run into the trees and then switch off the engine. We have to get rid of them."

She looked up into the sky, but there was nothing, not even stars.

Igor felt branches whipping the windshield and managed to avoid a medium-size tree that materialized in front of them like a ghost.

"Stop! We are in. That's enough. Switch off the engine and take a deep breath."

The stillness around them almost hurt Igor's ears. No wind, no sound at all. Then they heard the helicopter coming closer, and judging by the way the sound of the rotors was absorbed by the forest, it was flying very low.

A powerful nose searchlight broke through the forest but stayed anchored on the narrow road they just left. The illumination less than fifty meters away gave Igor a quick perception of their location. The road they left a few minutes before was high above them.

"We are safe, Igor."

She appeared to be in less agony than before, but he knew she needed a doctor quickly.

"Ancient training, Igor. Either you hide in the open or in an impossible place like this. They would never think we left the road on this side. It's quite steep, and I could never climb up again."

She pointed to her leg, and another smile lit up her perfect teeth like stars.

"It's time to call your boss, fifty."

She rooted around in her jacket and found her satellite phone. She tried to switch it on, but no light appeared on the small screen.

"Shit! I'm out of power. We have to reach Khrel, charge the phone, and get that damn bullet out of my leg."

For another few minutes, they listened to nothing. The chopper had vanished and was probably searching other roads or, even better, had returned to base.

"Now back my baby out of here. It's permanent four-wheel drive, and the reverse gear is the lowest anyway. She will make it."

Igor had his doubts but started the engine and after a few jerks on the gear handle managed to put the Zlin into reverse.

"Softly now. She has a hard clutch. Let go slowly and take the same way up. We didn't turn anywhere, so we will hit the road easily."

Igor let the clutch go as gently as possible, and the little car started to climb the hill. He turned his head, but Oksana instructed him to look forward to get the feeling of a straight climb. The fifty-year-old Zlin climbed the hill as if it were a highway, and after a few moments the rear wheels gripped gravel on the road. Igor jerked the steering wheel hard to the right and hit the path almost perfectly.

"Now you know why I told you to keep the Jeep straight on the way down. One turn and we might not have come up again."

Igor was relieved, thankful, and amazed that this woman, despite her bad injury, could keep her head clear and make the right decisions at the right time. He wanted to hurry now to get her to the doctor.

"Now just feel your way along this highway," Oksana said, laughing again. "It might take us another twenty minutes to reach Khrel."

Igor tried his best in the darkness but could not avoid hitting a few bumps left and right of the road that made the Zlin bounce. Oksana was a tough bird, but the thuds and blows were not what a doctor would have prescribed for her.

After endless turns and ferocious smashes, they hit a wider road that was half visible in the dark night. White gravel made for an easier drive. Igor switched gears and dared to speed up. Then Oksana's right hand hit his knee hard.

"Stop! Switch off the engine. Now!"

Then he saw it. The helicopter was on the ground near a farmhouse, and they could see several figures, illuminated by light from the house and from the airplane, standing around smoking. Oksana's professional calm was contagious. Igor reacted quickly. The road went downhill, not steep but enough to let the Zlin roll without the engine. He steered the vehicle off the road to the right side. Once again they were in the forest but not as deep as Oksana would have wished.

"Well done, Igor. That might have saved our lives."

Her compliment provided Igor with additional energy. He jumped out of the car and pushed it with all his strength farther into the trees, hoping the slope wouldn't get too steep.

He told her to stay in the car while he climbed up to watch their pursuers. Oksana had no objections, but she instructed him to keep low and not to leave the Zlin's entry path.

Igor realized that if Oksana didn't get help soon, her life as well as her leg would be in danger.

"Igor, come back here now."

Her voice was cracking, and he could feel her agony.

"Here, take this."

She handed him one of the submachine guns she had taken from the mercenaries back at the hotel.

"Just in case."

He reached the top of the hill and was surprised he hadn't noticed before how steep it was. The Zlin was covered, but that's not what worried him. Oksana had to get help quickly. He tried to adjust his eyes, which were not the best, damaged by hundreds of hours staring at computer screens, looking for signs of firewalls in codes, Trojans hidden behind thousands of small characters.

At least he was not shortsighted and could see action down at the farmhouse.

Igor got excited when four figures jumped into the helicopter and the rotors started. The noise was earsplitting, not only from the helicopter but from below him. The Zlin was coming up slowly in reverse again. *How on earth was she managing to do that?* he wondered. The clutch was so hard that it took great strength even for him to press it down. But here she came. He knew immediately she wanted to use the chopper noise to get back on the road.

He slid down on his back toward the approaching vehicle and grabbed the driver's side door with both hands. Luckily the night was still as dark as it could get. The chopper was lifting off and completely masked the screaming noise of the Zlin. He managed to push Oksana back onto the passenger seat and kept his foot on the gas pedal. Igor could hear Oksana's moaning even over the noise of the helicopter and of the shrieking Zlin engine.

Why couldn't she have waited?

The chopper passed several hundred meters off to the side, flying low with its searchlight on again.

They reached the top again, and Oksana immediately switched off the engine.

"They are gone. You need help. Let's go."

"We need to stay alive. I know these people, Igor. There are only three roads out of Alushta—one down to Yalta, the other up the coast, and the third inland to Simferopol. Why do you think they are looking here? This is an unknown way. They were sure we wouldn't travel on the main roads."

"You think they left someone behind there?" Igor nodded toward the sparsely lit farmhouse.

"That's what I would do. Let's find out. I'm afraid you have to go first. My leg makes it a bit hard for me to walk down there."

She handed Igor the Makarov with the silencer attached.

"Don't hesitate. I know you are not a killer, but they are. If you see one of them, take him out. The farmer is friendly, and he's what I need now. He is a vet."

Igor nodded silently and walked confidently down to the farmhouse, using a deep ditch that ran parallel to the road as cover. The gun's cold metal gave him a strange feeling of power and self-assurance. He had shot the weapon before with his boss on a pistol range in Kuala Lumpur. He even hit a few targets, but a human target was something new. Despite his confidence, he hoped it wouldn't come to that.

He neared the barn beside the farmhouse, which provided excellent cover for a close approach. He climbed out of the ditch and ran over to the barn where he could hear animal noises. *Goats or sheep— livestock*, he thought. Igor knew he should not alarm them since they could be as alert as watchdogs, although without fangs.

He crept silently around the barn and approached the only lit window in the farmhouse. Standing beneath the window, Igor tried to breathe calmly before taking a quick glance inside.

Oksana was right. The farmer and a round, middle-aged woman, whom Igor assumed was the farmer's wife, were sitting at a dining table with two teenagers beside them. The mercenary was stomping up and down behind the family with his back to the window. Igor couldn't hear what was said, but the family appeared frightened enough to tell him this guy was dangerous.

Igor couldn't waste time. The family was in danger and so as Oksana. Without quick help, her leg wound might develop gangrene, which could mean amputation and death. The farmer was a vet!

Igor raised his Makarov, a deadly gun from this distance of less than two meters. Luckily the CI thug was not wearing protective gear, so Igor could go center mass. In his mind he replayed the action at the hotel a few hours earlier. The three mercenaries were wearing vests. Oksana hit them all in the head. What a great shot she was!

The movie switched off and Igor took aim and pulled the trigger multiple times. The shattering glass made the most noise; with the silencer the Makarov merely coughed.

The intruder went down, hitting the table with his upper body. The farmer wore a shocked expression, while the mother and the kids fell off their chairs.

The farmer looked at Igor's equally panicked face and pleaded, "Don't shoot. Don't kill us."

"Is there more than one? Was he alone?"

Realizing Igor did not represent a threat to his family, the farmer grew calmer.

"No, just this one. He threatened to kill us if Oksana was not found within the hour."

So the mercenaries knew Oksana's identity; they knew she had killed their comrades at the hotel.

"Oksana is out there, badly wounded. She has a bullet in her upper leg. Can you help her?"

Looking at his wife, he said, "Let's get her hot water, vodka, and my things. Now!"

His wife was still in shock, but the teenage boy grabbed her and pulled her up from the floor. They hurried out of the room.

Igor and Vladimir, the farmer and vet, jumped into his old Fiat and drove up the road where they saw Oksana lying on her side and waving her hand. When they reached her, they realized she was only half conscious and was muttering something inaudible. They put her on the back seat of the Fiat and drove to the house.

Igor had to make a decision now.

Pointing to the body, he asked, "Did this guy tell the others to pick him up, or did you hear them talking?"

"They spoke English, I think. I don't know what they were talking about. This one spoke bad Russian. That's why they left him here."

"We have to get away from the house. Now. Do you have another place where you can work on her?"

"We can drive up to see Leysa. She is an experienced assistant. She's only ten minutes from here. I have to inject Oksana first."

Vladimir shot some liquid into Oksana's vein, and Igor told him to bring her out to the Fiat while he ran up the hill to get the Zlin. He raced the two hundred meters, jumped into the little car, and drove down to the farm. Oksana was already on the back seat of the Fiat. Igor took the two kids in the Zlin while Vladimir's wife got into the Fiat and cradled Oksana.

"One more thing." Igor was in command with Oksana unconscious and the farm family in half panic.

"We have to get rid of the body. Come with me," he ordered Vladimir.

They heaved the dead mercenary onto a pushcart, and Vladimir led the way. Behind the house was a deep ravine. They dumped the deceased over the steep edge and heard the body break through the woods on its way down.

"Hard to find there," Vladimir said, and they returned to the vehicles.

Vladimir took the lead, and Igor followed in the Zlin with the kids. They were very quiet and obviously still in shock over what had happened in their home.

No time to talk, Igor thought, and he concentrated on the headlights in front of him. The road was not as bad as before, and they quickly put distance between them and the house.

After a few more turns Igor saw a small farmhouse in a clearing with a huge barn beside it. No lights were on. Vladimir steered his Fiat straight to the barn, his headlights illuminating a large wooden door. He stopped the Fiat and ran toward the door, which he pushed open, making enough room for both cars.

At that moment lights shined in the small windows of the farmhouse. A young woman appeared in the entrance, shouting something in Ukrainian. She came closer and Igor saw that she could not have been older than thirty. The woman looked wild with her hair all over her face. She wore a long man's shirt and thick wool trousers.

"Vlad, what's going on? I heard a helicopter earlier, but I didn't dare switch on the lights. Who are they?" She pointed at Igor and Oksana.

"Later. Help me bring her in," Vladimir said. "We better leave the cars here. The helicopter might come back. Better open the cellar for Vladena and the kids."

Leysa immediately agreed and took Vladimir's family deeper into the barn where, hidden behind heaps of hay, farm equipment, and a tractor, an almost invisible gate opened.

"Leysa stows some valuable things in there. No need for you to know. The cellar is hard to find and is soundproof. I want them in there while I work on Oksana. Come now and help me with her."

After Leysa closed the vault door behind Vladimir's family, they left the barn and carried Oksana into the house. The small home was incredibly clean and neat. Leysa guided them into a room with a single bed in it. They laid Oksana gently on top of the white sheets, and Vladimir took off her clothes and the provisional bandage she had applied earlier. The leg was not a nice sight. The bullet wound was open and recognizably infected. Luckily Oksana was unconscious and couldn't feel the pain.

Vladimir began to clean the wound with pure alcohol Leysa provided, applying it with a soft white cloth.

"This might wake her up. I have to give her some more morphine."

He injected her with a generous load of the painkiller and then probed the wound with a long pincer. Igor had problems watching, but he wouldn't avert his eyes a millimeter.

"Here it is!" Vladimir exclaimed. "I have the bullet. It's stuck in her thigh. A through shot would have been easier, but she is a strong bird."

He worked the pincer deeper and then pulled it out gently, presenting a 9mm bullet and proudly dropping it in an aluminum bowl beside the bed.

"Now we have to stabilize her. I must clean deep inside the wound. Hold her down because this is going to hurt," Vladimir told Igor. "Grab her shoulders and make sure she doesn't move."

He took something like a huge Q-tip, which he soaked in alcohol, and penetrated the open wound with it. Oksana woke up and gave a piercing scream as Igor held her down with all his might.

"Just once more," Vladimir announced and inserted a new alcohol-soaked Q-tip in Oksana's open wound. Then he grabbed another syringe loaded with a yellowish liquid and injected her in the wounded leg.

Oksana was awake but didn't make a sound. *Yes, a tough bird,* Igor thought.

"Antibiotics are meant for animals, but they work just fine for everybody," Vladimir said.

Oksana was whimpering now and her body was twitching. Igor continued to hold her down.

"Now the stitching work, Leysa." Vladimir held out his hand, and Leysa handed him a thread and a curved needle. After a few minutes, he told Igor to let go of Oksana. Igor hadn't noticed she was in a deep sleep now and looked quite peaceful after the ordeal of the surgery.

"She will be okay. Her leg is safe, but it was a close call. I should pump some more antibiotics into her once she is awake. Leysa, we need a vodka."

For the first time Igor saw this simple man, who was up to any task, smiling and looking relaxed.

Leysa quickly fetched some vodka from the kitchen.

"That's part of what she's hiding in the cellar—her famous vodka in addition to all sorts of smuggled goodies. Right, Leysa?"

"You should not ..."

Vladimir cut her off, saying, "This man risked his life to save Oksana and us. He killed one of them. Without him we would be dead by now. So let him enjoy his well-deserved vodka. Nasterovye!"

Vladimir raised his glass, and they all enjoyed the delicious liquor.

"What are we going to do if the chopper comes back?" Leysa was rightly worried.

Full of confidence and pride after saving Oksana, Igor remembered some basic training given him by his boss and friend, Petrossian fifty.

"You are right. They will come back to pick up their pal from Vladimir's house. When they see everyone is gone, they might come here. So we hide, and you play act. We should all go to the cellar except for you, Leysa. But first we have to get rid of the cars."

"I know where. Come," Leysa said.

They carried Oksana back to the barn where she joined Vladimir's family underground. Igor was amazed at what he found there. The huge basement was filled with expensive goods and produce, and in the back was a comfortable room fitted with luxurious furniture and a huge TV set.

"I have a hidden air supply and surveillance cams around my property. It's originally a nuclear shelter the Soviets built in the eighties. Ideal for my goods."

Leysa smiled at Igor's big eyes.

They laid Oksana on a wide bed, one of two in the huge living room-bedroom combination, and told Vladena to watch her closely and to cool her head with fresh water.

They hurried upstairs and jumped into the cars, Leysa leading the way to a nearby clearing in the forest. They drove the two cars deep into the trees until they were invisible from the ground and the air.

They jogged back to the house when they heard the staccato of rotor blades. The chopper was still far away but close enough to create a wordless panic.

Igor took Leysa by the hands and preached what he learned years earlier when he and his boss were in a similar dilemma in Libya.

"We'll hide in the cellar. You will be in the dark house. Switch off all the lights, and switch them on when you hear the chopper close by. Go out of the house, rub your eyes for them to see, and look up into the sky.

Switch on the lights only when you hear the helicopter right above you. Clear? Just play innocent. You haven't seen or heard anything except for the helicopter. Now let's hurry. They have certainly seen the situation at Vladimir's by now."

Igor and Vladimir raced back to the barn and descended into the hidden basement.

The cellar was indeed soundproof, but although they couldn't hear the chopper approaching, the sophisticated surveillance system showed its arrival on a big split-screen TV. Following Igor's instructions, Leysa lit the house shortly before the helicopter touched down. They could see her watching the chopper land right in front of the house. Two guys emerged from the cabin and approached her with weapons in their hands. Leysa appeared quite sincerely scared and lifted her hands high over her shoulders.

Igor could sense the tension in Vladimir's body.

"She is good. They will believe her."

Igor tried unsuccessfully to calm Vladimir down. He was jumpy and maybe ready to go up and take them on.

Igor sensed his intention. "That would do no good, Vlad. We might be able to kill them, but where would we hide a chopper?"

Leysa and the mercenaries were in the house where video surveillance was limited. They emerged a few minutes later and walked over to the barn. *This might be interesting*, Igor thought.

The cameras in the barn were equipped with sensitive night vision lenses, so Igor and Vladimir could see every movement above them clearly on the screen.

The mercenaries appeared to be satisfied with what they saw, or better, what they didn't see. They left the barn and returned to the chopper, its rotors still turning.

Then the unthinkable happened, the horror Igor wanted to avoid.

Just before they climbed into the helicopter, one of them raised his gun and shot Leysa right in the face. She dropped dead instantly, falling on the sparse grass in front of her house.

Vladimir screamed and ran to the staircase that led to the barn.

Igor realized he had to stop him or they would all end up dead. He ran after him and grabbed him by the legs, pulling with all his strength to keep him away from the hidden door.

"Stop it, Vlad. You can't do anything. We will get them. I promise and she does too." He pointed toward Oksana.

Igor stopped Vladimir just in time. A few seconds later the chopper took off. One of the sensor cameras followed the bird until it disappeared over the dark horizon.

They went upstairs, telling the kids to stay put and to watch Oksana.

Vladimir sobbed and cursed the murderous bastards at the same time.

Leysa had been hit right between the eyes. She was unarmed and harmless, and Igor couldn't comprehend her killing.

Vladena seemed to have regained her composure.

"We have to bury her. She had no relatives, and if we go official with this we might all be in trouble."

She was right. There was too much going on that night in and around Alushta for them to be involved.

Vladimir and Igor dug a deep grave behind the barn where there was no easy access. They wrapped Leysa in the nicest tablecloth they could find in the house and gently lowered her into her last resting place. It took them another hour to close the grave and to put grass on top of it.

They returned to the cellar where Oksana was conscious. They decided not to tell her yet about Leysa's fate.

"What happened? Where have you been?" She looked at Igor and demanded answers.

"Later, Oksana. You have to regain your strength first."

"Did you charge the satellite phone?"

Igor had completely forgotten about the phone, and when he admitted that he faced a hailstorm of rage from the woman who had saved his life at least twice that night.

He plugged in the charger and started loading juice into the vital device.

"Give it ten minutes and then let me have it," Oksana demanded.

CHAPTER 14

THE JOURNEY WITH HYDER

The Dassault was cruising at forty-six thousand feet, and neither I nor Fedorov was in the mood to question our prisoner. There would be enough time at the base.

We enjoyed a hearty breakfast prepared by a new flight attendant, a Russian girl with Petrossian schooling. Although she knew the identity of our captive, she treated him with the same respect she gave the other passengers.

We both were anxious to hear from Igor, and Fedorov was worried about Oksana.

We tried for more than two hours to reach them via the satellite phone, but there was no signal on the other side.

Then, just as I finished my third coffee, the phone showed signs of life. An urgent beep almost made me drop my cup.

Hyder watched me with a devilish smirk on his ugly face.

"Yes! Igor?"

"This is Oksana. Hello, Matt."

"So glad to hear your voice. Where are you? Is Igor okay?"

"Please give me, Yev. I need to talk to him."

I handed the phone to Fedorov, who began conversing rapidly in Russian. They spoke for several minutes, and I understood only one side of the conversation.

Fedorov switched off the phone and dealt with our captive before telling us what Oksana had reported. He shoved Hyder to a back seat and bound him with plastic cuffs, which he tightened hard.

His threat to throw him from the plane when we didn't need him anymore effected total obedience from the Mukhabarat number two.

Fedorov then came forward and briefed me and Ketut in detail.

"Let's turn around," he said. "Clearly our team missed or lost them. We are more valuable in Alushta right now than at the base."

He had made his decision, and I moved forward to the cockpit.

The pilot, a veteran Petrossian agent who flew not only executive jets but also high-risk helicopter combat missions, didn't need persuasion. He informed ground control in Vietnam about a sudden change of flight plan and turned the plane around.

His copilot hammered on a computer keyboard and produced a new flight plan that would get us to Sevastopol in six hours and twelve minutes.

"Fuel is good but we need a constant flight level of at least forty-nine thousand feet."

"Get clearance for China and Kazakhstan airspace. We need the northernmost route. Leave Pakistan to the south. Its ID procedure is a pain in the ass."

The copilot talked to all the ground control personnel in reach and signaled thumbs up.

"China is okay. Kazakhstan I'll do later. I'll send a fight plan to Sevastopol to ease our approach."

By Sevastopol he meant our people based there—no combat staff but reliable communications experts.

We were in for a long flight, and we discussed how to inform forty-nine, Galina Mikhailova. We decided to put more distance between us and a possible order to return to the old flight plan. It became my task to inform her but only an hour later when we had reached the point of no return.

Fedorov's thoughts again turned to Oksana. His Crimean protégée meant a lot to my friend.

"She came to us as a young girl with a lot of guts and a constant concern that her breasts wouldn't grow. You had your experience with Oksana in Libya. You know she is more than just an agent in jeopardy."

We chose not to have vodka but tried to sleep a few hours after I spoke to Galina.

To my surprise, she supported our decision, saying she had lost contact with the team assigned to Crimea.

"We can't reach them, and I'm afraid they might be in trouble too."

"We'll take care of it. I'll keep you informed about our progress."

With that, I ended the conversation and began wondering what to do with our prisoner. Apparently, Galina didn't want to discuss the issue with me, and I was unsure of my next move.

We made good time. The captain said we had cleared Kazakh airspace. Still, I couldn't sleep or even relax. I moved into a seat opposite Hyder and started to interrogate him. I made sure the plastic cuffs were tight and were constricting his blood flow. His hand began to turn a deep purple.

"Now talk. You are not going to Siberia but to a much less friendly place. If I'm satisfied with your story, we might let you go. Otherwise we'll let you depart from up here. Start with the CI-Alliance Ovest connection, and remember that the smallest lie will turn you into a bird."

Hyder said the cuffs were hurting, and I promised to loosen them after the first chapter of his story.

I woke up Fedorov and asked him to listen in.

"The Islamic State of Iraq and the Levant, ISIL, or the Islamic State of Iraq and Syria, ISIS, follows the fundamentalist Wahabi doctrine of the Sunni Muslims based in Saudi Arabia," Hyder explained.

"In 1999 ISIL surfaced for the first time as Jamah at al-Tawhid wal Jihad and pledged allegiance to Al Qaeda. The group proclaimed itself a worldwide caliphate based on Saudi Wahabi fundamentalism.

"Officially, the Saudi kingdom doesn't support ISIL or Al Qaeda, but a powerful group of Saudi businessmen, politicians, and clerics, all Wahabi zealots, have decided to support the caliphate financially and otherwise.

"When the US-controlled forces invaded Iraq, Saudi Arabia provided bases and logistics, therefore fighting Iraq as well. The main reason for this backing, however, was not to support the allies but to annihilate as many Shiites in Iraq as possible.

"Saddam Hussein was a Sunni, and his ruling Baath party consisted of Sunnis only. Shiites were outcasts, killed or imprisoned. However, they were a majority in Iraq.

"Ibrahim Awwad Ibrahim Ali Muhammad al-Badri al-Samarrai, later known as Abu Bakr al-Baghdadi, was born in 1971 as part of the Bobadri tribe near Samarra in Iraq. The tribe followed the fundamentalist Wahabi rules and was an early target of the Saudi intelligence agency, the Mukhabarat.

"Although the royal Saudi government was never, at least knowingly, involved with the connection, the fundamentalists in the kingdom were starting to support all anti-Shiite actions in Iraq via the Bobadri."

None of this was new to me, but I let Hyder continue. We had another four hours of flying time. I loosened his cuffs a little, and he thanked me, asking for some water. Alesha, the flight attendant, brought him a bottle. He continued.

"When Al Baghdadi was imprisoned at Camp Bucca in 2004, the Mukhabarat convinced the CIA he was harmless and a victim of Saddam Hussein."

Here I interrupted.

"Convinced? How and by whom exactly?"

"The Mukhabarat was in effect a weak arm of the CIA at that time," Hyder said. "Its operatives were led, trained, and schooled by the Americans. However, the Americans were highly dependent on inside Arab information that the CIA never—until today—understood.

"After Al Baghdadi's release from Camp Bucca, he disappeared for a while before being elected leader of ISIL by the Mujaheedin Shura Council."

I instructed him to skip history for now and to concentrate on the situation with Alliance, CI, and the CIA.

"Once Al Baghdadi took control as the first caliph, the situation changed dramatically," Hyder said. "In a short time, he formed an army financed almost openly by the Saudis or their renegades. However, the king, an ally of the Americans, put a stop to the financing, creating temporary turmoil in ISIL.

"The Mukhabarat then contacted its old allies in the CIA, most of them either retired or dismissed on ethical grounds. Their activities in setting up a sophisticated finance scheme were funded by the Wahabis and protected by the Mukhabarat, again the rebels.

"Many of the ex-CIA agents were employed by Cohen Industries and by the infamous contractor Cavity, which was still a service provider for the Pentagon in crisis areas like Iraq, Syria, and Afghanistan.

"CI and Cavity wanted to be involved directly, and the Wahabis together with the Mukhabarat agreed to cooperate, handing the two contractors valuable defense and oil contracts.

"Michael Cohen, the CEO of Cohen Industries, and Eileen Cahill of Cavity were often in Saudi Arabia, received by the king and hailed by the Wahabis.

"Together they created a state-of-the-art worldwide network that allowed money to be transferred easily to ISIL and other organizations."

He paused, took another sip of water, and added, "That's what your shitty company in Kuala Lumpur exposed. It was a secure system, but you had to hack your own software!"

"Just get to the point," I said.

"To mask sensitive transfers of huge amounts of money, CI bought several suffering traders and contractors all over the world. Some of them were acquired by CI, others by Saudi enterprises like Alliance Ovest.

"AO was near bankruptcy when we offered Manuel Ortega a deal he couldn't refuse. It required his daughter's influence to convince him. She had an affair with one of our princes, which quickly became history once the deal was made.

"Ortega is still running the company but under strict supervision by his new principals. He opened offices in Indonesia, Malaysia, Dubai, and Abu Dhabi—offices he never saw. Alliance Ovest was thriving again to the surprise of many of its competitors.

"Then your hack ruined it all. CI is too deeply involved to just get out. Cohen's army and Cavity are hunting you and your Russian hacker."

"Who is your mole in the CIA?"

Hyder was visibly shocked and hesitated too long before answering.

"There is no mole. All the sources are ex-firm."

"We know you are lying. I've heard enough. Can you fly?"

"You wouldn't do that."

He stared at me with wide eyes and seemed to grasp the fact that I would.

"I'll instruct the captain to leave the flight level and go to ten. That's the safest way to get rid of you."

I left him with Fedorov and went forward.

The captain announced, "We will descend west of Aqtau over the Caspian Sea in fifteen minutes. Take your seats. The drop will be steep. Flight attendant, secure all."

Hyder was watching me when I returned to the rear of the cabin, but he showed no sign of defeat yet.

We strapped in and a few minutes later the nose of the plane was pointing almost vertically toward the Caspian Sea. We felt weightless, held back from crashing into the cabin ceiling only by our seat belts.

Hyder's face betrayed pure horror.

"Okay, stop it. I'll tell you everything."

"Too late. We already know everything, and you're no more than extra weight for us now."

"Please. Don't do it. I'll tell you all."

His eyes, like ours, were deeply embedded in the lids by the steep fall.

"I'll give you a chance, but one more lie and you fly."

Fedorov called the captain on the intercom, and the Dassault slowly began a sharp climb back to flight level forty-nine.

Hyder coughed and drank more water.

"We have the director of special ops on our side. He is vital to us—and I might be dead now anyway."

Special ops, often referred to as black ops in the movies. Since I was out of the loop too long, I looked curiously at Fedorov for a name.

"Frank Brewer. Almost impossible but let's pass the info to Shearer. We have no time to lose."

I set up my laptop and composed a highly secure message to Mark Shearer in Washington, DC.

The captain came back on the intercom and said, "We have clearance for Sevastopol if you change your mind."

We were considering the possibility. Sevastopol would give us entry without the hassle of immigration, and I had no idea what to do with our prisoner. On the other hand, the FSB would probably want to know what we were up to. We needed a quick decision.

"Okay, great. Tell them we'll come by and drop off a passenger for the FSB, compliments of Petrossian. Just touch down and go. Then we'll fly over to Simferopol."

"Copy that," the captain replied.

"You're giving me to the FSB?"

Hyder's face displayed sheer terror.

"You might be able to cut a deal by giving them all you have. Offer to let them turn you. They just might let you go—on a tight leash, though."

"I'm dead here with the FSB or with my people."

I almost felt pity for him. The FSB was not a nursery. Quite the opposite. The old style of KGB interrogation was still very much alive, but we had no choice. If we wanted to rescue Oksana and Igor, we had to leave Hyder behind—dead or alive.

I played with the idea of dumping him in the Black Sea, but I had given him my word. I would let him try to make a deal.

The captain announced landing clearance and said a Colonel Burov would see us on board.

Good, I thought. *So we can hand over Hyder without leaving the plane.*

I offered Hyder a vodka. He first declined it as a good Muslim but then agreed to a large gulp.

The Dassault came in low over the harbor, which was crammed with Russian warships, tugs, and other vessels. After a sharp turn to the right, we touched down at Sevastopol Airport in Belbek, a Russian air force base. I glanced out the window and couldn't see one civilian aircraft.

Fedorov seemed relaxed.

"Burov. I've heard about him. He is old school. He was a captain or a major back in the eighties. This should be okay."

The Dassault taxied to a remote area on the west side of the airport where three vehicles awaited us. Obviously FSB.

The plane came to a halt, and the hydraulic staircase opened together with the door. A lean officer in the uniform of an FSB colonel climbed up the stairs and entered the cabin. Burov.

"Dobryy den (good afternoon)," he said, looking friendly enough.

This might just go well, I thought.

Fedorov greeted him, shook his hand, and thanked him for letting us touch down.

"We have a present for you." He pointed at Hyder.

"You are Petrossian, right?"

This was the critical phase. I made an instinctive decision. Relying on instinct had saved my life more than once.

"Yes, we are, and that's why we wanted to land here. Our cooperation has been excellent in the past, and we want this to continue. Hyder here is the deputy commander of the Mukhabarat, and he has some interesting intelligence for you—among other things the name of the Saudis' CIA mole."

I waited for Burov's reaction, but his face remained totally unemotional.

"Where did you get him and what for?"

I briefed him on our mission, which touched on Russian interests in the Middle East, mainly in Syria. Hyder was an asset for the Russians.

"He is cooperating and willing to share," I added. "That's why he is here."

Maybe I shouldn't have gone that far, but Hyder's eager nod confirmed my introduction. It also surprised me because it showed he spoke Russian.

"You are on to Simferopol?"

"Yes, colonel. I have an IT lab there, and we do contract work for the FSB. We have to finalize a preparation."

He swallowed it.

"Yes, I have heard of you. My brother is a resident of Simferopol. This plane is Petrossian?"

"Yes, colonel."

I smiled and offered him a first-class vodka as a welcome drink. He gladly accepted. We clinked glasses and our conversation got even friendlier. I didn't want to push the deal our captive was offering him, but I thought Burov understood the offer only too well.

After two more shots, we all shook hands and I clapped Hyder on the shoulder, congratulating him on making the right move. This showed the FSB colonel it was Hyder's decision, not mine.

The colonel and Hyder, looking more comfortable than ever, left after wishing us a safe flight. Hyder had also downed two vodkas, which might have made him more willing to help us unload him.

"You still have it, fifty," Fedorov said. "I'm proud of you. Not too easy to turn the FSB on to your line. I know now you are back."

I wasn't that sure, but I felt good in my old function of persuading difficult people.

"No more vodka," Fedorov declared. "We have to be ready in Simferopol."

Ketut had been watching me with her lovely dark eyes.

"You are really good. People told me about you during my training at the base. They were right."

I was in the mood for another vodka after her compliment, but Fedorov was right. We had to stay alert.

Fedorov fiddled with the visa set that was on every Petrossian plane and soon finished working on Ketut's Indonesian passport. She now had a valid Russian visa for a tourist stay of thirty days. She knew of this Petrossian capability but was still amazed at how quickly the job was done. Fedorov and I already had valid Russian passports. The captain, the copilot, and the attendant were all Russians.

The flight took only twenty minutes, and Burov's call ahead made everything easy for us.

We were on the ground and whisked away by immigration with stamps and welcoming smiles.

Burov's brother was ready with a brand-new Lexus that smelled like it came straight from the dealership, although there was no Lexus dealer in Simferopol.

"I talked to Igor's engineers. They are very worried and so am I. If you need our help, call me here."

He pressed a business card into my hand with all his contacts neatly imprinted alongside his name and title: Alexey Burov, procurement director, AISA Engineering, Moscow, Simferopol office.

Sure, I said to myself.

The Lexus had a cooler with water, soft drinks and, of course, a bottle of vodka.

I took the wheel and we headed for Alushta.

CHAPTER 15

WASHINGTON, DC

M ark Shearer, retired deputy director of the CIA, woke up when the ultra-safe station just outside of his bedroom started to beep. Only a few people had his contacts and could reach him that way—and only if a situation was urgent enough to disturb his sleep.

He walked out to the station, which was double secured with Petrossian's seventh heaven cloud. Only harmless items could be found on his computer. When the NSA was hacking into the CIA, the FBI, and its own accounts, it revealed lots of embarrassing and even career-ending material, but he remained untouchable despite his connection to Petrossian. *They have some genius working for them*, he thought.

He read Matt's mail and scratched his head. A split second later the message was stored in seventh heaven, inaccessible to anyone but himself.

What? Impossible, he thought. Frank Brewer, an old-timer like himself, was a great friend, the godfather to his daughter, and one of the few pals his late wife had accepted.

Goddamn it! I hope Matt is wrong about this, he murmured. Then he walked into the kitchen to brew some coffee.

The retired special ops director needed time to digest what he had just read. He knew exactly who Hyder was and also recognized that Petrossian was unbeatable at interrogating its subjects.

Matt was a trusted old friend like Frank. They were both champions in their field and often performed on the same side. Not always, he remembered. They almost killed each other in the eighties in Chad when Mark was the CIA resident in Ndjamena, advising the brutal and infamous president Hissène Habré how to extract information, mostly from innocent citizens.

This remained a dark chapter in the books of the CIA or, more accurately, its contractors.

Mark wondered whether the Chad incidents played a role still today in these revelations.

Matt, at that time the Swiss Frederique, had rescued some Libyans from the fangs of Habré, but Frank's assassination squad, consisting of CIA special ops and Habré's killers, managed to get the upper hand at the Libyan border and killed more than fifty so-called insurgents—women, children, young and old men. Matt had gotten away with a few of his comrades and with a young Petrossian agent named Oksana.

She was the key witness in the later court-martial of Habré, a de facto indictment of the CIA.

At the time Oksana was officially a Red Cross helper in southern Libya. Her real identity had later been released to Mark by Fedorov, another high-ranking Petrossian who had developed into a close friend.

Frank's status and reputation were not hurt by the events in Chad, for it was later revealed that the CIA's contractor, Cavity, not the agency, had performed the atrocities. Frank went on to become director of special ops, a very powerful position within the CIA.

Now this!

Mark grabbed the phone and speed-dialed Frank Brewer on a secure line.

"Yes?" Frank sounded alert despite the early morning hour.

"Frank, it's Mark. Time for lunch? It's quite pressing."

"Can do, but make it one o'clock. I have a meeting with the new bunch of presidential security advisers. Combined IQ of a couple of unborn chickens—eggs! I know we are secure here. They all fit the newly elected POTUS."

"Tell me more over lunch. I'll make a booking at the Town Bistro."

"Look forward, old friend. Hope not to run into the president," he said with a laugh.

Mark knew he could not get in touch with Matt otherwise he would recognize the special code for it in the message. So he waited, took a shower, and got dressed.

The mention of Cohen Industries worried him most. CI had become a trusted contractor to the White House and its new occupant and of course to the Pentagon. Besides manufacturing weapons systems and electronics and running an army of Pentagon contractors, CI owned golf courses and hotels just like the new president.

Mark had held many meetings with Matt on CI golf courses in Florida and California. He recalled Matt saying, "The most innocent place for a very guilty meeting is a golf course."

He also recalled Matt's skill with the little white ball, which earlier in life had allowed him to play in the US amateurs, although he had not reached the second round of match competition.

With hours to kill, Mark went to his station and excavated whatever was available on the Frank Brewer-Petrossian relationship.

The creases on his forehead grew deeper as he uncovered information. It was not good. There was a lot of bad blood between Petrossian and Frank's special ops, though it was impossible to highlight one issue that stood out.

This woman, Oksana, had been tortured by Cavity, but Matt and his fighters—mostly Libyans but also some Russians—had pulled off a dramatic rescue. They had killed a dozen Cavity agents in northern Chad, but the commander of these agents, officially CIA officer Frank Brewer, was in Ndjamena, the capital, and therefore untouchable.

Mark made mental notes about Oksana, Fedorov, and Abu Said, a Libyan army commander, and poured himself another coffee.

Given his stellar career, how in the hell could Frank be a mole?

Mark prepared himself for the lunch meeting. The Town Bistro was popular with all kinds of people in DC. It attracted fewer politicians and more artists, actors, and wannabes. Thus it was a place where everybody would go unnoticed by the DC snoopers and gossips.

At twelve he backed his Mercedes out of the basement garage beneath his Georgetown brownstone. His late wife, Amelia, had come from a wealthy family. He was just a poor scholarship student when they had met at Yale. She was an architect and he was a lawyer, and the two of them had found the jobs they had been dreaming of. Or so he thought.

When Mark was twenty-four and fresh out of Yale Law School, the CIA had approached him with an enticing offer. He could work for his beloved country at a high salary with a chance to travel. Amelia hadn't been too enthusiastic about this career path, but her father, a Republican state senator in Arkansas, had persuaded her to accept Mark's decision.

Their life had been good, and he rose rapidly from agent to member of the NSA, advising three presidents during his successful career. Not that any of them ever listened to him.

Now he was faced with a task that gave him stomach problems. Frank a mole!

He knew all the intelligence coming from Petrossian was accurate. After years of secret cooperation with the firm, he listened carefully to its agents and usually followed their advice.

Mark arrived at the Town Bistro about half an hour early, giving him time to examine other guests. The owner greeted him with enthusiasm, like an old friend. Amelia had loved this place, and they had made it a tradition to dine there at least once a week.

"So nice to see you, Mr. Shearer. I held your favorite table at the very back. We have fresh lobster, oysters, and mozzarella. Can I bring you a martini as you like it?"

"Thank you, Roberto. With three olives, please."

Roberto hurried away and a pretty young lady escorted Mark to his table.

The former CIA assistant director sat down with his mind racing. How would he raise the issue? How would Frank react? He sipped his martini and chewed the three olives to the stones.

A black Escalade stopped in front of the restaurant, and Frank jumped out of the rear like the paratrooper he had been before heading CIA special ops.

Frank entered the restaurant and waved to Mark, striding through the place and ignoring the pretty lady. How very much like Frank!

Mark sat with his back to the wall, knowing Frank didn't like to expose his rear to the open space of the restaurant. Frank pulled a chair to the side of the table, providing himself with a partial view of the room.

"Hi, old friend. What's up? I'm starving."

He signaled the waiter and ordered the same martini Mark had.

Mark decided not to delay.

"Frank, what's your involvement with CI? And with the Saudis?" He took a sip. "Is Cavity alive again?"

His friend's face turned purple and then white.

"What do you know?"

"Enough to let you run to a beach in Aruba—or in Jeddah."

"Petrossian?"

"Exactly. And you know they are never wrong, so you better tell me everything before the red lights start blinking."

Frank Brewer, the godfather of his daughter, took a deep sip, ordered another martini, and started to tell his story.

Back in 2011 Cohen Industries' CEO, Michael Cohen, had approached him after a meeting with the CIA, for which Cohen was an important consultant. He knew Frank was in his last years at the agency and offered to make him a member of the board of Cohen Industries after his retirement.

Frank was flattered and thanked Cohen profusely for his generous offer, accepting it without contemplating any side effects.

Cohen agreed to pay Frank a generous retainer while he was still at the CIA, "just to make sure you don't change your mind."

Frank accepted and his lifestyle changed dramatically. He had a small yacht moored in Baltimore Harbor and always had lady friends even before his wife passed away.

Then the requests for information arrived. At first the questions appeared harmless.

Frank had a bad feeling about this but convinced himself that revealing such data did no damage and that the requests were therefore within the proper boundaries of his relationship with his future employer.

In 2012 all that changed.

Three CIA agents operating in northern Iraq were killed while they were asleep in a supposedly safe house. Frank had given CI the location and the names of the agents earlier.

The agents had been getting close to a significant ISIL leader and were planning his assassination.

With the killings, Frank had his first suspicions that Cavity had been revived since such missions had been their specialty.

The killing of the three CIA officers raised hell at the agency, and Frank, as the assistant director of special ops, was ordered by the director and by the president to head to Iraq to investigate the circumstances of their deaths.

Cohen offered the CIA safe and discreet travel on one of his jets, and Frank accepted. When he boarded the plane, a Boeing 737 long range, Frank found Cohen waiting him with a martini in his hand.

The flight to Erbil in northern Iraq was sheer torture for Frank as Cohen revealed his plans for him. He assured Frank that his offer stood and that Frank would be a member of the CI board and probably a future presidential security adviser.

He outlined his strategy for keeping the war against ISIL alive. A group of Saudi financiers lined up by CI had provided all the necessary international connections to finance ISIL until the end. What end? Cohen did not want to talk about that.

While they were on the plane, Cohen had Frank sign a bunch of papers that made him a director of several offshore companies that Cohen said were untraceable.

When Frank inquired about the potential involvement of Cavity, Cohen told him not to go there.

Frank's retainer was increased to $2 million a year paid in advance. The banking orders were arranged from the plane to an account in Frank's name in the Caymans.

Now all he had to do on this trip was to establish that the agents were killed by Iranian insurgents, who were fighting everybody in Iraq, including ISIL, Al Qaeda, and the Americans.

CI mercenaries already had five Iranian suspects, kidnapped from an Iranian vessel in the Gulf. The five supposedly confessed and wanted to die as martyrs. Their confession was videotaped, transcribed, and signed by all of them.

Then the five Iranian terrorists attacked a guard and got a hold of his weapon—not to flee but to kill themselves and to enter Allah's kingdom as martyrs. All of this had happened just before Frank and Cohen had taken off from Washington that morning.

Thus Cohen made it clear to Frank that the case would be wrapped up without an investigation.

Job done, and position earned.

Since that day Frank had been a marionette of Cohen and knew he better follow orders, or else.

Cohen made it clear to him that the CEO of CI was untouchable but that Frank might spend the rest of his days in a maximum-security prison somewhere in Nebraska—if he were not executed.

At that moment in his tale Frank started to sob. The tears rolled down his cheeks and dropped into his fourth martini.

He tried to make a joke but failed badly.

"Pity I'm not a Muslim, because now would be the time for me to become a martyr and be greeted by the virgins. Do you know I never had a virgin in my life?"

He laughed and choked after swallowing more of his martini.

"Last night CI, or most probably Cavity, blew up a chemical weapons storage near Ar Raqhaa in northern Syria. The nerve agent sarin was in the CI stock. You might have seen the horrible pictures on TV. The attack was my doing."

He ordered another martini and wiped away more tears.

"Cohen does everything to escalate the war and to let IS, Al Nusra, Al Qaeda, and other assholes take over the Middle East, except for Saudi Arabia. He secured huge oil contracts in the kingdom as well as in Iraq. But now comes the hammer."

Frank took a large gulp and almost appeared relieved that he had Mark listening to him.

"This morning we briefed our new president."

Another swig. His eyes were glazed and his lips trembling.

"The National Security Council, of which I'm now a member, compliments of Michael Cohen, advised the president to attack Syria with Tomahawk cruise missiles. I tried futilely to steer the decision in a different direction, saying we might hit the Russians and what have you."

Frank's voice trailed off and he was sobbing again.

Mark realized he had to get him out of there. People were starting to notice the rather strange conversation, turning their heads and whispering.

"Listen, Frank. Let's go to your house and try to find a fair solution, maybe a way out of this mess."

Frank hit the table violently with his fist. "Fuck you! There is no way out for me anymore, and you know it."

Mark gestured to a slightly troubled Roberto to stay away. He clutched Frank's arm and propelled him to his feet, leading him out of the Town Bistro.

Roberto, sensitive host that he was, had ordered a valet to bring Mark's car. The two had to wait a few minutes before Mark loaded his old friend into the Mercedes.

"We can send your car back to Langley later. Now stay calm."

Frank leaned back in the passenger seat.

"Fucking Petrossian, fucking CI. Fuck them all!"

"Shut up and let me debrief you at home. You realize that by doing this for you I will be an accomplice, a huge liability to the firm. But we will do a full debriefing on the record, which I will personally present to the director at the right time. That might help you prepare a defense."

Frank suddenly appeared quite sober as he replied to Mark's offer.

"There is no defense in the whole fucking world that would ever get me out of this, so just let me do my thing. Maybe there are really some virgins waiting for me on the other side."

The early afternoon traffic was dense on Connecticut Avenue, and Mark had to slow down before making a right turn toward Georgetown. A big city bus was approaching them in the left lane. When Mark was forced to stop behind a government sedan, Frank simply said good-bye, opened the passenger door, crossed in front of the Mercedes, and sprinted right into the path of the approaching bus. He was hit head-on by the huge vehicle.

The bus gave Frank what he thought was the only way out.

He was dead at impact, his body lying under the bus. In seconds a large crowd gathered with an anxious bus driver in the middle of the road.

Nobody seemed to focus on the Mercedes that remained in the right lane. Mark was tempted to keep a low profile but restrained himself from running off. Too many surveillance cameras were active in the city. He parked the car illegally at the curb and got out to do the inevitable—be a witness.

Mark instantly realized his friend's suicide would put him in the crosshairs of Michael Cohen and of the CI and Cavity mercenaries. CI would correctly conclude that Frank was spilling his guts to him before he killed himself.

After verifying Mark's identity, the police didn't keep him for lengthy interviews, and once his contact information had been established, he was free to go.

His Georgetown house was out of question. Cohen might already have put surveillance on it. Langley wouldn't detain him until the full picture became clear. That would take days.

He had to get rid of the Mercedes.

Mark computed all the potential outcomes, all the possible ways of getting killed by CI or Cavity. They would have to move quickly to contain the damage. He would do the same.

On Pennsylvania Avenue, he took an abrupt left turn into the basement parking lot at the Four Seasons. He couldn't make out any vehicle following him. Maybe he had gotten lucky and the incident had surprised and paralyzed them for a moment, though he very much doubted that.

He pulled into a narrow space between two vans, grabbed his belongings, and rushed for the elevator.

He pressed "Lobby," and the jingle accompanying the elevator's arrival snapped him back to reality.

All his communications equipment was back at his house, which was out of bounds.

He went straight to the hotel's business center where he had to do some convincing since he was not a hotel guest. Finally, after he displayed his credentials, the staff let him use a small cubicle with a computer.

The first thing he did was establish a connection to his home cameras, which was easy. He could gain access anywhere with the proper password.

The house appeared undisturbed. The minicams were sweeping every room, providing him with a 360-degree view.

Then he moved to the two outdoor cameras, one in front and the other at the rear of his property.

Nothing. All seemed clear.

Mark checked on the few cars that were parked at the curb and found nothing suspicious. Maybe it was too early, but he was not the type to persuade himself with the easiest explanation. Cohen would have to act swiftly to avoid the biggest political implosion DC had experienced in decades.

He moved from the cams to an entirely unsafe Internet communications connection. There was no choice. He had to do it.

He composed a message to Matt at Petrossian. The address had been stored in his memory for years, but he had never had to use it. He had saved it for extreme cases when all other channels were off limits—like now.

Mark remembered that the innocent-looking email address was forwarded via a dozen or so servers to Petrossian's famous seventh heaven, which not even the NSA had been able to hack into. He hoped it worked.

The crudely encoded message said that the mole was exposed and dead; that he, Mark, was a target; that he had no means of communication, and that he would proceed to the family. Only Matt would understand what *family* meant.

He hit "send" and deleted everything on the hard disk, even reformatting it. Someone using the public workstation would curse him for that later.

Now he needed transport and, much more important, he had to divert the CIA, CI, and Cavity away from him to buy time. The police certainly would have contacted the agency about Frank's suicide and about the CIA retiree who was with him at the time of his unfortunate demise.

Mark had killed his mobile phone minutes after the incident on Connecticut Avenue. He had disposed of the SIM card and had switched off the phone. He knew the NSA could locate phones in no time, and he was sure CI with its connections could do the same.

He used the land line in his cubicle and called a number he hadn't dialed in years.

Mark almost prayed this would have no dangerous consequences for the person who might save his life.

"Yes?"

The voice was not familiar to him and sounded hesitant.

"Hi! I would like to speak with Sister Veronica." He tried to sound like a regular caller.

"May I ask who is calling? Sister Veronica is in the middle of a class."

The nuns taught underprivileged children and helped drug addicts, ex-convicts, and fallen angels.

"My name is Harold Smith. I'm an old friend of Sister Veronica."

"If you give me your number, I will ask her to call you back in half an hour. Is that okay?"

"I'm afraid it's quite urgent. Please tell her it's a family problem. She will understand."

"Oh, right. Hold on, please."

A choir sang in his ear while he waited and got more nervous.

Then he heard a friendly voice with a slight Russian accent.

"This is Sister Veronica. How can I help you?"

"Privet kak dela, sestra?"

His Russian was flawless, and Sister Veronica immediately responded, "Prekrasny, tovarishch. Sposiba."

This established, the sister, a former Petrossian agent, understood the urgency of the call.

"I know who you are. No more names now. You need to come in?"

"Yes, and quick. I have to get in touch with the base from your place."

"When will you arrive? I'll prepare what you need. You can stay here."

"I'm in DC, no transport. Can you provide?"

"I can, but your line is not secure."

"Remember little Elaine?"

Elaine was a street girl Mark had rescued years earlier from a violent gang that was about to rape and probably kill her. He had shot three of the gang members before he had moved little Elaine to a safe house in Georgetown where she was picked up by Sister Veronica and two other nuns.

"Yes. When will you be there?"

"Half-hour if everything goes well."

"Gray van. Woman driver. One of us. She won't stop. Just hop in."

One of us. He didn't ask if that meant the nunnery or Petrossian. He didn't care.

The line went dead.

It was time to move.

The old safe house was just down the road at Foggy Bottom.

Mark ripped the phone cord out of its socket and placed the receiver neatly back onto its cradle. He had already wrecked the hard disk of the computer. One more act of sabotage would not harm him any further.

He carefully left the booth and walked over to the reception area like a regular guest. From there he had a clear view of the entrance and of the taxis piling up outside. He calculated his move cautiously, and when he saw nothing suspicious he casually walked to the revolving door, eyeing a cab in front of the line. A special sense developed over decades in his line of work made him hesitate at the last moment. He saw the black SUV entering the lane. There were thousands of such vehicles in Washington, but Mark's highly tuned mental alarm system was sending danger signals.

He strolled back into the lobby and took a seat in one of the comfortable leather chairs, grabbing the *Post* from a tray and hiding his face.

The SUV came to a halt right in front of the door, and two dudes in black suits jumped from the rear. Cohen or Cavity. How the hell did they figure out he would be at the Four Seasons?

Mark crossed his legs and hid himself behind the *Post*. The two guys went straight to the business center. They were better than he thought. Or they had help from one of the agencies.

He needed a phone. And quick.

An attractive middle-aged woman sitting in one of the chairs beside him was sipping a coffee and talking on her smartphone.

He stood up and faked a stumble, gripping the glass table on which she had placed her half-full coffee cup. The coffee spilled all over her, the cup flew off the table, and she started to scream. Mark apologized profoundly, grabbed her phone, and ran through the lobby to a delivery entrance.

All this took less than thirty seconds. He was out at the side of the hotel, running to a narrow alley used for deliveries.

He ran all the way to Twenty-Fifth Street. The little bar where he sometimes used to wind down after a tense day at Langley was still there—dark, discreet, ideal.

Mark entered the small, cozy bar, ordered a Bud Light, and went to the washroom. He splashed some cold water on his face and rearranged his suit. His short hair didn't need any correction.

"Hi, sir! Long time."

The heavy bartender recognized him and shook his hand vigorously.

"Yes, I missed your place. Too long abroad. Good to be back."

Mark took his beer and sat down at a rear table, the one he always used.

He took the woman's phone and dialed the nunnery again.

This time Sister Veronica picked up.

"They are on to me. Change of venue."

He gave her the address of the bar.

"Okay, I'll redirect. Be ready in ten minutes. Again, no stop. She will pass the bar slowly."

Mark checked his watch, put ten bucks on the table, and waited.

After nine minutes he stood up, shook hands with the bartender, and left.

He saw the gray van coming down Twenty-Fifth. An elderly woman was behind the wheel, and she clearly recognized her passenger. The van picked up speed and came almost to a halt beside him, the sliding rear door opening. He hopped in and the door shut immediately.

"Better stay in the back. The windows are tinted," she called from the driver's seat.

"Thank you." He didn't know what else to say.

"It's a two-hour drive. I have placed refreshments for you in the cool box. Relax. We are safe. No one knows me or the van, and I'm good at spotting tails."

She chuckled, and strangely enough Mark felt safe for the first time since the suicide of his friend and former colleague. He took the SIM card out of the stolen phone and switched it off.

By now the woman had surely reported the theft and his pursuers were on the trail again. He threw the phone out of the window while the van was moving up to Arlington Bridge.

In a few minutes, they would enter Virginia and would head for Richmond.

He tried to make conversation with the lady. She must have been at least seventy but looked fit and professional.

"Are you Petrossian?"

"Long time ago, yes. I know you and I know fifty very well. I'm retired, but are we ever really?" She laughed.

She knew Matt. That put her high on the ladder.

"Are you at the nunnery?"

He could see her pretty smile in the rear mirror. "No, but Veronica is an old friend. I handle the kids and guys like you. My name is Tatiana. I'm American since birth. My parents came to the United States during the war. We are Jewish. Now you know why I'm not at the nunnery. My father was Petrossian until his death, and so was my mother. Maybe you've heard my family name, Morozov. Of course I'm Morozova."

Morozov. Vitaly Morozov.

"I knew your father, Vitaly. A very good man. He was working with us. He has a star plaque at Langley. He died in East Germany."

"That's the one," Tatiana said, still smiling.

She obviously enjoyed the chat, but Mark could see she was extremely alert, constantly checking her rear mirror, driving just below the speed limit, and taking minor roads on the way south. She was mature, seasoned, and professional.

He had never heard of Tatiana, which meant Petrossian had kept her out of sight all these years and she had managed to stay undetected. He wondered what function she performed but didn't ask.

A breathtaking sunset and the steady hand of a veteran Petrossian agent provided him a comfort he hadn't felt in a long while. It was time to stop Cohen and Cavity, the traitors, and the devilish scheme they were pursuing.

After about two hours they reached the outskirts of Richmond.

Tatiana didn't enter the city but took a road to the west of it. The nunnery was about twenty miles west of Richmond, located in a forest, hidden from the roads around it.

After a few miles, she turned onto a tight gravel road, took a few turns, and stopped the car.

"I'll call Veronica from here just to make sure we are safe."

She grabbed a satellite phone from the glove department. All Petrossian agents communicated with these devices, Mark noticed.

"I have the delivery ready. You want me to supply today or tomorrow morning?"

Mark detected her eyebrows rising slightly, her lips forming a tight, thin line.

"Okay, you can warm up the bread tomorrow morning then."

She turned to Matt, her face showing concern.

"They are not in the nunnery but close to it. Two SUVs with DC plates are patrolling the access road."

The code they were using was sound and the satellite connection untraceable, at least for the moment.

"Okay." Mark was calm and not utterly surprised they were compromised. Cohen must have several moles in the agency.

"Where can we go? I have to get in touch with fifty."

"Let me think. My house is in DC. Too far. Let's find a motel far south of Richmond. And we should get rid of the car. I'm afraid if they are here they might know my car by now."

She was right.

"Are you armed?" A sudden thought struck Mark. Why run if there was a chance to take them?

She gave him a sly smile.

"Are you sure?"

Tatiana fumbled under her seat and took out a Makarov semiautomatic. She pointed at his seat.

"Raise it. There is more."

He moved aside and pulled up his seat to find a small arsenal consisting of two Makarovs like hers, two Uzis, and about twenty fully loaded magazines.

The stun grenades might come in handy too.

"Hell! You drive around with this in your car?"

"I'm an elderly woman, all taxes paid, never had a speeding ticket, never crossed the law. You really want to do this?"

"Let's do it if you agree. Find out more from Sister Veronica. How many and where?"

Tatiana dialed the nunnery again.

"Sorry for calling again. How many baguettes did you order? Our new girl misplaced the order. I'll send her tomorrow morning. Where should she deliver? Main entrance or at the beekeeper hut?"

She listened intently, nodding her head.

"Okay then. Thanks again, Sister Veronica. The girl's name is Sandra. She will be there by seven tomorrow morning."

They were good. Mark nodded his approval.

"According to Veronica, there are two SUVs with tinted windows. It's impossible to make out the numbers, but they are parked at the main access road. That's about two miles from here. Ready for a walk?"

She drove the van deeper into the forest, and they covered it with branches.

Mark was thrilled to see action again. His earlier days had been filled with dangerous adventures, so one more in the November of his life might just give him something he had missed for many years. Matt was his age, and so was Tatiana. *What the hell?* he thought. *Let's do it.*

They armed themselves but not too heavily. Tatiana carried her Makarov, while Mark took one of those plus a silenced Uzi and two of the stun grenades. These were highly illegal weapons all over the world but very effective.

Tatiana led the way through the forest. Although it was dark, the almost full moon provided enough light for them. They made slow progress through the dense forest, but Mark could see he was with an ice-cold professional, albeit one who was about seventy years old. She avoided making noise, sidestepping loose branches and almost automatically maintaining the right direction.

It took them nearly two hours to reach the vicinity of the nunnery. The access road was almost floodlit by the moon. They could see only one of the SUVs parked at the side of the road. But where was the other? Mark and Tatiana could not attack without knowing the position of the second car.

Tatiana's satellite phone made a vibrating sound in her pants pocket. Veronica wouldn't have called her if she knew what they had in mind.

They took cover behind bushes, and Tatiana tapped the reply button.

"Da, da ... Okay, thanks."

"What the hell was that?"

Mark felt his adrenaline pumping hard.

"It was Matt. They are in Igor's villa in Alushta and have a satellite view of the situation. Igor ..."

"You know Igor?"

"Of course. He installed our communications and security system in DC. He is the greatest hacker of all time. He was here last year with Matt when your firm was on to us. At least the wrong guys were. They have NSA satellite access now from Simferopol and can see the nunnery. Your former assistant, a Mrs. Corn something, called Khabarovsk and gave them info."

"Cornward, Emily Cornward. Long retired and missing in action as well. She was a confidante and was almost fully briefed about Petrossian. Very loyal. Might have to take her for dinner after this."

"Do you realize we are all oldies here? Where are the young Petrossians?"

"Petrossian is changing from the way we knew it. Today all the youngsters, like Igor, are sitting in front of computers and launching their attacks in cyberspace. We are the last of the old breed, and it feels good."

Tatiana's satellite phone vibrated again. Her natural frown lines deepened, softened by her contagious smile.

"Okay. I see them now. We go. Heads up!"

The other SUV came up the road and parked beside the first.

It was time to go.

Tatiana again led the way. Luckily the ground along the access road was lower than the road itself, so they could approach the two vehicles with less chance of being seen.

They were only about fifty yards from the SUVs when Tatiana's satellite phone vibrated again. She lay on her back and listened, not uttering a word.

"No go. Matt is monitoring their communications. They will be leaving in a moment."

Shit! They were too close to abort. If one of these guys stepped out of the car he might see them. They huddled close to the bank, right below the SUVs, totally motionless.

Mark raised five fingers in front of Tatiana's face, indicating five minutes. She nodded, eager to finish what they had started.

Then both engines revved, and the two SUVs rolled slowly down the road toward them. The vehicles passed overhead with the headlights lighting the otherwise deserted gravel road. Mark could feel Tatiana's body relax, but they didn't move for another five minutes.

"They gave up on us. I wonder what changed. They knew we would come here, and now they are leaving," she whispered.

Mark had a strange feeling that reminded him of his field days in the Middle East and Pakistan.

"Hold it," he hissed. "I think it's a trap. These guys are too good to just leave."

Tatiana agreed. They waited, frozen to the cool ground, straining their ears. Getting closer to the road might be the end of them.

The damn moon was too bright to allow them to move. They scanned the sky, looking for a cloud to darken the celestial floodlight above, but the sky was clear and the millions of stars added to the light.

"We have to separate." Tatiana pointed at him and then up the road.

"You might be fitter than I am. Crawl fifty yards and try to get a peek at the building."

Mark bobbed his head and began crawling close to the roadside, away from her.

His earlier bad feeling was confirmed when he heard a male voice whispering in the dark. It was impossible to determine the direction of the sound, but yes, they were still there.

Now Mark was happy for the moonlight. He signaled to Tatiana with two fingers and then three, meaning at least two of them were there.

He dared to glance at the road.

Clearly, they still expected Mark and Tatiana to arrive by car. He could see a glowing cigarette that lit up the face of a second chap standing near the main entrance of the nunnery. Mark and Tatiana had the advantage, but hell, together they were more than 140 years old.

Mark's adrenaline was flowing hard, keeping him alert. The two CI or Cavity men—he hoped they were not CIA—were about forty yards away. In his prime, it would have child's play for him to take them out with two rapid bursts. But now he wasn't too sure.

They couldn't be CIA, not on US soil and at a nunnery. He was sure they were Cohen dogs of war or, even worse, Cavity, most probably ex-military. And young.

Mark aimed the Makarov at the smoker. He and Tatiana had chambered rounds earlier. She was well trained.

The silencer was not great for accuracy, but it was better not to raise hell with two loud shots.

Suddenly Mark was ice cold, his heart rate dropping instead of rising. He took two deep breaths, let the air out about three quarters of the way, and pulled the trigger. No head shots from this distance, just center mass.

Blop, blop. The Makarov coughed and both guys were down almost simultaneously.

Now their cover was blown, and there was no reason to hide anymore. If there were more than two, he and Tatiana might be dead.

Mark, who was in good shape for his age, sprang up and ran over to the two bodies. One man was dead. He had hit him right in the heart. The other was coughing blood but was alive.

Tatiana was right behind him.

"Good shots. Couldn't have done better."

Her strained smile lit up the night even more.

The door to the nunnery opened, and Sister Veronica, dressed in tight jeans and a golf shirt rather than a habit, grabbed the corpse and pulled it toward the building.

"I watched you. Great shots! We must get rid of them quickly. Come."

Tatiana and Mark lifted the badly injured mercenary and dragged him inside.

"Lung shot," Veronica muttered. "Let's try to get some info before he checks out."

Yes, she was a nun now, and a devoted one, but in these situations she was also a Petrossian.

Two more sisters helped with the body and the wounded man.

"They are okay. Armenians, Petrossians all their lives," Veronica assured Mark.

They dragged the dead man and his badly wounded comrade into the narrow hallway of the nunnery. Veronica shut the door and triple locked it. The door was made of steel and quite heavy.

"Sister Kohar and Sister Tangaking will dispose of the body. Let's bring this one in here."

Veronica opened a solid wood door that led into an empty room.

"Let's hope he lives for a few more moments," she murmured, pulling him into the cell-like chamber.

But it was too late. Once in the cold stone chamber he gave his last breath.

"That's it. We shall bury him too."

Veronica, at about seventy, was the youngest of them, and after taking care of kids, drug addicts, and fallen angels, she was a cool operator experienced in crisis management.

"Sister, I need access to com ..."

"Veronica," she interrupted. "I'm not a nun right now. Follow me."

Veronica's office was stunning to say the least, with dazzling art on three walls, Persian carpets, and leather sofas. However, the fourth wall was what grabbed Mark's attention. At least a dozen screens and humming computers took up all the space.

"You want to talk to Matt? Here he is."

She pointed to one of the monitors where the familiar face of fifty, his old friend, was smiling at him.

"Hello, Mark. Nice to see you made it. Dobryy vecher, Tatiana. What a girl! Mark, stay with Veronica until we have more feedback. I know you are safe there. Make sure to wipe away all traces." He meant to get rid of the bodies. "Don't get in touch with the agency, because we don't know yet who is on what side. CI has its tentacles everywhere including the White House."

Mark glanced at Veronica, who didn't look like a saintly nun right now in her tight jeans and her loose leather jacket. She gave him a nod.

"We'll take care, Matt. Keep us lit up." She smiled and closed the connection.

CHAPTER 16
ALUSHTA, EARLY MORNING

I was joined by Ketut and Fedorov in front of the camera screen, and we all shouted a happy welcome over the time zones. Fortunately, Igor's system was intact, reliable as always, although his main console was destroyed beyond repair. However, in typical fashion, Igor had protected his key emergency equipment in the adjacent room with a fireproof cabinet, invisible to an intruder. I was with him when he installed it and had my doubts whether he would ever need it. We did now.

The trip from Simferopol to Alushta was uneventful, but Ketut and Fedorov watched the road, the few cars, and the surroundings vigilantly. All our satellite phones were on since we hoped to hear from Igor. I didn't know Oksana was with him until my phone beeped. Khabarovsk.

"Da, govorit!" (Speak!)

The woman from the base told me as much as she knew about the situation near Alushta, which was not a whole lot. Oksana wore a tracker for such situations, but it had died hours earlier. However, the woman could pinpoint an estimated location west of Alushta from where the tracker had sent its last sign of life.

Then she briefed me about the occurrences in Washington, DC, and urged me to get in touch with Mark Shearer. It took her about twenty minutes to give me the details.

We arrived in Alushta shortly after sunrise, and I drove by Igor's private nest without losing speed. Fedorov and Ketut observed the neighborhood with eagle eyes. They saw no people, and the houses all looked empty. No surprise. The busy holiday season was still weeks away.

On a second pass, we noticed Igor's door was somewhat ajar, confirming my fears.

There was still no sign of life in the streets, so we decided to enter in full view. After all, we were three trained Petrossians and heavily armed.

I parked the car near Oksana's café, and we walked back to Igor's abode.

We had our weapons drawn when we pulled the door open.

The inside was a mess to say the least. Demolished furniture and wrecked computers gave me little hope of finding a way to communicate. Then I recalled Igor's emergency communications consoles in the small living room where nobody would expect to find state-of-the-art IT equipment. The little salon, overlooking the Black Sea, was located right over the boathouse and featured a balcony. The floor-to- ceiling windows were intact, and the cozy room looked untouched.

I went over to the man-high bar and found the button that let it swing open like a magic door. There was the gear we desperately needed.

Ketut watched the street, her Glock in both hands, while Fedorov checked the rest of the house.

"All clear," I heard from both.

I loaded up the sophisticated communications computer, turning on three monitors above it. I was familiar with Igor's installation because he had fitted my house in Kuala Lumpur with similar stuff.

I found an encrypted file from Khabarovsk with an urgent note saying "Read first." As if I wouldn't.

The file was a detailed description of the situation with Cohen Industries, the CIA, Cavity, the Saudis, and a whole bunch of international corporations that played a role in financing the Islamic State. And not only that. According to this material, CI, the CIA, and the Saudis were evidently into much more than financing these terrorists.

Petrossian obtained recordings that pointed in a frightening direction. Cohen Industries was developing mini nukes that could be delivered with smaller ballistic missiles or even artillery shells.

I studied the file after Igor's decoding program made it readable. Meanwhile, Fedorov tried to reach Igor or Oksana with the base's help. It became clear the two were somewhere between Alushta and Simferopol and were still being hunted by the CI and Cavity mercenaries. Extraction was our highest priority but was impossible without a general location.

Fedorov urged Khabarovsk to place a satellite over the region. Khabarovsk promised to hack into a Zenit III surveillance satellite located somewhere above Crimea, mostly monitoring troop movements in eastern Ukraine.

My eyes flew over the pages of the decrypted file, which gave me the creeps to say the least. I didn't want to spend too much time on it and had a hard time digesting what I read.

Cohen Industries, renegade CIA agents together with Pakistani intelligence, or maybe just a few fanatics generously paid by CI were plotting big time against peace in the Middle East. Financing the Islamic State looked like a diversion, a way to stir the pot in Syria and Iraq. The main goal was to launch a nuclear attack on Iran, officially orchestrated by the Islamic State. The second or maybe the first target was Israel. Ultimately these attacks would produce a "big conflict," as the file put it.

I had wondered why the caliphate would need that much money to continue its useless battles. This explained it all. The IS received funds, but the major part went to a special unit based somewhere in Saudi Arabia or Iraq that planned to hurl nukes over the Persian Gulf or toward Israel.

The file contained detailed intelligence about the offshore companies involved, including Alliance Ovest, which had triggered all this.

I read enough to understand why the CI mercenaries were so determined to eliminate us, particularly Igor. He appeared to have exposed the plot with his spyware.

"Okay, guys, we have to move. Igor and Oksana are somewhere between here and Simferopol. We must extract them. I'll brief you on the way."

I told Fedorov to leave the house as it was and ordered Ketut to get the car.

The Mercedes SUV was the ideal vehicle for the roads we would take. Khabarovsk had told us Igor and Oksana took country roads toward Simferopol. I knew the area quite well for the vineyards in the picturesque hills between Alushta and Simferopol. Igor and I had long enjoyed the region, relishing the wines and liquors produced there.

Fedorov drove up the hills behind Alushta, heading for Rozovyi, a small village famous for its produce.

Then my satellite phone beeped. The base.

"We have the satellite up. The last faint trace of Oksana's phone was near Rozovyi but not in the village. Look out for foes. There is helicopter movement in the area and several cars that don't belong there."

"Copy that. I guess the last signal from Oksana was west of Rozovyi."

"That's right. Maybe five kilometers to the west. We'll try to zoom in, but the FSB is already aware of our hack. We have to be quick."

I thought I knew where they were.

On one of our trips into the hills, Igor had pointed out a farm with a small vineyard that produced illegal Crimean cognac. He had never been there before, and when we had approached we were turned away rather rudely. The farmer had been too afraid of Ukrainian government officials. Igor and I might have looked like officials in our clean clothes and our new car.

"Rozovyi it is," I said. "I remember Oksana telling me about the illegal distilleries and contraband. After all, she grew up in that environment and was once a smuggler."

I called the base again, but there were no new developments. The FSB had shut down access to the Zenit III.

I was slightly amazed at how swiftly the Russians reacted, but then I realized it was our doing. My company, the outfit in Simferopol, was contracted to do exactly that. Sometimes Igor could be too useful.

Fedorov pushed the Mercedes to maximum speed on the narrow country road, while Ketut looked out for trouble from her perch in the rear seat.

We saw action just before reaching the vicinity of Rozovyi. Two dubious-looking dudes were lurking at the intersection before the village. They didn't display weapons, but I was sure they were heavily armed and ready to kill. I told Fedorov to slow down and to approach them as inconspicuously as possible. One of them placed himself in the middle of the road with his right hand raised, indicating we should stop. He must have been left-handed or he wouldn't have used his right hand to signal us—a dangerous mistake.

"Stop!" he shouted, and we rolled up to him at walking speed.

"Gde idti (Where are you going)?" he asked in heavily accented Russian.

Fedorov told him we were from Simferopol and wanted to buy cognac and other spirits. He laughed and pantomimed drinking from a bottle. Ketut and I had our weapons ready close to our seats, all set to kill him and the other asshole.

"Do you speak English?" he asked. He sounded less than confident and probably didn't have clear directions about what to do in such a case.

"Only I speak English," Ketut said from the back seat. "I'm visiting from China. I speak Russian as well. I love this region. It's beautiful."

"Where do you go for cognac?" the thug asked, making a quick rebound after he had found someone who spoke his language.

"I really don't know. Let me translate."

Ketut spoke rapidly in Russian, addressing Fedorov, who replied in even more hurried tones.

"My friend tells me there are several farms that sell cognac. We are looking but no specific place."

Meanwhile, the other thug drew closer to our car. I was ready to take them out, but he yawned and stretched, indicating severe sleep deprivation.

"Okay, go. We are here to check for terrorists. The Russian government needs some English-speaking experts."

A totally pathetic explanation, but we were happy to swallow it. Ketut smiled at them, and the two goons, captivated by her Asian beauty, smiled back and waved us on.

Fedorov resumed driving, and we made good time on the tight gravel road. When we arrived at a junction, he stopped to decide whether to head west or north.

"Where to?"

"I don't know," I said. "Take the right. They might have tried to reach Simferopol. That would be north."

A low-flying helicopter was circling overhead and came pretty close. Ketut opened her window and waved, showing her pretty, smiling face. The aircraft turned once more and then headed west.

We saw a small farmhouse down the road with a huge barn to its left.

The satellite phone beeped. I listened to base while Fedorov approached the farm, showing no hesitation over potential watchers.

"We are on the right track," I said. "Base had contact with Oksana. It must be this farm. She is injured but okay, according to base. Don't slow down, Fed. Just approach as if we were the tourists we claimed to be."

We turned into the apparently deserted homestead, and Fedorov stopped the Mercedes beside the massive barn. I wondered what could be stored or hidden in such a huge building, which looked out of place beside the little farmhouse. A few pieces of farm equipment, an old tractor, and other stuff I couldn't identify were neatly parked outside.

We left the car and strolled toward the farmhouse when a deep voice from the barn stopped us.

"Ne dvigaysya! Ruky vverkh (Don't move! Hands in the air)!"

Vladimir, the vet, had a huge shotgun aimed at us, no doubt ready to fire.

His arms high above his shoulders, Fedorov said, "We are looking for Oksana and Igor."

This straightforward approach was risky, but I agreed it best not to lose more time.

"Who are you?" The shotgun was aimed right at Fedorov's chest and didn't waver. One round from that monster and Fedorov would have been minced meat.

"Please tell them Matt and Fedorov are here."

This was not necessary since the surveillance system had already confirmed our identities. A door to the barn opened, and a beaming Igor emerged.

"It's okay, Vladimir. They are good. This is my boss and his friends."

Slowly Vladimir lowered his World War I meat hacker while Igor pumped my hand vigorously.

"Let's go into the barn. It's not safe out here. They are still flying around in their helicopter, the bastards."

Vladimir ushered us inside where I was a bit surprised to see just a barn with farm tools, bales of hay, and bottles.

"Where is Oksana?" I asked Igor.

"Follow me. In the basement. It's an old Soviet nuke shelter, as if that would have helped," he said with a chuckle.

Behind all the stuff an electric-powered, heavy steel trap door opened, revealing a narrow staircase that led down to the former shelter.

Fedorov rushed down the stairs and called out, "Oksana, we are here."

"Here, Fed. I'm okay. Glad to see you. I tried to call base, but from down here I get only a minimal signal."

"Don't worry about base now. Matt is talking to Khabarovsk right now upstairs."

"The mercenaries might be back. Igor is their main target because they want access to seventh heaven."

"I know, Oksi. Just relax and don't move too much."

He smiled affectionately at her. She was the daughter he never had, and he would give his life for her.

Fedorov could see she was in pain and pressed her gently back down to the field bed she was lying on.

I was upstairs, briefing Khabarovsk and getting information about the action in Virginia. According to Veronica, Mark had left the nunnery and nobody seemed to know where he was headed. Veronica would only say he wanted to clean up the mess.

Classic Mark. He was hot-headed and emotional but the best field agent I had ever met. Once his emotions were under control, he was an extremely cold and ruthless operator.

I had a feeling I knew where he was going. Tatiana was with him, easing my alarm. She was equally effective but much less likely to let her emotions get in the way of sound decisions.

I heard the helicopter approaching and realized we should prepare for a fight. I rushed into the barn.

"Fed, come up here. They are back. Ketut, check your weapon and drive the Mercedes into the barn."

She pushed the huge door open and drove the vehicle into the shelter.

Vladimir came up the stairs with a Degtyarev M27 machine gun.

About 1925, I thought. The round magazine was mounted on top of the gun, a legendary weapon during the winter war against the Nazis.

"Does it work?"

Vladimir gave me a weird look. "It's practically new. Works like a Swiss watch."

"Do you know how to operate it?"

"Leysa cleaned it regularly. She has over two thousand rounds in the basement. We shot it together. I know this baby."

"Don't remain in clear view. Stay in the barn. I don't want them to see your baby too early."

"I just want to kill the bastards."

When he told me about the cold-blooded killing of Leysa, I agreed with him wholeheartedly. He gently caressed the old weapon.

The chopper was getting close, its engine screaming behind the hills to the west as it made a very low approach.

The helicopter appeared behind the hills to the west, and we soon heard the deafening noise of its rotors over the barn and the farmhouse. The pitch of the rotors changed when it performed a tight turn, pointing its nose right at the barn. It slowed down and hovered tightly over the now-deserted space in front of the barn.

My comrades were all in the barn while I took cover behind several huge barrels beside the structure. After what I heard from Igor and Vladimir, I was not in the mood to sacrifice another friend.

The chopper landed softly in the open space between the barn and the main house. The thugs on board couldn't possibly have known about the three tourists who had just arrived.

The pilot let the engine run, the rotors turning idly as the right front and the left rear doors opened. Two men in black jumpsuits climbed out with their guns pointed at the buildings. With the pilot, that made only three of them. That might give us the advantage we were looking for.

An idea crossed my mind, and I hoped Vladimir would not open up with his Degtyarev and accidentally or willingly destroy the chopper. That aircraft was our way out of this place. I needed the pilot either to leave the chopper or die.

"Don't shoot. Don't move," I shouted over the engine noise to the others in the barn. I felt quite safe in doing this given the racket the chopper made.

My Makarov still had its silencer attached, which was not necessary with the chopper's engine running. We had to take out the two thugs without panicking the pilot into a quick takeoff. My position would allow me to sprint to the chopper and take out the pilot while Fedorov and Ketut finished off the other two. The only variable was Vladimir. Fed and Ketut would grasp my plan right away, but if Vladimir opened up, the chopper was done.

Luckily the two mercenaries didn't suspect much trouble and approached the barn door.

"Yest kto nibud zdes (Anybody here)?"

So at least one of them spoke Russian. No accent. He was Russian.

"Yes, I'm here. Hold on. I'm in the back."

Vladena. What the hell was she doing?

Hearing a woman's voice obviously gave them assurance that the barn represented no danger.

The two entered the dark barn, which was my sign. I dashed the twenty meters to the helicopter where the pilot was focused on the barn door. Too late he saw me with my gun pointed at his head through the open switch window in the chopper door.

"Let the engine run and climb out slowly."

I had to shout and he understood I meant business. The pilot, another Russian, slowly opened the door and jumped to the ground.

"You'll pay with your life for this," he threatened.

He was calm and professional, and I had to immobilize him quickly. There was still no indication of any trouble in the barn, but with Fedorov and Ketut in there, I was confident things were under control. As I expected, Ketut materialized in the open door and gave me the thumbs up.

I pressed my gun against the pilot's head. Merely displaying a weapon to a professional adversary could be deadly. If a gun was even an inch from his body, he could divert the weapon in a split second. However, if the gun touched his body there was no possibility of a counteraction. I ordered the pilot into the barn where his two buddies were safely tied up with rope. Due to the noise of the chopper I didn't hear what had happened in the barn.

"Vladena is a hero!"

Fedorov gave her a hug and a salute.

"She brought the two heavies back to the dark where Ketut and I took them out. They are alive but will have headaches like a freight train later."

He laughed and tied the pilot to the tractor with a cord.

I glanced at Ketut. "We have transportation. It's an Ansat. I think I can handle it, but I need a copilot. Are you up for it?"

I knew Ketut had helicopter lessons when she was in Kryilni, as we all had. The Ansat was not a complicated thing to fly, but I might have been a bit rusty. It wasn't a gunship and had very limited military use. The eight-seater was powered by Pratt & Whitney turbines, which made it very reliable.

"I'm up to it. Let's move. I have a feeling we might not be alone for very long."

She was right. We had to create a diversion. The three mercenaries were alive, and I had no intention of adding to my killing record, although Vladimir was hard to restrain. He still was extremely upset over what they did to Leysa. He was trigger happy, and I had to convince him to restrain himself.

We returned to the barn to check on our captives. One was still unconscious, the other groaning with a bloody head wound. The pilot was unharmed, and I made extra sure his rope cuffs were tight enough.

Fedorov and I spoke almost inaudibly.

"Ketut is checking the fuel. It should be enough to reach Sevastopol if we take a straight line. I'll radio Burov to give us clearance."

A side glance confirmed the pilot was listening in attentively.

Once again, I checked the ropes and faked satisfaction. I left the unconscious thug loosely constrained so he could get free once he came to.

"You guys have a good time. We'll send the FSB after you as soon as we land."

The pilot gave me a smirk and said, "Udachnogo poleta (Have a good flight)."

He seemed to be the sharpest of the three, and I was not sure whether he swallowed our little act. The last thing we wanted was to involve the FSB, although we maintained excellent relations with the agency. If the CIA was infiltrated, the much more corrupt FSB might have been an active partner in its game. This would explain why the CI agents could operate undisturbed for two days.

I patted him on the head. "Next time you don't live."

The Ansat was ready to go with Ketut in the pilot seat. I didn't mind. She might have flown such a bird more often than I.

I took the copilot's chair, and Ketut lifted the sleek chopper up, pointed its nose downward, and swept over the barn in a southern direction toward Sevastopol.

About ten kilometers out, Ketut banked the chopper hard to the right, up north to Simferopol.

"We cannot use the airport, of course. Where you want me to go?"

Igor fumbled with Oksana's satellite phone. Two of his engineers would pick us up south of Simferopol.

"I'll guide you there," he said. "It's a forest with several wide clearings, not farmland. It's unlikely anyone will notice."

The flight was short, and I was confident the CI guys didn't know yet about the fate of their comrades.

Igor guided Ketut to a dark forest with tall fir trees.

"There. Go very low toward the tallest tree. There is a clearing with a small pond."

He pointed somewhere ahead, and Ketut followed his instructions.

A small clearing opened up below us, and we could see a tiny pond half covered by the forest.

A few kids fishing looked up stunned at the approaching chopper, which barely missed the top of the trees. They scattered away from the pond and took cover in the trees, or so it appeared.

Ketut banked the helicopter hard to the left and let it hover for a few seconds before it gently touched the grassy ground. A smooth landing.

Igor was out first, talking on the phone.

"They are on the way. Might take them about twenty minutes. We sometimes come out here to grill and to reload our brains. The kids know me."

He stepped close to the edge of the forest and called some names.

Four boys and a girl emerged from the woods.

"Dyadya Igor (Uncle Igor)," they yelled and shook my friend's hand heartily.

"Wow! With a helicopter! Is it yours?"

"It belongs to my friends. They wanted to see your fishing place. Did you catch anything?"

They showed him a basket with a few meager fish in it.

We all left the helicopter, Fedorov supporting a still-dizzy Oksana, the others shaking hands with the kids.

"Want a beer? We have a cooler that Vlada borrowed from the Central Hotel."

Yeah, borrowed, I thought, but I kept my suspicions to myself.

Vlada explained enthusiastically that he had landed a job at the hotel as a night porter.

"The food is great and I can go to the kitchen whenever I'm hungry," he said merrily.

"And he brought us specials today—boiled eggs, ham, bread. Vlada is such a great guy," one of his friends said, adding, "And he got us beer."

They displayed a big cooler filled with bottles of Nevskoe Imperial, one of the better Russian beers. We gladly accepted two bottles, which we shared. I was surprised how thirsty I was. Oksana waved off the beer in favor of a cold Coca-Cola.

Then I took the boys aside and told them they would be better off going home.

"The helicopter belongs to a bunch of very bad and dangerous guys.

We don't want you to get into difficulties when they show up. And don't tell anybody about this."

Igor spoke to Vlada and made it clear that sticking around was very risky. He made the cutthroat sign, which he hoped would convince the teenagers. He persuaded them to help cover the chopper with branches from the fir trees.

"We'll pay you for your help." He took out a wad of rubles.

"I'll give you twelve hundred rubles if you can do it in half an hour."

They immediately began breaking and cutting branches, pulling them out to the chopper and covering the aircraft with a considerable part of the forest. When Igor's engineers finished, the helicopter was invisible from the air. I added another thousand rubles and had to stop them from cutting more trees.

We thanked them, and Igor promised to join them in fishing and grilling very soon.

We entered the two cars, and Igor instructed us where to go. I called Khabarovsk, requesting a plane. The base told me a Gulf from Istanbul was on its way and due to land in Simferopol in less than an hour. Now we had to make sure we got on the plane.

Igor called Burov, apparently a close buddy besides being a valuable client in the FSB.

"No problem. Burov will wave us through without any formalities, but our flight must stay within Russia. An international flight plan will take too much time and hassle."

Igor looked at me inquiringly.

"We'll manage once airborne," I said.

I called base again to arrange for a speedy flight plan to Moscow.

Igor redirected his guys straight to the airport where a black Lexus, the favorite car of FSB brass, was waiting for us. He knew the officers, and clearly they had orders to escort us to the Gulf as soon as it touched down. After a tense wait, we watched the sleek plane on its final approach to Simferopol Airport.

We all bid farewell to Vladimir and Vladena but not before I instructed base to transfer one hundred thousand rubles to their bank account in Alushta. Vladimir pumped my hand, and Vladena had tears in her eyes when we left.

A gate opened on command by the FSB officers, and we were whisked through, rolling onto the tarmac straight to the taxiing Gulf. The hydraulic staircase came down, and in less than two minutes we were on board.

The captain informed us that his flight plan to Moscow was approved and that we were ready for takeoff.

The plane was now under my command, and I told the captain a new flight plan would be presented once we were over the Black Sea.

Once in the air we all felt calm, and a Turkish flight attendant served us ice-cold vodka and brought us menus. Yes, we were hungry. When the captain had his new orders to fly to Frankfurt, we all looked forward to food and rest.

Frank Brewer's suicide stirred a hornet's nest at the firm. The tension in the director's office was so thick one could cut it with a knife.

Mark Shearer's disappearance added to it. Michael Cohen, the CEO of Cohen Industries, intervened with the weak president, according to Pete Aiello, the CIA director. He demanded Mark's immediate arrest, painting him as a dangerous traitor and a threat to national security.

The office was packed to the last chair with the assistant director, Walter Wills; the first assistant director, and several high-ranking agents together with a bunch of analysts.

Early that morning Wills had received a phone call from Mark, who briefly outlined the situation for him. Mark clearly didn't want to be traced although he was on a satellite phone. The NSA monitored all satellite phone conversations in the United States and in hot spots abroad. Though the phone was hard to locate in a short time, especially with the Petrossian software in it, Mark was a cautious operator.

The most disturbing information Mark provided concerned Alliance Contractors in Delaware. Wills knew some members of the president's family were shareholders and consultants to the shady corporation, of which Cohen Industries was the majority owner.

When Mark had spoken with Frank at the restaurant, he had been clever enough to secretly record the conversation. He still had access to sensitive equipment, which he would use only in delicate situations like this one.

He made it clear his life was in danger because of the information he had received.

Wills had once been Mark's protégé at the agency, and that was how he had gotten his position as the number two man, running special ops under Aiello, a man he didn't trust.

Wills briefed the assembled CIA officers, leaving nothing out and creating turmoil in the crowded room.

"Are you saying Shearer is on the run? Why doesn't he come in?"

The director, as usual, had asked the most naïve question, stirring snorts from the others.

Wills raised eyebrows when he replied, "I would run too. Wouldn't you?"

The session got very testy when Wills outlined the role of Alliance Contractors, the French outfit Alliance Ovest, and the Saudi bank Dhahabi Khalij. Although interrupted by the director several times, he didn't budge and ordered the analysts to dig for information on the businesses involved in this mess.

They left the director's office and headed back to work on the issue.

"I have to warn you this will bring diplomatic trouble between us and the other countries involved," Aiello told Wills.

Ever the politician, this presidential appointee was already pissing in his pants contemplating his walk to the White House.

"The president surely has no idea about this evil constellation, as you call it. I have to involve State," Aiello said.

"I might remind you we are the major intelligence agency in the country," Wills said. "If we don't react swiftly, the shit will cover us." He meant the director himself.

"Finish your report before noon. I will schedule a meeting with the president," Aiello replied, as if he had the authority to do so.

When everyone had left, the director grabbed his super-secure phone. He pushed the private Cohen speed dial and got Michael Cohen after the second ring. Cohen knew whenever this phone rang it was an emergency.

"Hello, Pete. What seems to be the problem?"

Despite his casual tone, Aiello could feel the tension in Cohen's voice.

"It's fucking Petrossian. They hacked into Dhahabi Khalij. Shearer apparently is part of it, and Brewer spilled his guts before he took himself out."

"Are you totally secure there? This is a hot potato."

"We are safe. I'm alone and …"

The thick wooden door to his office opened, and his assistant, Melly, stuck her head in.

"Sir, we have a problem. Mr. Al Hamzah from Saudi intelligence is here. He insists on seeing you. Sorry to interrupt, but he is in very bad mood."

Aiello showed his annoyance. "I made it clear I didn't want to be disturbed."

"Sorry, sir."

The door flew open and Al Hamzah stormed into Aiello's office.

"This is important enough for us to talk right away. I assume you want to avoid diplomatic consequences. Our ambassador, Prince Ali, is seeing the secretary of state as we speak."

Aiello waved his assistant away.

The two shook hands, and Aiello asked Al Hamzah to sit.

Al Hamzah was the Mukhabarat man in DC. He was a basically useless intelligence agent, but why should he be good? He got all the intelligence he needed from his US allies, especially from this office.

"You hacked into Khalij!"

"I heard, but it was not us. I would never authorize such a move. It was Petrossian."

"I thought they were finally extinct. All of them are of retirement age, and my sources tell me the firm is shutting down."

"Apparently not. At least not yet. We got intel that they wreaked havoc in Crimea where your clumsy agents were involved too. So don't blame us for your blunder."

Al Hamzah took a deep breath.

"You realize your asshole Brewer may end our careers. I might get away with living in Switzerland, but you could see one of your super max prisons from the inside for the rest of your life."

"We will terminate Shearer. Cohen's people and my trusted operatives are on to it. He is the critical issue. We will have him before nightfall. Tell your ambassador not to raise hell with the secretary. The more you stir the pot, the more the shit falls out."

"You can guarantee Shearer?"

"It's done. The NSA is monitoring his phone, and we will have his location in a couple of hours at the most."

Aiello pushed a button on his desk phone. "Melly, absolutely no interruptions," he barked into the speaker. "Now let's call Cohen and get an update on Shearer."

Cohen again picked up immediately.

"Proceed," he commanded.

"Al Hamzah is with me. We are on speaker."

"Good. Hamzah, you better cooperate with your bunch of camel herders or I'll take you down with the rest of us."

Cohen clearly wanted to show who was in command and who was in the position to throw insults.

"My men are ready," Al Hamzah said. "They are the best assassins in the country. We need a location. Two of my agents are watching Shearer's house in Georgetown right now."

"You are just too stupid! He will never show up there. It's a waste of manpower."

Cohen was enraged, and Aiello had never heard him like that.

"Send your idiots to Richmond and tell them to be on standby there. Telll them to be as inconspicuous as possible and not to wear carpets on their tiny heads. Fucking Petrossian is slightly ahead of us now, and they are good at kicking your fucking Arab asses. And so am I if something goes wrong!"

They heard deep breathing on the speaker. Then Cohen said, "Pete, make sure you get the NSA downloads streaming. Shearer needs to communicate to stay alive. Report every detail to me on this line. I have the best out in the field, and we don't play with amateurs. Some of my contractors are ex- marines. Two of them disappeared last night. I'm sure the Petrossian gramps had their fingers in it. We are trying to break their cloud, but my engineers are stuck, and I understand that not even the NSA was able to get in. So you know what to do. The key to our staying alive is to take out Shearer. Go to work!"

Cohen hung up, leaving the CIA director and his Saudi colleague speechless.

Al Hamzah stood up.

"I'll leave now and get my men ready. Make sure you get a location on Shearer. Then he is as good as gone."

Aiello sunk in his leather chair, contemplating the consequences if Shearer was not found quickly.

Fucking Cohen with his war plans, Aiello thought. When Cohen got him aboard he was a Republican senator from Arkansas. Cohen promised him the CIA directorship and of course paid him handsomely from the beginning. Aiello had developed reservations after he was fully briefed on Cohen's plan. CI's research into mini nuclear warheads was far advanced, and two of them had been tested underground in North Korea. They had paid a heavy price in transferring the technology to the crazy North Koreans with the stipulation that the nukes would first be used in the Middle East. They had also paid a hefty amount of cash.

When Aiello had mentioned his reservations, Cohen had threatened him with all kinds of repercussions. This had brought him back on track, and now he was a traitor and a hostage.

He called the head analyst, but he had no news from the NSA or from the field agents blanketing Virginia. It was illegal for the CIA to operate on US soil, and so Aiello had to make sure only his most trusted agents were working on the situation.

Aiello took out one of his adored Havanas and lit it up. He found this was the best way to relax his overstressed brain.

Then his phone rang.

"Sir, it's Miller from surveillance. We've got a location on Shearer. He just made a call to another satellite phone from the Norfolk area. The NSA is trying to pin it down."

"Thanks, Miller."

He hung up and called Cohen.

Men were on the way, and the net around Shearer was tightening.

Shearer had been in naval intelligence before joining the CIA. He might still have connections in Norfolk. Aiello's brain was overheating again.

He decided not to inform Al Hamzah since his agents might just fuck it all up.

His request to see the president had been approved, but Aiello regretted asking for a meeting. With Shearer's time dwindling, everything seemed to be falling into line. He had to rethink the briefing he would give the president. However, Brewer's suicide demanded an explanation. Stress, guilt in another form, sex? Aiello was good at misleading people, and the president was even better at being deceived.

Aiello ordered Melly to get his car. All seemed to be fine. But before he left he called Cohen once more and told him about his meeting with the president. It was good to display loyalty to the mighty industrialist by telling him all he knew. Aiello was sure tonight he would sleep well again.

CHAPTER 18

FRANKFURT AIRPORT, EARLY MORNING

The Gulf G280 landed shortly after midnight at Frankfurt Airport. Igor prepared the necessary Schengen visas for Ketut and Oksana. Fedorov and I used our passports to get through immigration. It was unclear where we should go from there.

"We have to get Oksana to a hospital," Fedorov said. "She is better but is still losing blood. I know where to go."

He was very worried about his protégé and wanted her in safe hands. He called a German doctor friend who agreed to pick her up at the airport. Dr. Fischer arrived minutes later and packed Oksana into his Mercedes.

"Keep your head up, girl!" I said. "We'll get in touch as soon as it's safe. We need you back!"

I gave her a kiss. We all were sad to leave her behind.

After a long conversation, Galina Mikhailova, the head of Petrossian, advised us to rest for a few hours in Frankfurt while she decided on our next move. Apparently, Mark Shearer needed assistance, but Galina assured us he was in good hands. Looking at Fedorov and myself, I wondered how old these good hands were. She agreed with our decision to leave Oksana with Dr. Fischer.

"He is a good guy. Oksana will be safe with him.""

We got a suite at an airport hotel and let Igor set up communications via satellite phone. Frankfurt was an NSA hot spot, one of the crucial entry points into Europe where the NSA monitored millions of phone calls, emails, and text messages.

We drank coffee by the gallons while Igor tested his laptop connection and made sure seventh heaven was untouched. He gave me thumbs up, signaling we could communicate for at least fifteen minutes before the NSA might be on to us.

I called Galina and inquired about Mark's situation. He was with Tatiana Morozova and Veronica Maximina, the deadly nun, at a Norfolk motel near the navy base. I had to agree he was in good hands, but even the best hands can be broken.

Although I knew the dangers, I dialed Mark's phone. He picked up after one ring.

"Hi, Matt! Glad to hear your voice. Where are you? We could use some help. I'm afraid they are close. Let's keep this short."

"We are in Frankfurt, on the way. Khabarovsk told me you are near the harbor. Did you fill in Walter? He is the only one you can trust."

"He is informed and in danger too. I told him to join us for the time being. But you know him. Righteous and honorable. He is preparing his report, which might be his death sentence. Now I hope the NSA is listening in." Mark chuckled.

"Keep your head down and stay with the girls. They are good and not afraid to pull the trigger. We should be there in about ten hours."

I disconnected. I had been on the line too long. The NSA would be on high alert for us.

Igor was downloading more files from Cohen and related companies, but that was a danger too.

"Igor, stop it. It's not safe."

"I know. They are already on to me, but I diverted them to a server in California. I hope that keeps them busy for a while."

"Time to go. Galina gave us the green light for the United States."

I made sure Igor logged out. Then I went to the window overlooking the hotel entrance. I saw two black SUVs pulling up.

"I'm afraid they are here. Igor, you know you are their main target."

Everyone jumped up and ran to the window.

Six guys in suits entered the lobby, all bald or with short hair. They were ex-military, probably special forces, judging by their appearance.

We had to move. We made sure the silencers were securely attached to our Makarovs and the magazines were fully loaded. Igor packed his laptop and stored all his equipment in a bag. Then we left the suite, running to the staircase. I knew they would also use the stairs and realized I had made a mistake in taking a top-floor room. We proceeded one floor down, and then I told everyone to take cover and to keep quiet.

We heard footsteps below us and estimated maybe half of them were coming our way. We had our weapons ready and would shoot without hesitation. They were there to kill us.

Then Ketut made a move that took us all by surprise. She opened the door to the hallway, spoke in German, and laughed.

"Ja, ja, ich bring die Bettwäsche hoch. Mach Dir keine Sorgen (Yes, I will bring the linen up. Don't worry)," she said, opening and shutting the door.

I realized she wanted Cohen's men to think a hotel maid was the only person on the stairs. *Clever girl but a bit reckless*, I thought. She took some noisy steps and shut the stairway door decisively.

We all waited for movement from below.

"Just a maid. We are clear."

Americans. They were coming up now, feeling safe, and therefore taking hard, fast strides. We were ready with our weapons pointed toward the lower landing, and when we saw them I knew Ketut's effort had paid off. The four of them were bunched together.

It took us six shots to put them down. I noticed Ketut was the only one taking head shots, while Fedorov and I went for center mass. The pretty Balinese was a stone-cold killer.

We emptied their pockets for IDs and carefully went down the stairs, our weapons at the ready.

Igor packed all the wallets in his laptop case. We would have to inspect them later.

Seven floors down we reached a service door that led to a huge kitchen. We strolled past the wide-eyed cooks and helpers to another door that opened into a delivery area. A food van was parked just behind the door. Igor ran to the driver's door and put his thumbs up.

"Keys," he said, smiling.

I was proud of my friend. Although he was not a trained agent, he had a professional's cool and was not the nerd many people took him for.

Fedorov jumped into the driver's seat with me beside him, and Ketut and Igor sitting in the back amid the aromatic delicacies the company was delivering to the hotel.

"I give it ten minutes max. Then we have to change transport," I said.

With Fedorov driving much too slowly for my taste, we left the lot and entered a road that ran parallel to a runway at the airport.

"The airport is out," I said, and Fedorov nodded his assent.

"Do you know how to get to railway station?" I asked.

"I know. I was stationed here for three years. Frankfurt is like my hometown," Fedorov said.

"As soon as you see taxis, stop. We can't stay in this car."

Taxis were no problem. The airport road was packed with them.

Fedorov parked the van about fifty meters from the first Mercedes cab. We strolled up to it and told the driver to bring us to the Hauptbahnhof.

"Do you take dollars?" I asked. "We are short in euros." In fact, we had none.

"No problem, sir. Money is money."

He laughed. I noticed he was not a German. Pakistani probably. Frankfurt was like New York.

It took us more than half an hour to reach the huge railway station where I paid the driver and gave him a handsome tip.

"You shouldn't have done that," Fedorov said. "High tip and he remembers us."

He was right, and I realized I would need to remember the rules if we wanted to keep the upper hand against our foes.

We entered the high, wide hall at the Frankfurt station, walking casually like a group of friends going on a trip.

"Where to?" Ketut asked.

"Düsseldorf," Fedorov answered. "I know this region very well, and Düsseldorf is a great place to vanish in the open. However, we need a flight ASAP."

"We make arrangements on the train. The airport here in Frankfurt is out of the question. I'll call Galina from the train. We need another phone. The satellite phone is painting red lights all over the map right now."

Igor again surprised me with his quick thinking. He took one of the wallets out of his laptop case and produced several credit cards.

"Let's use these. They might not be on to them yet."

"Good thinking, Igor."

I grabbed the wallet and went to what I thought was a ticket booth. The girl behind the window directed me to an ATM-style box where I could purchase tickets with my credit card. I decided to let Igor do the job, and he returned with four first-class tickets for the train to Düsseldorf.

"Where is Ketut?"

I was edgy not seeing her with us, but she came back from the ladies' room with a mischievous smile on her pretty face.

"I got a phone. A lady placed it on the sink while she put on makeup."

Again, great girl!

The train was leaving in a few minutes, and we were all seated in the comfortable first-class section, compliments of a Hank Willers from Chicago. I wondered how Igor had gotten the PIN for the credit card so quickly. He explained that he had hacked some of the cards while we rode in the taxi and said it had taken him less time than drinking a cup of coffee. Yes, he was one of the greatest hackers in the universe.

I worried that Willers's bank would call about every transaction, but Igor had taken care of that by adding the special security code for transactions done overseas.

While we relaxed on the train, I called Galina.

"You called up hell at the Steigenberger! A hotel employee found the bodies and summoned the police. The hotel is swarming with uniforms, and the Germans have put out a terrorist bulletin. I know what you need. The old taxi"—she referred to the Gulf G280—"is out of order. Tell me where."

Fedorov took over.

"You remember where we had the best sauerbraten in 1999? We were celebrating your promotion to head for Western Europe."

"How could I ever forget? Okay, I'll send a text with details."

"Where the hell was that?" I inquired.

"Düsseldorf, a place called Mullers and Fest. It became my favorite restaurant in Germany. The food was so delicious and heavy there that it always called for double shots of vodka afterward."

"Let's have lunch there. The dead thugs will pay for it."

We all agreed. We were hungry and tired, and we Petrossians understood that hiding in the open was the safest way to avoid trouble.

Once in Düsseldorf, we got a table overlooking the Koenigsallee, the city's famous shopping lane. The restaurant was packed with rich-looking people, and our clothes, unchanged since we left Crimea, made us look less privileged. But, credit to the Germans, we were Americans in the company of a pretty Asian woman, and that gave us access to one of the prime tables.

Fedorov was not exaggerating about the food. It was fantastic. I ordered an Italian red wine from which Ketut abstained. She was too tired to enjoy wine, and I appreciated her attitude. However, Fedorov and I knew we could handle a glass of wine and stay alert. Again, the idea was to hide in the open and to behave as if nobody on earth was looking for us.

Although I enjoyed the food and our present circumstances, I was anxious to hear from Galina. While we finished dessert, and Fedorov resisted the temptation of a grappa, the satellite phone beeped. I rushed to the men's room and answered Galina's call.

"The Dassault will touch down at Zurich Airport in an hour. You are cleared to fly back to Russian territory. You are listed as passengers under your passport names."

"Russian territory" meant the United States in old Petrossian jargon. "Our passports" signified that we were to use others. As if I wouldn't know. Maybe Galina had lost a tad of trust in our capabilities. I would have to have a serious talk with her.

I killed the message without replying.

We had to proceed to the airport quickly.

Igor paid the bill with a card that belonged to him but was impossible to trace. We decided not to use the credit cards of the deceased since our pursuers might have started monitoring any transactions.

The business jet lounge was expecting us. We felt safe. So far, no sign of troubles. Maybe they bought the Zurich tale if they were listening.

I switched the TV to CNN and saw a live report from the airport hotel in Frankfurt. The police had identified us as likely Chechen terrorists being pursued by a special American anti-terror squad. My ass! But this disinformation showed me again how powerful the Cohen-Cavity network was.

The captain, a guy I had never met before, entered the lounge and told us our flight was ready. He was French and said our trip to Washington, DC, would take six hours and ten minutes. I would have to give him a new destination during the flight.

We were airborne within minutes, and Fedorov and I finally ordered ice-cold vodka, which was served by a pretty French girl. Ketut and Igor were fast asleep, which gave me the chance to strip naked and to wash my rather dirty and used body in the spacious lavatory.

At ten it was time to beep Mark. I prayed he was alive and would answer my call.

To fly to Norfolk was too risky with the Cohen gang, the CIA, and probably half a dozen other agencies combing the area for Mark.

Thus we decided on Richmond, Virginia. I informed the captain, who was obviously prepared for a change of flight plan. He confirmed the new destination without delay.

The flight over the Atlantic Ocean was peaceful, and we all fell fast asleep in the comfortable leather seats.

The captain's voice woke me up and saved me from a nightmare in which the Cohen thugs took us prisoner and tortured Igor for access to seventh heaven.

The French flight assistant brought me freshly brewed coffee and some Danish.

Beside me Fedorov stretched and yawned.

"Where are we?"

"About an hour out. It's time to talk to base."

I drank the hot, fresh coffee, chewed a Danish pastry, and dialed Galina.

CHAPTER 19

RICHMOND AND NORFOLK, VIRGINIA

"We have your location and a satellite over your destination. All looks quiet except for some commotion at Veronica's nunnery. I had brief contact with Shearer. I've sent his location to Igor. The NSA is hyperactive and tries to enter us on all fronts, but we are safe so far. A car is ready for you at landing. No names. He will get in touch with you. I suggest you turn to CNN's live feed from the nunnery. Some assholes burned it down and killed at least three nuns. You will find a very trigger-crazy Veronica. Try to calm her as best you can."

This was probably the longest conversation I had ever had over a satellite phone with our top lady.

I switched on the TV and watched the report from the nunnery. The building was a blazing inferno. Veronica's life work was now up in flames. Knowing her, I realized the task of calming her might be a huge one. She certainly had motivation to kill.

Igor and Ketut awoke and were shocked to see what had happened to Veronica's haven for children.

"I'm going to kill them with my bare hands," Igor muttered. I hoped it would never come to that.

The Dassault took a narrow turn to the left and landed smoothly at Richmond International.

We were whisked through the VIP immigration and were met by a young black guy.

"Your car is ready for you, fifty. Follow me."

What? He couldn't have been more than thirty years old, while all the Petrossians I still knew were beyond retirement age.

"My name is Bernhard Mathison. I've been with the firm for more than ten years, running a small op in DC. It's a legit business with a strong link to the base."

He smiled, and his snow-white teeth almost blinded me.

"Do you know where we are heading?"

"Yes, sir. I have been briefed. I'm supposed to be backup. I'll monitor the area and inform you of any movement. I'll occupy a room just opposite your target. Here is the information."

He handed me an envelope with the address of Mark Shearer and the two seasoned female Petrossians.

"I took the liberty of programming the navigation system in the car, but I advise, not to go too close first."

Wise ass, I thought, though it was good to finally meet a young Petrossian.

"What's your code?" I asked Bernhard.

"I'm seventy-eight, sir."

"Cut the sir, Bernie! May I call you Bernie? We all go by first names and codes."

"Sorry, sir. I mean fifty."

"From now on with phone or any other communication, just codes. Understand?"

He gave me his blinding smile, and I was starting to like him.

"Oh, by the way, forty-nine ordered me to make some purchases—personal stuff. It's all in the car. I have reserved three rooms at the Silverstar Motel about thirty miles east of here."

We were opening Christmas presents in the Cadillac Escalade—jeans, T-shirts, underwear, shaving kits, socks, and Timberlands for all of us.

"Oh, I can't wait to finally take a shower," Ketut said.

She hugged her things as if they were gifts from heaven.

Bernie had thought of everything. We found an arsenal of weapons in the Escalade, well hidden in the doors and easy to retrieve. But first things first.

I let Ketut drive because Route 64 was an easy stretch and the perfectly programmed navigation system made it even simpler to find the Silverstar Motel. I wondered how Galina had found the place and whether it was more than just a spot to shower, shave, and change.

I would find out soon enough. After just twenty minutes the navigation system started speaking in a smoky female voice.

"You are approaching your destination in two hundred yards. Keep right."

We saw the huge silvery star to our right, and Ketut took the exit that led straight to the motel. Bernie was already there and guided us to the last cabins on the left, away from the highway.

"Here, rooms 212, 214, and 216. Sorry I couldn't get four. The motel was heavily booked. But forty-nine insisted on the place."

Fedorov and I took 212, Igor and Ketut the others.

I finally felt fresh again after a long shower and a shave, and I waited for Fedorov to clean himself up. He came out of the shower, grinning and in a good mood.

"I know now how dirty Crimea is. I think I left a ton of dirt in there," he said.

Through the blinds I noticed Bernie sitting in his car. He had parked at a discreet distance but with a full view of the cabins. I decided he was tougher than he looked. Galina wouldn't involve an inexperienced youngster in this situation.

Ketut had quickly washed and changed and was knocking on the connecting door.

"Are you guys ready or still applying makeup?"

She was in good spirits! I knew Galina wanted to create this effect on us. It was very important not to enter a critical situation in a lousy mood or a bad temper.

"I'm ready, but Fedorov is still smearing lipstick on his big mouth."

Ketut opened the door and I was stunned by how lovely she was.

Then there was a heavy knock on the door. Fedorov glanced outside at Bernie, who was sitting calmly in his car, and I held my best friend, the Makarov, in my hands. Bernie's posture gave Fedorov enough assurance, and he gave me the thumbs up.

I cracked open the door, standing beside it at the wall with my weapon ready. Then I heard a voice I knew from many years earlier.

"It's just me, Matt. I bring some intel. Let me in."

Walter Wills, the number two at Langley.

I pulled him in and gave him a bear hug.

"Walter, this is a great surprise!"

Walter was the CIA official who made it possible for Petrossian to operate on US soil. He had always been friendly and supportive. He was one of the few people I could trust right now.

"Let's make it short. I took official leave for a day to set this up. Galina asked me to assist you, but I must be back at Langley tonight. All hell broke loose after Brewer's suicide, and practically every agency in the United States is hunting Mark Shearer. Now listen good."

He took a deep breath, and Ketut handed him some mineral water.

"We know Mark is somewhere in Norfolk and can't move. The firms have deployed more than hundred agents in the area, while the NSA has put top priority on communications in and out of Norfolk. I also know he is with Veronica and the daughter of Vitaly Morozov, Tatiana. They are very good but against this army I'm afraid not good enough. Once you find out where Mark is holed up, you must create a diversion. Galina could get information through to Mark. I have two more black Escalades on standby for you, but this might end badly. We must get Mark out of there alive. He is on the top of the hit list just like Igor here."

He shook hands with Igor and complimented him on his skills.

"I know where he is," Igor said. "I got Galina's message just a few minutes ago. It went through about two hundred servers and is not traceable. Mark is in an old Petrossian safe house near the harbor, and according to Galina, only Veronica knew of its existence. I have the address."

Walter was quiet obviously anxious.

"With Mark and Igor dead, the Cohens can proceed with their deadly plan, so it's imperative that these two are protected 100 percent. I suggest Igor come with me. I'll place him in one of our safe houses far away from DC and Langley."

"Over my dead body!" Igor said.

"That's exactly what might happen, Igor," Walter replied. "They want you and Mark dead. You have the entire file on their ops, and Mark has Brewer's testimony recorded."

"No way! I'm with the task force. I won't hide in a cozy house somewhere in the countryside while my friends risk their lives. That's final."

Igor made me proud and worried at the same time.

"What will happen if they get you? What about the files?" I asked him.

"No problem. They're in seventh heaven, and I already gave access to base."

So this was settled. I knew I couldn't convince Igor to go with Walter. Besides, a CIA safe house might not have been the securest place at the moment.

"Igor comes with us and I guarantee his safety," I told Walter.

"Okay, if you say so. I must fly back. My plane is in Richmond, and I'm not sure whether the director is monitoring my moves. We are not friends." He embraced us all. "Oh, before I forget, the Cohen people are taking the lead in this operation. They will do the killing, or at least try."

He never mentioned Cavity, and I wondered whether he knew anything about the group's status. I let the question go for the time being.

Walter opened the door and a blue Richmond taxi pulled up. *Ever the field agent*, I thought.

Bernie made the "all safe" sign, looking a bit like a hockey referee, and we prepared to leave. We didn't have to show our faces at the reception desk. Bernie took care of everything.

With the sun setting, we traveled on Route 64 toward Norfolk. My satellite phone beeped. Galina.

"I assume you have the destination. Base accessed your navigation system, which will give you the safe house you will use for the diversion. Now for Igor. We need him safe for communication. Therefore we have arranged a room at the Courtyard Hotel. No beach view but clear sight to Mark Shearer's hideout. Proceed to your place first. It provides a view of the safe house but only from the flat roof. From there Igor takes a cab to the Courtyard. The room key is at our safe house. No check-in needed. Clear?"

Very clear. I was relieved Igor would be out of the firing line.

The trip to the safe house was uneventful. I drove the Escalade into the open garage, and Igor walked over to a Patriot cab, the only car on the nearly deserted street. The Petrossian plan was proceeding like clockwork.

Igor drove away with his laptop, his satellite phone, and other equipment I never understood.

Gallina assured us the Cohen people hadn't pinpointed Mark's hideout, which was why the street was quiet. She said Khabarovsk was planting "electronic rumors," whatever the hell that meant, which would point these thugs to the north of us. However, she warned that might not keep them at bay for long. We had to move.

I could see the safe house from the porch. The tranquil street gave me the creeps. What if they were in the adjacent houses and took us out as soon as we stuck out our noses?

Anyway, no time to show nerves.

"Let's go. Weapons ready."

Then I followed one of my spontaneous, usually brilliant hunches. I was still in good spirits, which is constructive but can also make a person less sensitive to natural alerts. However, my legendary sixth sense had saved my life numerous times. Or so I believed.

"Ketut, you stay here. Monitor the area and keep us informed via satellite phone."

I pointed to the small suitcase Bernie had delivered. Where was he by the way? I told Ketut to ready some of the grenades and to prime the RPG, which came in an unobtrusive plastic tube. It was a Russian RPG 30, the Abrams killer, with four grenades.

Holy hell! Did they want us to start World War III?

As Ketut unpacked the arsenal, I wondered how the RPG might fall into place.

I gave Ketut a cautious kiss on her forehead. Then Fedorov and I casually strolled out of the house, both of us carrying heavy briefcases filled with ammunition and additional guns.

I was sure Veronica or Tatiana already had us in their crosshairs, and I winked to show we were aware of that.

The safe house was only two hundred yards from our place, but the longer we walked on this eerie street the more sweat we produced. My sixth sense was screaming. I grabbed Fedorov and pulled him on a run for the last twenty yards.

"We have been made! Run!"

We reached the door, which Tatiana opened and shut hard behind us.

"They are here, two houses down just behind the bend," she said.

"Behind the bend" gave me hope they couldn't see us when we arrived. Ketut might be safe.

"Quick! We have a way out. A boat."

Mark and Veronica appeared, and we hurried down the stairs to a short landing where a Zodiac, with two heavy Evinrudes at the aft, was moored. My phone beeped but I ignored it. We jumped into the Zodiac, and Veronica pulled away from the jetty at full speed.

Right then the house above us exploded, glass, concrete, bricks, and wood flying high into the air and raining down on us like hell fire. Apparently we were not the only ones with an RPG unless the house had been rigged before and they wanted us to do together.

The Zodiac flew the Elizabeth River doing at least forty mph.

"Fuck!" Veronica said. "We are on our own. Dunno where to go from here."

"Sister!"

I gave her a deep frown. "That isn't the kind of language a pious nun should use!"

My lame rebuke seemed to relieve the tension, and everybody laughed, though the response was a bit forced.

"Up to the Jordan Bridge, then left into Lakeside Park. I'll alert Bernie," Fedorov said.

He pushed buttons on his phone and shouted inarticulately into it.

"Bernie is on his way up Bainbridge Boulevard. He will be at Lakeside. Don't worry! My former territory."

Veronica made a hard-left turn under the Jordan Bridge, and we entered the inlet to Lakeside Park.

Lakeside was just a few hundred yards away. I saw Bernie standing on the rocky waterfront, waving his arms wildly. He stood next to his Chevy.

A few seconds later the Zodiac hit the shore hard, and the heavy inflatable rushed up the pebbles toward Bernie.

"Quick! No one was tailing me, so I think we are safe, but I have bad news."

He looked as if the teacher might spank him.

"What is it?" I barked.

"They got Ketut. As soon as you entered the safe house three of them went into her place. I couldn't do anything. I was too far away."

Shit! That changed everything. I was not ready to sacrifice the brave, noble, and yes, pretty woman, and I knew what a bargaining chip she would be. Shit, shit!

We all crammed into Bernie's Chevy.

"Where to?" Fedorov asked.

"I don't know," Bernie said, pushing the Chevy hard.

"Let me make a call," Tatiana said.

She took her satellite phone and punched in a number that obviously wasn't in her speed dial.

"Da, eto ya, Tatiana." She spoke rapidly in a language I had trouble understanding.

"Armenian," Fedorov said.

"We will go to Kitty Hawk, North Carolina," Tatiana announced. "It's a long trip, but we will be safe there."

"We have to get Ketut and Igor first," I said.

"Matt, you know better than that," Tatiana said.

She gave me a stern glance and I knew she was right. If we didn't communicate with the Cohen people, Ketut might be safe.

Then my phone beeped. Igor.

"What the hell happened? Are you guys okay?"

Igor remained undetected, and I planned to keep it that way.

"Igor, stay put. We are fine. Your room is safe. Wait for further instructions. We are on the way to a new location. Don't make a move. Enjoy the hotel but just the room. Absolutely no communication!"

I disconnected and turned to Tatiana.

"Who were you talking to? Petrossian?"

"A friend. Armenian." She laughed loudly. "You will be surprised. He is retired, but of course a high-ranking Russian mafia boss never is. He has a huge network that might be able to help us."

"It's Valenti, right?" Veronica said with a snort.

"The one and only," Tatiana shot back.

"Valenti Assarian, former boss of the Armenian East Coast mafia. At least that's what the press said. Heroin, cocaine, prostitution, arms. What the hell, Tatiana?"

"He is an old friend and I trust him. And by the way, his main business is mining. The rest is rumors. And just to put you at ease, he is not mafia but one of us. The mafia rumors were planted deliberately."

"I read about him," Bernie said. "The FBI tried for years to build a case, but to no avail. He really is in mining. There are even pictures of his estate in Kitty Hawk. Splendid!"

I decided not to dig any further and tried to place at least a piece of my ass on the back seat of the crowded Chevy. If this went on for hours, I would need physical therapy on arrival.

"Don't use your phones anymore," Tatiana said. "Valenti has state-of-the-art communications equipment that we can use once in the house. They were on to us via our calls. I hope Igor stays quiet."

I hoped so too. I said a short prayer.

The drive all the way on Route 158 took us almost four hours. When we entered the mile-long bridge that led to Kitty Hawk, I looked forward to relief from the pain in my lower back. The two tough ladies beside me were also suffering.

"At the Walmart turn left. Look for a sign saying 'Duck Woods Country Club.'" Tatiana was guiding Bernie.

There it was. The Duck Woods Country Club. The area didn't appear too prosperous, but a few houses looked like palaces from a D movie.

"Take the next right. There, the gate. Pull up."

We stopped in front of a huge iron gate with more cameras than glittery balls on a Christmas tree.

A guard approached the gate from the inside. I saw no weapon but I was sure he was packing.

Tatiana left the car, which provided me with immediate relief. Veronica felt the same, letting a long sigh go.

Tatiana exchanged a few words with the guard and the gate swung open.

The house we saw when we entered was not the residence but the guardhouse. It was larger than my house in Kuala Lumpur.

We drove half a mile to the real residence, a palace, or maybe more like a citadel with a turret commanding the site.

Bernie stopped the car near a door that looked like a cathedral entrance. It was open and a white-haired gentleman in a gray suit stood in front of it. He must have been in his eighties.

Tatiana rushed to him and they hugged like father and daughter.

"Tata, moy malen'kiy golub (my little dove)," he said. "Welcome to my humble home. It's yours and your friends'."

Humble home? I thought. *In some cases, crime seems to pay.* I still didn't get the sense that he was one of us.

Valenti led us into a huge hall. I could see a golf course and the water behind it.

"Val, we are so grateful for your help," Tatiana said. "We need to communicate with our network, and then we can have a drink with you. Please."

"Of course. Follow me. Whatever calls you make, they originate in Russia. Don't worry. Are all these people ours?"

Valenti looked at us. "This must be Fedorov," he said.

Tatiana nodded and gave Valenti a kiss on the cheek.

Valenti led us to a thick metal door in the great hall. He pressed his hand on a reader and the door slid open. I was amazed to see a communications chamber that outstripped even the communications center in Khabarovsk. It was cold in there and, besides the hum of computers, very quiet.

"This is the safest room in the country. Half-meter concrete walls and the ceiling even thicker. No sound can escape, and all communication is totally secure. You can't use your satellite phones or mobile phone in here, but my lines are directly connected to our own satellite. I learned a lot from Petrossian," Valenti said, winking at Tatiana. "I'll talk to you later. Now I'll let you work."

Valenti left the room, the metal door slidinfg shut behind him.

Tatiana had obviously been here before. She sat behind a console with a huge monitor in front of it and operated equipment only Igor would understand. Within seconds she produced Galina's face on the screen.

The rest of us stood behind Tatiana and waved hello to the top Petrossian.

"Good that you are there. I must remind you that after you leave this place, you will forget about it."

We briefed her in detail with Ketut the top priority. Galina listened without interrupting, and then we stopped to hear her counsel.

"We've got to move quickly on Ketut, and I advise you to accept Valenti's assistance."

"The mafia?" I dared to ask.

"No, Matt, not the mafia. Tatiana will give you an explanation, which all of you again will erase from your memories. We are monitoring all the moves of the Cohen and Cavity people. I don't know for sure, but we might have a location for Ketut. Since her captors can't communicate with us, we have to take the initiative.

"I have extracted Igor from his hotel. He will join you in about two hours. As we speak, he is being packed into a chopper on the rooftop of his hotel. The pilot is one of us. I suggest you listen closely to Valenti, but first let Tatiana brief you so you don't think a man who is the guiding star of Petrossian is somehow involved in the mafia. Get back to me after the briefing. I'll send all info about Ketut in the next few minutes. When Igor arrives, he can handle that."

Connection gone. We stood like schoolchildren who had watched the most amazing magic trick.

"I will brief you on Valenti," Tatiana said, "but first you must swear all I say is just for now and will be deleted from the little hard disks you have in your heads."

We were still speechless and nodded our assent.

"Valenti is the grandson of Gavril Petrossian, the founder of our organization. His mother was Eva Nikolayeva Assarian, a Russian Armenian princess of enormous wealth, just like her husband. After the Armenian genocide and the fall of the Russian czar and his family, Gavril moved to the Far East and started to build the establishment we call Petrossian. His influence was so great that not even the Soviets went after him. In fact, they used him on diplomatic missions to the West on many occasions. He became close to Molotov, the first Soviet to know about the secret society Petrossian. Molotov recruited agents away from Felix Dzershinsky, the all-powerful head of the KGB. Molotov saw the value of a parallel outfit to the KGB, a clumsy, incompetent organization at the time, and that's why most of our older agents are of Russian—though not Soviet—origin.

"Valenti, for many years, was number one. He invented the number system.

"He made Petrossian reputable and trustworthy in the shady world of intelligence. Most of you are all old enough to understand what a vital role we played during the Cold War. Without us in the middle, hidden from the eyes of prying newscasters and journalists, the Cold War might well have become a hot one."

She gave Fedorov a bright smile.

"Fed, you remember what you did in Cuba during the missile crisis. You, we, Petrossian, turned the boats back. It was not Kennedy. It was us. But we have never wanted credit for what we do. I think the training in Kryilny, that godforsaken place north of Khabarovsk, has done us all good. And the toughest agent ever to come out of there is Valenti. Do you still have the medal Khrushchev gave you in New York?"

Fedorov nodded and I thought I saw a tear in his eyes. But no, not stone-cold Fedorov. I smiled.

A little hesitation showed in Tatiana's face.

"He is my uncle, my mother's brother. For all these years we have had to avoid direct contact until now. Believe me, if somebody can help us, and in this case the world, it's Valenti. He is still extremely rich and probably wealthier than ever before, but not from mafia activities. We deliberately kept the rumors alive. As you know, Petrossian was funded by numerous governments, though more or less under the table. But the global picture has changed. The European Union now stretches far into the east, and more and more naïve Americans believe only the United States can save the planet. Government funds are drying up and so is Petrossian. Bernie is one of a handful of dedicated, clever young people motivated enough to take on the organization's functions. Valenti is financing Petrossian's inevitable funeral. We are the last, which means we must be the best. Veronica and I have dedicated our lives to this case, and so have you. We have also risked them many times. We are the only impartial and independent intelligence service the world has ever had."

She smiled her fetching smile and led us out of the chamber.

"Ketut is our top priority," I said, "but right now we deserve a drink. Let's relax until Igor starts communicating with the bastards."

Sitting on a covered porch the size of a hockey rink, Valenti invited us to try a very rare vodka.

We put down our vodka glasses when we heard a clattering sound over the ocean. A huge Bell 525 approached Valenti's estate and landed softly on the manicured grass just below us. Igor jumped out of the front door with his laptop bag around his shoulders and ran up to the portico.

"They got Ketut and you just sit here and drink vodka?"

"Calm down, Igor. That's why you are here now. We know what they want, and you have to talk to them."

Valenti got up and extended his hand, which Igor reluctantly shook.

"Welcome to my home, Igor. I have heard a lot about you. This might be our last mission, and you will play the most important role in it."

Igor looked inquisitively at me and I nodded.

"Okay, what do I have to do?"

He would never ask "Who are you?" or "Why am I here?" I loved Igor.

"First, sit down and tell us what you have seen," I said. "Did you see the guys entering our safe house?"

I had to appease him before he went into the communications chamber and started hacking.

Igor filled us in.

"Three or four guys entered the safe house after you left. I tried to call you, but it was too late. When the other house blew up, I couldn't see anything, but I knew they had taken Ketut."

Taking him by the arm, Valenti said, "Come with me, Igor, and do your best. We don't need to communicate with them right now, but hack into everything."

"I'm limited." He pointed to his laptop.

"No, you are not," Fedorov said with a laugh. "Go with one. He will show you."

"One? Like Petrossian one?"

Igor looked at Valenti with his eyes wide.

"Mr. Assarian is one of us. Well, actually we are part of him," Fedorov said. "Explanation later, Igor. Just go and do what you are good at."

Valenti led Igor into the communications chamber.

"Wow, neimovernyy! Incredible. May I use this?"

"It's all yours, Igor. I want you to hack into the Cohen communications system and into everything else—including the CIA. This center is super secure and so powerful that I was able to penetrate your seventh heaven."

"Impossible! Nobody could ever do that."

Igor was shocked to hear that this very old man even knew about his seventh heaven.

"Don't worry. We were the only ones monitoring you, and yes, it's unbreakable, but Galina has given me access. Now get familiar with the equipment and start entering on all fronts. Our top priority is the location of Ketut. I like the girl too. She is very resourceful and loyal."

He left Igor and joined us on the portico where he poured himself another vodka.

CHAPTER 20

CIA HEADQUARTERS, IN THE EVENING

Assistant director Walter Wills returned to his office just after 8 p.m. to find a very anxious secretary waiting for him.

"The director wants to see you right now. I couldn't reach you by phone, but he knows you used one of the jets."

"Calm down, Betty. I'll handle it. Go home and take a day off tomorrow. I won't be around."

"But the director ordered no leave for all, sir."

"Did he? Well that counts for officers only. If I need you I'll call. I know your boy has soccer tomorrow, and you've missed too many games already. Leave now."

A deep frown creased her forehead.

"Please be careful, sir. Something is going on that I don't like."

"You're telling me, Betty. Enjoy tomorrow. It will be better if you are not around when all hell breaks loose."

She reluctantly left the office and he gathered his thoughts.

Five minutes later Walter entered Aiello's office.

"Where you been? The jet log tells me Richmond."

"That's correct, Pete, and I'm here to tell you that you should resign right now."

Pete Aiello didn't trust his ears, but he looked alarmed.

"What the fuck are you talking about, Walter? I'm still the director, and without a presidential order I shall remain so."

"What about an investigation by the Justice Department into your dealings with Michael Cohen?" He paused for a second to dramatize the impact. "I have all the evidence that could lead to a lengthy prison term in one of the super cages you fought so hard to build."

"All false rumors, Walter."

"No, Pete. I've just come from a meeting with the Petrossians. They have enough material to put you away for good."

"They are illegal and have no status whatsoever. I could arrest you for this and put *you* away for good. Petrossian is a dinosaur and virtually extinct. The president himself outlawed this bunch of criminals as soon as he entered the White House."

Yes, Mills thought, *after you told him to do it.*

"I know all that, Pete, but they are very active and far from extinct. They hacked you and everybody else involved in your deceitful scheme, which is nothing other than treason. Arrest me right now if you have the guts, which you have never had."

Aiello pushed a button on his desk phone.

"Bring them in. He knows."

The door opened and in walked Walter Wills's darkest dream. Stomping into the director's office was Michael Cohen, the CEO of Cohen Industries, with three of his goons.

"Well, assistant director Wills, your time is over. We are very close to success and can't be stopped now by a minor official like you. What you don't understand is that we will change the world. No more fucking Arabs dictating our finances, no more armed conflicts in the Middle East, no more American soldiers dying abroad. The Islamic State is just our vehicle to end all this. It doesn't matter what you have learned from those deplorable Petrossians. Your voice will never be heard. We have a Petrossian in our hands, and she is a nice little bargaining chip. You are not, Wills."

With that, Cohen gestured to his gorillas to take Walter away.

Walter offered no resistance, knowing that would be useless, and let himself be shepherded out of the office. The director's secretary looked worried, and for a moment he considered giving her a warning sign, but that would have endangered her too.

The thugs escorted Walter outside the building. They were equipped with the latest security tags and cards, compliments of Aiello. They shoved their captive into a black SUV but not before confiscating his SIG.

"Don't get comfortable," one of the goons said. "The ride will be short, so enjoy! It's your last one."

The SUV left the George Bush Center for Intelligence, the CIA headquarters, and headed onto the George Washington Memorial Parkway. The ride indeed was short. They soon arrived at a mansion on the Potomac that Walter had always admired whenever he passed it. The pillars in front made it look like the White House. He had always wondered whether there was an Oval Office behind these dark windows.

"You may have noticed that we don't mind that you see this place. That's because you'll leave here dead or stripped of your brain."

Walter didn't react to the remark but focused on the surroundings. The SUV entered a subterranean garage, and they pulled him out of the vehicle.

"Mr. Cohen will have a word with you before you check out."

A heavy metal door led to a brightly lit cell. Walter saw a bed and a toilet in a corner and, to his surprise, an Asian woman with a bloody, beaten face. Ketut.

"Get acquainted. She is a shitty Petrossian, and I'm sure she can help you get out of here."

The goon laughed and kicked Walter in his back, shutting the door loudly.

Walter looked at her with a worried expression on his face.

"What did they do to you? Did they beat you, Ketut?"

"Sure, and waterboarding. They think they are good at it."

A deep-throated laugh escaped her bloody mouth. "I'm able to hold my breath for more than two minutes, so I faked terror and drowning and they stopped. When I still wasn't giving them the right answers, they kicked me a bit. But I'm sure you know where I'm coming from."

Ketut observed his reaction carefully before she continued.

"Their main objectives are Igor, an IT wizard and a hacker, and Matt, Petrossian fifty. The two of them hacked into some Saudi bank and other places. I don't know the whole scheme, but it is alarming. I'm worried about Igor. He is not a Petrossian, and he was alone when they got me."

"You might be safe for now, Ketut. They must get rid of me, but this place is too close to Langley. I'm quite sure I won't be here for long. So hold on if you can, and reveal information only bit by bit. I'm much too risky for them to keep me alive. You, however, might be a trading chip."

"I'm not. I took an oath a long time ago, and I will live up to it."

Her bloody face displayed defiance, just what he had showed his Arab jailors years ago when they had held him in a cell in Iraq. He hadn't been crushed despite the hourly torture. He had held on until Matt, Fedorov, and a few other Petrossians arrived. The ferocious team had slaughtered twelve of his captors outside his cell door and had left them to dry in the scorching desert. His collaboration with Petrossian had grown into a partnership greatly benefiting the CIA, but that had ended when the new president outlawed the organization on Aiello's advice.

Ketut had to use the toilet and asked Walter to turn around.

"They unlinked something inside me, which makes me pee every few minutes." She tried to smile.

Walter turned away and wiped away tears he shed over this incredibly brave woman.

He decided not to give her more details despite the chance that the information might keep her alive a bit longer if she started to talk under torture. Too much was at stake, not only for them but for the world.

They sat together on the bed and talked about their lives, their families, and their friends. This went on for hours without Cohen's goons entering the cell.

"Maybe they forgot about us."

Ketut tried to make a joke, and they both gave slight smiles.

Walter still had his watch. Maybe they were not as professional as they would like to believe. To strip a detainee of his personal belongings enhances psychological pressure. *But what the hell*, he thought, *they'll kill me with or without my watch.*

He raised a more pressing subject.

"Do you have any idea where Matt and Igor could be now? Any place you've heard of before?"

"No. I have no clue. I only hope they are safe and can finish this. They are with the two Petrossians— Sister Veronica and the other woman. I forget her name. Must be the waterboarding. It can hurt the brain."

"Tatiana Morozova," he said.

"That's the one. But they are not young anymore. What could they do?"

Walter was amused by this remark, which gave him a brief shot of adrenaline.

"Yes, I know. They are all beyond their expiration dates, but believe me, they are still deadly. Tatiana was in the field, mostly with us but also with others. She is a stone-cold killer if she must be. Never mind her age. I wouldn't like to be her adversary if her life, or a Petrossian mission, was at stake. The same goes for pious, holy Sister Veronica—lethal if necessary. You are too young to know this, Ketut, but when they enrolled and committed themselves to Petrossian too long ago, it seemed they couldn't live without taking other people's lives. The deadliest rivals they faced were in the Soviet Union. Although Petrossian had an agreement with the KGB, its agents hunted Petrossians like nothing else. The ever-changing leadership in Soviet intelligence created a lot of unrest not only in the world but mostly at home. Trust me, these two veterans are lethal."

Ketut was amazed at what he told her and wondered if she could or would ever become like these two ladies.

Walter consulted his watch and wondered what's going on out there. Another two hours had passed without a goon in sight.

CHAPTER 21

KITTY HAWK, IN THE MIDDLE OF THE NIGHT

We left Igor alone in the communications room, but I grew irritated that he had been in there for hours without results.

"Shouldn't we watch what he is doing?" I asked Valenti.

"I have followed Igor's career for a long time and I say no. We shouldn't disturb him. He will produce something."

Valenti, the old man we now saw in a different light, seemed unruffled, but I was becoming more nervous every minute.

"Matt, I was behind the wheel for a long time, so I know when to pull over to look for new directions. Trust me, with Igor we are on the right path."

As if I wouldn't know. He was my friend and partner, my star, but I was concerned anyway.

I strolled down to the boundary of the property, which led to one of the holes on the golf course. I was sure that in the daytime the spot offered a breathtaking view over the fairway and out to the Atlantic Ocean. I could hear surf crashing onto the shore. I stepped closer to the standard-looking fence that signaled private property and heard the hum of electricity powering the laser beams that presented the real barrier. I guessed all hell would break loose when one of them intersected with an intruder. State-of-the-art security. The lasers might not have been lethal, but they were strong enough to paralyze a trespasser within a split second.

I was about three hundred yards from the main house when I heard shouting from the patio.

Fedorov was clearly visible, waving his arms and yelling something unintelligible.

I ran back to the house and was slightly out of breath when I stumbled onto the brightly lit terrace.

"Igor found something. Come."

He pushed me into the great hall. Valenti opened the communications chamber and we all entered.

Igor sat in front of half a dozen monitors, hammering on his keyboard and murmuring something only he could grasp.

"I'm in," he said. "I'm in Cohen deep with video and sound. Cohen, Aiello, and some of their bastards are in a meeting. They have Walter Wills and Ketut. I have recorded everything so far. You can listen in. I don't have the location yet, but it's near the CIA headquarters."

We stood like statues behind Igor and watched our foes. Igor had somehow succeeded in hacking into the heavily protected Cohen system and now had a camera feed at a still-unknown location.

"Can you pinpoint the site?" I asked. "Near Langley is just not good enough."

"I'm working on it. Listen!"

He turned up the volume and we eavesdropped on the heated conversation.

"He has to go now. Fucking Brewer spilled the beans to him. The fuck even recorded it," Aiello said.

"How can we get rid of him if the recording is still out there somewhere?" Cohen asked.

"The bitch is our bargaining chip. Petrossians pride themselves on never leaving an agent behind. You have to tell that if they don't give up the recording, she will join Wills in his wet grave."

Aiello was visibly wrecked, and the only chance he saw to escape from this mess was to get rid of his assistant director as quickly as possible.

At the risk of insulting Igor, I asked him whether this was all recorded.

He frowned at me and put his thumbs up.

"I need at least another half-hour to get a location of this meeting. Cohen's system has a ton of firewalls. The video feed was easy because they never suspected an attack there. Let me work on it. I have put up a phrase alarm, which means whenever a place is named aloud my system will become red."

We withdrew to some chairs behind him, but none of us was leaving the chamber. Watching the conspirators on a live stream was fascinating.

Igor worked frantically with the equipment and suddenly announced, "I have a feed into the CIA—the outside cameras. It's impossible to get into the building. But I can enter the records and the playback. I'm sure they took the assistant director on the premises. Where else would that have happened?"

He hacked the recordings of the last few hours. Walter Wills had taken the jet for the short hop to Richmond and had deliberately created a deceptive trail with a flight plan to a destination much farther away. I knew the way he thought and planned. A two-hour drive wouldn't require a flight on a CIA jet, so he probably would have been back at the office around 6 p.m.

"Go to 5:30 p.m. and play it from there," I instructed Igor.

When we reached six-twenty on the video, we saw Walter walk into the headquarters via the main entrance.

"Now cover all exits and play forward!"

Igor looked at me with his brows raised and said, "Check the monitors. All exits are covered."

It sounded like a reprimand or maybe a lecture. I should have known better. Igor knew what he was doing.

Only a few people left the building by the side doors. Most of them, coming and going, used the main entrance with its sophisticated security equipment.

At 6:46 p.m. we hit the jackpot. Walter was escorted by three men, presumably Cohen's, out of the building at the east doorway, reserved for top-clearance agents. *Aiello, the fixer,* I thought.

"There, can you follow them?"

Igor hit some keys and the picture changed to the top-clearance parking area where only five cars were parked. They packed Walter into the back seat of a black SUV, an Escalade, and drove off.

"Follow!" I almost screamed.

Igor could follow the car until it hit Colonial Farm Road. Where the hell were they going? DC? There we lost the car.

"Any way to catch them on traffic cameras?"

I started to annoy Igor. He hit some keys, and the traffic camera at the entrance to Washington Memorial came up on one of the higher monitors.

"These cams are easy to hack. I access the library."

I guessed correctly that he meant the library storing the recordings. He wound back to 6:45 p.m., and a few minutes later we watched the Escalade approach the Washington Memorial heading west along the Potomac. Igor switched traffic cameras, which were in abundance near DC and the firm, but we lost the car.

"That means the Escalade stopped somewhere between here and Arlington," Igor declared. "I guess somewhere at the Potomac." He pointed at a map of the area.

I looked at Valenti simply because I didn't want to exasperate Igor any further with my layman's questions.

"Do we have satellite access for the area?" I asked.

The old man smiled, knowing very well why I addressed him instead of Igor.

"Of course we have. DC is covered by satellite images 24/7. I'm in already but there is no playback function, at least not from here."

He zoomed in on the Potomac shoreline and scanned a dozen or so large estates with well-conserved parks and wide entry roads.

"Get me all the info about the owners of these places. I bet one of them belongs to Cohen."

My instruction was intended more for everyone in the room than for Igor alone.

"Working on it, boss."

Igor was in his element and clearly enjoyed what he was doing.

Just a few minutes later we had all the data on the estate owners, but no Cohen was listed.

Shit!

The owner of the biggest estate, the one I was sure belonged to Cohen, was listed as Eileen Cahill. The others were under names none of us knew except for the one nearest to Arlington, which belonged to a senator from California. He was a clear opponent of the president, which meant he couldn't be on board with Cohen.

"Whatever! We need to get on the ground there as quickly as possible," I said.

I touched Valenti's arm and said, "We need your chopper, sir."

"It's on standby, and it's a pity I'm a bit too old to join you. I'll call the pilots."

After a rapid exchange in what I assumed to be Armenian, our departure was set in fifteen minutes. Armenian pilots! Nothing could surprise me anymore.

Igor started to shut down his equipment, but I instantly objected.

"Igor, stay here and monitor whatever you can. That's an order! We need your input once we're on the ground. Meanwhile, work on the backgrounds of all the other estate owners and find a link to Cohen."

The name Cahill rang a loud bell in my tired brain.

He knew I was right, and to my amazement he simply replied, "Okay, boss."

Valenti helped us check our weapons and added some high-tech laser guns and night vision goggles.

As much as I wanted to leave Mark behind, I realized I wouldn't get anywhere with such a demand. He was hot to see action, and I knew he was one of the best, although like all of us, long in the tooth.

Fedorov and I did a short mission briefing, emphasizing the main goal: freeing Ketut and Walter.

"Is DC ops still active?" I asked Tatiana. "If so, please arrange transportation, two cars, as soon as we know where we touch down."

"Consider it done."

I felt all of us were ready for a mission that might well end in death.

The flight was swift and undisturbed by turbulence or bad weather.

"I can't get closer to DC than Springfield without springing alarms," the pilot said. "Hope that is okay."

"Springfield. Call your guys," I told Tatiana. "We'll send them coordinates once on the ground."

"One-hour max," she said. "I've notified them. They are already south of DC. And by the way, not guys, girls!"

The Bell swept low over the landscape, and the pilot made a few turns until he found the touchdown spot, a green field just south of Springfield. We stayed in the chopper and communicated with Igor and Valenti.

Igor was excited about something he found out.

"Boss, the woman Eileen Cahill, who owns the biggest mansion there, was formerly Eileen Caldwell, previously married to a Maximilian Caldwell. He was with either the CIA or another firm."

"Oh my God, not that I'm a believer," Tatiana responded. "Caldwell headed a super-secret outfit that did only black ops in the nineties and before. They ran the blackest of all black sites all over the globe, Cavity."

She looked at Veronica and got a stern nod.

"Caldwell was bad news not only for us but for the US government, the CIA, and the whole national security establishment. He passed at the turn of the century, but we knew his wife was the driving force behind him—as is so often the case." Tatiana snickered.

I had to admit I had never heard of Caldwell or his wife. I knew about Cavity but was not deeply interested in its structure.

"You realize we might not be up against Cohen," Veronica said. "This might be the old Caldwell firm, Cavity. I always wondered how Cohen could recruit all these pros. I had a run-in with some of the Cavity operatives back in 1992. I have the same doubt about Cohen. This is too big for him. If it's the Caldwell firm, this is an extremely dangerous situation."

Igor sent us data about Cavity, a clandestine organization established under Richard Nixon that operated quietly for about a decade until Maximilian Caldwell took over. The firm was under scrutiny for the mysterious deaths of politicians and for the disappearance of hundreds of people all over the world.

"Eileen Cahill—that's her maiden name—comes from a politically radical family, anticommunist, anti-Islam, against everything opposed to their way of thinking."

Valenti cut in, his voice filling our headsets.

"Matt, Fedorov, do only close recon until we find out more. These guys are lethal and only a frontal attack might stop them. Meanwhile, we could get more intel on their Saudi operation. Apparently, a mini nuke has been tested in Kim land, small enough and deep enough underground not to disturb seismic surveillance too much. The Chinese and the Russians noted the explosion but didn't pay much attention to it. We'll try to monitor shipping channels because I think one or more of these devices are on the way to the Saudi kingdom."

"What you mean by close recon only?" Tatiana said. "They have Ketut and Walter. We have to go in!"

"No. We should try to get official help on this, meaning somebody in the US government who is not corrupted by these people. We need a force."

"Understood, Valenti," I said, using his name for the first time, "but time is against us. We'll decide once on site."

I ended the communication because I didn't want to get into an argument with the legendary Valenti Assarian and because the two cars Tatiana had arranged were arriving.

We told the pilot to remain on standby but further south. I didn't want to lose our way out by having him stay too close to the action.

This was a completely new picture. Cohen was probably just a tool in the scheme hatched by Eileen Cahill. I flipped through Igor's report about her. She was the devil incarnate with huge amounts of money available for her plans. As the main shareholder and the chairwoman of the board of Vickers Pharmaceuticals and with seats on two dozen other major corporate boards, she made Cohen look like a pauper.

Igor's report ended by saying, "The annihilation of the Islamic world is her main objective."

We jumped into the two Mercedes SUVs. They are driven by two women whom I guessed were in their twenties. Tatiana introduced us quickly and gave them the directions. I was tempted to ask questions but left it at that after Veronica shook her head vigorously. Two youngsters. Maybe Petrossian was not extinct yet.

Because it was nighttime, we didn't encounter much traffic and reached the George Washington Memorial Parkway in no time. Fedorov ordered the drivers to park about five hundred yards from the mansion.

We hid the cars among other vehicles parked in a yard adjacent to a dark, squat building. We saw no guards.

I was about to tell the girls to stay in the cars and to wait for our return, but Tatiana stopped me short.

"They are good and much speedier than you. They will come. We might need them and their competence with recon and, of course, with weapons."

I observed them strapping on ultra-light submachine guns with silencers beside their SIGs. No Makarovs. *Must be the new generation*, I thought. The SIG, the Swiss precision tool, was part of the CIA and FBI armory. I preferred my Makarov.

In contrast with us, the original gang, the girls wore all black. They didn't speak a word, but their preparation seemed professional and I had no objections.

We started down the parkway but out of sight, following the lush parks and gardens while the girls stayed on the lookout for cameras. They knew what they were doing.

We arrived at the gate to the Cahill mansion where four cameras were turning in all directions. We took cover in some brush.

"No way to get in here," Fedorov whispered. "Total coverage. We have to create some diversion."

Right then we were flooded with extremely bright light and heard a female voice over the communications system.

"Mr. Fedorov, I expected you. Please come in and join me for an early breakfast. The gate will open, and I really would like you to stay together."

The gate slowly opened and we tried to gather ourselves. I noticed the two girls had disappeared. Tatiana winked at me as if she knew that would happen.

The rest of us entered the estate where we were intercepted by four men whom we would earlier have assumed to be Cohen thugs. They aimed their weapons at us center mass for a quick kill if necessary.

"Please drop all your weapons here as well as all your communications stuff."

We unloaded our weapons, took out our earpieces, and let the men frisk us. They did so quickly and efficiently. Two more goons appeared and grabbed our stuff as we were escorted to the main house.

I wondered if they had captured the girls or whether the two had gotten away.

"Welcome to my home, Yevgeni Fedorov and Matt Burke. Yes, I know your names as I know everything about my nemeses."

There she was, Eileen Cahill. An elegant woman in her seventies, she wore a cocktail dress and looked ready for a grand party.

"And, of course, the pious nun, Veronica, with her deadly killer bitch, Tatiana. And a new face. Is it Bernie? Come join me for a drink. But let me first say that I don't need any intelligence from you. The sweet Balinese girl and, of course, Walter Wills, have told me everything."

I knew she was lying. I was prepared for action, but the four goons acting as her bodyguards gave me no way out. My only hope was that the two girls had gotten away and maybe, just maybe could inform Khabarovsk.

"Please sit down. It would spoil the ambiance to have you stand while we enjoy a little conversation. I'm really happy to have you as my guests."

"Are Ketut and Walter alive?" I had to ask because listening to this bitch made me sick.

"Oh, they're well and in good hands—something I can't say about Michael Cohen."

She made a face that recalled a creature I had seen in *Star Wars*.

"Just about now poor Michael has had a car accident not far from here." She actually sniffled. "It's so dangerous nowadays on the roads, particularly when you are drunk and driving. I shall miss him. Sit!"

Her voice changed, and I had the feeling she indeed was an alien.

I nodded and we all sat down in the huge chairs provided in the hall.

"Let me tell you a bit about what happened and, of course, about what will follow. I'm sure you are dying to hear it all." She snickered.

A butler of some sort was serving drinks, but we asked for water.

"Remember Chad, Yevgeni? Since then I have really wanted you gone—not only dead but tortured, humiliated …"

Her voice trailed off, and she took a deep sip of her pink cocktail.

I knew what she was referring to.

"When we were active in Chad and desperately tried to keep that asshole Hissène Habré in power, you spoiled our party. Yes, it was us, not the CIA. By 'us' I mean Chamber 19, an ultra-secret, government-funded black operations and intelligence organization later named Cavity. My husband, Maximilian, God bless him"—she crossed herself—"headed it with me as his senior adviser and mentor."

She took another sip and seemed to wipe a tear from her eye.

"Then you Petrossians entered the picture and ruined our plans. With you was your little Ukrainian sweetie, Oksana. I wonder where she is. I was hoping to catch her too. But never mind. I have you now. Africa was to become our playground, and Chad, that godforsaken place, was our practice ground."

Another sigh and another mouthful of the pink liquid.

"Then you and your little whore spoiled it all."

Hearing the word *whore*, Fedorov was about to attack her, but one of the goons behind him pushed him roughly back into his chair.

In 1989 Petrossian had contracted a job in Chad from the DGSE, the French national intelligence agency. The assignment had been easy enough at the beginning—monitoring the atrocities of the Habré regime and reporting them to the French. We did not have to engage in any action.

But this was more easily said than done. Fedorov and Oksana were sent to Ndjamena, a rotten, dirty city that hardly deserved to be called the capital. From Ndjamena they went north, close to the Libyan border, where the killings were in the thousands some days.

They soon found out that Habré's killers were being assisted by Americans who did not like to waste bullets in the massacres. Thousands were drowned, their bodies floating in the lakes and rivers.

Petrossian had not known that an American organization other than the CIA had been operating in Chad. In fact, Fedorov and Oksana had captured two mercenaries who were CIA agents or who had originated with the agency. The other Americans, now known as Cavity, a government-sanctioned black ops group, shipped arms and even jet fighters to Habré. The objective had been simple enough: to help Habré kill all nonconformists and to use Chad as the base for the group's future operations in Africa.

The murder of dozens of Libyan soldiers around the border area, however, had changed the picture. Fedorov and Oksana had crossed the border into Libya and, against orders from Paris, had briefed Gadhafi in Tripoli, but not before they had left some twenty Cavity operatives dead, drawing attention to the group to the international press.

Libyan forces had entered Chad on the information, and another African war had nearly erupted. French intervention the same year had put an end to the Habré regime and to the strategic ambitions of Cavity.

Despite ignoring the French mandate not to interfere, or maybe because they did, Fedorov and Oksana had received French medals. In absentia.

Now it looked like we finally had to pay for that.

Eileen Cahill accepted another pink drink from one of her lackeys and offered a toast. "Let's celebrate the death of my dearest enemies tonight. You will die together while I watch your agony from here."

She pointed at a huge screen that came to life on her command.

The picture was very clear and showed a concrete room where Ketut and Walter sat on what looked like a military field bed.

"You see they are alive and well. My people had to rough up your

Asian bitch because she thought she could fight us. But where she is going she won't have to be pretty anymore."

The woman's laugh reminded me of the hissing of a Komodo dragon.

"Now let's see whether you might tell me something about Petrossian in this country. If you do, you will die painlessly. Otherwise my experts shall take their time for my amusement."

We sat in silence, and I admired Fedorov, who kept a smile on his face.

"Could I have a vodka, ice cold, please?"

He was ice cold.

For the first time a very tense Mark Shearer, who had insisted on accompanying us, spoke. "I'd like to have one too, and for what it's worth, madam, I have Frank Brewer's confession. It's inaccessible."

The Cahill woman rasped something to one of her goons, her face turning into an ugly mask.

"I'll have one too." I smiled at Eileen as if this were a garden party. What the hell, why not?

The goon reappeared with four vodkas in iced glasses, just the way we liked it.

We raised our glasses and said, "To long life and happiness!"

CHAPTER 22

OKSANA

Dr. Fischer brought Oksana to his private clinic, just south of Frankfurt in a dense forest. She was very weak and cursed the Cohen goon who shot her.

"You will be safe here, Oksana. I know a lot about you from my friend Yevgeni. When the Berlin Wall was still up he brought me many, uh, patients who needed discreet treatment."

Oksana heard his voice but was almost unable to reply.

"Thanks. Just make it quick. They need me."

"Trust me, I know. A week and you are back."

She was too exhausted to protest and sank back in the car seat.

The entrance to the clinic was barred by a gate that opened on a remote signal Dr. Fischer sent. The winding road up to the hospital led through a green woodland.

Two female nurses put her on a roll stretcher and raced into a ready operating room.

Then Oksana blacked out.

Dr. Fischer changed into hospital scrubs and washed his hands. He never wore latex gloves for surgery, because they numbed his sense of touchs. His nurses prepared Oksana meticulously, washing and disinfecting her wound.

Just before noon, about the time her friends were arriving in Düsseldorf, Oksana was rolled into a room that appeared more like a luxurious hotel apartment than a hospital cell.

Dr. Fischer was content with his work. From his private bureau, he called Galina on a very secure line and told her Oksana had had a close call but was alive and safe.

"Helmut, I owe you a big one. She is our most valuable asset and despite her age, the future of Petrossian. Please don't keep her too long. I have a feeling she will be needed soon. Thank you!"

Dr. Helmut Fischer emigrated to West Germany years before the wall fell. He was an East German and one of the Stasi's most favored surgeons before he escaped. And not a minute too early. The Stasi, which was much more efficient than its mother, the KGB, at least in East Germany, had found out about his connection to another intelligence organization, Petrossian. Although the KGB had never been able to establish a clear picture of Petrossian, some zealot in the agency had approved the doctor's arrest. Fedorov, stationed in Germany, had rushed to extract Fischer from East Germany via Hungary.

In the following months, Valenti Asssarian had funded the new clinic in Frankfurt, which had saved the lives of many Petrossian agents and friends.

Hours later Oksana woke up and, unsurprisingly, was confused. She looked around and found herself in a luxury suite that bore no resemblance to a hospital room. However, the tubes sticking out of her made it clear enough where she was. Almost as soon as she opened her eyes the door opened, and Dr. Fischer walked in.

"Good afternoon, Oksana. How do you feel?"

"You tell me. Thanks for helping me. I think I'm okay."

"You are better but not okay yet. I highly recommend a few days' rest. I talked to Galina, and she agrees."

Oksana immediately knew he was lying, although this was a kind untruth spoken by the man who had saved her life.

"Now rest, my dear. In a couple of hours, I shall connect you with Galina. You are still weak, and we must recharge you. For starters, you need to eat and drink. I know you guys like vodka, but for now it's water and juice. Nurse Anna will bring you food. Enjoy!"

He left the room and Oksana realized she was starving.

Nurse Anna brought a variety of German delicacies such as small sausages, paté, and dark bread. Her throat parched, Oksana grabbed a large glass of orange juice and emptied it.

"Go slow, Oksana. There is more. Dr. Fischer thinks you have to eat, not gobble." The nurse smiled.

And that's what she did. Oksana enjoyed the heavy, filling meal, which reminded her of the rich food of her homeland, Ukraine.

After finishing what she called her snack, Oksana fell into a deep sleep, disturbed by wild dreams about her friends. When Dr. Fischer gently touched her, she almost hit him in the stomach.

"Oksana, wake up." He softly shook her arm. "Galina needs to talk to you."

Dr. Fischer handed her a phone with the cable plugged into the wall. He understood her concerned look.

"Secure line. Goes through my data center. Igor installed it."

Oksana took the receiver. "Hi, forty-nine. I'm okay. What's up?"

"Oksana, I want you to listen carefully. Tell me if it's too much and I'll stop, okay?"

"Yes, copy. Go ahead."

"Fed, Matt, Ketut, Walter Wills, Mark Shearer, and three others are in the hands of Cavity. You haven't heard about them. It's not the Cohen people, as we thought. It's the bunch that almost got you and Fed in Chad. Follow me so far?"

Oksana's shock showed on her face.

"Yes, understand. Please proceed."

"We know where they are. I'll send the location right after this. They killed Michael Cohen. It was supposedly a car accident. The DC police are all over it."

Galina filled her in for another fifteen minutes.

"Galina, I'm fine. My leg hurts a bit, but otherwise I'm operational. Arrange transportation."

"Give me Helmut. I want to talk to him."

Oksana handed the phone to Dr. Fischer, who protested but knew the decision had been made.

Galina spoke with Oksana again.

"I have dispatched the Gulf, which should touch down in Frankfurt in thirty minutes. You'll get all the latest intel on the flight. Stay safe this time and, udachi, good luck!"

"Well, Dr. Fischer, I thank you very much for what you did, but now it's time for me to leave."

"Okay, Oksana, I understand. Please be aware that your wound has been reopened and is still extremely vulnerable. Walk with care and don't run." He gave her a straightforward smile.

"I never run, Dr. Fischer, not from my enemies!"

The clinic had prepared a gift package for Oksana—jeans, shirts, street and running shoes, underwear, and toiletries.

Dr. Fischer checked her passport fastidiously. The French document didn't require an entry stamp or a visa for the United States. Oksana was now Brigitte Delveaux, a jet-set millionaire on the way to America on a private jet.

Helmut Fischer himself drove her to the airport where they parked at the jet aviation slot for VIPs traveling on their own planes. He hugged her and placed a kiss on her forehead.

"Be careful, Oksana, and get my friend Yevgeni out of trouble. I owe him my life and wish I could be with you."

"Thanks again, but 'careful' is not in my repertoire." She laughed and strolled out to the Gulfstream, which was being refueled.

She was expecting more agents on the plane and was slightly surprised that she was the only passenger. Once they were airborne the captain said she could use the communications system. Oksana opened the files Galina had sent and started to read.

Valenti Assarian. She had heard Fedorov mention the name a few times. She assumed he must be about a hundred years old by now, a legend still alive and active.

It took her almost an hour to digest all the files and to grasp the situation. Oksana felt horrible that she hadn't been there.

She read the intel about Cavity again and felt some satisfaction that Michael Cohen had been killed by this group. Eileen Cahill was a new name to her, and Oksana dug into the intel about this person with great interest. All of it came from Valenti Assarian, of course via Galina.

"ETA in five hours, ten minutes at Reagan International, DC," the captain said over the intercom. "You will be picked up by two of us, Misha Kucherenko and Gaby Jones. Misha is originally from Kiev, Gaby from Boston. They know the site and will brief you on the way. And Galina orders you to rest."

Yes, Oksana felt very tired, and Galina was probably right. The flight attendant reclined her seat so it became a flat bed and covered her with a soft blanket. Oksana was asleep almost instantly.

Before they landed at Reagan International, she was roused from her deep sleep, which this time had been without nightmares, and served a breakfast of coffee, eggs, and croissants. She dug in like a starving refugee arriving at a safe haven. She checked with the captain to see whether there had been any new communications from Galina or Khabarovsk. There was nothing that would change the situation.

"Misha and Gaby are completely briefed and are monitoring the situation at the Potomac," the captain said. "We are landing in a few minutes, and I wish you all the luck you might need."

He left for the cockpit, and the sleek plane banked hard to the left for final approach.

As a VIP passenger, Oksana was whisked through immigration where Misha and Gaby were expecting her. She was startled to see two girls in their twenties. *That's something else,* she thought. Oksana, in her sixties, usually got treated as the "young girl" among the November agents in Petrossian. Maybe there was a pipeline of fresh talent, one she'd never noticed.

The girls introduced themselves with great respect and led her to an Audi SUV parked just outside the private jet terminal.

"We know about you," Misha said, "and we both have been to Kryilny for two years. We are very honored to have this assignment together with you. Your life is in the history books at the base."

Gaby took the wheel.

"Base is watching the estate by satellite, and there is no new development since last night," she said. "Fedorov, fifty, Mark Shearer, Ketut, Walter Wills, Veronica, Tatiana, and Bernie are still inside, but we don't know where. The mansion is huge. We passed it a few times with infrared sensors, but apart from the guards we couldn't find anything."

They hadn't mentioned Valenti or his involvement. Oksana didn't want to bring up the subject yet. She was amazed that the legendary Valenti was living in the United States and still pulling strings.

"The estate is riddled with cameras and awash with guards," Misha said. "We got away last night because I spotted a night vision camera away from the gate, but it was too late to alert the others. Early this morning Gaby and I took a boat ride on the Potomac, passing the estate just twice, not to be too conspicuous. We think we may have found a small weakness in the fortress. The concrete wall at the river is almost five meters high and hard to climb. Further, we spotted only two cameras, one upriver, one down."

"It's daylight now, which means we can't move, and even too close observation is too risky," Oksana said.

"Yes, we realize that," Misha said. "We have set up a safe house about a mile from the mansion from where we have satellite access on our laptops. We suggest the three of us proceed there and watch. The feed comes from a station in North Carolina, not from the base. Strange."

"It's better you forget about that for the time being."

"We cannot pass the estate again since they check every car," Gaby said. "They stand there openly with their cameras. We passed by early this morning. I turned on the radio, and we were singing. The plates are no problem. They're registered to an accountant who lives down the road, near Langley."

Gaby took the Arlington Bridge and headed west. The George Washington Memorial was to the left, but from there Oksana couldn't see the estate.

"Do you have another car? I want to drive by just once to get a feeling."

"Yes, at our safe house. It's an old Chevy with Virginia plates. But I think the two of us should stay away. We definitely are on their recordings."

"That's fine. I'll go alone."

Five minutes later they arrived at a ranch-style clapboard that looked like a home for the destitute.

"This is your safe house?" Oksana didn't trust her eyes.

"Wait until you see inside," Misha said, giggling.

With a remote on the dashboard, Gaby opened the garage. The Audi was out of sight in a few seconds.

Well, maybe it's better than it looks, Oksana thought.

"This is Tatiana's hideout," Misha said. "She built it and we sometimes use it. Come in and see for yourself."

Misha opened the access door to the house with her thumb print on a hand reader. The heavy metal door hissed open and revealed a surprising sight. The modern furnished living room tempted Oksana to relax, but for that was no time yet.

"Come," Gaby said, wiggling her finger.

"All secure," Misha called out. "We can open. Gaby, let's go."

Gaby pressed a button somewhere, and the living room floor opened noiselessly. A staircase led to a brightly lit floor beneath. Oksana was impressed by the functionality of the place. They descended to the lower area, which was lit with numerous monitors, flat screens, and blinking computers.

"Galina knows this place and was here when Igor installed the hardware. I hope he is okay."

Did Oksana detect a crush on Igor in Misha's body language? That could be a problem. If Oksana was going to initiate a rescue operation, emotion had to be sidelined. She decided to tell Misha that Igor was not one of the captives. She was still undecided whether to tell her where he was. Apparently, the girls didn't know about Valenti, and without a nod from Galina she would keep it that way.

"Now come here, Oksana."

Gaby pointed to a big monitor that displayed the entrance to the mansion.

"Misha parked a pickup opposite the entrance and left the half-empty building via the back door. We have two cameras streaming, but the angle is low and limited."

She pointed to another screen that showed the Potomac River and at the far end the mansion with its huge wall at the riverbank.

"All cameras can be operated from here," Gaby said.

She zoomed in on the mansion and the wall.

"We record, of course, and Igor's software is cueing on 'unusual behavior,' which means …"

"I know what it means, Gaby. I'm familiar with Igor's work. So any unusual behavior?"

Gaby operated something that looked like a joystick for a computer game and scrolled backward through the recording.

"Here. See? The front entrance this morning at six-thirty-four. That, according to the software, was unusual, although I don't see it. The blue van entered the estate and left again at six-fifty-one. That's the only 'unusual' we have so far. Nothing from the riverside."

"Let's start communicating," Oksana said. "Link me up to Galina, and I need a glass of water for my medicine."

Oksana sat down in front of one of the familiar communication stations, and Gaby handed her a glass of cold water.

Galina came up almost immediately.

"Dobroye utro, Oksana. Kak dela?"

"Good afternoon, Galina. Thanks. I'm fine."

CHAPTER 23

THE WHITE HOUSE, IN THE MORNING

The president was behind his desk in the Oval Office, gently stroking the wood of the historical furniture and desperately trying to appear relaxed and in control. The national security chief, the directors of the FBI and the CIA, General Huntington, who headed the NSA, and the leaders of a few other minor but more clandestine intelligence agencies were waiting for him in the adjacent conference room.

Aiello, his appointee, was the only one who knew of Cavity's existence. The ultra-secret group had existed since the 1970s but had almost disappeared after the death of its head, Maximilian Caldwell. Then his widow, an ambitious vulture with too much money, had revived it after Gitmo became too floodlit by the international liberals. Cavity had become active again in the darkest places. The group ran container ships that were simply black ops prisons, ideal for torture and even better for making bodies vanish forever. The few black sites in Bulgaria, Romania, and Cambodia were comparably soft prisons, and some inmates even got flown out. To where? Only Cavity knew.

The new and much more disturbing intelligence gossip coming from Russia concerned Cavity activity in Syria and Saudi Arabia. This clandestine Russian connection, however, didn't talk about Cavity but about Michael Cohen. Apparently not even the FSB knew about the revival of Cavity. The president, a friend of Cohen, was informed about a stealthy operation involving Cavity and Cohen. He never told his security council, let alone the other agencies, only the conspirators around Aiello.

He made a decision. He had a hard time doing that and had already lost the good will of most Americans during his first few months in office, mostly because of his wrong decisions.

His secretary stuck her pretty head in the Oval Office.

"Mr. President, they are waiting ..."

He stopped her cold and said, "Send Aiello in first. Now."

She withdrew her head, and a few seconds later Pete Aiello, the CIA director, entered the Oval Office.

"Mr. President, good morning."

The furious president ignored his outstretched hand.

"Pete, before we go in there, I want to know everything about Cavity, Saudi fucking Arabia, and the circumstances of Michael Cohen's death. Understood?"

"Yes sir, as you wish."

Aiello's account took much longer than the president anticipated. He quickly went over to the conference room and dismissed the waiting intel heads, rescheduling the meeting for the afternoon.

"Aiello, you fucking asshole, what did you do? You want me out of office even before the Russians make that happen? A nuke attack on Iran? Are you fucking crazy?"

"Sir, it's the right solution to the Middle East problem. We ran all scenarios a thousand times, and only loyal CIA officers are involved. Once we get rid of Petrossian, we're home free. Those people are the only remaining troublemakers. All the rest is behind us."

He was desperate to please the president.

"And, of course, Mark Shearer, the former head of special ops. He was the one who broke Brewer, but he is in our hands now."

"Petrossian? What the hell is Petrossian? Something to do with caviar?"

The president hit his forehead hard and started to laugh.

"You fucking assholes do this all behind my back, and even better, you involve the bloody North Koreans. You stupid son of ..."

His voice trailed off, his whole body shaking, sweat sticking to his face.

"Trust me, Mr. President, it will work. The great United States of America will once again come to the rescue of the world. We have a carrier group near the Persian Gulf as we speak."

"Shut up, Pete! Tell me about this Petrossian!"

Aiello told him all about it, and the president got more apprehensive and ever closer to his first heart attack.

"We have the key Petrossian agents in our hands. By 'we,' I mean Eileen Cahill. She holds three of them plus Walter Wills, my assistant director, and Mark Shearer."

"So tell me, Michael Cohen was murdered. His death was no accident, right?"

"It was necessary, sir. Too many arrows pointed at Cohen. We needed a diversion. Nobody knows about Cavity."

"Except those Petrossian people, right?"

"Yes, sir, but we are about to eliminate them permanently. We know the location of their base. The Russians will play their part in that."

"The Russians? You know how much damage the Russian connection has already done to my office. Leave the Russians out!"

"That's not possible, sir, because the Petrossian base is in Russia."

Now the president was getting closer to cardiac arrest.

CHAPTER 24

KITTY HAWK, NORTH CAROLINA, NIGHTTIME

Igor was still sitting in front of his sophisticated equipment when Valenti entered the communications room. He had monitored Cohen channels for hours but had learned nothing.

Valenti stood behind him and put his hands on Igor's shoulders.

"You need a rest, Igor. Come outside and have some coffee while I brief you on the latest developments. Base was trying to get into a system but failed. So our hopes are with you."

"What system? Where?"

"Coffee first and then I'll tell you. What I didn't tell you is that our friends are in the hands of the enemy. The enemy is not Cohen but an organization called Cavity, a former government intel group that obviously went rogue. Now come, coffee and some eggs. Then you return here and open them up."

He forced Igor out of the room and led him to the patio where a table was set with sausages, eggs, juice, and coffee. Igor realized he was very hungry and allowed himself half an hour max to recharge his batteries.

Valenti briefed him about Michael Cohen's death and about the capture of the small Petrossian group, together with Mark Shearer, supposedly in the house that held Ketut and Walter Wills.

"Do we know where?"

"Of course. Two of us got away and have installed a limited camera feed on the property. But it's your task to get in. I hear from base that the mansion is extremely well guarded, physically and electronically."

"Good. I need something real. I've had enough of checking on the Cohens. That brought absolutely nothing new. I have a camera feed but nothing else so far."

Igor gobbled down his food and grabbed the coffee pot.

"Let me try again. I want to break them open."

"As soon as you have something, let me know. We have a team ready." Valenti stopped and looked at Igor. "And Oksana will be back in a few hours."

That got Igor's attention. Oksana was back in the theater!

"Okay, I'm already in the base intel, and yes, it's hard to break but I will do it."

When Valenti closed the communications room door, he heard the chopper touching down in front of the deck. The pilots told him it was unsafe to hold Igor in Virginia, because the state was crawling with troopers, local police, and feds after an accident involving a VIP.

No wonder, he thought. Michael Cohen, a friend of the president and one of the most influential people in America, was killed. Murdered.

Valenti went to his private office where his communications system was on. It wasn't quite as complex as the one in the chamber, but it was equally safe. He contacted Galina.

"Still up?" she asked.

"Up until we end this. I've let Igor try to hack into the mansion, and I had some thoughts. Listen and try to focus on a new theory." He let out a deep breath.

"It all started with Igor hacking into one of Matt's customers because he got suspicious about some transfers. He discovered a huge network— companies in France, banks in Switzerland, offshore outlets in Belize and Delaware, and so on. Do you get what I'm trying to say?"

He looked at Galina's tired face more than ten thousand miles away.

"You think it's too much of an effort simply to finance the Islamic State. I agree."

"You know why you are where you sit now, Galina. It's because you are a quick thinker. Yes, you are right. It's got to involve much more than simply financing these fanatic Sunnis. There is a much greater scheme behind this that we have to unravel. I can't give Igor two tasks right now, although he would be capable of doing them. I want you to have Khabarovsk dig deep into Cohen affiliates and into other covert business activities. Maybe China, Southeast Asia. I don't know offhand."

"I agree with you, Valenti. Let me work on it, and tell Igor to copy me on all he gets."

They ended the transmission. Valenti was deep in thought. He was convinced that financing the Islamic State, a huge risk, was a smoke screen for something much bigger.

There was a hard knock at his office door, and the hidden minicam showed Igor standing outside. Valenti hit a button, and the heavy metal door hissed open.

"I'm in their security camera system plus two inside the house," an excited Igor said. "However, there are about twenty more, and they are hard to break. The basement cameras are almost impossible to access, and I suspect our friends are down there."

Valenti stood up.

"Show me what you have and relay it to here."

He gave Igor an IP address, a floater that changed every few minutes once contacted.

"That's the safe house in Virginia where Misha and Gaby, our DC girls, are hiding out and where Oksana will arrive soon."

Misha and Gaby, Igor thought. *Two more girls*. He didn't dare speculate about their age. Valenti seemed to have read his thoughts.

"They are young and well trained. Two years at the base. Oksana will be in capable hands, but she will take command as soon as she arrives. Now send me what you have immediately."

"Already done."

Valenti pulled up a chair and sat down beside Igor, watching the monitors. The outside cameras showed no movement at all. They were all state-of-the-art night vision, providing a clear view around the whole property. Igor pointed to the center monitor.

"That must be the hall or something where we watched the earlier meeting. I'll try to get into the recording. There was activity—look, glasses still on the table. It looks as if somebody just left."

He's right, Valenti thought.

"Can you access the whole thing?"

"I'm trying but it will take time. Meanwhile, my software for movements within the Khalij bank red- flagged a cash withdrawal from several accounts linked with the scheme. Here, take a look. Seventy-two million US dollars in cash. For the IS? How many suitcases is that?"

Valenti saw his suspicion confirmed. The IS was smoke screen to keep everyone busy while Cavity together with Cohen, and perhaps others, was underwriting a much bigger plan.

"Send that to base, Igor. I will get into it too. Try to track the cash if that is somehow possible."

"Done for one and for two. All data are automatically on auto transfer to base. I have footing from Khalij that shows two wooden crates." Igor moved the video to the cue. "See? They were loaded on a Toyota truck just about the time they were plundering the accounts. It must be the cash."

"Which branch of Khalij is it?"

"Al Jubail, the headquarters of Dhahabi Khalij. I have cameras on the harbor and record everything. As soon as the crates show up, I'll get a warning from the monitoring software. The harbor cameras are well positioned, so I should be able to catch it clearly."

"Don't trust the cameras too much. I have a feeling these guys are extremely vigilant. Record all the vessels moored in the harbor and analyze them."

"Okay, sir. You are right. Sorry I didn't see that."

"Get me details on the ships, the owners, points of origin, destinations, bills of loading."

"Consider it done, sir."

And as Valenti conjectured, all the cameras went dead just a few minutes later. There was no video stream from the Al Jubail harbor anymore.

Igor checked the recording system at the mansion. The special software was on auto penetration. The system worked well, and full access would probably be available shortly.

Igor started to check on the vessels in Al Jubail. In one part of the harbor two long oil jetties stretched out into the Persian Gulf where several huge tankers were constantly fed with Saudi light crude. The other part was commercial and fortunately not too big.

Behind Al Jubail was nothing but yellow sand with no place to deliver goods except for some green parts of the desert where the Saudis bred sheep and probably other edible or milkable animals.

The two Thai freighters were exactly that, carriers that brought sheep up from Australia to the kingdom. They would leave empty. *Yes*, Igor thought, *what else besides sheep can you carry on a sheep carrier?*

The Kuwaiti and Bahraini vessels' freight was unclear as were their destinations. Igor found out they had already been mooring for five days. Suspicious? He thought not.

The South Korean ship was a medium-large freighter owned by a company in Seoul called Hun Wha Shipping. Igor checked the company. It ran over a dozen freighters, mostly in Asia.

The *Chong Gang Gang* originated in Incheon and delivered lawn mowers. Lawn mowers? Now Igor was fully awake. In addition to the mowers, it unloaded medical equipment made in Korea. The ship's destination was Incheon, and it would leave Al Jubail today. Igor cursed the blanked-out cameras at the harbor.

All his findings and comments went automatically to the base and to Valenti's private study.

Igor tunneled deeper into the Korean shipping company. Hun Wha was one of only three shippers in South Korea that had an official license to run into North Korean harbors with humanitarian cargoes specified as food, medical equipment, meds, and clothing.

He red-flagged the info. Base sent a message.

"Good job, Igor. We'll satellite monitor the *Chong Gang Gang* from now on. There is loading movement going on. Several big crates heaved in by ship's own derrick. Thanks."

Valenti entered the chamber.

"Okay, Igor, concentrate on the mansion. Base is over the Korean ship with only a dark satellite window in about two hours, but that might still be too early for a high sea transfer. I hope so."

"Yes, sir, I mean Valenti. My software is still analyzing the mansion's firewall. Should be through shortly. It can't fail unless they have engineers observing my footsteps, but I don't think so. Oh, and by the way, I was in the harbor computers at Al Jubail. Hun Wha has a ship there almost every month."

Valenti slapped his shoulders. "Really good job, Igor."

The chamber was windowless, so Igor couldn't observe the sun rising far to the east over the Atlantic Ocean. Valenti sat on his patio, not noticing the display of natural beauty but worrying about the Petrossians held in the house on the Potomac River in Virginia.

He was informed that Oksana would be on the ground and in the safe house in less than two hours. He would need to brief this amazing woman in detail so she could make the proper decisions.

Valenti had to fight fatigue. After all, he was more than eighty years old. The butler brought freshly brewed coffee and warm kasha with ham and butter. Valenti called Igor and again ordered him to eat breakfast. Igor loved the fresh kasha in butter and milk. *Very Russian*, he thought, *and awfully good.*

His little gadget attached to his belt beeped and blinked in bright yellow signals.

"We are in. Thanks for the breakfast, Valenti. I have to work on this."

CHAPTER 25

AT THE CAVITY MANSION

Eileen Cahill never needed much sleep. Most predators are night creatures. She sat behind her desk in her secure office on the second floor of her mansion.

Her husband, Maximilian, had built this stronghold when he oversaw Cavity, but he neglected Eileen, who had been his unofficial right hand. They had bought the estate on the Potomac River with her family's money, and with her Machiavellian intelligence they had turned Cavity into their own instrument.

While the super-secret organization originally was funded by the Pentagon for the purpose of conducting secret operations abroad that might have been too risky even for the CIA, Eileen swiftly turned its assets against domestic targets as well.

Over the years Eileen had taken the reins from her husband while several high-profile US politicians had disappeared or had died in tragic accidents, leaving a vacuum to be filled by Cavity-approved successors.

Eileen was close to her goal of creating a completely new world until the obnoxious Petrossian got involved. Now she thought that snag in her plans might be eliminated with the captives in the basement. She realized keeping them alive, at least for a short while, might be more advantageous than exterminating them right away. She would have to set up a communication line with Valenti Assarian.

Cavity needed only two weeks to execute probably the boldest political scheme in history. Eileen was a zealous disciple of Sun Tzu, the Chinese general and strategist. She cursed contemporary politicians and military commanders for ignoring his doctrine, which called for turning one's enemies against each other instead of against oneself.

She knew the key to changing the world lay in the Middle East, not in Korea or in any other little hot spot on the planet. Eileen believed foolish world leaders were wasting military resources, money, and lives and ignoring the real issue in favor of a trivial battle against the Islamic State that reminded her of the crusades in medieval times. She saw huge effort with few results.

However, she was more than content with these useless investments of money and lives, for they would provide her the perfect platform for war on a much greater scale. Islamic State terrorists would look like stage hands in the drama that would unfold when the real battle in the Middle East took place.

Eileen opened her secure PC, and a display on the final plot put a lizard's grin on her face.

Just two weeks to go and the Arabs and the Iranians would turn on each other with ferocity. And yes, Americans would have to play a major role in the play she was directing. That would happen after the assassination of the useless president by the Iranians.

She took pride in the simplicity of her scheme and congratulated herself for being the only person on the planet who could comprehend the plan and its consequences. The world would be altered in a way that left her as the sole person wielding power.

Eileen went over the timing of the planned assassinations of the US president and of King Salman of Saudi Arabia. The Persian dummies, provided by the otherwise hapless Islamic State, were all in place. She loved to refer to the Iranians as the Persians, a foul and rotten society that had to be wiped out once and for all.

Then she went into the PRK files. Eileen had invested huge sums in North Korea to facilitate its development and testing of mini nukes that would fit into missiles.

Money, cash, was transported monthly from Saudi Arabia to the North Korean bank in Macau.

Yes, Petrossian had detected something wrong, but its experts couldn't hack cash transfers. They uncovered Khalij and concluded the money was all for the IS.

Eileen scrolled down and found the timing for the missile delivery to Saudi Arabia. A sheep carrier from Australia was in the Indian Ocean with an ETA in the Persian Gulf in four days. All was on schedule.

The North Koreans had successfully tested a fifty-kiloton tactical nuke, which fit into their missiles. Cavity planned to use a controllable tactical nuke, rather than the much more powerful strategic nukes, for the first strike. This would trigger the inevitable.

Eileen decided Pete Aiello must go. His limited brain capacity made him too dangerous. She would have him shot in the head. Once the plan was executed, Cavity would control all US government agencies, including the security council.

Once the president had been eliminated, the vice president, a loyal Cavity man, would appoint her as his second, a position she would occupy at least until calamity steered the republic in the right direction.

Now it was time to move the Petrossians and to get rid of Walter Wills.

The generals she picked for the task were all loyal, some of them because she had a grip on their families and would not hesitate to reduce them to rubble; others were motivated by money or the promise of even higher positions.

She double-checked on the container vessel moored in Baltimore. The ship was taking on freight, numerous empty containers with a destination of Singapore.

Some of the containers were equipped with state-of-the-art torture tools, far worse than what they had used in Guantanamo, the pleasure retreat, as she called it.

Her captives would never see daylight again and would beg for a quick death once Cavity learned all about Petrossian.

Ketut was the one exception. She would move the Balinese Petrossian to Baltimore to create confusion in case the despicable Armenian got wind of the transport. The others were needed here for the next step in her devilish plan.

Eileen pressed a button on her desk, summoning her most trusted ally, Commander Lewis, a member of the president's security council. He immediately entered her office, a round room furnished like the Oval Office at the White House.

"Madam, we are ready to move them. However, there was an intrusion into our surveillance system. We are working on it. I know it's not one of ours. Maybe Petrossian."

"I was expecting that. Override the sound system with ultrasound. I don't care that they have eyes. They will not suspect our mode of transportation."

She waved him away and watched the monitor that showed the estate entrance. Any minute now the catering truck would arrive and would unload crates of food and drink. The truck would park exactly above the spot that hid the basement exit, opening its belly for the female Petrossian.

The cameras were placed so the underside of the truck wouldn't be visible to any prying eye.

Time to call Valenti Assarian.

A woman answered the phone.

"Assarian residence. How can I assist you?"

"Tell Valenti Cavity one is calling."

The Russian music in her ear almost made her sick. One minute, two—the wait was interminable. Finally she heard a familiar voice.

"Eileen, what a surprise!"

"Indeed, Valenti, long time, much too long. I hope you are in good health."

"Thank you, Eileen. I'm in better shape than most people our age." He sounded cheerful, but Eileen knew he was a cold bastard and usually not up for idle chatter.

"You know why I'm calling, so let's cut the crap. I have your guys and the little bitch from Bali in my basement—my torture chamber. So it's up to you. Either cease all actions that might be a thorn in my side or at some future date pick up their mangled remains."

"What you want me to do, Eileen? Just name it." His voice was still extremely calm.

"First, stop all investigations into Khalij, and I mean now. Second, get out of my system—again, Valenti, now. Third, immediately call off all field activities on US soil. Got it?"

"And what do I get in return?"

"A quick and painless death for your agents. You do realize I could never release them just to bite me in the ass again?"

"I understand, Eileen, but as you know, I'm not involved anymore in actions that concern Petrossian. However, I'll pass on your message to Galina. I assume you remember her well."

"Do you really want your people tortured before they die?"

"No, of course not, but I have no control. It's all Galina and I can predict her reaction. I'm sure you won't like it, Eileen."

She should have known better. The old goat was trying to stall her and felt free to mock her.

Eileen was fuming, one of her weaknesses, she knew, but she tried to stay calm.

"My contact with Galina usually is restricted to Christmas and my birthday," Valenti said with a chuckle, making Eileen even more furious. "I don't maintain close contact with base anymore."

Valenti realized he was playing a dangerous game with a savage foe, but there was no other way. To show any softness would give Eileen immediate leverage, and he did not want to do that.

"As you wish, Valenti. I shall order the treatment right now."

Eileen slammed the receiver on its cradle, leaned back in her presidential chair, and took several deep breaths.

At least she had told him where his people were and where they would stay. Now it was urgent to make sure the perimeter was secure.

She watched the delivery truck enter the estate, rolling up to the right side of the mansion where goods were brought regularly. The small army she maintained on the grounds needed to be fed, so there was nothing suspicious about another supply delivery.

The driver and a helper unloaded cartons of food and carried them into the house under the watchful eyes of her men.

After one of her guards had signed documents, the driver turned the truck onto the wide estate lane toward the gate.

A guard buzzed her intercom and said, "Madam, all clear. She is loaded."

CHAPTER 26

KITTY HAWK, TWO HOURS EARLIER

Igor was excited that he had gained access to the cameras at the mansion along with the perimeter security. However, the security controls were inaccessible—too many high firewalls. Still, he had eyes on the ground and on most of the mansion's rooms.

For some reason, he was not able to bring up parallel sound. Again, a high-level firewall. The cameras were always easy because too many walls could cause the surveillance system to collapse.

Valenti stood behind him and watched the monitors, which displayed a view of the inside, though without a connection to the basement.

"The basement is wired differently, if at all. I don't find any cameras. They might have a wireless system working down there, and it would take me hours to break in."

Igor slapped his knee in frustration.

"And here the perimeter is secured with wireless electronic devices that would alert the bastards at the slightest movement. The wall at the Potomac is riddled with boobies, deadly high voltage and nearly invisible to the naked eye."

"You know, Igor, when I was young I loved them."

"What? What did you love?"

"High-voltage boobies," Valenti said with a laugh.

Igor was embarrassed. "Sorry, Valenti. Just talk. I meant booby traps."

Igor's face took on a deep red, but Valenti slapped his shoulder. "Igor, you do a fantastic job, but keep in mind that you can survive life's direst situations only if your witty spirit remains in intact. Report any development to me. Oksana has arrived at one of the safe houses near DC. I'll confer with Galina about how to proceed."

Valenti left a discomfited Igor alone and returned to his study to call Galina.

Igor tried all his tricks to penetrate the mansion's mainframe, and they would work if he had more time.

Since he was making no immediate progress there, Igor went back into Hun Wha, the Korean shipping company. That was much easier. He dug into schedules, freight, and harbors. Zilch! Nothing unusual in the movements of the ships.

The *Chong Gang Gang* was headed for Incheon where it would halt before a short stop in Macau. It had no other cargo on board other than the potential money crates.

Igor examined all the Macau stops Hun Wha vessels had made in the last six months. The *Chong Gang Gang* and three more ships with the same owner stopped eight times at Macau on their way back to Incheon.

He identified all the banks in Macau that might have a connection to North Korea and found only one, the All China Investment Bank, formerly named the Portuguese Overseas Banking Institution. He found no clear evidence that the bank was managing PRK money, but the open Internet provided him with gossip that the ACI was suspected of administering PRK funds managed by a half-brother of Kim Jong-un.

Despite all the sanctions placed on the PRK, China was known to be providing more than just a helping hand to the isolated regime. Igor secretly approved. After all, a total blackout would only hurt the poor people in North Korea more.

He plowed through the bank's management organization and found a Korean name, Kim Il Sung, in the listing for the board of directors. *Wasn't that a coincidence?* Igor thought. He extracted whatever else he could find about the bank and its directors but again ran into serious firewalls. The firewalls at banks were usually minor hurdles for Igor, but these were dangerous electronic fences that automatically triggered a track response at any attempt to enter. He didn't fear being tracked, but his stab at the system might trigger an alarm that closed all the doors for good.

Valenti entered the chamber again and he seemed very agitated.

"Igor, go back to the mansion. I talked with the head of Cavity a few minutes ago. She confirmed she was holding all of our friends except for Misha and Gaby, our young agents in DC. She claims they are still alive but will be tortured for information about Petrossian. I know she was lying when she told me they would remain in her personal custody. That would be much too risky, even for her."

They watched the monitors and saw a delivery truck marked Five Shells Delicacies Catering enter the compound. The truck rolled up to the supply entrance at the house, and two guys unloaded crates of food and drink.

"Check on the company—ownership, management, location, and whatever else you can find."

Valenti seemed extremely stressed, and Igor recalled his earlier advice about maintaining a witty spirit.

"Maybe they'll throw a party for their guests?"

Valenti appeared stunned for a moment and then smiled, his calm restored.

"Igor, I'm proud of you! You are one of us. I know you are suffering under these circumstances, but you are doing the right thing. You think rationally by keeping your psyche calm and flexible."

Igor came up with the data about Five Shells Delicacies.

A catering company registered in DC, it supplied balls and congressional and corporate events in big style. The owners were listed as a Delaware corporation and Cohen Industries. What a surprise!

"Okay, that's something. Can you move the cameras outside from here?"

"Yes, and that's strange. They know I'm in, so why would they let me do that? It would be easy for them to block me now."

"Remember a Petrossian adage that says if you don't want to be revealed, hide in the open. They want us to see them. We have an angle on the truck that covers both the side and the rear, but what can't we see?"

"The underside. All the cameras are positioned high to provide a full view of the estate, so no reason to have them at ground level. You think …?" Igor was dumbfounded. "I know how to see the bottom of the truck."

He hit some keys and a different view came up on one of the monitors.

"The dash cams in the truck opposite the estate that Misha and Gaby left yesterday. They are low and give us the underside of the delivery truck."

The picture was not very clear, but the space between the truck's bed and the ground was visible.

"Can you zoom in?"

"No, these are simple dash cams, and we are lucky they still work after all this time. I can enhance the stream later but no direct zoom."

They watched the screen that displayed the underside of the truck, and then Igor saw movement.

"Here, see? Something is moving under the truck. People. They are loading our friends from the basement."

Valenti was already on the line with the safe house, explaining the situation to Oksana, describing the truck, and giving her the plates.

"Igor will use street cameras to follow the truck. Keep an open line in the car."

Igor had already accessed the street cameras around the mansion. There were many—small wonder since the site was so close to the paranoid capital and even closer to the CIA.

They watched the truck leave the compound and turn right onto the George Washington Parkway. The ample cameras provided streaming and clear video.

"Maybe Eileen wasn't thinking of everything," Valenti said. "She is a devious woman with a cunning mind, but she is just a human being."

Valenti appeared calm again as he directed Oksana and the two young Petrossians. They were only twenty minutes behind, and the truck was considerably slower than Oksana's Mercedes SUV.

CHAPTER 27

OKSANA AND THE GIRLS

Oksana was thankful for Valenti's call. She was hungry for action, and although her hip hurt slightly, she was more than ready. Misha drove while she and Gaby checked their weapons—SIGs for the two youngsters, Oksana's silenced Makarov, plus Israeli submachine guns that made almost no sound when fired.

They followed Valenti's instructions, and Misha tried hard not to exceed the speed limit. A police pullover would be the end of the pursuit.

Oksana was calm, even icy, as she always was when entering battle, and this might just become one.

Valenti confirmed only two men were transporting the captives but said they would undoubtedly be very dangerous, well trained, and on the highest alert. He did not know how many prisoners were in the back of the truck.

Valenti was online through their encrypted satellite communications.

"They're heading west up George Washington toward the first bridge, I guess toward Woodrow Wilson Bridge. How far are you out?"

"It's on our way," Oksana said. "Ten minutes and we should be there."

The traffic cameras were a great help to Igor. He was able to track the truck by flipping from one camera to another.

"They're headed east onto the bridge, but we think they have an escort."

Of course they would have, Oksana thought.

Igor pointed to a black SUV, a Lexus that was following about fifty yards behind the truck, making every turn and keeping the same speed.

"Black Lexus SUV behind. I didn't expect anything else." Valenti was calm and in command.

"Base is lining up satellite coverage just in case, but it will take a few minutes. It's one of theirs, and I don't want to have the whole family on our tails while we go in."

"Okay, copy that, Valenti. We see the bridge ahead. Traffic is moderate. Should be close any minute. Take out in DC? I hope not."

Oksana, sharp as ever, knew an ambush in the city would end badly, but if they entered a complex or a building, there was no other choice.

"No, not in the city. Only if absolutely no other way. Oksana, stay back once you see them. The truck is easy to spot. Blue with 'Mayflower' in white letters on it."

"Five Shells Delicacies Catering," Igor added, "with a shell logo."

"Got it. We see them and the Lexus behind."

The truck and the Lexus were now on 495, the Capital Beltway, heading east, not into the city, making it more difficult to stay out of sight. Oksana decided to rely on Valenti's surveillance and told Misha to fall back.

Interstate 495 had enough cameras to provide them sufficient information about the whereabouts of the truck.

They were out of sight while Igor fed them positions every minute. Traffic was light on the interstate, making the pursuers' situation even more precarious.

Gaby was impatient and urged Misha to get closer, but Oksana calmed her down.

"We must wait for the right time. The main target is the Lexus. That's where the firepower sits. Once we are close enough, there is no second chance. In for kill."

The girls nodded and Gaby went over her weapons again.

"Intersection to Baltimore Washington Parkway ahead. I don't have video. Suggest you get slightly closer now."

Igor warned them just in time, and Misha put her foot down. The Mercedes shot forward until they could see the Lexus and the blue catering truck ahead.

"We see them, Valenti. Any suggestions. No cameras, I guess. They would be ideal here."

"If you have the chance to take out the Lexus now, do it."

Valenti realized that entering a city again would diminish the chances for a clear and fast takeout.

"Now sing and let your bodies move to the rhythm of the music. We're three happy women on a morning drive."

Oksana switched on the radio, and they sang and gyrated to the rhythm of rock music. Misha drove just slightly faster than the Lexus whose passengers must have noticed the approaching Mercedes by now.

The three women smiled and pretended to sing along to a tune they could hardly hear.

Misha pulled alongside the Lexus, and the girls smiled at the four guys, blowing kisses and waving. The men didn't react when Oksana gave her command.

"Now! Kill!"

The right-side windows came down, and the deadly bullets hit the Lexus in a coughing staccato, shattering the vehicle's side windows. Blood flew inside the swerving car. The driver tried desperately to stay on the road, but he eventually lost control and the Lexus tumbled over the shoulder into a ditch.

Misha stopped the Mercedes and was out in a split second, her SIG aimed at the Lexus. The driver was still alive and twitching in his seat. Misha finished him off with a bullet between his pleading eyes.

A truck they had overtaken a mile back pulled up beside them.

"You need any help?" the driver shouted.

"Thanks, we have it under control," Oksana said. "Bad accident. Probably fell asleep."

Oksana waved him away when she heard the high pitch of rotor blades coming in low toward them.

"Shit! They have air cover and we are sitting ducks."

She yelled at the truck driver, "Wait! Yes, we need your help."

She signaled Misha and Gaby to enter the truck while she aimed her submachine gun at the approaching helicopter. The chopper was only a few hundred meters away when she made her move. Oksana jumped into the ditch and climbed up the other side, running into the low bushes that lined the freeway. She deliberately moved slowly so the chopper would see her disappearing into the woods.

"Oksana, come back," Gaby screamed, but Misha understood Oksana's incredibly brave move. No wonder she was a legend.

"She wants the chopper crew to follow her. They haven't seen us yet."

It was time to act. Misha held her SIG at the truck driver's head.

"Just drive and be quiet. We are government agents pursuing terrorists." She flashed fake FBI credentials.

Misha didn't care whether the driver swallowed her lie, but the cool metal of the SIG did the job. He pulled away from the scene of the cruel accident.

Gaby handled communication with Igor and Valenti, explaining the predicament, which silenced Kitty Hawk for a moment.

"We don't have satellite coverage, but it should be up in a moment." Valenti sounded relaxed.

"My chopper is on the way to extract Oksana. Don't think about her now. She is Oksana. We have your coordinates, and we will find her and bring her home safe. We think the blue truck is heading for Baltimore, and I think I know why. Tell your driver to stay on the Beltway."

He was obviously impressed and assured them of his cooperation.

"The blue truck? I saw it before the accident."

He pushed his vehicle to maximum speed, sweeping past other trucks and cars and ignoring headlight flashes and horns.

They couldn't catch up with the catering truck. The two deliverymen had certainly noticed the ambush of their escort.

Valenti was on the line again. Misha turned off the loudspeaker. The driver was already highly motivated to assist the two attractive federal agents.

"We have satellite eyes. The truck is heading toward the harbor, as I suspected. I suggest you try to change transport as soon as you enter the city."

"Roger that. Will do."

At the outskirts of the city Gaby told the driver to stop. She spotted a few cabs parked near a playground.

"Drop us here, please. You have been a great help. I have your details, and your company will hear from us."

Gaby took a picture of his driver's license, which was attached to the dashboard.

They said good-bye and walked casually over to a taxi parked under the trees bordering the playground.

"Harbor area, please," Gaby told the driver.

"Lady, that's a bit vague," he said, laughing. "Baltimore Harbor is a huge area with several hundred docks, jetties, and moorings. Any particular place there?"

Misha was on the satellite phone with Valenti, who directed them to the container ship wharf.

"Go to Dundalk," he said. "It's the outer harbor where the containers are. We are trying hard to figure out which carrier it is. It's positively a container ship. Cavity has used them for years as black sites."

Misha gave the driver directions.

"I was sure you were more yacht girls than freighter hands." He laughed again and seemed to have a good time with the two Petrossians.

"It's quite urgent. An extra fifty for you if you hit it hard," Gaby said.

"I'll my best, ladies, but we have an extremely thorough police force in Baltimore, and I can't afford to get another ticket."

Nevertheless, he kicked his Ford into gear, and in a short time they arrived at Dundalk, just outside the gigantic container wharf.

Misha handed the cab driver a hundred and told him he had done a good job. He thanked her profusely and handed her his card.

"If you need to get out of here, give me a holler. Enjoy the harbor."

Now what?

Misha dialed Valenti, who told her to stand by. Igor was covering the harbor area, looking for the blue truck.

It was sizzling hot on the naked pavement outside the harbor, and Misha and Gaby were dehydrated.

"Let's find a cooler place to wait, and I need a drink," Misha said.

She spotted an eatery near the entrance to the container harbor. That would do. They walked over to the old-style diner, an ancient rail car with booths lining the windows.

They entered and received a warm greeting.

The friendly waitress, who was at least seventy and dressed in what looked like a German dirndl, led them to a booth by a window.

"What would you like to have?" she asked.

"Two Cokes, please," Misha said. "Ice cold."

"We only serve them ice cold, honey."

She smiled and walked over to the counter, quickly returning with the two sodas.

Just after her first huge gulp Misha's satellite phone beeped.

"We have the truck." Igor was excited. "It's inside the harbor somewhere among thousands of containers. They are unloading our friends. You need to get inside. I'll try to get a more accurate location. Move in now."

Easier said than done, Misha thought.

The harbor entrance was guarded, and the lorries delivering containers didn't offer the cover larger trucks would.

"Let's move," Misha said. "We have to get inside somehow. Igor is tracking the catering truck and observed the delivery of the captives. Let's find a way."

For a few minutes, they watched the lorries entering the harbor zone. There was no way to jump on one without getting caught.

"Let's do it the hard way. We hijack a lorry. I think it's the only way to get in," Gaby said, taking command.

They strolled toward the gate, maintaining just enough distance to avoid suspicion.

A huge lorry with a gigantic container on its back turned slowly toward the gate.

The two girls reacted in synchrony, leaping on the right door step, opening the door, and sticking their SIGs into the driver's face.

"If you do what we say, you will live and see your family again," Gaby told him. "If not, we won't hesitate to shoot you and take over your lorry. Now drive us in and be careful about your health."

They climbed into the slumber compartment behind the front seats and made sure the driver heard the clicking as they loaded their weapons.

"We'll let you go once we are inside," Gaby said, "so don't be a hero and you can look forward to a long life."

The truck turned into the gate area where papers were checked, words were exchanged, and some chuckling eased the tension for the girls, who were behind the driver, cool and determined.

The lorry slowly picked up speed and rolled down an alley lined with containers stacked up to the sky.

"Stop here, Arnauld." Gaby found his name on the license attached to the dashboard. "If you stay quiet about this, we won't come after you, understand?"

Arnauld mumbled something that sounded like an okay. One more hard thrust at his chest with the chubby silencer on the SIG made him nod again, this time eagerly.

Gaby and Misha climbed out of the high cabin and ran into the labyrinth of the stacked containers. The lorry gently rolled away. It was a gamble, but they decided to let the driver live. They hoped the corpses would stack up later.

Once in the shadows of the stacked containers, Misha dialed Igor.

"We are in and need directions quickly."

"Understand. Now try to give me a hint where you are."

"Did you see the lorry that stopped quickly? That was our way in. We are less than fifty yards from the stopping point."

"One second." He was breathing heavily. "Yes, I think I've got you. You should move south about two hundred yards. And stay covered by the containers. I haven't seen any guards inside the harbor compound, but there is activity all over. The blue truck is still motionless, and the hostages have been loaded into one of the containers on the third stack. It's at the top. Makes sense if they want to load it soon. Watch for a row that is only three stacks high. It's a bright yellow box."

They ran down the passage between the stacks, checking carefully for company at every open spot and for Arnauld, who might come with a posse.

Then they saw the Five Shells truck parked beside a forklift far bigger than those at a typical factory. That must have been how the thugs lifted their friends to the top container.

The truck appeared abandoned, but they knew better than to fall for too easy prey.

Misha's phone vibrated in her pocket. Valenti.

"Sorry for keeping you in the dark so long. The ship's name is *Inchi Maru*. It's a container vessel, 150,000 tons dead weight and under a Panama flag. We may have gotten lucky. The *Inchi Maru* is still entering the harbor and should dock in about an hour. Try to get the situation under control before that."

"Copy that, sir. Four casualties already today, more to come. Green light?"

"Go ahead with everything you have."

Who was that? Misha had never heard his voice, but he seemed to know what he was talking about.

Gaby pointed upward to where the bright yellow container sat.

"Air conditioners. That's a positive. It's for people—still living people."

The container's air conditioning unit was fed by a thick electric cable reaching up to the movable prison.

"They are alive. It looks like they wanted them buzzing at least for a while."

Misha smiled a mischievous grin that Gaby knew showed absolute determination and total commitment to the mission. She also understood that it would be no easy task to bring their friends down to the ground and out of there. They weren't dealing with Arnauld. Blood would be spilled.

Gaby remembered an episode in Kryilny when she first saw Misha deploy her special smirk. Misha almost killed a seasoned instructor during a hand-to-hand combat session that went too far. It took half a dozen people to get Misha off the unlucky trainer as she applied the deadly tiger claw to his throat. She had just flashed the same smile, which clearly signaled death.

For a few minutes, they watched the blue truck. There still no sign of its crew. Then Gaby got itchy.

"Let's take the truck and wait for them there."

Misha nodded and they moved cautiously toward the vehicle. *Where the fuck are they?* Misha wondered. It didn't make sense to leave the truck where they had unloaded prisoners into one of the containers. She had a dreadful feeling they might be walking into a trap.

Suddenly her phone vibrated again.

"Misha, get out of there. Hide in the second row behind our container.

They somehow seem to be expecting you. Igor spotted them just around the corner to your right. Move! We'll try to track them."

Again the voice she couldn't place, but she followed instructions. Misha grabbed Gaby and pulled her behind the row of containers to their left.

"They know or suspect. According to the guy on the phone, they are ready to ambush us, so let's shuffle the cards again. We will trap them."

At that moment, a chopper whirled overhead on a low flight path.

"I think it's the helicopter from the freeway. I hope they didn't get Oksana," Gaby said.

She was extremely agitated but ready for action. Luckily the noise from the chopper muffled any other sounds.

They ran toward the catering truck, took positions behind it, and had their weapons ready.

"I'm not sure whether they saw us, but who cares now? Let's finish this," Misha said.

She took the lead, running to the next stack of containers where they found the two men from the blue truck aiming their guns right at them.

"It's over, sweeties. Drop them slowly."

The one talking had an Uzi pointed at Misha and Gaby, while the other displayed a shiny H&K full automatic.

But they didn't know the Petrossian girls, who slowly lowered their SIGs as if surrendering. Then they fell flat on the hard pavement and released two fast double taps, hitting the two Cavity soldiers center mass and rendering them helpless.

Misha finished them off with two head shots as the chopper touched down about three hundred yards away.

There was a commotion in the yard, with people running to the chopper from all sides.

"Only two of them. Must be this Cavity everybody is so excited about. They are carrying heavy stuff," Gaby said.

She pulled Misha out of sight.

"We have to get up there and open the container."

She pointed to the yellow box above them and handed Misha the Uzi she had taken from the fallen thug.

"Keep them busy. I'll go up."

Gaby ran over to the huge forklift and started the engine. The heavy diesel belched black smoke from its exhaust pipes.

Misha noticed the chopper crew advancing toward her position with a bunch of yard workers behind them. The workers looked confused, but the chopper crew flashed IDs, which kept them at length.

Misha realized she couldn't use the Uzi with all the workers behind the crew. She had to let them get closer and take out the bad guys with the SIG.

She couldn't make out whether Oksana was in the chopper, but she had a feeling the fabled woman had gotten away.

Behind her she heard the forklift moving up slowly, and Gaby was now fully visible to the chopper crew. They spoke on satellite phones, probably requesting orders. Only fifty yards away now. Misha had to make a decision. Shooting them in full sight of the yard workers would inevitably get the cops involved, but what other choice was there?

She let them come around the corner of the first stack, which put the workers out of the firing line. Misha opened up with the captured Uzi and hit them fully with the first burst. Luckily the Uzi was an almost noiseless weapon, and the sound of the moving forklift covered the coughing of the shots.

They went down hard, but there was no time to finish the job with head shots.

She ran to the forklift. Gaby reached the yellow container and blasted away the lock with two or three shots from her SIG. The right door swung open, and a beaten woman emerged from the opening. *That must be Ketut,* Misha thought. *But where are the others?*

"Only one!" Gaby screamed over the noise of the forklift.

Shit! Only Ketut was in the container with no trace of the others. Gaby pulled Ketut out onto the forklift, and the huge platform moved downward with the two women on it.

Misha could hear sirens approaching and knew the three of them had to leave quickly.

She helped a badly beaten Ketut to the ground and raised her weapon toward the oncoming yard workers.

"We don't want any more trouble. Move back. These are the bad guys."

She pointed at the two wounded thugs. Pity she couldn't finish them off now.

"They are FBI. You shot them!"

"That's what they said," Misha replied.

The worker standing in front of the growing crowd looked determined to get the two female terrorists and to be a hero.

Misha didn't hesitate a second. She released a short burst from the Uzi over the heads of the workers, hitting the container just above them and their leader.

"You!" she shouted at him. "Get me to your car or you die a hero."

The rest slowly retreated from the threatening weapons. Misha grabbed the man by his arm with her SIG at his temple.

"Now move if you want to live. Where is your car?"

He pointed to a faraway spot where dozens of cars were parked. They started to run, Ketut having armed herself with one of the guns from the Cavity thugs.

The police sirens were very near, and Misha realized that leaving by car might have become impossible.

She changed her plan and pulled the worker toward the water.

"We need a boat and getting us one is your only chance to survive."

He clearly understood his predicament and started to cooperate.

"There is a boat, but you have to let me go once you are on it. Please. I have three kids …" His voice trembled.

"We get a boat and you go free. Now hurry."

Fortunately, it was a much shorter run to the water than to the cars. They made it in a few seconds.

"There, the harbor master's boat, but there's a crew. Don't kill them, please."

The large Boston whaler with a weather cabin was moored at the pier behind a huge container ship that was being loaded. A short ladder was attached to the concrete dock, and they sent the worker down first, following him onto the deck.

Two elderly crewmen appeared from the cabin and froze when they saw the pointed guns, slowly raising their arms.

"Start the engine and head down toward the sea!"

Gaby gave the command, but Misha, slightly more experienced, corrected the order.

"No, up to Inner Harbor. Gaby, we are too exposed going out to the sea. I think police choppers will turn up shortly."

"You are right. Sorry. We have to get rid of them, though," Gaby said, pointing to their three hostages.

"No more killing. They are innocent. I'll send them up the ladder now."

The engine was running, and Ketut had unfastened the mooring ropes. Gaby sent the three shaking guys up the ladder just as the first howling police cruisers entered the yard.

Misha took the wheel and pushed the heavy but fast whaler away from the dock, turning it hard to the right and proceeding at full speed up the harbor.

"I know a place on Boston Street," she said, "not a safe house but a bar where I used to hang out a few years back. The owner is a friend, or I hope will still be. It will take us just a few minutes to get there."

The boat plowed through the brown harbor water, leaving a yellowish surf behind it.

"Thank you," Ketut said. She looked weak, her T-shirt ripped to pieces with blood all over it.

"Not now, Ketut," Misha said. "We are glad we have you. We'll talk once we are safe."

Misha steered the boat into the inner harbor. Hundreds of pleasure boats and a few yachts were anchored on the left bank.

"There to the right. That's Boston Street. I'll run the boat up there and we'll jump out. Hold on!"

She took a hard right and proceeded at full speed toward the stony shore, which was walled with concrete blocks. She found a spot where the blocks were only a yard or so high and rammed the boat starboard into the wall.

"Out! Now!" she screamed and pulled Ketut onto one of the low blocks. They reached the street, and Misha led the way to the other side, which was crammed with bars and shops.

"It's the Harpoon, just a few yards from here. Let's not run now. Hide in the open."

A smile appeared on Misha's face when they arrived at the Harpoon, and few moments later they were swallowed by the dark, cozy bar and its mahogany panels.

Only two other guests sat at the counter. A guy who looked like a pregnant elephant, his shirt stretched to the max, stood behind the counter and stared at them.

"Misha, is that you or are my eyes getting worse?"

"It's me, Dan. Our friend here fell into a ditch and hurt herself," she said, pointing at Ketut. "We need to wash up and get a drink."

Dan lifted a lever and came out from behind the bar.

"You poor thing. This looks bad. Come with me."

He pulled Ketut gently to a side door marked "Private." Gaby and Misha followed.

"That's not from a fall and you know it. Better tell me everything so I know how deep I stand in the shit."

"You are right," Misha said. "It wasn't a fall. It was torture. We need to melt away for a while. Can I count on you?"

"Did you ever have to ask?"

He opened a door that led upstairs to his living quarters, a tastfully furnished apartment with a great view of the harbor.

"I don't want to know, Misha, but you can stay here as long as it takes. The two drunks downstairs are friends of mine, and I'll find the right story if necessary. You remember my private bar. It's stocked as well as downstairs. Take care of her and relax."

"You have some friends, I must say!"

Gaby's smile was back. They undressed Ketut, and Misha found medical supplies in Dan's bedroom. It took them almost an hour to clean up Ketut, tend to her numerous wounds, and dress her in one of Dan's shirts, which looked like a tent on her.

"Now we need a drink!" Misha said.

Juice for Ketut and two ice-cold beers for them.

"Whenever you are ready, Ketut, tell us what happened to the others."

CHAPTER 28

THE CAVITY MANSION

Eileen Cahill was content. She watched the Mayflower truck leave her estate with the Petrossian and ordered coffee. Everything seemed to be under control, and the Indonesian bitch might come in handy as a bargaining chip later.

She had formed a new plan for the assassinations. Although the Iranian scapegoats were in place to kill the president and the king of Saudi Arabia, the Petrossians provided a much more attractive option.

Eileen was extremely pleased with the new twist in her vicious plan. Petrossian would be eliminated once and for all. Cavity would not prevent the assassination of the president but would lead a crackdown after the horrendous crime and, in doing so, would kill the Petrossian assassins and expose their global network. Just brilliant!

The involvement of two high-ranking CIA officers in the killing of the president would again provide Cavity with an official status after many years in the dark.

Her way to the top was now unstoppable.

It was time to have a talk with her captives to tell them about her strategy.

Eileen left her office but not before checking with the crew in the Mayflower truck. All was going according to plan. They hadn't spotted a tail, and why would they? After all, they were driving a harmless delivery truck.

She took an escort with her down to the basement where the Petrossians and the two CIA dummies were kept without water or food.

Eileen opened the heavy steel access door and walked in behind the bulletproof glass panel. On the other side it, her prisoners were lying on the concrete floor.

"Good morning, all of you. Your Indonesian lassie was useless for me, and she will find herself at the bottom of the Potomac with a heavy weight attached to her divine body."

She relished the horror in their faces. Only Fedorov showed no emotion. Once again, Eileen realized he was the most dangerous of the bunch.

"Now let me fill you in on what will happen next."

Her lizard sneer almost made me jump through the glass plate separating us, but Fedorov slowly shook his head, and I conserved my energy for what I hoped would be other opportunities.

"You all will go down in the history books, and going down is exactly the right expression."

She grabbed a chair and sat down outside the cell, which was sound-connected but escape-proof.

"You will assassinate the president of the United States."

She paused to watch our reaction and continued when there was none.

"I'll let you do that, you know," she said, laughing like the mentally disturbed woman she was.

Eileen detailed her malicious strategy. We would be the scapegoats for the president's assassination. The Iranians would kill King Salman in Mecca the same day the president would be shot in Washington, DC.

In retribution, rogue but nationalistic Saudis close to the IS would carry out a nuclear attack on Iran, sealing the fate of the Middle East and of Petrossian.

I wasn't sure what to think, but I was slightly impressed by her plan to seize power—Cavity the crime solver, Eileen the national hero and, of course, her organization the leader of US intelligence.

She told us how we would be found just after the killing of the president, how we would put up a fight with the heroic Cavity agents, and how, naturally, we would lose the fight and our useless lives.

"Where will that happen?"

I could feel Fedorov's serenity and almost touch his ice-cold mind.

"You will find out when we ship you to your funeral and, of course, to the president's."

A soldier entered the room where our captor sat sneering at us. He whispered something in her ear, and I was pleasantly surprised to see the lizard woman's face get pale, her predator eyes trained on us.

"We'll talk later about your funeral arrangements."

With that, she left the room and we were alone again.

"I'm sure something good just happened," Fedorov said with a wink.

Eileen Cahill stormed upstairs where she grabbed the phone and started shouting.

"How could that happen? Do I have amateurs in my ranks? Fuck! Find them!"

She was outraged at the news that the Mayflower truck's escort had been ambushed and the protective crew killed.

The chopper crew reported looking for the attackers in the woods beside the highway but said the forest was too dense to see any of them.

"Ten minutes max for the search, then out and follow the truck. If you see them, shoot to kill. No prisoners. They must have known about the truck."

But how? she wondered. The plan was waterproof and there were no watchers outside the mansion. Her cameras were all over the area. Fucking Petrossian!

Eileen decided to call Valenti to stress her intent to kill all of the prisoners.

Again, she had to wait for a few minutes until Valenti Assarian finally came on.

"How did you know? Now you are trying to free your people, but I hold the most valuable, Fedorov."

"My dear Eileen, I don't know what you are talking about. I was hoping we could make a deal. I know very well about the security measures you have taken at your family home. Simply impenetrable. What are you insinuating?"

"Let's not pretend, Valenti, okay? You tried and you failed. Now it's time for me to take action. You call off your agents or I'm going to kill Fedorov."

"You would make Oksana very unhappy, and you know what she is capable of when she is annoyed."

"Good bluff, Valenti, but I know for sure that Oksana is in Germany, and we will hunt her down there."

Petrossian obviously hadn't gotten hold of the truck yet, Eileen decided. Valenti didn't know that only the Asian bitch was being transported. Nothing lost yet. She produced an ugly smile.

"Listen Valenti and listen well. I'm going to finish Petrossian once and for all, and you will all go down in the history books. In a few days Petrossian will indeed be history."

She hammered the receiver onto its cradle and shrieked a command to get her video from the chopper.

The chopper was still hovering over the forest beside the freeway, and Eileen knew that finding the attackers by air would be next to impossible.

"Get out of there and off to the harbor. The truck should have arrived by now, but since they knew, expect trouble. Kill immediately."

The nose mounted camera gave her a clear view of the flight path the chopper took—a straight line to Baltimore Harbor. She hoped the Petrossians who ambushed the escort were all somewhere in the forest, hiding from the chopper.

She scrolled through the chopper recordings from right after the attack. No other car was nearby, so the Petrossians couldn't have been picked up. The freeway was almost deserted except for a truck that seemed to have stopped for a brief moment. The attackers had abandoned their Mercedes, which was being searched by the highway police.

The truck. How could the chopper crew have overlooked that?

"Did you see a truck at the site?"

"I think so," the helicopter pilot replied. "There was a container truck rolling by when we arrived."

"Could it have stopped? This is vital."

"I guess so, but as I said, when we arrived it was rolling."

"Look out for it. It may go to the harbor, but don't lose too much time."

"Copy that, ma'am."

The pilot and the shooter tried hard to remember what the truck looked like.

"I guess we fucked up back there," the shooter said over the intercom. "Let's go to the harbor and bring her down inside. If there is trouble I'll open up."

He checked his submachine gun and was satisfied that his baby was ready to spread hell.

Meanwhile, Eileen communicated with the crew in the Mayflower truck.

"No, ma'am, we had no tail. Positive. We are in the harbor. The captive is on her way up to the third floor. About two minutes to go. We are clear."

"Give me a heads up once she is stored."

"Yes, ma'am."

While this was happening we held a conference in our cell. I had made out the hidden cameras earlier and had found the dead angle, which was just beside the prison cell toilet. *How considerate*, I thought.

Fedorov sat on the toilet while the rest of us stood beside it. We whispered and hoped the system wasn't too sensitive. If Igor installed it, even the slightest sound would transmit.

"They have moved Ketut," I said. "That means their plan is heading for the next step. We have to get out even if it costs some of us our lives."

I was serious and my friends understood, nodding in accord.

"That Cahill woman is going to kill the president and blame it on us. If it wasn't for that, I might look the other way."

Fedorov and his sarcastic mind.

I looked at the others.

"I know you might have a different perception of things. Besides planning to kill the president, she's going after Petrossian. A double kill for Cavity."

"Look, Matt, our lives have the same value as yours, meaning not much right now," Walter said. "We would be better off going down now before they slaughter us at the assassination site."

Walter was adamant and Mark nodded his agreement.

"I'm retired and know much too much after Frank's confession and breakdown—even if it's irrelevant now since Cohen was merely Cavity's tool. Frank didn't know shit about Eileen Cahill and Cavity. I'm in. Let's attack them with full force."

Fedorov took off his belt as he sat on the toilet, the camera's dark spot. He pulled something out of the leather that looked like a two-inch needle.

"Remember the frog poison, Matt? I still carry it."

When he and Oksana were in Chad they hid for days with a tribe in the north that was notorious for its poisons, which were sold all over Chad and in neighboring countries.

Members of the tribe extracted the poison from so-called flying frogs that lived in the marshlands of northern Chad. Fedorov once told me he had used the poison on one of his torturers and was amazed at how quickly and efficiently it worked. He and Oksana had procured enough frog poison to kill thousands. Now I saw a faint opportunity.

"One needle for how many?"

"At least three of them within seconds, but I have to be careful not to hit myself."

His smirk was reassuring.

"At some point, they have to take us out. All we must do is refuse to be cuffed. I will hit one of them, which may result in gunfire. The objective is to seize some of their guns and then to shoot our way out of here.

"There is no guarantee we can get out of here unharmed, so I'm happy to see your commitment. I don't give a damn about this president's life. Petrossian is the priority. If this Cahill woman manages to destroy us, she might take down the world."

We all nodded and returned to our positions on the cold concrete floor.

"For what she did to Ketut, the lizard lady is mine, and I don't want to waste a bullet or my precious frog juice."

Fedorov was adamant about that, and I knew him too well to doubt his intent.

We were very thirsty, and I recognized the objective of our captors.

A cold, dry cell, with a dehumidifier sucking out all the moisture, would turn us into willing cooperators if we were offered something to drink.

I whispered instructions to my cellmates. "Lick your hands and your arms," I said. "We still produce vital salt. Fake weakness for the cameras. Focus your mind on the upcoming action. Believe in it, and pray that we get a break."

The toilet was no help. It was a military-style dry version used in desert camps and didn't require water to function.

The hours passed with our jailers nowhere in sight, and we all grew frailer.

We didn't have our watches and had no daylight to judge the time.

But just when we thought we could do nothing more than lick the salt from our bodies, the steel door outside the glass panel opened.

"You!" one of the armed jailors said, pointing to Fedorov. "You are first to go. The future president of the United States wants to do the honors herself. The rest of you back to the wall."

He menaced us with his submachine gun, seemingly unaware of the bulletproof glass.

Eileen had picked Fedorov! She must have felt very secure if she had chosen the deadliest among us, but on the other hand her emotions dictated her decision. Fedorov was her longtime nemesis, and now she would destroy him, unquestionably after torturing him first.

We all moved to the rear wall and stood around the toilet while a portion of the glass panel hissed and moved sideways into the wall. Fedorov put up a show and balked at leaving the cell. In response, the loudmouth captor took two steps forward with the other two behind him. Oddly enough, they pointed their weapons at everyone except Fedorov.

When he reached the opening in the glass panel, Fedorov made his move. Slowly, as if surrendering, he lifted his arms above his shoulders and then let them come down with all the force he could muster. I noticed the shining needle sinking into the loudmouth's neck while Fedorov's right elbow struck the guy standing at his side. The first captor was down in a split second and the other knocked totally off balance, but the third was able to react.

His shot, from a handgun, missed Fedorov, but Bernie, our young Petrossian, standing beside me, was hit in the chest.

I had no time to tend to him but leaped like a hungry predator to the gap in the panel and then onto the shooter. His second shot, which was deafening, hit my shoulder, but it was too late for him. Fedorov's needle was already in his neck, and bubbles formed on his lips almost instantly. These frogs really were lethal.

Mark finished off the guy who had made contact with Fedorov's elbow, twisting his head in a quick move that instantly severed his spine.

I ran back to the cell where I found a dying Bernie, blood spurting out of his mouth, his pulse almost nonexistent.

I closed his dying eyes and gently stroked his forehead.

"He is gone. We'll get his body out later."

The earsplitting sound of the two shots must have alerted the rest of the bastards. We armed ourselves with the handguns and the single sub and proceeded slowly to the open steel door. I peeked out and found a deserted, brightly lit hallway but no stairs. There was an elevator at the end of the hall, the one that brought us down to our cell the previous night. I wondered how deep underground our location was. I hoped very deep so maybe the shots were not heard. But I had overlooked the cameras in our cell that would have displayed our move on the lizard lady's monitors.

"You are bleeding," Fedorov said, checking my arm, "but I think it's just a scratch."

Only then did I feel the pain in my shoulder.

"It's nothing. I think it went through all the way. However, I'm worried about my golf." I tried to be funny, but my face said something else.

Fedorov tore away my shirt and inspected the wound.

"Yes, I believe you are right. It went through clean. Maybe the bone is intact. Let me put on a tourniquet to stop the bleeding."

He tore a piece from my shirt and bandaged me so tightly I almost didn't feel the pain anymore.

We were more than surprised that until now our captors had taken no counteraction. Maybe nobody was watching the monitors. A slim hope. We had to get out of this vault.

I tried the "up" button at the elevator door, and the doors opened with a whoosh. What the hell?

We entered the cabin. There were only three buttons to choose from—one, for the lowest level, where we were, and two others with no description. I decided to push the top one, wherever that might bring us.

"Open fire only if absolutely necessary but be ready," I said.

I placed our firepower at two sides of the elevator because the doors could open either way.

Mark had the submachine gun, an H&K, a top-quality German weapon, aimed at the side where we entered. Fedorov, Walter, and I aimed Glocks at the other side. Veronica and Tatiana stood ready to fight.

The elevator's ascent took longer than we anticipated, so we knew the prison was deep underground. Finally it stopped, and the door on the side from which we entered opened onto a hallway that must have been on the second or third floor.

The hall was furnished with antiques that reminded me of my ex-father-in-law's house in Rome. The small hairs on the back of my neck rose.

The situation got even stranger as we slowly proceeded down the hall toward a huge wound stairway that led to the place where the lizard lady had served us drinks the previous night.

The sound of sirens outside made me extremely nervous. I ran to a window that overlooked the entrance to the mansion and saw black SUVs escorted by motorcycles and followed by the presidential limousine entering the grounds.

I immediately realized the devilish plan the lizard lady had hatched. Our escape was calculated so we would be trapped in the house while the president was assassinated. Eileen must have used some ruse to bring the president here.

Fedorov and the others instantly saw our predicament.

"Someone has to warn the president," Walter said, "or he and we are done."

At that instant two doors opened behind us, and half a dozen heavily armed Cavity goons emerged from them.

"You can see there is no way out for you. Drop your weapons and do exactly as I say," the leader said in a calm tone.

Fedorov and I raised our arms, still holding our captured guns. Walter and Mark did the same. Then, with no command needed, we opened fire on the Cavity operatives, well knowing that they outnumbered us and that we could be mowed down in an instant. But that was still better than being shot as the president's assassins.

Obviously, they didn't expect our reaction, which made their first volley inaccurate to say the least. A bullet entering a human body makes a nasty sound that cannot be adequately described. That's what I clearly heard. Mark Shearer, my dear old friend, was hit. He stumbled and fell forward, which rescued him from the next bullet.

He was down beside me and still emptying his Glock into the Cavity operatives. Their fire receded, and fewer and fewer bullets hit the far wall of the hall. We seized the opportunity to retreat.

As I suspected, the noise from the sirens and from the heavy vehicles had muffled the sound of the shooting.

We entered a room that looked like a guest chamber with a huge poster bed, Persian carpets, and Gobelins on the walls.

We checked the windows and saw that a Secret Service agent was about to open the door of the presidential limousine.

"They are going to kill him here, and we are the scapegoats. That's why they let us move in here."

Fedorov agreed with me.

"We need a distraction. A fire! Look for matches and anything that burns quickly."

We pulled Mark onto one of the Persian carpets where Walter examined his wound.

"Not too bad. Flesh only, probably the kidney. He is bleeding hard. I'll take care of him. Go light a fire."

Tatiana found a heavy table lighter and grabbed a Gobelin that looked old enough to catch fire easily. Indeed, the flames rose in just a few seconds, smoke crawling up the wall.

Veronica opened the window, and I hoped the smoke could be seen from below.

The president left his car and walked toward the entrance where, unseen by us, the lizard lady welcomed him to her humble home.

God praise the ever-vigilant Secret Service.

"Fire!" one of the agents shouted, pointing up toward our position.

The president was pulled back to the limousine and shoved inside. Eileen Cahill came into view, staggering out from under the roof in her high heels and looking at the smoke escaping our window.

She barked a few unintelligible commands, which were probably misinterpreted by the Secret Service men. They pulled her to one of the SUVs and loaded her like a piece of wood into the vehicle, which raced down the driveway toward the exit. Apparently, Eileen Cahill was regarded as important enough to be saved from a fire in her own house.

Walter was still working on Mark, using his shirt to stop the excessive bleeding.

Tatiana high-fived me, saying, "That worked. Now let's save ourselves."

Some half a dozen Secret Service men remained on the grounds, probably waiting for the DC fire department. Without a miracle, we would soon be discovered.

We heard the Cavity goons outside our door, undoubtedly preparing for a final attack but also realizing we had the advantage for the time being. Anyone entering the room was doomed.

"Leave me here and try the window. The Secret Service knows me, and I can explain my presence."

Mark tried to be hero once again.

"We leave together, or we go up in smoke together," I told him.

The Gobelin was engulfed in flames, and the smoke was getting thicker every minute, making it difficult to breathe but giving us a chance to climb out to the narrow roof without being noticed from below.

"That's a million dollars up in smoke," Veronica said with a grin as the Gobelin burned.

"Let's go out to the roof," I said.

We hauled Mark out the window and told him to stay put until we all were out. He protested but to no avail. We made it to the narrow, steep roof, fully covered in white smoke, when I heard the sirens from the fire engines.

"Quick, around the corner," I said. "There we'll be in a blind spot from below."

I dragged Mark with all my strength. Fedorov was the last to leave the room, climbing like an alley cat toward our new position.

"Two minutes max for the fire department," I said. "We have to hide and then find a way down."

The part of the roof we occupied was almost flat with huge chimneys from the fireplaces below. We seated Mark with his back to one of them while I desperately sought a way down. I didn't care about being seen now. We looked like legal residents caught by the fire and trying to get to safety.

The first fire engine entered the compound, and we were revealed to the Secret Service men down below.

One of them pointed the firefighters in our direction.

They sent a ladder from the fire engine up to where we were on the roof.

"We have an injured man here. Bring him down first," I shouted at a firefighter, pointing to Mark.

He spoke into his walkie-talkie, and like magic, a hydraulic arm with a stretcher attached appeared right where Mark lay.

We heaved him onto the stretcher, the hydraulic arm swung away with Mark on it, and we climbed down the ladder.

Medics, probably overtrained, hung blankets over our shoulders as if we were freezing to death and led us to an ambulance with its rear doors wide open.

"Here, drink. It will help to clear your respiratory system," a firefighter said as he handed us water bottles. Our lungs were okay, but we all appreciated the water, gulping it greedily.

One of the firemen noticed our weapons and opened his mouth to ask questions. I headed him off, saying, "We are part of the security team for the president's visit."

I flashed an ID that showed the letters CIA. He was satisfied and let us enjoy the cool water.

"We need to leave," Fedorov said, pulling my arm. "Mark is in good hands, and I ordered them to bring him to George Washington University. We need phones urgently."

I asked the firefighter in the ambulance to lend me his phone. "Mine is back in the fire," I said.

I dialed Igor's phone.

"Hello?"

"Igor, it's me. I'm ..."

"Boss, where are you? Are you okay? Valenti is crawling up the walls here. Ketut is safe ..."

"Hold it, Igor. We are safe for now."

I looked back toward the mansion where some of the Cavity operatives stood in the doorway, knowing they could not attack us now.

"We have no communication and no transport but we are out."

"Here is Valenti."

"Matt, are you out?"

Valenti was edgier than I thought he could be. I described our dilemma in as few words as possible.

"Take the ambulance with Mark Shearer to WU Hospital. The chopper is nearby, and we can use the helipad there. Call when you arrive."

I had to make it clear that we were stripped of communications equipment and therefore could not make a call.

"It's all timing. Hold on. How long will it take us to reach WU?" I asked the fireman who gave me his phone.

"Twenty minutes, maybe a bit less."

"Did you get that, Valenti?"

"Okay, clear. I'll direct the chopper to the helipad there. Are you all okay?"

I decided not to tell him about Bernie, the only casualty up to now.

"We can't leave Mark at the hospital. They will get to him immediately."

"Understood. I'll arrange for a safe house and a doctor. The pilots will know. Now move."

We all crammed into the ambulance and told the driver to rush.

With some malicious pleasure, I noticed the helpless Cavity men behind us, waiting to get slaughtered by the lizard lady once she returned.

Siren blaring, the ambulance was racing up George Washington Memorial when I again asked the medic for his phone.

"Okay, Valenti. Where to?"

He gave me an address in Foxcroft Heights, which was about fifteen minutes away.

"Take Interstate 395 west to Foxcroft Heights," I instructed the driver.

"But WU is the other way, sir."

"Just do what I say."

"Your friend needs medical attention quickly, sir. I have to inform my captain."

I showed him the captured Glock and said, "National security. Take 395 and don't ask any more questions."

I knew WU would be a graveyard for Mark if we delivered him there. Nothing could stop the Cavity operatives now, especially after the disaster at the mansion.

I also ordered the siren turned off. We made good time just with the flashing lights and reached Foxcroft Heights a few minutes later. I called Valenti again, and he told me the chopper would touch down at a soccer field just opposite Arlington National Cemetery in less than five minutes.

We arrived just in time to watch the sleek Bell helicopter swing in and land on the deserted soccer field.

The ambulance pulled up to the chopper, and we unloaded Mark and carried him to the aircraft. With all on board, I tossed the mobile phone to the ambulance driver and thanked him for his cooperation.

We took off, and the chopper made a sharp turn to the west. I slipped on the intercom while the pilot connected me to Valenti.

"Where to, Valenti?"

"Manassas Battlefield Park, just a few minutes' flight. An old friend of mine takes care of the Civil War museum at the park. He is a retired surgeon. He's been informed and is expecting you. Call from there. There is one satellite phone in the helicopter for you to use. The chopper crew will drop you off and then pick up Oksana. No questions now. I'll talk to you later, but she is okay."

I noticed the relief in Fedorov's face.

"Oksana is back and Ketut is safe. Well, what else could go right?"

Mark sounded hurt, but he'd tried to make a joke. That was good to hear.

The Bell approached the Civil War battleground where General Thomas J. Jackson had acquired his nickname, Stonewall Jackson. We could see ancient artillery pieces on the peaceful lawn beneath us and a low-roofed stone house toward which the chopper was heading.

After a soft touchdown, we carried Mark to the house where an elderly gentleman with gold-rimmed glasses ushered us in. He'd obviously been briefed by Valenti.

"I'm Dr. Marshal and this is my wife Betsy."

A friendly woman maybe half his age, dressed like a hospital nurse, greeted us with a bright smile.

"Bring him in here, please," she said, pointing to a brightly lit room stuffed with Civil War artifacts, miniature soldiers fighting the battle all over again and a high bedstead that resembled a military field cot.

Betsy took Mark's blood pressure, cleaned his entry wound, and prepared a plasma infusion.

"Betsy was a surgical nurse at Walter Reed. She knows what she is doing," Dr. Marshal said. Between the two of them, I was quite sure Mark was in capable hands.

"Now go to the living room, and let us do our work. Sorry I don't have vodka, but there is cold beer in the fridge."

He winked at us and we left the battlefield couple alone with Mark.

I dialed Valenti on the satellite phone and got Igor.

"Hi, boss! I'm relieved that you are all okay. I hope your CIA friend pulls through. Listen, Valenti is talking to the Cahill woman, and I'm glad to hear she is really pissed. Oksana is okay …"

I interrupted him. "Igor, calm down and tell me everything slowly. So Oksana is back from Germany? Where is she?"

Igor told me about the ambush on the freeway, the rescue operation in Baltimore Harbor, and the heroic action by Oksana to pull the enemy chopper away from the others.

"Okay, where are the three girls—Ketut, Misha, and Gaby?"

"All I know is a bar in Baltimore. Not even Valenti knows the connection. Apparently, an acquaintance of one of the girls works there. I heard they will be extracted soon. But I have lots of info about movement in the Persian Gulf and in Al Jubail and about some strange shipping connections. You will be flown here as soon as we have the girls and Oksana."

I told him to ask Valenti to call me ASAP, opened a cold beer, and sat down on one of the ancient leather chairs that decorated the living room.

It was the best beer I'd had in a long time!

Veronica and Tatiana enjoyed the ice-cold beer just as much.

"I vow to go back and break the lizard's neck, but not before I've had fun with her," Veronica said.

The nun had made her vow, and I knew she was a deadly killer.

CHAPTER 29
KITTY HAWK

Valenti had just finished talking with Eileen Cahill. She was adamant that Petrossian's days were numbered despite the small setback at her mansion.

The president had agreed earlier to meet the almost officially reinstated head of Cavity at her residence for brunch and a briefing. All had been planned to perfection, and the narrative was set—the Petrossians assassinating the president and Cavity killing the murderous traitors.

Igor tried in vain to record the call, because she was speaking on one of the newest NSA-developed secure communication tools, which automatically overlaid a conversation with an unremovable audio track as soon as a recording device was detected.

"The Gobelin your agents burned in my house was a piece owned by Catherine the Great when she reigned over Russia from Kiev. For that alone I will erase Petrossian once and for all."

Veronica had been right—at least a million dollars!

Valenti tried to convince Eileen to release Bernie Mathison's body for a proper funeral, but she refused and told him to fish the agent's remains out of the Potomac.

Valenti, usually serene, slammed down the receiver. The veins in his forehead were swollen, and drops of sweat gathered on his brow.

He prided himself on bringing his agents home, and now one of them, a promising young professional, had been killed in action by a monster.

Igor shook his head, indicating he was unable to record.

Igor was heavily engaged in tracking a freighter in the Persian Gulf that was carrying sheep from New Zealand to Saudi Arabia. He hacked into a Russian Razdan satellite that was covering the gulf, Iran, and the Saudi coast.

The images from this newest Russian surveillance system were astonishing, even better than what the NSA together with NASA produced. Igor was following all Hun Wha vessels in the gulf. The *Chong Gang Gang* was on its way from Al Jubail, but he was still in the dark about its destination.

"Igor, watch the CNN report from Saudi Arabia," Valenti said. "There's been a bombing in Mecca."

The reporter, a veiled Western woman, quite obviously was in shock while reporting live from Mecca where just a few minutes earlier a blast had occurred on the holy ground around the Kaaba.

Igor turned up the volume.

"An explosion of huge force struck the holy ground around the Kaaba where thousands of hajj pilgrims were praying. We have no report at this point on how many dead or injured the horrendous attack has left. However, we know his majesty, King Salman, was near the Kaaba when the blast struck."

The reporter paused and listened attentively to the voice in her headset. She wiped sand or soot from the blast from her eyes. The intense wind made a clear view almost impossible.

"We hear now that his majesty is safe and has been escorted out of the Kaaba by hundreds of heavily armed security guards. The death toll might well be in the hundreds with the grounds packed to capacity. We will update viewers as the situation develops."

Valenti remained composed and in control, although Igor could sense he was shocked.

"Igor, it's of the utmost importance that you track this sheep freighter and watch for any rendezvous-vous with a vessel or a chopper."

Valenti's satellite phone beeped. Matt.

"Did you see the news? We know what they are about to roll out. First the president here, then the king there, and then the programmed retaliation against Iran. We need intel about which group was responsible for this atrocious attack."

"I agree with you, Matt. That's why you have to get back here immediately. The Bell is loading Misha, Gaby, and Ketut right now outside Baltimore. I could warn the president, but as we know, he is not the brightest light in Washington and listens only to Eileen Cahill."

"There is no use, Valenti. All he wants is to kill the nuclear deal with Iran, and this is his opportunity. I bet Iranians will soon be captured and blamed for the hit on the Kaaba."

"Igor is tracking a Hun Wha sheep freighter that is on the way from New Zealand to Al Jubail. We are still in the Russian Razdan that monitors the Persian Gulf and the Saudi coast, but I'm afraid not for much longer. They'll try hard to shut us out."

"Talk to the FSB, but it has to be very high up."

"They too are not enthusiastic supporters of Petrossian right now after we exposed some of the corrupt people in their ranks. But I'll try."

Igor frantically tried to break down the newly rising firewalls, and he was successful. After all, he had designed the security for the Razdan satellites. However, the FSB now knew who was hacking its sky baby. Follow-up contracts with the FSB might become hard to obtain unless Petrossian could produce some miracles.

He guessed he might have access to the satellite for an hour at the most before the Russians pulled the plug and rendered the Razdan blind for him.

The news from Saudi Arabia grew more disturbing by the minute. The attack represented a threat to world peace.

Correspondents from all news channels reported panic and chaos not only within the Kaaba but all over Mecca. The unrest spread quickly to Riyadh, Medina, Jeddah, and other Saudi Arabian cities. The king was slightly injured and flown out by a fleet of helicopters to a nearby airbase.

Valenti received the encouraging news that his team was safely on board the Bell and on the way to Kitty Hawk. He needed Matt and Fedorov to help decide how to tackle this unsettling situation.

The president would listen to the Cavity leader, and the Russians would not trust Petrossian now, especially after learning who had hacked into one of their satellites. Further, after the Bali incident and the capture of a Mukhabarat leader, Colonel Hyder, the Saudis would probably ignore Petrossian and would prepare for war with whomever they thought was behind the assassination attempt at the Kaaba.

An approach to the Mossad might provide payback, but the Israelis were more interested in planning for war than in avoiding it.

"Igor, where are the sheep? Do you still have a visual?"

Valenti understood it was imperative to follow the vessel even if there was no clear evidence of foul play.

"Entering the Gulf of Oman and in the last fifteen minutes dropping from nine knots to five and getting slower. I'm sure they are expecting a rendezvous-vous."

Valenti concurred with this analysis and realized time was running out.

"How long can you stay in?"

"I guess another hour unless the Russians kill it, but that wouldn't make sense. My guess is they are eager to find out what we are looking for. If I'm right, that would give us the time we need."

Valenti was thankful for Igor's brilliant mind. He was right. The Russians might as well let them use the Razdan until they knew what Petrossian was after. Then there would be time to contact them and to offer the Kremlin a great diplomatic opportunity.

"Watch and inform. I need a drink."

Igor couldn't care less. He was busy observing the strange movements of the freighter on his screen. It was impossible to make out the name of the ship, but he had an idea. He was already deep into Hun Wha's rather elementary IT system, which contained no particularly hard firewalls, and his software could crack all the simple passwords within minutes.

With one eye on the freighter's maneuvers, he examined Hun Wha's ship deployment in the Indian Ocean for the last three weeks.

Here it was. Igor thought he had found the sheep carrier on a log that had it going from Auckland, New Zealand, to the Persian Gulf, although without any defined unloading destination.

The vessel had 5,500 New Zealand sheep, lambs, and other livestock in its hull. This made sense because toward the end of Ramadan mutton was in high demand in the Arab nations.

Igor scrolled through lists of vessels to find a match with the schedule he had unlocked. He identified the ship as the *Jae Eun*, an eight-thousand-ton multifunctional bulk carrier, refitted for the transport of live animals.

The captain was a former South Korean navy commander, Kim Yah On, a veteran seaman from Incheon in the service at Hun Wha for more than twenty years.

Igor immediately transmitted all his findings to the base and to his save cloud, seventh heaven.

He noticed that the *Jae Eun* had stopped and that the Russians had finally joined him in observing the Korean vessel's weird maneuvers.

The signature of FSB intrusion on the satellite was strong enough to convince Igor the Russians were equally interested in the surveillance.

The *Jae Eun* lay motionless about 150 miles northwest of Muscat in international waters, not too close to Yemen or Iran.

Igor thought it was time to call Valenti. What he had long suspected seemed to be happening right now. A sleek submarine emerged on the lee side of the freighter. Igor's software quickly identified the type, a Romeo class sub of 1,800 tons, the largest the North Korean navy was operating.

Valenti stood behind Igor, fascinated by the action on the screen. The Razdan pictures were the clearest of all satellite surveillance in the world. They could see every detail on the ships and could almost identify individuals on the freighter.

Igor pointed to the tube-shaped cargo attached to the upper hull of the sub.

"These are Hwasongs, North Korea's most accurate ballistic missiles, with a range of five hundred to a thousand miles, more than enough to reach Iran from anywhere in the immediate Arab world. Their cargo capacity would allow a mini nuke, one of those Cohen developed and probably tested in North Korea."

Valenti scratched his head, thinking hard.

"Are the Russians watching too?" he asked.

"Yes, they are in, and since I overrode their surveillance access they are piggybacking on mine. I don't think they will shut us out soon. I would take them hours to restore their own settings."

"Any Russian navy ships in the immediate area?"

"None. They are all in the Mediterranean and Black Sea for Russian anti-ISIS support and to keep Assad in power in Syria."

"Well, the Americans can be counted out with Cavity slowly taking control of their intelligence operations. The Saudis? Maybe."

In the background a CNN report appeared on a huge monitor.

"Saudi Arabia has announced that the bombers who devastated the Kaaba a few hours earlier have been identified and apprehended. According to the Saudi News Agency SPA, the attackers are of Iranian origin. However, no terrorist group has claimed responsibility yet. The statement by SPA says the Saudi intelligence service, Al Mukhabarat Al A'amah, received assistance from a not-yet-identified US intelligence operation. The five attackers were killed during the arrest process. One of the slain attackers apparently had identification for MOIS, the Iranian Intelligence agency, on him. We are joined by Stephen McGard, CNN's Middle East expert, who will outline the grave consequences this murderous attack will undoubtedly bring. The death toll has risen to more than two hundred pilgrims. Stephen, thanks for being with us ..."

Valenti turned down the volume.

"Eileen Cahill's shrewd planning had paid off up to now, although the assassination attempts failed."

Igor pointed to the screen where two cranes from the freighter were heaving the tubes on board the sheep vessel.

At that instant, the screen displaying the house surveillance feeds showed the Bell approaching the helipad.

"Great timing," Valenti mumbled and went outside.

We were slightly cramped in the normally roomy Bell helicopter. My wound was getting on my nerves, and I could almost hear every beat of my pulse.

We were all back in Kitty Hawk except for Mark. His injury proved to be too severe to allow him to travel in the chopper for more than an hour. We left him with the battleground caretakers, who promised he would be good to go in two or three days.

Another doctor friend of Valenti took care of the damage to Ketut's face.

Dr. Kerian, another Armenian, was about the same age as Valenti. He had been the top medical professional in Kitty Hawk for almost half a century, taking care of sick or injured golfers and sport fishermen. I wasn't sure whether he was part of the circle, but I didn't care as long as he was doctoring Ketut.

Before he started to work on Ketut, he looked at my scratch. It wasn't much more. The bullet entered my left upper arm and tore out a piece of flesh. I was feeling pain, but it couldn't stop me. The doc cleaned the wound, stitched me up, and released me to my friends, who were gathered in the communications chamber behind Igor.

We invited Walter Wills, an outsider to join us, Valenti greeted him warmly.

"Let me set the facts straight," Valenti said, addressing me and Fedorov. "The Cavity assassination schemes failed, the one against the president because of you and the one against the Saudi king because the people executing the bomb attack either had bad intel or were too agitated to hit the button at the right time.

"Eileen Cahill may be quite happy that the president hasn't been killed just yet. That gives her more leverage on the Iran nuclear agreement. We all know this president sooner or later would have torn up that piece of paper anyway, and now he has motive to do it sooner."

The butler interrupted briefly to bring us water, coffee, and soft drinks, though no vodka.

"By financing the Islamic State over the last three years, Cavity got all the intel agencies to focus on Syria and Iraq while the organization built up its base in Saudi Arabia. At least that's how it looks. Al Jubail is Cavity's entry point for any hardware it needs to escalate the already hot conflict."

Igor pointed to the TV screen. CNN had more breaking news.

The reporter stationed in Saudi Arabia now appeared exhausted. Pushing her blond hair back under her veil, she stared into the camera and said, "Just minutes ago the Iranian foreign minister, Ali Mechradani, made a televised statement denying any involvement in the bloody attack at the Kaaba and blaming the United States and Saudi Arabia. He said the two countries were involved in an unholy violence, targeting Iran during the sacred month of Ramadan. The tension between Saudi Arabia and Iran rose to new heights before the beginning of the fasting month when Saudi Arabia cut the Iran hajj contingent by almost 20 percent. Meanwhile, the United States has put its forces in the Persian Gulf and in countries where American troops are stationed—Saudi Arabia, the UAE, Bahrain, and of course Syria and Iraq—on highest alert. A Saudi and allied retaliatory strike on Iran is imminent, according to our Middle East expert …"

Valenti hit the volume button again.

"Let's concentrate on the PRK sub that just loaded two Hwasong ballistic missiles. The rockets are most certainly equipped with mini nukes developed by Cohen in North Korea. Igor, what's the ETA of the vessel in Al Jubail if we cannot somehow delay it?"

"The *Jae Eun* is quite slow, so I estimate three days, seventy-two hours."

"Who's your top FSB connection? I want you to contact him and have a private talk. There is no doubt the FSB knows by now what we are after."

Igor seemed reluctant to answer, knowing he just hacked into one of the FSB's satellites.

"Colonel Antonin Burov. But I'm not sure he has the right relationship at the very top. He is a straight guy, but after this"—he pointed to the satellite surveillance screen—"I really don't know."

"We have nothing to lose, and the Russians might be the only party willing to listen to our conclusions. Call him now."

Valenti was resolute about this and directed Igor to a soft leather chair in front of a packed communications desk.

Igor hit some keys on his laptop, and the contact details for Antonin Burov appeared, ready to be clicked on. He had his laptop connected to the chamber's security system, which would guarantee no tracing.

We listened to the dial tone on the other side of the world for what seemed like forever until finally a woman answered.

Igor explained who he was and said it was urgent that he talk with Burov. We waited anxiously while she located him.

Finally, we heard a low male voice. "Privet, chert voz'mi, Igor!" Burov said. "What the hell, Igor, you have the nerve to call me here while you are hacking our system, the one you integrated. Should you ever set foot on Russian ground again, I shall arrest you and put you away for good without a trial."

"Listen, I can explain, and this will probably make you a general. I had no bad intention in using Razdan. It was essential to our operation to stop a major war in the Middle East, one you can prevent."

Burov was silent for almost a minute.

"Don't tell me it's Petrossian. I can't sell anything that comes from that organization right now. The American president talked to our president about two hours ago, telling him Petrossian and the Iranians were behind the killing in Mecca and the unbalancing of the whole region. I'm inclined to believe this, knowing what experts you are in destabilization. So you better come up with something I can use, but don't involve Petrossian. Understand?"

Igor looked at us, and Valenti nodded assent.

"Okay, no Petrossian at this time."

Then Igor told him the whole story from the hacking of the Saudi bank to the revival of Cavity. We frantically wrote notes for him during his monologue, which Burov never interrupted. I took that as a good sign.

Then Burov broke in.

"Are you telling me Mark Shearer and Walter Mills are with you?"

"Walter Wills is with me while Mark Shearer is still near DC after surgery. He got shot by Cavity agents when he and the others were escaping ..."

Burov seemed to have heard enough. "Let me talk to Walter Wills to confirm your story," he said.

Walter sat down at the laptop. "Colonel Burov, this is Walter Wills, CIA."

"Tell me, Wills, what was the code name for your safe house in Leningrad in 1984?"

Wills, the hardened CIA agent, looked at Valenti, who urged him ahead.

"The distillery."

Silence on the other side.

"Hello, colonel."

"So you are Walter Wills."

"Yes, I am, colonel, and you came pretty close to stopping us before we brought Eva Kriznova out of the Soviet Union to Finland. It was a close call, but we beat you."

Burov was silent again before returning to the original subject.

"Let me bring this to a higher level. I've always trusted Igor, and maybe with you on board I can sell it without being sent to Siberia or losing my head. Igor, I'll get back to you. Well, on a second thought, I rescind that. I don't trust you Petrossians at all, but maybe this will work."

Click. He was off.

Valenti was on the line with Galina, who was also monitoring the Korean vessel. He spoke rapidly in his mixture of Russian and Armenian.

"I have my jet ready at Dare County," Valenti said. "I want Matt, Fedorov, and Oksana on it right now. Meanwhile, I'll work on clearance for Bahrain. We have choppers in Qatar, but with the present situation it might be problematic to enter Saudi airspace from there. Galina will arrange transport to Jubail."

A strong protest arose from Misha and Gaby.

"What about us?" Misha asked. "Why leave us here where we are useless?"

Valenti contemplated the issue. "Okay, you two join Matt and Yev. No wild actions and every action only on the command of elders. Understand?"

The two girls smiled, happy to join in field action. "We won't let you down," Gaby said. "Thanks."

Valenti called the two chopper pilots, who were cleared to fly jets as well. They were ready to go. It took them a few minutes to work on a flight plan that would bring us to Santa Cruz de Tenerife in the Canary Islands for refueling.

"You can shower, change, and eat on the plane," Valenti said. "There are weapons stored including your beloved Makarovs. Galina will facilitate a transfer to the helicopter. The plane has top-security communication, and the attendant is Armenian, a mother of four, a great cook."

I didn't ask about the bar, but I assumed it would be well stocked. The long flight might give us the chance for a relaxing drink.

We drove out to Dare County Municipal Airport where a Bombardier 6000 sat ready, a fuel truck having just left the plane. It was an even sleeker aircraft than the Falcon, with a range of six thousand miles and a speed of close to mach one.

Anoush, the attendant, greeted us on the stairs. She was in her fifties with a lovely, friendly face. I didn't want to intrude on her privacy by asking about her Petrossian past or present, but since she was so close to Valeni, I presumed she was or had been a well-trained agent.

The plane's amenities were extraordinary with full reclining chairs, a dining-conference corner, a sophisticated communications compartment, and a bathroom with a shower.

Fedorov and I were scrutinizing the plane's cupboards—closed in case of turbulence reasons, I suspected. Anoush noticed and reacted instantly.

"I will serve drinks right after takeoff, or would you prefer to take a shower first"?

"I guess a drink first and then the shower would be ideal," I said.

Fedorov planted his tired body in one of the comfortable leather chairs, strapped himself in, and closed his eyes.

Oksana and the girls did the same, exhausted as they were.

"I'll join you for the drink, and we girls will go to the bathroom first, okay?"

I smiled at Oksana, whom I greatly admired. "Ladies first," I said, "but leave us some water."

"If you leave us some vodka." Her radiant smile filled me with optimism, though we faced a mission that might well end our lives. "Ketut is a great girl!" Oksana added. "We should be happy and proud to have her in our ranks. I hope she recovers."

So did I.

The Bombardier sped down the runway and started a steep climb into the clear but dark sky. The captain told us the flight to the Canary Islands would take approximately five hours at an altitude of sixty thousand feet.

After we had showered and shaved, Anoush served meat and green peas, something very Armenian, together with dolma and lula kebab. The only non-Armenian part of the delicious dinner was the delightful Barolo, my favorite Italian wine.

All of this called for a stiff after-dinner vodka, but raising eyebrows, I chose instead to have a tasty Italian Grappa. Oksana joined me.

"That was unusual," she remarked. "I was in the mood for it after the Barolo.

All of us were in a deep sleep when the Bombardier touched down softly in the Canary Islands. The captain announced that the stop would take about an hour and that he had to go to the airport authorities to clear the flight plan. We had again fallen asleep when the captain got clearance to fly to Bahrain. I was dreaming of a sandy desert with camels carrying Korean missiles.

The girls were fresh and sat at the communications panel reviewing the latest reports from Igor. Burov talked to Walter again and hinted at the possibility of cooperation, though out of Iran. Russia was Iran's strongest ally, and somehow this made sense to me.

I pondered the possibility of flying to Iran and trying to get to Al Jubail from there. I jumped up and joined the girls at the communications station.

"Get me Valenti and pull up a map of southern Iran."

I checked Iran's coast and found an air force base at Bandhar Busher about 160 miles from Al Jubail.

Valenti came up on the screen.

"Valenti, just listen and then try to analyze my idea. Okay, the Russians might cooperate but out of Iran. What if we don't comply? There is an air force base at Bandha Busher, and I'm sure the Russians are there. It's about 160 miles to Al Jubail, and we could get there in time on a fast boat or on a helicopter equipped with Zodiacs."

"We have already discussed this option with Burov. He needs time to clear it with the Iranians. They are in a war mood and are mobilizing everything they have, and it's a lot, believe me."

"I hope Burov explains to them that mobilizing wouldn't help much once Tehran is in ashes."

"Let me work on it and proceed to Bahrain. We still can change plans in midair."

On the flight to the Persian Gulf we decided to abstain from alcoholic beverages. I was watching the news from all over the world and was fascinated at how the stock exchanges from Tokyo to London to New York were plummeting. The assassination attempt on the Saudi king combined with more than three hundred dead pilgrims made the world poorer by hundreds of billions of US dollars. Graphics for blue-chip share prices all pointed to the bottom.

I was reminded of an old friend from Houston, Texas, who lost and then won again during the financial crises in the previous century. Concerning his ups and downs in the stock market, he said, "As long as you don't sell, you don't lose."

He was right all the time and made a bundle after every recovery. This time, however, an upturn might be closer to the rising of Phoenix from the ashes, the nuclear ashes.

During the flight the captain told us he had gotten permission to enter Iranian airspace but recommended I verify this with Valenti, who had just popped up on the screen in front of me.

"You are clear to land at Bandar Bushehr, but be prepared for some tough questions by the MOIS as well as by the Republican Guards. Burov's counterpart at Bandar Bushehr is Colonel Nikolaev. Burov says this man has lots of clout at the FSB. He doesn't seem to be too happy about us but got instructions from Moscow. So play it cool and let's hope he will cooperate. Walter is talking to Moscow directly, and they seem to be playing along."

We diverged from our original flight plan, possibly causing concern in the Emirates, Bahrain, and Qatar. The Bombardier banked slightly to the left out over the Persian Gulf, heading northeast toward Iran airspace.

"Flight time twenty minutes," the captain said.

We decided to use our Russian passports and stashed the others in a safe Anoush provided.

Then, at the last moment, the captain got instructions from Bandar Bushehr to head for Kharg Island, a tiny landmass in the Persian Gulf with a strategic Iranian airbase where there officially was none. The island was much closer to the Saudi coast than Bandar Bushehr was.

Kharg was known to have a huge oil terminal, built by the US company

Amoco. There was only one city on the island and an airport that could easily handle military aircraft of all kinds, although the facility was not classified as an airbase.

The Bombardier leaned heavily to the right and made its final approach to Kharg.

CHAPTER 30

KHARG ISLAND, IRAN

Our plane rolled out to the end of the runway where a military escort awaited us.

"An armada of military vehicles pulling up. This doesn't look too good," Fedorov said as he stared out the window. "I assume the Russians are not here."

I checked and had to agree with his analysis of the situation.

Six or seven military vehicles loaded with soldiers flanked our plane. The captain came back to the cabin.

"They want me to lower the stairs. I think I have no choice."

"Lower it and let's meet the welcoming committee," I said.

Oksana was online with Valenti, who was surprised to hear where we had touched down.

"Kharg is a dangerous place. Oil terminal, disguised airbase with batteries of middle- and long-range missiles that can effortlessly reach Israel. Leave one of the girls behind if you can. She can update me."

The captain lowered the staircase, and soldiers immediately surrounded it. They made way for an officer who had arrived behind them.

I was still on the line with Kitty Hawk, and Igor affirmed satellite coverage of the scene outside our plane.

"I have very clear streaming video here. The Russians are obviously playing along. A soldier is climbing up the stairs."

I could hear military boots stomping their way up the stairs and into the plane.

"Do you have weapons with you?"

"Good evening to you, and thank you for letting us land on this beautiful island. And yes, of course we have weapons with us, as you certainly know."

Fedorov addressed the fervent Iranian officer in Farsi. Misha came forward from the rear of the cabin and welcomed him in the same language.

"I'm Major Mehmedi of the Iranian Republican Guards. I order you off the plane now. Until further notice you are my prisoners. Should you try to escape, the guards have orders to shoot you."

He clomped deeper into the cabin, his gun shifting from right to left as if he were searching for a target.

Misha looked at me inquiringly, and I signaled her with a nod and two raised fingers, which meant "Yes, we should disarm the major, but give me a minute or two to clarify the situation."

Fedorov understood what was going on between us, and he addressed the major again. "Am I right that you are the commander of Kharg, major?" he asked, smiling.

"I am the military commander here, and my orders were to apprehend you right after the plane landed."

"Sir, may I offer you some iced tea? It must be hot out there for you and your men."

Misha played her role exquisitely, the meek woman offering a drink to the mighty warrior. I smiled, though more inside than out.

Major Mehmedi took the glass of iced tea, and Misha almost effortlessly seized his gun and pointed it at him.

"Well, major, since you are the commander here, I kindly ask you to send your soldiers away from our plane. There are seven of them outside, and we could easily get rid of them ourselves."

My Makarov looked scary with the stubby silencer attached.

The major was easy to persuade, and we sat him down in a chair so he could recover from the shock of being disarmed like a toddler losing a lollipop.

"Do you have contact with the FSB in Bandar Bushehr, major?" Fedorov asked in businesslike fashion.

"I receive my orders directly from General Rahimi in Tehran. If I fail here, my family and I will be executed." He whined like a third-grade student who didn't make the fourth.

"Now do us all a favor and send your troops back to the barracks. Tell them that all is okay and that you will follow with the foreigners. Understand?"

The major went out to the top of the stairs with Misha's SIG pressed to his body and the rest of our guns ready to come alive. A lieutenant at the foot of the stairs acknowledged Mehmedi's command. The soldiers withdrew to their vehicles and were out of sight in a moment. Only the major's Subaru and his driver remained in front of the Bombardier's nose.

"Now let's go inside and start to communicate," I said. "We are here to save Iran from a nuclear disaster, major. Instead of being executed, you might well get a promotion and a nice desk in Tehran—if Tehran is not reduced to rubble."

Gaby had Valenti on the screen with Igor sitting beside him at the sophisticated controls in Kitty Hawk.

"We've got everything, Matt, Yev, and well done, Misha. Walter is talking to Burov, trying to clear up the situation there. The Russians are still highly reluctant, but I think they will let us operate."

"Are you saying they'll let us do the job but without their cooperation?" I asked Valenti.

"At least initially, yes. You go in with the Russians waiting for the right moment to join."

Those fucking Russians! I was furious. We had come this far with the FSB starting to believe us only to be told we were on our own.

"And how are we supposed to get to that fucking sheep ship if the fucking Russians don't provide a platform?"

"That's the point. You don't go to the ship. You go to Al Jubail and stop the attack there. An interception on the high seas doesn't produce the same publicity. The Russians want to expose the Saudis. Only then will they consider wet action."

"What if we don't succeed in Al Jubail? What if the Saudis or whoever can launch the missiles? Did the fucking Russians think of that?"

"Matt, I know how you feel, and I feel the same rage. The Russians or the Iranians will outfit you with a chopper and Zodiac to make a landing south of Al Jubail. They have agents there who will bring you safely to the city and the harbor. At least that's what I have been told."

At that instant, we were jolted by a thunderous sound that caused our plane to vibrate.

Gaby came back and reported that a MI 38, a Russian heavy transport helicopter, had arrived with Russians and Iranians on board.

Colonel Nikolaev proved to be the asshole Burov had politely suggested he was He sent Iranian MOIS agents up the stairs of our plane before venturing into the danger zone himself. After the MOIS had given him a safe sign, he started up the stairs, entering the cabin with a smug smile on his peasant face.

"I do what Moscow tells me, but I think you are on a fishing expedition to save Petrossian from extinction. My pilots will drop you off on the Saudi coast. I have no confirmation about our agents on the ground yet."

His smile told us he hoped we would all be killed before reaching the kingdom.

"You leave here just after midnight. A Zodiac on board the MI 38 will hold your crew. Are the women staying here?"

"The women have about triple the value of every agent in your shitty organization, and I strongly recommend your cooperation before I unleash them on you."

Fedorov was furious and didn't try to hide it. He pointed his Makarov at Nikolaev's head and motioned him back toward the communications compartment. With Misha and Gaby brandishing their SIGs, the two FSB agents and their MOIS counterparts stood paralyzed.

We quickly set up a link to Valenti and Burov, clearing up the misconceptions and squabbles about the operation. Nikolaev got ever smaller after he heard Burov was in charge.

A connection to the FSB agents in Al Jubail cleared the pickup at about thirty miles south of the city. The FSB offered a safe house near the harbor in Al Jubail.

Perfect. So I thought and disbelieved.

Just before we disconnected I had an idea.

"Burov, get in touch with your asset in the Mukhabarat, the one we delivered in Sevastopol. I forget his name."

Of course I would never forget Hyder, but such requests promoted cooperation.

"Hyder, Colonel Hyder. Good point, Mr. Burke. Will do right away."

Evidently, he had learned my real name. Burov was using it to signal the Russians knew more than I might like. Never mind now. We were all hot to move.

Shortly after midnight the heavy MI 38 lifted off, carrying our team and a fully inflated Russian attack Zodiac. During the flight Igor confirmed our GPS, but the night sky didn't provide him with enough illumination to follow the heavy chopper on satellite images.

The Russian pilot announced we were thirty miles from the coast, skimming the surface of the Persian Gulf. The MI 38 slowed down, and we got the green light to depart. Fedorov lowered the Zodiac into the water, secured by a single rope. Oksana went first, then Gaby and Misha, followed by Fedorov and me. After the crew had cut the line, the dark airship turned rapidly and vanished into the night.

I started the powerful outboard, checked our compass heading, and moved the Zodiac toward the Saudi coast. We saw no lights in any direction. Igor monitored our position and immediately corrected the slightest deviation in our heading.

After less than half an hour we finally saw the outline of the dark coast. Igor confirmed our position. Then Oksana, who was surveying the shore through her night vision binoculars, gave a short warning.

"Lights, a vehicle."

I stopped the Zodiac and let it float in the calm water with the engine idle. We watched the coastline through our Russian night vision gear. There were at least two vehicles either at the shore or approaching it.

"Something is not right. We were supposed to be met by two Russians. Why two vehicles with full headlights on?"

Oksana was right to be concerned.

I slowly steered the Zodiac back into deeper water, running the engine low to avoid making too much noise.

Fedorov got on his satellite phone with Igor and Valenti. According to Burov, all communication with Russian agents on Saudi soil had been cut about half an hour earlier, just when we left the MI 38.

Valenti advised us to head out to sea and to follow the coastline north.

Oksana stared at me inquisitively, already knowing what I would decide. I turned the Zodiac around and headed south.

Fedorov nodded his assent. If the Russians on shore had been compromised, Mukhabarat agents would know about our plan and, being simple-minded, would think our move up the coast was the only logical one. Or so I hoped.

Never make the obvious move if your opponents are as shrewd as you are, an old Petrossian adage advised.

With Mukhabarat agents, however, I tended to make the opposite assumption unless they had Cavity operatives with them. But life is a gamble and I decided to go a step further.

I steered the Zodiac slightly closer to the coastline.

"What are you doing?"

Gaby was on the edge, but Oksana took her arm reassuringly, knowing exactly what I was trying to do.

The strategy seemed to work. The vehicles moved parallel to us down the shore, the occupants probably trying desperately to keep us in sight. I gave them enough of a view to follow us.

After a few minutes, I pulled the small vessel hard to the left as if we had finally noticed our pursuers on shore and took her farther out to sea. We quickly lost visual contact with the vehicles. I turned the boat around and moved up the coastline again, far enough away not to be observed from the shore.

Igor confirmed the coordinates of our original landing point, and when we saw no lights I decided to go in hard. With any luck the Russians would still be around, hiding from Mukhabarat agents.

Our rubber boat hit the sandy beach softly enough not to damage the delicate hull. The Russian night vision goggles came in handy, providing a clear view of the environment.

Fedorov checked with Igor, who could make out a small structure about a hundred yards inland that might be a car or a hut.

Oksana and I went in the direction Igor had indicated and found an abandoned Range Rover with dune tires. We carefully approached the vehicle, and I was not surprised when we discovered two bodies inside. The Russian welcoming committee had been taken out.

Now we had to make a hard decision—either proceed up the coast in the Zodiac or do the crazy thing and take the Range Rover.

Fedorov lifted his head toward the coffin car. The decision was mader. We checked with Igor, who confirmed the two Mukhabarat vehicles were approximately seven miles down the coast, giving us time to disappear with the Rover.

We quickly carried all our weapons to the car, and Oksana took the wheel. The narrow coastal road was unlit and not easy to navigate, but we decided to drive without headlights up toward Al Jubail.

Igor came back online to warn us the Saudis had turned around, apparently having finally discovered our diversion. They had the advantage of knowing the road and could use their headlights, so it might not take them long to catch up with us.

"We need to find an ambush spot," Misha said. She was already assembling the shoulder-held RPG Burov had provided. The Russian RPG 7 was very effective and extremely light. Its range was only about two hundred yards, but that would do if we could find the right spot.

"There, the curb."

Gaby pointed ahead to a bend in the road, away from the water. But I feared they wouldn't fall for that. As naïve as they usually were, they were probably not that dumb.

Oksana came up with the solution.

"We let them come close. Then I drive away, hitting the brake lights several times, and you take them out."

Simple. But if we missed the lead vehicle, Oksana was done.

"Okay, we do it."

Fedorov, always closest to Oksana, agreed with her plan. We took positions in the dunes and waited for our pursuers to show up.

We soon saw their headlights approaching and sent Oksana out to be bait.

As the lights drew closer, I saw to my shock that the vehicles were not on the road, at least not the same one as Oksana. They came in full speed, maybe a hundred yards inland, avoiding the curvy coastal road and out of range of the RPG.

I warned Oksana and told her to go full speed with lights on.

"Try to lose them in the city. We'll walk."

What else could we have done?

Losing Oksana and the vital transport was a major setback.

We conferred with Igor and Valenti, but they were out of immediate solutions too. Then Gaby came up with an idea that made sense.

"Let's divide them. Misha, take a shot at them from here to pull at least one of them back to us."

"Brilliant, Gaby!" Fedorov said. "Let one loose, Misha. We'll take out whatever comes our way."

Misha aimed high from her shoulder in the direction of the speeding cars, and the missile flew with a hissing sound into the black sky, exploding near the Saudi cars.

Apparently it had some effect. The cars stopped, giving Oksana a slight head start on getting lost in the nearby city. One of the Saudis soon resumed the pursuit, but the other indeed turned toward us, bumping over the dunes right into the wolves' lair.

The Toyota pickup stopped not less than a hundred yards from our position, and four guys jumped out, weapons ready, night goggles on. But we were prepared.

We heard commands in American English. Cavity operatives. I was afraid that would be the case. On the other hand our motivation to kill had just increased.

We lay low in the dunes, half covered by the powdery sand. We were too experienced to waste energy on commands or signs. It was very clear that those on the left would go to the left and that those on the right would go to the right.

"It came from here, I'm sure. Spread out. It's either the fucking Russians or the Petrossians."

They spread their line, making it impossible for us to execute an ambush in one fell swoop. The first shot came from my left. Gaby put the one on her side down. The others disappeared in the dunes.

Again, Petrossian teaching kicked in. Instead of digging in, we split into two groups. Gaby and Fedorov crawled to the left, while Misha and I moved as quickly as possible to the right.

Having received the first shot, the enemy had to take cover before moving again. This was a crucial advantage. Misha and I shifted as much as possible to the right but not too far away to maintain a line of fire. I was sure Fedorov and Gaby would apply the same tactic.

Then we lay still, focusing on the potential enemy positions, which were now more to our left than straight ahead.

"We need their car. Quick kill."

Misha understood and nodded silently.

Then they came. The three of them raced over the dunes toward our original position, their weapons spitting automatic fire. They threw hand grenades over the dunes, creating a huge wave of sand that almost blinded us. But we had them in our crosshairs. Fedorov and Gaby opened up simultaneously with us, and it took just a few seconds to eliminate the three Cavity men.

The powdery sand was in our overalls, our eyes, and our mouths, but we didn't have time to clean ourselves. We ran to the Toyota pickup, the most feasible vehicle in desert warfare and even more effective than the American Humvee, besides being much more affordable.

We gathered the Cavity weapons and threw them in the loading space behind the cabin. I took the wheel while Fedorov communicated with Igor.

He was following Oksana with enhanced satellite images, another sign the Russians were game. He had her on the phone and pinpointed her position on our handheld communication pilots.

Google maps showed a clear and pixel-free image of Al Jubail.

"Burov is directing her to the FSB safe house in the northern part of the city. She is proceeding there but might have to leave the car behind. The streets are deserted at this time of the night, and a car is too easy to spot. I have sent you the location."

I drove boldly into the quiet city, ready to take on more Cavity thugs.

There was moderate traffic on the Dharam Jubail Expressway—trucks, tankers, and a few passenger cars. Fedorov guided me to a street simply named Road 183. It led all the way to the north in a straight line. Gaby was talking to Oksana, who was somewhere ahead in an industrial area called SINA. Despite its designation, the area had plenty of small houses and neat little gardens.

We easily found Oksana and were happy to be a full force again.

Luckily the city was quite big, and I thought we just might have lost the vehicle that had pursued Oksana.

The safe house was in Huwailat, an opulent residential area with lots of green space. The two-level family home was set off from the townhouses that lined the wide boulevards.

We had to get rid of the truck. Although there were many similar Toyotas parked in the neighborhood, the pickup was easy to spot. Gaby and Misha took on the task after we retrieved our weapons and approached the stone building.

The gates were locked, but Burov provided us with the access code, which I punched in while Misha and Gaby pulled away from the house.

"There is somebody home."

Fedorov pointed to a second-story window where a light went on when I pushed the gate inward.

"Shit. Call Igor and let him know. We can't get into a firefight in this neighborhood."

We hid ourselves behind some nicely manicured bushes and waited for any reaction from the house.

"Nikolai, eto ty?" (Is that you?)

A sleepy female voice sounded from the entrance door, and a woman covered in a silky white robe staggered out to the parking bay.

"My druzya ..." Fedorov told her we were friends.

"Okay, come in and have a drink with me. Bloody Nikolai left me alone the whole night."

She was not stable on her feet, so we pushed the gate open and rushed her back into the house.

"Where is Nikolai? I was alone, watching TV, and had a few drinks."

A drunk Russian blonde, voluptuous and obviously pissed about Nikolai.

"He will come later," I said.

This was not the time to tell her Nikolai would never return home.

Why the fuck didn't Burov tell us about this?

We set up shop in a room that obviously served as the communications center. It was not quite as high-tech as Valenti's in Kitty Hawk but was refined enough.

I switched on the communications desk and started to compartmentalize the equipment in front of me. It was astonishing that the Russians were running a safe house in Al Jubail that really was an operations center, and doing so quite openly.

I wondered what else might surprise me on this eventful night.

In a few minutes, I had the gear under control and dialed Igor. He popped up on the big screen, looking tired and stressed.

"Hi, boss! You better hurry up. The Korean sheep carrier will dock tomorrow around noon and has already received priority clearance from the harbor master. Where are you? I'm asking because I detect interference in your communications system."

"Igor, we expected that. We are in a Russian safe house, but I think it's more than that. This is not the classic safe house, and communications are open. We have found an intoxicated Russian woman here. You or

Valenti should find out from Burov who the fuck she is and how we should treat her."

"Valenti is here, and he is on it."

"And send me all files concerning the Korean ship, crew info, whatever you have."

"Done. It's in seventh heaven for you to open."

Fedorov was listening and had his small laptop open. He typed in the codes for seventh heaven and downloaded Igor's information.

Valenti came on with a grave face.

"I'm afraid the Russian safe house is compromised," he said. "The Mukhabarat or Cavity or both are aware of the hideout and might stage an attack any minute. Get out of there and get rid of the woman. She is a liaison between FSB, the Mukhabarat, and probably the CIA and Cavity. Leave now and find someplace else to bury yourselves."

Igor was on the screen again.

"I'm not sure whether Cavity knows about the house. We monitor activity in the city and haven't seen anything definitive. However, numerous cars with police lights are cruising around, mostly in the southern part of the city. I agree with Valenti. Run!"

To my surprise, Burov's face suddenly appeared on the screen.

"Hello, Matt. I hope you'll forgive my intrusion, but after all it's our equipment you are running. Valenti is right. The house is compromised but probably only to the Mukhabarat. I don't think the CIA or even Cavity knows about it. Hyder is cooperating and commands his camel herders around the south of the city. However, that can change at any minute. Now listen carefully."

He paused and took a sheet of paper from which he read.

"I'm going to violate everything that's in the books, at least in ours. You have to go to the Rolling Dunes Golf Club, which is west of your present location."

"Are you kidding me? A golf club here?"

"You would be surprised at what else you could find in this hellhole."

No, I wouldn't.

"Now pay attention. The manager of the club is an American, CIA, in his fifties, and I hope one of the good guys. His name is Frank Warner, and he cooperates with us from case to case. I'm trying to alert him right now, but so far I've gotten no response. I'll text you his contacts. Get out of the house now. We'll keep Cavity's people busy in the south as long as possible, but sooner or later the Saudis will fall back to the safe house. My guess is sooner rather than later."

Oksana was worried about the girls. They hadn't returned from their mission to dump the truck.

"We can't leave them behind. I'll try their phone, but either it's dead or they don't hear it."

We needed transportation to the golf club. Fedorov scouted the neighborhood for any viable form. A car theft probably never occurred in this city surrounded by desert and sea, particularly not in the affluent quarter we were in now.

Oksana finally got through to the girls. They hadn't discarded the truck yet and were driving near the seashore to find a suitable place to dump it.

"Stop them! Tell them to bring the truck back," I said.

Fedorov nodded. "No way to get a car from here," he said. "Tell them to hurry."

The truck pulled up in front of the house a few minutes later. We climbed in, and I directed Misha to the west of the city, toward Rolling Dunes Golf Club.

We carefully rounded every corner with weapons drawn, ready to deal with an ambush or a roadblock.

Fedorov decided to let the woman in the safe house live. She was too drunk to give reliable information about us to Cavity or the Mukhabarat.

I realized we could not enter the golf club unless the manager, Frank Warner, knew we were coming. Fedorov asked Igor and Valenti to have Burov call ahead with an introduction.

Certain groups within the CIA and the FSB maintained special relationships, and an unknown contact might not be welcome. But Burov apparently had an established line to the CIA man, and we would have to use it.

We parked our truck near the lavish golf club. The entrance gate, which was secured, reminded me of the door to a palace. Through our night vision goggles we could make out at least two armed guards. They didn't appear to be sleepy. Quite the contrary. That they were pacing in front of the closed gate and were watching the only access road implied they had been warned about unusual activity in the city.

My satellite phone beeped. An unknown caller.

"Yes?"

"Frank Warner, Rolling Dunes. Tell me who mentioned my name to you." I heard mistrust in his voice.

"Burov, FSB," I replied.

"Okay. Right now it's impossible for me to let you in. The whole city is on high alert, I assume because of you guys. You have to hide for a few hours until sunrise when the gate opens for members and guests. I also understand that you're driving a compromised truck. Dump it, hide, and wait for my limousine to pick you up. If you don't have a safe house, go to the northeast of the city. A park along the coast might provide a more or less safe hideout. I'll contact you just before 6 a.m."

He hung up. I checked the truck's navigation system and found the park which, according to the detailed information, was open twenty-four hours.

I drove the truck, which felt by now like a hot piece of coal in my hands, into deep bushes that looked as if nobody had ever disturbed them. Then we waited and communicated with Kitty Hawk.

Mark Shearer confirmed Frank Warner's position but could not substantiate Burov's belief that the CIA man was reliable. With Aiello still at the helm of the powerful US intelligence agency, it was impossible to know for sure who was trustworthy. We would have to take our chances with Warner.

The sky to the east slowly filled with color. A light rose was followed by a deep red, and we saw the sun rising over the water.

My phone beeped. Warner.

"We open in a few minutes. I'll send a black Lincoln Town Car to fetch you. The driver is one of us or, more accurately, one of mine. He is trustworthy. His name is Ali. He is a Palestinian and has been living in the kingdom for more than thirty years. Now give me your coordinates."

Fedorov made sure Kitty Hawk could listen in, and we received the thumbs up from Valenti. What else could he opt for given our situation?

It took Ali fifteen minutes to reach us. He stopped the car on the access road to the park and opened all the doors so we could see he was alone. *Either a pro or well instructed*, I thought.

We entered the air-conditioned car with four of us in the back and Fedorov in the front. We decided he looked distinguished enough to pass for a golfer or a guest.

However, his appearance didn't matter because we found the gate open and the two guards saluting us the way they would VIPs.

The limousine didn't stop at the main entrance to the luxurious clubhouse but drove straight to a basement parking area where a Westerner in golf slacks welcomed us.

"Frank Warner. Welcome. Follow me. I have the guesthouse prepared for VIPs—you. Have breakfast, shower, change clothes, and then fill me in."

Warmer was a no-nonsense guy and recognized what we needed most. Maybe we were lucky with him.

The guesthouse was an opulent villa, almost a mansion, with

a swimming pool and all the amenities Saudi royals would enjoy. We showered, changed into golf apparel fresh from the pro shop, and enjoyed a breakfast of Western and Arab specialties. The only person serving us was Ali. Warner was wary.

Before communicating with Kitty Hawk, we briefed Warner. An ever-alert Oksana stood ready to terminate his life if we had the slightest doubt about his commitment and cooperation.

It turned out Pete Aiello had sent Warner there about a year earlier after the two had argued about the integrity of the CIA. We had Mark Shearer listen in, and he confirmed the story with his sources.

Al Jubail was a dead end for Warner career wise, and he could not stop Aiello and his traitors in DC. Indeed, Warner said his position had no value except that he could play golf whenever he wanted and could enjoy booze in his extravagant enclave in the alcohol-free kingdom.

He was eager to be involved in something that might give him a reason to exist.

We informed him of the Cavity plot and made it clear we would do everything possible to stop the missiles from reaching ramps somewhere deep in the desert.

Igor confirmed the *Jae Eun* was scheduled to dock in about twelve hours.

Warner started to look better by the minute. He told us the harbor master was a keen golfer and loved a cold beer or two.

"I can bring you to the harbor as my guests, let's say from Jordan, just to mask any accent. Would that help?"

It would indeed. We would go on a harbor tour.

CHAPTER 31

WASHINGTON, DC

The president was hosting the world's most dangerous conspirators in the Oval Office. After the fire at Eileen Cahill's house, he had been rushed back to the White House. Eileen had followed him with her own security detail.

He had a feeling the sudden fire at the mansion was not a coincidence, because he didn't believe in happenstance. The president was an extremely paranoid character who saw conspiracies behind every move made by his foes and even by his friends. But now his old business sense kicked in, and he decided to be extremely careful.

The invitation to the Cahill mansion had been initiated by Pete Aiello, the CIA director, whom he distrusted more and more by the minute.

Now Aiello, Eileen Cahill, and Cecil Cohen, brother of the deceased Michael and the new CEO of Cohen Industries, sat in the Oval Office.

The president wanted to have Admiral Weisskopf, the acting head of the NSA, at the meeting, but Aiello was adamant about keeping the gathering to a minimum, citing national security. This planted deep frowns on the president's forehead.

It was almost noon, and while coffee and tea were served, the president needed a bourbon, neat.

Eileen asked that no recording be made of the meeting. This was an unusual request, but the president agreed and let her have her way. He had learned the once-notorious intel agency Cavity was back and under her control. During the eighties when he was a presidential adviser, he had helped shut down the agency, which operated with clandestine funds and regularly locked horns with the CIA, the KGB, and Petrossian. He had never understood the origin or the purpose of this last intel outfit.

Now, with the support of Aiello, this loathsome woman had called a meeting to bring him up to date on Petrossian and on the bloody attack on the king in Saudi Arabia.

"Mr. President, we thank you for seeing us on such short notice, and I apologize for the mishap at my home." She gave him her lizard grin.

"The events in Saudi Arabia call for your special attention, sir. We have the perfect solution to the precarious political and military situation in the Middle East."

Eileen paused for dramatic effect, sipping her tea and pacing around the Oval Office as if she owned it. When she turned toward Aiello and Cohen, she briefly drew the president's eyes away from the side table where the crystal tumbler holding his bourbon sat. She slipped a tiny bit of powder into the glass.

"Mr. President, we have initiated a plan that will change the world for the better," Eileen announced. "Iran will be obliterated by a Saudi nuclear attack within the next twenty-four hours, and then the entire Middle East will be in our hands."

"The Saudis don't have nuclear weapons. We made sure of that," the visibly disturbed president responded.

He was about to take a swig of the bourbon, but Eileen stopped him. It was too early for him to go. She loved theatrical settings and had always fancied herself a legendary actress.

"Hear us out, Mr. President. You will love the plan."

Aiello's moment had arrived. As he spoke, the president sank back in his chair, his fragile heart beating like the drums of Hades. Aiello shocked the president to his core with the doomsday scenario, and the chief executive gulped the bourbon.

When he finished, Aiello said, "Mr. President, you will enter the history books as the greatest American leader of all."

Aiello desperately wanted to tell the president he would enter the history books now, but he bit his lip.

The president felt a sudden sharp pain and reached for his chest. He fell back into his chair, suffering heavy convulsions and gasping for air.

He appeared to be having a heart attack. Aiello started what he thought was a futile attempt at resuscitation, pressing rhythmically on the president's chest.

The White House doctors stormed in and worked on the president, apparently in vain.

"Get the vice president, the chief of staff, whoever is around. Quickly!" Aiello ordered Secret Service agents in his high-pitched voice.

Eileen sat in her chair feigning shock and wiping her dry eyes.

The doctors wouldn't declare the president dead and summoned an ambulance. The first lady was informed while she was visiting a school for handicapped children in Houston.

Vice President Eric Balton, a puppet whom Eileen Cahill held in contempt, stood in the Oval Office, wringing his hands. He had known this would happen, but he remained as helpless as usual. He looked pleadingly at Eileen, but the lizard lady offered no response.

The chief of staff tried to establish protocol, but like all the others who were not part of the murder conspiracy, he was completely unprepared for the situation.

"Mr. Vice President, you must take the oath right now," he said, facing a fearful Balton.

"But we don't know if he is dead," Balton replied nervously.

He had discussed this scenario several times at Eileen Cahill's mansion and had even practiced for it, but now he didn't know how to react.

Eileen quickly found her footing.

"Mr. President, you are in charge now."

She looked at him with her cold green eyes, which gave him the creeps.

The first lady was scheduled to arrive in four hours. Eileen regarded her as the only obstacle to her scheme. Hannah was a strong woman without whom the weak president would never have gone far.

"What happened?" she asked the White House internist over the phone. He was a surgeon from Bethesda whom Hannah had personally chosen.

"This is clearly cardiac arrest, natural heart failure. Your husband has had heart trouble for the last three years."

The doctor paused and a little smile crossed his bearded face.

"But I think he'll pull through. I'm in touch with the heart surgeon in the ambulance. Your husband is alive but will be incapacitated for little while. I think this would justify swearing in the vice president."

Eileen looked inquisitively at Cecil Cohen, who shook his head.

The addition of hydrofluoric acid makes a small amount of cyanide almost impossible to trace, and Cohen Industries had developed an additional corrosive acid that almost instantly destroyed any trace of cyanide; no DNA test had ever shown cyanide with the drug created by CI.

Michael Cohen had assured her the drug was always deadly, noting it had been tried on several subjects in Afghanistan and Syria.

Eileen Cahill suddenly saw her house of cards collapsing. First the attempt on the Saudi king's life had failed, and then the Petrossians had gotten the better of her in her own house. Now this. She maintained her composure on the outside, but the alarm signals in her brain told her to regroup somewhere far from here.

Even before the first lady arrived in Washington, Eric Balton was sworn in and became the first acting president of the United States.

The plan called for the new president to declare Eileen Cahill as his choice for vice president. But this chance was gone with the president alive and regrettably recuperating and with Balton only the acting president.

However, all was not lost. The nuclear launch in Saudi Arabia had to go as planned while Balton still held the Oval Office.

Eileen shot him a glance like a lightning bolt.

"You will have to stay on top of the crisis in the Middle East. Cavity together with the CIA will update you on developments."

She immediately got support from Aiello.

"I suggest a limited briefing before you meet with the Joint Chiefs on how to proceed."

To their surprise Balton suddenly became more assertive.

"First, we have to make sure the president is recuperating swiftly. All other business comes second."

He looked stern, deliberate, and almost capable of being president.

Eileen was worried and so was Aiello. They had never heard this commanding tone of voice from him before.

The new president dismissed them.

"I will brief Congress immediately. Chief, make arrangements!"

Eileen Cahill left the White House with a bad feeling in her stomach, and more murderous thoughts entered her mind. Once she was in her limousine, she got on a secure line with Aiello.

"We have to get him back on track. Do whatever is necessary," she said in a hoarse voice.

Back at her mansion she locked herself in her office and watched CNN's coverage from the Hill.

Seeing Eric Balton arrive to brief Congress made an awful day even more miserable.

Eileen grabbed a heavy crystal ball from her desk. It was a gift from an Indonesian black magician that supposedly guaranteed she would triumph over her foes. Disgusted, she threw the crystal ball at the television screen, shattering it.

Mercifully the dummy president had not been briefed to the maximum extent. He had only a vague idea of what the plot entailed. He did not know IS fighters were building the missile ramp in northern Saudi Arabia with Korean and American engineers executing the last steps before the world became a different place and Eileen Cahill seized power.

She regained her confidence and convinced herself that after the nuke attack on Iran she would be the most powerful person on earth.

Eileen would ignore the failures of the day and would concentrate on the vital engagement in Al Jubail. She dialed the satellite phone of Ben Warton, a veteran Cavity agent who would put his body in the line of fire for her.

"Yes, madam. We have a slight problem. I think we have Petrossians on the ground, but we'll get them before tomorrow morning. The ship will dock in a few hours. Everything is going smoothly."

CHAPTER 32

AL JUBAIL AND NORTH SAUDI ARABIA

The harbor master was a Palestinian who had lived in Saudi Arabia all his life. He took up golf when the Saudis built the Rolling Dunes club with the help of a famous American golfer and course designer.

The course was still partly desert style with brown sand greens, but the Saudis had watered and so nine holes were green and flanked by huge palm trees. Golfers were annoyed to occasionally find scrub.

Mahmud spent all his free time on the golf course. He told us his wife and two sons had returned to the state of Palestine.

We left the girls out of this get-together but included Oksana, who, like the rest of us, was pretending to have come from Amman in Jordan.

We told Mahmud we had been in Mecca when the bombs went off but had been in the hotel because the Kaaba ground was limited to certain pilgrims while the king was visiting.

"All transportation out of Mecca was restricted, but some Saudi friends helped us with a car," I said. "The route to the east was the only one open, and we hope to fly out of here to Kuwait."

My Arabic was slightly accented, but posing as a Jordanian with roots in England, I didn't raise suspicion.

Oksana was a visiting professor at the University of Jordan in Amman, originally from England too.

Mahmud was happy to meet new people and asked us if we played golf. We said we didn't.

"We would like to see the famous harbor and its oil terminal if that's possible," I told him.

"I can bring you this late afternoon just before Maghrib. Then we can visit the mosque in the harbor, which is one of the most beautiful in Al

Jubail, for prayers. I must go back because we need high security for a Korean freighter that arrives tonight."

"We won't occupy more of your time, Mahmud, and it was very nice to meet you," Oksana said.

She smiled at him, her blond hair covered by a flowery hijab.

"I'll send you a car before five. Will you will come too, Frank?"

He looked at the golf club manager, who enthusiastically nodded his assent.

After Mahmud left, Frank led us to his office, which was furnished with communications equipment that carried standard NSA code encryption. We had to talk to Valenti and Igor quickly.

Frank opened up his computer and said, "Okay, look at this. From the director personally. Somehow Langley knows you are here. Look at the message."

He used the NSA tool to decrypt the message.

"To Frank Warner. Enemy agents on ground in Al Jubail. Petrossian. MKB and friendly agents will get in touch. Assist. PA."

MKB was the Mukhabarat, and the friendlies obviously were Cavity operatives.

"I'll reply that I heard rumors but haven't seen anything."

He looked slightly worried as he typed his reply.

"I know the Mukhabarat quite well—a nasty bunch that makes my life as manager of the golf club difficult more often than not. They abhor foreigners, even Muslims. You might become easy targets."

Shutting the computer, he said, "Follow me. You will stay in my quarters. You'll have communications there that are much better than what I have here. Your two female companions are already there. Ali is the only one who knows I have guests. He is trustworthy."

We trailed behind him through an underground passage that led to a spacious and elegant bungalow with a private pool abutting the golf course.

Wearing hajibs, Gaby and Misha sat in the living room.

"All okay? We were a bit uneasy here."

"Mukhabarat agents have never been here, and I better get back to my office in case they show up," Frank said. "The fridge is well stocked with soft drinks and food. Just stay inside until I come back."

The multifunctional golf club manager left us in his house where the girls already had activated the sophisticated communications system set up in a hidden bedroom closet.

"We didn't do voice and face communication yet but shot a burst message to Igor, explaining the situation," Misha said.

Fedorov and I crammed into the narrow closet. The satellite equipment had been fired up, and all we had to do was dial Kitty Hawk.

Valenti and Igor appeared on the small screen in front of us.

"The first thing you should know is that Warner is safe," Valenti said. "Walter Wills double-checked. Warner hates Aiello for putting him in the Saudi sand, and he doesn't know but suspects the director is corrupt. Now follow Igor's instruction. I want you to have a good look at the harbor."

Igor guided us through the complex protocol of connecting to the Russian satellite, which took us almost ten minutes. Then a clear stream of Al Jubail appeared on the screen. With Igor's help, we zoomed in and enhanced the picture.

Now we had a clear view of the harbor, and what we saw gave us second thoughts about visiting that night.

"You can see heavy security in and around the harbor. The Saudis have even deployed two tanks to secure the access. We don't think a harbor tour is feasible under the circumstances."

Valenti looked slightly troubled now, and Igor continued.

"The president had heart failure at the White House. The vice president was sworn in but couldn't announce Eileen Cahill as the new vice president because the president survived. Since then, Cavity has been going crazy. We monitor these people closely, but their activities are so intense that it's almost impossible to get a clear line. Two senators were shot and killed in DC. Everything points to Iran after the new US sanctions."

A heart attack? I wondered whether that was another assassination attempt by the lizard lady.

Valenti held a glass in his hand.

"After all this and almost twenty-four hours without sleep, I deserve a vodka. Now hold on for the next shock. The Russians are pursuing their own agenda. The Russian communications we have intercepted, FSB and foreign service, shows clearly that they plan to do what they do best—act as opportunists.

"The safe house they provided in Al Jubail was a trap, but luckily the Mukhabarat is what it is—stupid, though not to be underestimated. Agents raided the house just after you left. Now, having said all that, the Russian satellite connection will stop at any minute. And again, the Russians are not on the other side, but they are on their own. The Russians want the nuclear attack as much as Cavity does so they can take control of their part of the Middle East."

Valenti stopped, leaving us clueless about what to do next. Igor took over.

"We were able to use an NSA satellite for just a few minutes, and it showed unusual activity in the northeast of the kingdom, near the Kuwaiti border. The city of Kafji is also the official headquarters of our Saudi bank, Khalij. Coincidence? I don't think so. About thirty miles west of Kafji the satellite showed unusual activity. There is no oil field in that area, but construction with heavy security nearby drew the satellite's software to it. This may be a smoke screen, but we think it is a ramp for the Korean missiles, because we got a glance at some heavy vehicles that looked like ballistic missile platforms."

"You have to get there," Valenti said. "Our resources are exhausted, and any intrusion now into eastern Saudi Arabia would send up alarms. Try to get a car from Warner and leave by nightfall. Igor will guide you away from the main coastal highway. He is researching roads that lead north and away from the coast."

Fedorov tapped my shoulder, pointing at his laptop screen, which had dark. The Russians finally had cut our access to their satellite.

"Okay, Igor, guide us to the north," I said. "We'll get transportation. Over and out."

I switched off the communications system because I didn't trust it anymore. If we could monitor the Russians, they could oversee our communications, though it might take them some time.

Transportation. We needed a truck. The one we used before was out of bounds on a golf course.

I called Frank Warner.

"How can we get to the north without using the coastal road?"

"There are roads inland, but they are treacherous. I can guide you. Let me come along. I'm tired of being a useless club manager, and I'm hungry for action. I've gone up north several times and I know the way."

"Good. Any feasible transport?"

"Yes, the club truck. I've used it before. But let's leave after sunset. There is a lot of Mukhabarat activity right now."

I informed Fedorov and the others that a very frustrated but motivated Frank Warner would join us, eager to see action.

Igor sent us satellite images of the inland roads, which all appeared hazardous, and transfer information from a Belize corporation owned by Cohen Industries to a Macau bank. The corporation held bank accounts in Switzerland.

Wow! That was another piece of the puzzle.

I was sure this transfer was made a long before to display commitment. We figured out that later payments were made only in cash.

Thus the North Koreans had forced Cohen Industries to become visible, giving them dangerous leverage. *Clever Kim*, I thought.

We were busy cleaning our weapons when Frank entered the spacious living room, carrying a Russian RPG, four grenades, and a submachine gun I had never seen before.

"There are more Russian arms in Saudi Arabia than you can imagine. We can leave in half an hour. Everyone will be praying then, and the kingdom will come to a standstill. The Korean ship is docking in two hours, but there's no way for us to get into the harbor. I told the harbor master you have changed your minds and are preparing to fly out tomorrow morning."

Good. He was thinking. My trust in him rose a bit.

A battered Toyota truck with a double cabin and a flat deck was ready for us. At Maghrib, the prayer time, we left the manager's villa and started our drive on back roads out to the desert.

Igor reminded us to check with him in two hours when the Korean sheep carrier was supposed to dock. Fedorov rechecked the satellite communications, which were working just fine. Otherwise we were blind.

We were all hot for action, and I hoped Warner's false report about our intentions would distract the Russians. However, I knew the FSB might follow us with its sophisticated equipment.

Frank took the wheel and we started our trip, entering a desert lit up like gold with the sun just disappearing on the western horizon.

The roads we took were nothing more than pressed sand with the occasional dune slowing us down, but Frank was experienced on these tracks. Night fell within minutes, wrapping us in a strange darkness as we drove without headlights.

Igor reported ground activity about thirty miles north of our position.

We had driven another ten miles in almost complete darkness when Igor informed us about unloading activity in the Jubail harbor. The satellite image he sent showed four long tubes being hauled on flatbeds flanked by armored vehicles.

The showdown could begin soon.

We stopped, stretched our legs, and discussed our plan. The silence in the desert almost hurt our ears. We decided we could not use the truck much longer even with the noise of machinery not far away. Sound travels easily in the desert, and if our foes had set up guards as we assumed, we would be detected before we could react.

Frank advised that we drive another five miles or so and then hike the rest of the distance.

My satellite phone beeped. Burov.

"We know where you are, Matt, and I suggest you turn back. The

Mukhabarat is alerted. This is your only chance to get out of there alive. Turn back now."

I was still stunned that the Russians would allow the destruction of Iran, their ally in the region.

"You would have to stop us now, and knowing you don't have firepower in Saudi Arabia, we'll take our chances. And Burov, we'll record our conversation for the history books. You allow terrorists in Saudi Arabia to use nuclear weapons against your allies? Stop me now if you dare, you son of a bitch."

There was silence.

"Burov, do you hear me? Petrossian base is recording this call, and we will use it against you when the time is ripe."

Igor was on Fedorov's phone and confirmed the recording.

"The Mukhabarat is on to you," Burov said. "Hyder has been neutralized by the traitors in its ranks. I can't do anything to stop them. Turn back and give yourselves up. We'll help to negotiate your release."

Hyder was neutralized, which meant either killed or otherwise silenced.

I laughed. The Russians, the FSB, negotiating our release? What a joke!

I terminated the call and told Frank to drive the truck into a dune. Using their bare hands, the girls shoveled sand over the truck until it was swallowed by the Saudi desert.

We had at least twenty miles to cover on foot. Oksana took a backpack with ammo while Frank carried his RPG and four grenades.

The desert at night is cool and pleasant to travel. We made good time with Igor constantly online, directing us to the site from which nuclear missiles would be unleashed into Iran.

We hiked through soft and hard sand, climbed dunes, and slid down the other side, always protecting our weapons from sand and dust. The Makarovs were similar to the infamous AK 47s, Russian guns that could endure sand, mud, dirt, snow, hot, and cold. But the SIGs the girls carried had to be protected from nature.

Frank was in front and raised his hand after he climbed another sand hill. We halted and kept still until he came back down the dune.

"Guards. Four of them at twelve o'clock. Not overly alert but awake."

We were close. Strangely enough, there was no sound that would indicate construction activity or heavy machinery.

I climbed up the sand hill and looked through my night vision binoculars. Yes, four soldiers in desert camouflage sat in the sand, smoking and talking.

But where was the activity Igor told us about earlier?

"We can take them out," Misha suggested, but I was reluctant to do this without knowing what was beyond them.

"Let's go around them," I said. "Something doesn't feel right. We must be close to the site, but we don't hear anything."

We took advantage of the high dunes and circled around the four guards for about fifteen minutes. Then we heard the coughing sound of at least one heavy truck.

On my signal, we all were on our bellies, our binoculars out, scanning the dark horizon to the north.

Two M270 mobile rocket launchers were rumbling through the desert about two hundred yards from our position. That's the way they would deliver the missiles, I guessed. There would be no ramps or any kind of fortified launch base. The movement the satellite detected was from the launchers changing position for final launch.

The tubes we saw changing from the sub to the freighter must have been fit for the M 270. Only Cohen Industries, the company that manufactured missiles for the US armed forces, could have designed the Korean projectiles to fit the M 270.

Igor beeped me. I whispered in the phone, "Igor, we are close. We have contact."

"It's a trap. Get out of there now."

It was Valenti.

"The Russians are fully involved. My contact at FSB warned me about the scheme. They are involved with Cavity. The Saudis are blind. That's why they were misleading the Mukhabarat about your destination."

Fedorov listened in and nodded.

It all made sense now. The renegade Saudis, the Islamic State, and Cavity wanted us to be there when they launched an apocalypse toward Iran. Two birds with one stone. But where was the Islamic State? I was sure there was a contingent on site to be blamed together with Petrossian for the horrifying nuclear attack on the country they all abhorred.

"We'll proceed and try to interfere even if it's the last thing we do. Out."

I packed away the satellite phone and gestured for everyone to move over the next dune.

Fedorov pulled my arm and pointed westward. I was stunned to see several guys putting up the black banner of the Islamic State. They were only about a hundred yards from our position.

We stayed low and crawled closer. The four IS mercenaries were very young and were speaking English. I wasn't surprised.

"We have to take at least one or two of them alive," I said.

Oksana and the girls checked the surroundings. There was movement behind other dunes, but fortunately the night was dark, with the half moon covered by rare clouds.

Fedorov gestured for us to make a move. We couldn't crawl toward them without raising suspicion, so we stood up and strode toward their position.

They were hammering poles into the ground to erect the huge banner. One of them became aware of us and turned.

"Who is there?" He had the voice of a young boy, stammering slightly in English.

I replied in Arabic, hoping we could get closer. All four of them were facing us now, pointing handguns and a machine gun, which was much too heavy for them, in our direction.

In broken English, I told them to hurry up because they were needed at the launch site.

They reluctantly lowered their guns and we were on them. Fedorov took care of the two boys closer to us while I pointed my Makarov at the other two.

"We don't want to hurt you." My English sounded better. "Where are you from?"

I was amazed to see these young boys in Islamic State garb—cheap boots, worn pants, and dirty T-shirts—with ammunition belts hanging over their shoulders.

"We are IS fighters and are ready to die for Allah. We are destroying the devils in Iran tonight."

"Answer my question. Where are you from? One more wrong answer and the first of you will meet the virgins."

I was dead serious and knew these youngsters were radicalized, emotionally disturbed, and therefore very dangerous.

The one in front, standing in my firing line, moved his gun upward, which left me no choice. A bullet from my silenced Makarov hit him straight in the heart. It was too dark for a head shot. He went down with blood bubbles forming on his lips.

I had a bad feeling about the kill but realized it was necessary.

The others dropped their arms and raised their hands high over their heads.

"We are from Birmingham, but our home is Raqqa. We are with the IS," a blond boy nearest to me stammered.

"If you want to live, start talking. Maybe, just maybe, we'll let you go. How many of you are here and where are the rest of you?"

"We are the front battalion, thirty of us with our commander. We are all English, German, and French. Our commander is Syrian. We are heroes ..."

He suddenly began crying and drew a harsh rebuke from one of his mates, a slightly older fighter who was not more than twenty either.

"Kill us now. We don't care. Our place in heaven is secured while you will go to hell."

We had to take care of this one quickly. Fedorov never hesitated in such situations and dispatched him with a shot between the eyes. He had always been better at this shot than I was.

The other two were shaking now, finally realizing we were dangerous enough to send them to the other side.

My thoughts about their families back in England swiftly vanished with the approach of another IS warrior, who stumbled down the high dune. Despite his age, Fedorov was quick as a snake, pressing his Makarov at the man's temple and pushing him toward me.

"Whom do we have here?" I spoke in English but then realized this one was Arabic.

He was less heroic than his soldiers but stayed quiet.

"Listen, if you don't talk you will join these two, and you might have to share the virgins."

"You are dead, unbeliever. We know you are here. I'm Abu Said, commander of the hero battalion."

"As the commander, don't you see what the game is here? You IS heroes will be sacrificed to a cause besides your faith. The Saudis around you are not regulars but are traitors to their country, and the Americans commanding them want you to be the scapegoats for the attack. That means the ultimate end of the glorious Islamic State. You will be accused of unleashing the next world war and therefore will be eradicated."

I was talking too much but was trying to convince them to join our cause. Fedorov realized this was useless and shot the commander between the eyes.

The two radicalized Brit boys were ready to be used. I could feel that.

"Now where is your camp? Are there other nationalities among you besides the ones you mentioned?"

"No. We are the international battalion. Abu Said was the only Arab."

We could see the devilish plan of Cavity; European IS mercenaries would be slaughtered, and the gallant Cavity would arrive just a bit too late to stop the nuclear attack. The nuclear fallout in Iran would be minor compared with the political and military consequences for the world.

One point was clear and slightly encouraging: the Russians could not afford to be on the ground in Saudi Arabia. That left us with the renegade

Saudis, the traitors in the army, and the Mukhabarat. Piece of cake. I started to feel confident again.

"If you join us, you might return to England alive. Even if you are not seen as heroes, you might at least be pardoned."

I looked at them with my Makarov pointing at the chest of the nearest one. The two bobbed their heads, indicating they would choose life over the virgins on the other side.

At that point Frank Warner, whom we had left behind with the girls, came sliding down the dune behind us. He looked excited and anxious.

"Aiello got me on the phone. He knows where we are, and the asshole made me an offer."

He was out of breath and had to inhale deeply before he continued.

"He told me there was a future for me at Langley if I played the role he expected of me, meaning killing you and identifying myself to Cavity."

He was laughing, so I had to calm him down. Although we were hidden by dunes, our voices might carry far enough to alert Cavity operatives.

"Let's move on and kill any fighters we can, including these assholes," Frank said.

We outlined our plan to use the two boys. I still had enough doubt that I was tempted to kill them, but if we succeeded with these two we might be able to turn a few more.

Then it started.

The hero battalion raced over the dune in front of us, about twenty boys screaming at the tops of their lungs, weapons spitting fire. They were totally disorganized, sent to the oven by Cavity. The dune behind us was occupied by the three girls, who mowed them down as they raced to their deaths.

In a few seconds, the battalion of heroes was reduced to three or four lost boys, still firing wildly but hitting no target. Our prisoners were paralyzed, lying in the sand, one of them covering his ears with his hands.

The girls finished off the rest with single shots, and the desert was littered with ill-counselled young fanatics who had thrown away their lives for a bunch of calculating criminals and traitors.

Fedorov, Frank, and I ran back behind the dune where the girls were reloading their guns. Oksana was ready with the RPG for a second wave of Cavity or IS zealots that never came.

The stench of gunpowder filled our noses, verifying we were still alive. I used to love the smell of battle, but on this day it made me sick.

The two boys were totally beaten, and Misha was about to finish them off when I put a halt to the killing.

"Let them live, Misha. They are so young and so stupid. Maybe they will find their way back to a peaceful live if we can stop the rest."

We crawled around the dunes to get a better view of the site where we had last seen the two missile launchers. We spotted them ahead of us, positioned to the east, ready to absorb the Korean missiles and probably to end the world.

A few Westerners stood beside the huge war machines with their guns at ready, aiming in the direction of the short and merciless battleground. However, we were at three o'clock to their assumed target, which gave us a huge advantage, at least for the time being.

The huge, noisy engines on the two missile platforms had apparently muted the brief firefight. Besides the few armed Westerners, we couldn't make out more fighting troops.

We had no idea how many Cavity mercenaries, renegade Saudis, or IS fighters might be down there, so we had to make a quick decision.

The longer we waited, the more likely it was they would spot us, and then we might be in big trouble.

I ordered Oksana to ready the RPG. The M 214s were about three hundred yards from our position and in daylight easy targets, but in the diffuse illumination of headlights, the semi-covered moon, and the strange glow of the sand they presented a major challenge.

Oksana signaled she was ready to fire, and I gave her the go-ahead.

With a whoosh the missile left the tube, and its flaming tail traveled down toward the machines that were poised to destroy Iran. A split second later the grenade hit the first of the two launchers in the side, creating an orange fireball. Oksana had already reloaded the tube and was aiming at the second launcher when a helicopter appeared over a dune about half a mile away. It was no doubt a gunship belonging to the US forces in Saudi Arabia, pilfered by Cavity. I knew the sound only too well. This was an Apache gunship armed with missiles and the deadliest machine guns on earth.

Oksana quickly changed position with the RPG. We could do nothing but wait for the hellfire. Without the proper weapon, there was no defense against an Apache gunship.

The chopper was on us in a few seconds, but strangely enough it hadn't released one of its missiles yet. I watched the girls sprint left and right, leaving a gap in their position that would make it more challenging for the Apache to pinpoint a clear target.

To my right, Oksana fired the RPG, and to our delight she hit the chopper at its rotor blades, creating another orange fireball right above us.

The chopper tumbled and fell straight to the ground with its engines whining, a helpless mass of steel. A dark figure emerged from the wreck. The pilot was the only one on board, which explained why the Apache didn't release its hellfire. The Apache is not an efficient weapon platform without a gunner.

We approached the pilot, our guns ready, with no intention of killing him. He would be valuable if we could make it out of there alive.

He seemed unscathed and raised his arms when he noticed us. He walked toward us, raising his hands even higher into the fire-lit sky.

"On your belly, hands behind you," Fedorov ordered, his Makarov pointed at the Cavity pilot.

He obliged and fell hard on his belly. I used my belt to fasten his hands behind his back. We handed him to the girls with a warning not to kill him unless absolutely necessary.

We had no time to interrogate him but proceeded back to the dune overlooking the launch site where the one M 214 was still smoldering. However, the other launcher had been moved to a farther-off spot where it was hard to hit with the RPG.

Oksana agreed it was almost impossible to hit the launcher from our position. We moved back toward the desert road and took stands safely away from it but in range for the RPG.

Our actions may have had an impact on the enemy troops because there was no immediate reaction to the downing of the Apache.

My phone beeped. Igor or Valenti.

"Yes, we are still alive and have created some havoc. The IS boys, and I mean boys, are probably all gone. But all Cavity needs is our bodies to get back to its scenario."

"Okay," Valenti said. "Things became clearer after my talk with the FSB secretary. The FSB is not involved, but a turncoat group within the agency has linked up with Cavity, the IS, and other scum. It's all coordinated by the lizard lady with the traitors in the CIA. Is Frank Warner nearby?"

I hesitated a moment, looked around, and saw him lying in the sand near Oksana, making conversation.

"Not in earshot."

"Listen carefully. I get conflicting information about him. The FSB tells me he is with the rebels and is a close collaborator of Aiello. Did he talk to Aiello while you were on the road?"

"As a matter of fact, he did. He told us Aiello offered him a position at Langley …"

Valenti interrupted me.

"He has the position already. The reason for the phone contact was to establish GPS for Cavity. Terminate him immediately. He is on their side."

I closed the call and snaked over to Fedorov, giving him the bad news.

"He is with Oksana and the RPG," I said. "Without the rockets, we are done. Let's move."

We joined Oksana and Frank Warner, offering them water, but apparently Warner was warned. He put his Glock to Oksana's temple, smiling at us in a weird way.

"Yes, I know you found out. Pete Aiello is monitoring your satellite phones. Now drop all your gear or I put one in her brain. You never had a chance. We were visible as soon as we left the golf club. Uh, and thanks for taking care of the IS apprentices. Saves us ammo and they look good as dead villains in the desert."

He grabbed our stuff—the guns, the binoculars, the phones—and hit Oksana hard over the head with his gun barrel.

"Makes it easier for her to go when she is already unconscious, don't you agree?"

He laughed and shouted something in Arabic. A group of Saudis in camouflage appeared and cuffed us behind our backs, shoving us rudely down the dune to the desert road where a Toyota pickup was ready to transport us to neverland.

We arrived at the site where a huge bus served as the command center for Cavity and its cronies.

"Let me ask you some questions before we turn you into the evil conspirators we eliminated just a few minutes too late."

He laughed like the criminally insane.

I knew what was coming but my thoughts were with the girls. They were nowhere in sight, and my hopes rose just a notch. Maybe Warner underestimated them. They looked so green that anyone who didn't know them could be fooled.

The Saudis shoved us into a tent furnished only with a table, two wooden chairs, and a water tank. I was aware that we could face waterboarding, electric shocks to the testicles, and having our fingernails pulled out. But Fedorov and I had endured numerous such sessions in Khabarovsk and were well trained in how to resist the urge to talk.

Still no sign of the girls, which was good.

"Where did you position the two Amazons? Better tell me now before you are unable to speak."

Warner seemed a bit anxious about not having found the girls. Clearly, he didn't know what they had done in Baltimore and on the freeway before they rescued Ketut.

We stayed silent, not moving a muscle in our faces.

One of the Saudis pulled Fedorov to the ground and placed him on his back. He was already more than uncomfortable with his hands cuffed behind him. The Saudi put a dirty towel over Fedorov's face and poured water from a rusty bucket over it.

Fedorov remained totally motionless—no coughing, no squealing—which annoyed the Saudi applying the water. He kicked Fedorov in the ribs. Again, he had no visible or audible reaction.

After two or three minutes of waterboarding and kicking, the Saudi pulled the towel from his face and saw a smiling Fedorov.

"Thank you. I was real thirsty," he mumbled, which earned him a vicious kick in the stomach.

I looked at Warner, who was slightly startled by Fedorov's reaction.

"Why don't you just ask us what you need to know? Maybe we will enlighten you." I gave him the most charming smile I could muster.

"Fuck you! Your bodies are all we need now. You can't tell us anything we don't already know. You Petrossians are fucked for good. You're traitors who worked with the shitty Islamic State to start World War III. After tonight we will run the world with the CIA, the FSB, and all the other letter agencies as our servants."

Warner ordered the Saudis to cuff us to steel rods that supported the big tent. Then he stomped out into the glowing night.

The girls were still unaccounted for, and my hopes rose rapidly.

Oksana was brought in a few minutes later and rudely dumped on the ground, her forehead bleeding, one of her eyes shut. She was Petrossian's last active hero, and she always suffered most, I thought.

About an hour later the girls were still at large or maybe dead. Oksana, however, assured us they were extremely tough and professional and showed no nerves.

A heavy engine roared outside, and we presumed the Korean missiles might have arrived. This was immediately confirmed by a beaming Warner.

"Now it's just a matter of hours and you are lucky. I'll let you live long enough to watch the first nuclear attack since 1945. We might even see the mushroom cloud on the other side of the Persian Gulf. History will be made today, and you will enter the books, although we will be remembered as the heroes."

Despite the desperation gripping my heart, I laughed inwardly.

"Let me tell you a story before you kill us." I grinned at him and could see a glimmer in his eyes.

"Go ahead. It will be the last you ever tell."

"Some years ago, your uncle reported you to a therapist. He told him you thought you were a chicken. The doctor advised him to commit you, but your uncle refused. You know why?"

Warner was quiet, and a dangerous expression covered his face.

"Okay, I'll tell you. Your uncle said he would gladly agree if it wasn't for the eggs he was going to miss."

I let that sink in for a second or two and said, "See, it's in the family."

That cost me a heavy punch in my stomach.

A silenced gun coughed outside the tent, and we heard two bodies fall to the ground. Warner jumped while Fedorov and I started to feel warmth in our hearts.

Warner rushed to get his gun out of its holster, but he was too late. Misha and Gaby entered the tent and placed a bullet in each of his kneecaps.

"Didn't know if you still need him," Misha said.

"Well done. We need him," I said.

Gaby cut our cuffs while Misha, ever vicious, put her foot on one of Frank Warner's knees, saying, "One sound and I'll stomp on it."

Fedorov took care of Oksana, who was badly hurt.

"You'll never get out of here, assholes. The Saudis will take care of you, raping your bitches and skinning you alive."

Gaby closed his mouth with her hands while Misha kept her promise, applying her weight on his left knee. The crunching sound made my neck hair stand up straight.

Warner blacked out and lay still on the sand except for some twitching.

Except for the RPB, our weapons were in the tent. We armed ourselves, and I asked Oksana to watch over the CIA traitor and to kill him if necessary. Fedorov and I badly wanted to present him as a token to Eileen Cahill and Pete Aiello, but if keeping him alive might hurt our plans to stop the Armageddon, a single bullet would do.

We carefully opened the canvas at the entrance to the tent and peeked out. Seeing no one, we rushed out behind the Toyota truck.

The tubes with the missiles had arrived and were unloaded by a movable crane, which took them over to the remaining M 214 launcher. A few North Koreans, I guessed, were directing the Saudis and the Cavity agents.

I recognized the missiles as the new Hwasong 14s, which supposedly could reach targets thousands of miles away. The missiles appeared slimmer than in published pictures and obviously had been modified to fit into the launcher. This was the most reliable rocket the North Koreans had developed so far, and I was sure that with the additional technology provided by Cohen Industries, the flight over the gulf would be child's play.

We didn't have the RPG, which left us no other choice but to attack with what we had. Fedorov deployed us to three locations, which might just confuse our foes once we opened fire. The main targets now were the North Koreans because, I hoped, they were the only ones able to load the projectiles and to arm the warheads.

But where were the Saudis and the main Cavity force?

There was no time to discuss tactics. On Fedorov's signal we fired from our positions, Gaby and Misha acting as snipers and Fedorov and I unloading what was stored in our magazines.

I saw two Koreans fall hard without a sound. A third ran behind the M 214, screaming commands in Korean. I wondered who would comprehend his shrieking and reloaded my Makarov and the submachine gun.

The Saudis and the Cavity mercenaries ran in all directions. About half a dozen lay dead or badly wounded in the sand. I knew then we had probably succeeded. All the loading activity had stopped, and the place looked eerily deserted.

An American voice shouted, "Warner, where are you?"

A Cavity soldier stormed toward the tent but was stopped cold by Misha, who hit him in the head. I made a mental note to always be on her side.

We heard engines revving, and I expected an onslaught by the Saudis. who had machine guns mounted on Toyota trucks. To our surprise, however, the vehicles were leaving the site, racing toward the desert highway.

The Saudi traitors reacted quickly. Realizing their mission was over, they left the Cavity mercenaries behind. We didn't know how many of them were still alive and functioning.

The few faces we could see looked confused. I suspected they were as surprised as we were that the main force had not yet arrived.

My phone beeped, and since there was no immediate danger in sight I decided to answer. Igor.

"Boss, we have the Russians back in the boat, at least the straight ones. We have satellite access with an incredible infrared filter. We saw your action, and we can see where the Cavity soldiers are hiding. It looks like there are only six or seven left."

"Where are they, Igor?"

"I'm getting to that. They are about fifty meters behind the M 214. I think it's a dune. They are fixed, not moving, but might have a clear firing sight on your positions."

"Thanks, Igor, and tell Burov I want all the FSB IT projects in our baskets or he sinks."

"Copy that, boss. Be careful."

I gathered our little band and shared the news.

"We have to get behind them quickly from two sides."

Misha was thinking intelligently, and we deployed—Fedorov with Misha, me with Gaby. The small fires that our attack caused left the Cavity mercenaries blind in spots, allowing us to move to the left and the right of them. We agreed we would take no prisoners and would go for straight kills. That's what we were good at.

It took us a few minutes to verify what Igor had told me. There were indeed six and all in one clump, lying behind the dune with a clear view of the site. They were all focused on the battleground, and I could imagine they were pissed at their Saudi conspirators and at the Cavity main force. The only open question was, where was the remaining North Korean?

We made short work of the Cavity soldiers. Six were not worth all our ammo, but about ten shots took them out. Misha, the enforcer, the name I had just given her, walked calmly over to the killing site and finished the deal with a few close head shots.

Fedorov was worried about the vanished Korean as was I, but we were too exhausted to go hunting in the desert night. We walked back to the site and entered the tent, where Oksana was up on her feet, cool and calm as we all knew her.

"He was a good boy. I didn't even have to apply more pressure. He is ready to talk and to switch sides."

She gave us her lovely smile and added, "But aren't they all when it's too late?"

Then we heard noise near the M 214. We all rushed out and saw the missing North Korean working on one of the missiles. He was unscrewing the tube that held one of the Hwasongs. When he saw us, he shouted something in Korean, a language none of us had mastered. We didn't bother to take a language course now. Misha struck him with a single bullet, sending his body over the opened tube.

Was that the last one? I was so tired I was ready to explode one of the Hwasongs just to end the battle.

I called Igor.

"Can you see any more living and moving creatures around us?"

"No, boss. I think you got 'em all. But there is a convoy of Saudis on the way up from Al Jubail—according to Burov, the good ones. I told Burov to brief them about you, about Petrossian. I hope he did. Burov told me that the Mukhabarat took care of its traitors and that Hyder is in charge again."

I went back to the tent where I interviewed Warner. This was a step down from interrogation, which wouldn't be necessary since he would be easy to break in his state.

"Listen, Warner, you have one slight chance to spend the rest of your miserable life on crutches or in a wheelchair. I won't promise you freedom because you know that would be a lie, but I can guarantee life in a cozy prison where you have the chance to be pardoned before you die of old age."

He was paying attention.

"You have the unique opportunity to be a star witness but only if you expose Eileen Cahill, Pete Aiello, and everyone elese behind this devilish scheme."

I looked him in the eye.

"Understand what I need?"

He nodded. "You'll get it. I was in at the top, and I'll take my chances now."

I placed my smartphone in front of him and activated the recording app.

"Start talking, because if you don't spill here, you will never get the opportunity to negotiate terms."

He talked, and we listened for the better part of an hour. The scheme was planned and executed by Cavity with conspirators in the CIA, the NSA, other smaller intelligence firms, Russian turncoats, and Saudi fanatics who wanted to replace the kingdom with an Islamic caliphate and to burn Iran to the ground.

When we heard the convoy arriving, I put away my smartphone and told Warner he would be safe for now.

Misha video-recorded the whole story on her smartphone, and I should have seen what was coming, but maybe I didn't want to.

Just before the Saudi army and the real Mukhabarat arrived, she fired a single muffled shot between Warner's eyes, relieving him of further pain and saving us from long, painful sessions with whatever legal authorities might get involved.

"He had it coming," was her only comment. She packed her SIG into her holster and sat in the sand as if nothing special had happened.

To our surprise, Hyder Fatah, now a general, entered the tent, congratulating us, winking at me, and shaking our hands vigorously.

"Our friend Burov told me everything. You Petrossians did great work, but we Saudis prevented the most horrific crime the world would ever have experienced."

Fine with us. He could take the credit. We just wanted to get out of there.

"Because of an approaching sandstorm, we couldn't fly in with our choppers. I have comfortable transportation for you back to Al Jubail. Khalij is being raided as we speak, and its directors are under arrest. I guess similar action will take place in the United States and in Russia. Again, Allah be with you, and I don't mind if we cross paths again. The traitors in our ranks are being hunted down without mercy. We stopped the Cavity main force outside Al Jubail and had no choice but to kill everyone in it, including our own conspirators."

Good for them, I thought. *No lengthy trials and no executions. Job done.*

Hyder was clever, no doubt, and played his Russian connection, which was not entirely his doing, with the Mukhabarat. General Hyder Fatah, a commoner, not a prince, now headed the Mukhabarat.

He escorted us out to an air-conditioned bus that probably served tourists or rich pilgrims in the kingdom. I hid my smartphone and so did Misha. This was our wild card for the last round of a deadly game, and we hoped to have a winning hand.

CHAPTER 33

BACK IN KITTY HAWK, THIRTY-SIX HOURS LATER

The Dassault that was dispatched to Al Jubail stopped to refuel in Portugal where we woke up after a sleep that felt like anesthesia. We stretched our legs on the island of Funchal, and for the first time in eternity I felt like a normal living creature again.

Fedorov nudged me as we walked on the tarmac, looking up at a cloudless blue sky. "It's time for a vodka, tovaritch," he said.

Oksana was walking behind us, stretching her abused bones. "I heard that, and I'll join you," she said.

Though we were alive and felt relaxed, we weren't in the mood to celebrate. We were content to sit in our snug chairs and to enjoy the ice-cold vodka served in frosted glasses.

When the plane was on its final approach to Kitty Hawk's airport, we were ready to wrap up the events with Valenti's guidance.

Valenti, Igor, Veronica, Ketut, and Tatiana hugged us, kissed us, and called for vodka.

"There is a surprise waiting for you inside," Valenti said. He was smiling, which was very rare.

We entered the great hall where Galina, the head of Petrossian, was speaking with a man we didn't know. She greeted us warmly and made one slightly sarcastic remark to Misha and Gaby, which they took as a compliment.

"The death toll in the kingdom is officially forty-six, and I learned that you two were important contributors."

The two girls were in awe to meet Galina for the first time.

"Be quiet and accept my commendation. You embody all of Petrossian's virtues—boldness, trustworthiness, and cold-blooded determination. I commend you for your actions."

"But how do you …?"

Galina stopped Gaby cold.

"While you were asleep on your trip back here, Fedorov, reported every detail to me. So you see I'm always informed."

She smiled and turned to the gentleman beside her.

"This is Mr. Andrew Peterson, special security adviser to the recuperating president of the United States. He agrees with the president that Petrossian should get back its official status as an independent intelligence agency that cooperates with the CIA and the NSA—the real CIA and NSA—and with all the other three-letter firms."

Fedorov grunted beside me and earned a stern look from the head of Petrossian.

"Petrossian's headquarters for all operations will be in Washington, DC, close to Langley but not beneath it."

Galina paused, looking each of us in the eyes.

"I will step down as director and install Oksana as my successor."

This produced huge applause and, for the first time I could remember, a blush from Oksana.

Galina didn't waste many words on her career, but she revealed that a dozen freshly trained agents would soon leave Khabarovsk to help maintain peace on an unstable planet.

She filled us in on what had happened in the last thirty-six hours. Pete Aiello had been arrested and would be replaced as director of the CIA by Walter Wills, who was recovering swiftly from his injuries. Mark Shearer, the retired assistant director, had been called to the White House as senior security adviser. The acting president, Eric Balton, had stepped down. There was no evidence linking him to Cavity, but he couldn't bear the pressure of his office. The president would be back in the White House within days and until then would take care of business from his hospital room.

"What about Eileen Cahill?" I couldn't wait to hear about her fate.

"Eileen Cahill has been indicted for the attempted murder of the president and numerous other crimes. Conviction would put her on death row, but she is on the run. She left DC on her jet just after the news broke about the Cavity defeat in Saudi Arabia. She was scheduled to fly to Thailand, but she made a stop in Oregon at a private airfield. We don't have any trail to follow as yet. She has vanished."

Misha and Gaby were almost trembling beside me, and Galina addressed them directly.

"You two are assigned to find her and to bring her in dead or alive. You know what I mean."

I knew it too. The lizard lady was doomed.

"Bernie's body was recovered from the mansion and shipped to his mother in Iowa. I will attend the funeral the day after tomorrow. I hope you will join me."

Galina's encouragement was unnecessary, for we all would fly to Iowa to bid farewell to Bernie, who gave his life for Petrossian and for us.

The Russians arrested more than one hundred traitors. The Saudis didn't release any news about their actions, but we all knew the Saudis didn't simply arrest traitors and put them to prison. These people were all meeting the virgins, and I hoped the virgins were wearing horns.

The Saudis took all the credit for preventing the first nuclear attack since World War II, though they knew who was really responsible for stopping it.

King Salman's compliments and thanks to Petrossian were good enough for all of us, and he had pledged to engage Petrossian in highly sensitive business in the near future.

After another round of drinks with a slightly tipsy Peterson, Igor whispered in my ear.

"Burov got promoted to number two at the FSB and promised a load of IT projects for our firm. We have to stock up in Simferopol."

"Um, one last question." Oksana addressed the presidential security adviser. "What happens to Cohen Industries?"

He frowned at her as if she had inquired about his sex life.

"The administration might have a hard time proving any connection to North Korea, but we are looking into it. Don't forget that more than ten thousand people are working at CI. The president doesn't want a major job loss on his hands. Cecil Cohen denies any involvement with the Koreans. So ..."

I interrupted him rather impolitely and took out a flash disk with Frank Warner's confession, which more than implicated the Cohens, the North Koreans, the Saudis, and the Russians.

"This copy is exclusively for the president. There is video too should you have any doubts about its authenticity. And just in case you or the president tries to cover this up, I'm not Petrossian anymore after tonight and therefore just might leak it to the press." I stared into Peterson's nervously blinking eyes.

"I'm sure your info is in good hands now," Valenti said diplomatically, "and furthermore I'm convinced the US government will do everything to get to the bottom of this conspiracy, which almost led to World War III."

I left it at that, but Oksana, standing close to me, mouthed, "Don't worry."

After the last drink, a huge iced vodka, I fell into my bed in one of Kitty Hawk's luxurious bedrooms and dreamed of being back in Kuala Lumpur, though not before I'd delivered Ketut to Bali. Hell, I thought I might stay there for a while and watch her heal.

EPILOGUE

The next morning the Petrossians left Valenti's mansion and crammed into the Bombardier for a sad flight to Cedar Rapids, Iowa.

Bernie's body had been shipped to the small town about twenty miles north of Cedar Rapids the day before.

No one was in the mood for a drink but sipped hot coffee served by the pleasant Armenian flight attendant who had accompanied them to the Middle East.

Sister Veronica tapped her porcelain coffee cup with her spoon and got everyone's attention.

"Bernie truly was one of us, but please keep in mind that his mom has no idea. She believed her son was working for an international finance company in DC."

Veronica hesitated for a moment and then continued in a firmer voice.

"Bernie was recruited by me and Tatiana and was sent to Krilnyi for training. He finished second highest in his extremely effective class. Yes, he learned how to kill, how to defend himself, and how to fight for the ideals we are pursuing."

She took a sip of coffee with all eyes and ears on her.

"Bernie, however, was never just an executioner of the scum we deal with every day. No! Bernie had a brilliant mind and lofty goals. He wanted to have a family one day, to be a father. This all came to an end when the lizard lady, one of our vilest foes, took his life and ended his dreams, his mom's, and his girlfriend's"

Veronica eyes were wide and glistening, maybe with tears or with rage.

"His mom and his girlfriend believe Bernie was the victim of a DC drive-by shooting. That's what the DC police have agreed to report.

"My uncle, Valenti, the last of the great Petrossian generation, has decided to support Valenti's mom and his girlfriend to give them the life Bernie was determined to make for them."

Nothing more had to be said. They all understood, and the fury inside them remained under control until after the funeral.

The Bombardier gently touched down at the Cedar Rapids airport. It seemed the pilots wanted to soothe the passengers with a super soft landing.

At the airport they boarded four Escalades and traveled about forty minutes to Springville where they were greeted by Bernie's mom, his girlfriend, Alicia, and most of the community.

The funeral was conducted by the pastor who had baptized Bernie as a baby, and the Petrossians were deeply touched by the warmth and care of the young man's family and friends. None of the Petrossians attending the funeral led normal lives.

Fedorov wondered whether this was good, because many more of them might get hurt or killed. *This business is so much easier without family, friends, or close relationships*, he thought.

Bernie's mom's house was much too small to accommodate the big congregation. After the gathering, the Petrossians, including Bernie's top boss, Valenti, said good-bye, promising to monitor the small photo shop Mrs. Mathison was running. Malls and smartphones had almost killed her tiny business, but Valenti thought it could be revived by sending Petrossian-related jobs in her direction. A young technician would take over the new digital work line financed by Petrossian.

The Bombardier brought them all back to Kitty Hawk, and on this stretch the vodka flowed.

When they had reassembled in Valenti's mansion, the patriarch thanked them simply for being Petrossians.

"The Bombardier will bring you to your destinations, which I believe will be Zurich for Fed, Kuala Lumpur for Igor and Matt, and Bali for this brave woman." He smiled at Ketut.

"You all know how to change flight plans, so your final destinations are entirely up to you."

They all enjoyed the ice-cold vodka before a delicious Armenian dinner was served, accompanied by several bottles of 1978 Barolo.

Veronica, Tatiana, Misha, and Gaby would be flown to DC the next day on the Bell.

Oksana and Galina were supposed to stay a day or two in Kitty Hawk to discuss Petrossian's immediate future before briefing the girls in DC concerning the hunt for the lizard lady.

The next morning, they all said good-bye without hugs and kisses, knowing events in the near future might bring them together sooner rather than later.

Matt had a few parting words. "Friends, our recent adventures mark the end of my active career with our firm. I will hand over my shares of the Simferopol lab to Igor and will assist him in any way I can. I'm sure he will update you about my retirement location, but he has strict instructions to keep my communication channels free of any disturbance. It has been an honor and, yes, a pleasure to serve with you!"

With that, he walked out of the mansion to the car that would bring them to the nearby airport. Ketut, Igor, and Fedorov soon followed him.

Fedorov didn't change his flight plan, and they parted in Zurich where he owned a pleasant house. They did not indulge in an emotional farewell but offered the assurance that they would be there for each other if necessary.

Two of the others changed their destinations. Igor needed to go to Simferopol and to Alushta to rebuild his lab and his beloved house. He didn't know Valenti had ordered a powerful, brand-new boat, already named *Blue Thunder II*. It awaited him at his Alushta house.

Ketut and Matt decided to stay one night in Simferopol to enjoy a wonderful Ukrainian dinner before they continued on to Bali. Matt thought it was too early to return to Kuala Lumpur and Jakarta, so Bali, with its friendly people, great golf courses, fantastic duck menus, and ice-cold beer, was his final destination.

Although Ketut wanted Matt to stay with her in Ubud, he opted for the Legian Top and hoped his golf set was still in storage. He promised to visit her at least every other day and to check on her recuperation, which was in the hands of her doctor friend Mia.

Matt had one main reason for separating from Ketut at Bali Denpasar Airport: he had strong feelings for the Balinese beauty, but she was almost thirty years his junior.

They kissed just before Ketut entered Mia's car, and the kiss may have lasted a bit too long, for a huge tear escaped Ketut's eye. Matt saw it while pressing her fragile body close to his.

Let's wait and see, he thought, and gave her a final good-bye wave when the car left.

What the … was that? Matt had wet eyes.

Printed in the United States
By Bookmasters